The Eighty-Twenty Rule

Rubi Somerton

Author's Note

This book contains open-door love scenes and coarse language.

Written in British English — some spellings are deliberately different to US English.

Chapter One

I will always remember this moment. The moment I realise I am going to die alone. There is no one out there for me, and I am not out there for anyone.

Nothing dramatic has happened. Just a crystalline moment of truth. As I stare at the electric kettle boiling in front of me, I just know that no matter how old I get, it will always be 'English Breakfast with one, for one'.

'Will you go out with him again, Meg?'

I am startled back to my surroundings by my best friend's voice, and her enquiring eyes meet mine.

'Who, me?'

'Well, yes, of course, you! You are the only "Meg" here, and it's your god-forsaken story, you twat,' Elle says, full of good-natured mockery.

'I'd rather not.' I've just finished telling Elle about the date I went on last night with a tradie I matched with on one of those ridiculous dating apps that are apparently designed to help one find an eligible suitor. All it seems to do for me is put me through the endless pain and torture of talking to strangers, followed by making the decision to never talk to strangers again, only to find the next day that there's another bleeding stranger waiting for me, and I go through the motions again.

The last guy seemed harmless enough to begin with. He turned up in his own car. That was a start. He brought me flowers, and he didn't smell half bad. I would imagine he had bothered to shower, and had even brushed his teeth, though I couldn't be sure as I didn't get close enough to categorically confirm or deny until later that evening.

We went to dinner at the Italian restaurant down town. He did all the basics right. He asked me what I do for work. When I told him I work at the library, he asked me what I want to do as a real job. When I told him that working at the library *is* a real job, he laughed. Fine. They all do that.

He asked me about my tattoos. How many do I have? Eighteen. Do they mean anything? No. Which one was the most painful? That's private. Will you get any more? Inevitably. Do I ever provide more than one-to-two-word answers? No.

He asked about my family. Am I originally from Yorkshire? No. Where am I from? London. Do I like it here? Indifferent. Do I plan to stay? Inevitably.

I knew things weren't going well. I can always tell. They start to look around at the other diners. Then they start to check their phone, or their watch, if they're wearing one. Sometimes a low whistle escapes through their lips. They pick up the drinks menu and peruse it like it's page three of the newspaper. That's when I get nervous. And when I get nervous, I get awkward. Even more awkward than my baseline.

So last night, just like all the other times, I did what I always do. I attempted an escape.

'Gee, it's getting late,' I said. 'You must be up early in your line of work. Perhaps we should go.'

'It's only 8pm,' he replied, 'and you haven't *asked* me what I do for work.'

Why do people have to be so argumentative? I thought the British were known for unwavering politeness. If someone suggests it might be home time, shouldn't one just go along with it, so as not to cause offence?

'Your profile said, "tradie". What I meant was, I'm tired, and I have an early start at the library. Perhaps we should go.'

'Can I come back to yours?'

I'm sorry, where did I give any indication whatsoever that I wanted to bed you? Was it in my curt, one-to-two-word responses? Was it perhaps, the disinterested glaze in my eyes as you've been speaking, or was it my sullen, closed off body language?

Of course, I didn't say any of that. I simply said, 'Fine.'

Elle is looking at me with puzzlement, and I know what's coming. She's going to want to know what was unsuitable about this latest conquest of mine.

'What could possibly be wrong with this latest conquest, Meg? I thought you said he was "OK" in bed, which for you, is positively a rave review.'

I place her cup of tea– white with none– down in front of her and take the other wooden-backed seat at her small, round dining table.

The crystalline moment of truth crystallises further. There was nothing wrong with him. Nothing at all. He was quite suitable. The problem is me. I hate people. Almost all of them. I don't hate Elle. She's fine, which is positively a rave review. I don't hate Elle's housemate, and my other best friend, Gabby, though she is a viper. I don't hate my Mum and Dad. I don't hate my younger brothers. But everyone else – even my older sister – not a fan.

What I'm painting here is a picture of my indifferent, bordering on disdainful feelings towards most of humankind. A grim foretelling indeed. Just me. Alone. Each day drawing closer to a lonely death. Please don't be alarmed, I'm perfectly well.

'I'm just not cut out for dating, Elle. I'm going to give up and accept my fate.'

'Don't be ridiculous, Meg! You are drop dead gorgeous, the funniest person I know, and the sweetest–'

'You need to get out more.'

'I won't hear another word of this bollocks. I wish you could see yourself as I see you.'

Purely out of curiosity, I probe. I suspect the answer will be entertaining. Elle has a vivid imagination. She wants to be a writer, but for now, she has to be content with being a primary school teacher. 'How *do* you see me?'

Her lips twist in thought, and then her eyes light up. 'I picture you as the heroine of a high fantasy.' Her hands become animated as she elaborates. 'A street urchin turned assassin, with a strong sense of justice and an even stronger will to survive. Born with two heads, one removed shortly after birth, with sharp blue eyes that turn insides to mush with a single withering glare. When captured and sentenced to a gory execution, you hold your remaining head high, your glossy midnight-black locks draped over your shoulder– to hide the scar. The supple curves of your generous breasts draw the attention of the raucous crowd surrounding you, baying for your blood even as they lust after—'

'—OK, stop. You're getting me excited,' I say, as unenthusiastically as possible.

Elle giggles. She finds my lack of emotional repertoire and dead pan sarcasm hilarious. In fact, the more emotionless I am, the harder she laughs. I see it as a challenge. Elle can find absolutely anything funny. Her favourite things to laugh about are her own misfortune, and mine. Not necessarily in that order.

Anyway, she's not wrong about one thing. It seems that since my boobs finally made an appearance, at the ripe old age of eighteen and a half, suddenly being pasty white, six foot tall and gangly as fuck was acceptable to the male half of the population. Funny, that. I probably am some weirdo's fantasy girl.

'Seriously, though, you can't give up, Meg. You're a romantic at heart. You just haven't met "the one" yet, that's all.'

I raise my eyebrows at my beautiful best friend. God, she can be oblivious sometimes. Elle has never had an issue meeting 'the one'. She met 'the one' as soon as she started university, and the said 'one' proposed to her a couple of years later. And if it hadn't been him, it would have been another 'one', because Elle can't help but be right for any guy she flutters her lashes at. She knows it too, the cheeky git. Long, dark blonde hair, hazel almond shaped eyes, a smoking hot body and a smile that lights up her face like a ring light. She can be infuriating at times, and more than a little odd, but men find her quirkiness adorable. It must be a fine line, because my quirkiness seems to have the opposite effect.

Elle's been scrunching up her nose with every sip of her tea, so I suspect I've done something wrong. She stands up, and heads into the kitchen.

'I don't know how long you brewed my tea for, my love, but I'm wondering if you're trying to kill me, or you just despise me and wish to see me suffer …,' she starts to say, but then she stops. Her cheeks take on a crimson hue. She takes a deep breath and: 'GABBY!'

Enter Gabrielle Bello. Six foot two, long rich brunette hair, sharp dark brown eyes and legs for days. That's Gabby. She takes a few steps out of her bedroom and into the compact living room, which brings her within only metres of where I am sitting, since everything about Elle and Gabby's flat is compact. She puts her hand on her hip and raises her eyebrows in challenge.

Here we go.

'You've done it again! You do it on purpose because you know it upsets me. I hate you, you spawn of Satan,' spits Elle, meeting Gabby's challenge with her own eyes flashing

'What are you on about, you daft cow?' the spawn of Satan responds.

'You've mixed up the spoons with the forks,' Elle says. She looks down into the drawer and visibly shudders, then slams it shut. I jump as cheap laminated wood hits against cheap laminated wood and then rebounds from the force. 'You will fix it, or I'm moving out.'

'The sooner the better. Then I can live my life without your constant nagging. Fucking Type A prima donna.'

I think it's safe to say Gabby isn't very happy that Elle will be moving out once she marries Joe. Elle and Gabby have been best friends since primary school. They were inseparable before Elle met Joe, and have remained inseparable despite Joe, so I really don't know what Gabby is so worried about. Gabby likes to externalise her feelings. Maybe it's her way of making sense of them, though it never seems to get to that point. They just seem to remain completely irrational. Elle really should have moved in with Joe by now, in fact, but she has resisted on the basis of being a Good Catholic Girl. Elle is very selective about when she wishes to be one of those.

'You're going to miss me when I'm gone, Gabrielle, and I hope when you're sorting the cutlery, alone and miserable, you'll wonder whether if you'd done some things differently, I might've stayed,' says Elle. That's a low blow, delivered with just the right amount of guilt-inducing sorrow.

It doesn't have the desired effect on Gabby. She rolls her eyes so hard I fear she might pull an ocular tendon.

'I hope when Joe finally comes to his senses and realises he's shackled himself to a highly strung, delusional narcissist, he isn't going to dump you back on my doorstep with a note saying, 'no returns'.'

Wow. I take it back. *That's* a low blow.

Elle is breathing heavily, and her hands are clenched. She's staring down Gabby, and Gabby's not giving an inch. I've never seen them in a physical fight before. This could be a first. But then a slight smile curves at the corners of Elle's mouth, and the next thing she's in a fit of giggles. Then so is Gabby. I look from one, to the other, in complete bemusement.

'I did do it on purpose,' Gabby admits. 'I'll sort it later.' Gabby seems to notice that she and Elle are not alone. She looks at me. 'All right, Meg? How was the date?'

'All right, Gabby. The same as usual.'

'What did you do wrong this time?' she asks with her usual tact. And no, it isn't a rhetorical question, or playful sarcasm. She genuinely wants to know how I've ballsed it up. 'Did you put the condom on inside out again?'

'Leave her alone, Gabby!' says Elle, before I can respond that I won't be making that mistake again. She has returned to the table, having added sugar to her tea, and is sitting opposite from me. 'It would be the easiest mistake to make. I could quite possibly do the same thing myself.'

'How?' demands Gabby. 'You've had more sex than all of us combined. Surely you wouldn't make such a rookie error.'

'Certainly, I have had a depth of experience that perhaps you haven't,' concedes Elle. 'Joe and I have gone to such depths together that our sex life is now buried six feet under,' she says with a giggle at her own wit. 'You both have me for breadth of experience though, and I've never had sex with a condom. Joe took my 'V' with his 'V', remember.' Suddenly, her face drops. 'A depressing thought, if ever there was one.' Almost as quickly, she brightens again and pats my hand like a kindly aunt who is discussing the perils of condom donning with one over a cuppa. 'It could happen to anyone, lovely, and the fact that he laughed so hard just means he wasn't "the one".'

'Thanks Elle,' I say, withdrawing my hand from beneath the reassuring squeeze she is now giving it.

'Speaking of "the one",' says Elle, taking a sip of her tea, 'if either of you are talking to my Joe, I have a terrible headache. You've seen me, and I looked quite unwell. You suspect it may be an attack of the gout on top of a crippling migraine, and you estimate it could take anywhere up to two weeks to right itself.'

Elle is a lover of regency romance. It colours the way she talks on a regular basis and is largely to blame for why she's constantly raving on about finding 'the one'.

'Do you think you might need to take the waters in Bath?' I ask.

'I wouldn't be at all surprised, my love,' says Elle, with a perfectly mischievous grin spreading across her face.

Gabby shakes her head. 'How long do you think you can avoid sleeping with the man you're going to marry, Elle?' It's a reasonable question. I have wondered the same thing.

'Not forever,' says Elle with a shrug. 'I suppose I'll resign myself to it eventually. But a break will do me the world of good.'

Gabby throws her hands up in despair and goes back to into her room. I look at Elle with genuine concern. She has been joking about not wanting to sleep with Joe for a while, but at what point is it no longer funny? She's engaged to the man. She gives me a smile. It doesn't go to her eyes. She reaches her hand out again and places it over the top of mine, artfully deflecting the attention from her problems, back to mine.

'Don't worry Megsy, the right man is out there for you. I know it. In fact, I bet he's just around the corner.' She gives a slight sigh, and a wistful look comes over her face. There's one thing I know when it comes to Elle. Expect the unexpected. 'And I just know that when he materialises, he will have the most magnificent cock you could have ever imagined. The kind we usually only get to read about at Book Club.'

Chapter Two

Book Club. When I started working at the library a few years ago, the weekly book club was on its last legs. There was only one regular attendee, a woman named Margaret, or Margy for short. She brought with her a paid carer, but it was a different person each time, so I couldn't count them in our regular numbers.

I don't know Margy's age, but I suspect it is in triple figures. Diminutive in frame, with tight silver curls and deep lines etched in her face that tell the tale of a long, rich life, Margy is as brilliant as she is daft – discerning which is in play at any given time is almost impossible. She has a sharp sense of humour, and her favourite trick is making others think she is in mental decline, purely for her own entertainment. I knew her for months before I realised her eyes twinkle with mischief when she is toying with her prey.

I felt for Margy. Book Club on a Wednesday afternoon at 4pm was her only social outing for the week. So, at first, I allowed her to select the book, believing I was doing a good thing. It was when she selected the same book for the fourth month in a row, barely containing her mirth as she presented it to me as though it was the first time she had ever encountered it, that I cottoned on— I was the prey.

Despite realising I was her shiny new gullible play toy, I still allowed Margy her choice each month, digging deep into my professional reserves to feign interest in her favoured genres– historical fiction (contemporary for Margy) and mystery (yes, detective novels). Until one day, my carefully curated patience ran out, prompted by my boss's suggestion that Book Club was a waste of time and resources, and would have to be cancelled if numbers did not improve.

So, that month I placed my employment at considerable risk and told Margy that I would be choosing the book. I went with something a little more avant-garde. Something I knew would...er...stimulate the interest of the bookish community. Not a well-known title, but something a little more... climactic. *Cloaked Lust* was the name of it, and dark romance was the game.

Elle is never one to pass up one of my book recommendations, so she needed no further encouragement to join the rejuvenated book club, and once I got onto socials, neither did several other like-minded female members of the Leeds community. That very week, there were five attendees. Numbers have since grown to twenty regulars, give or take, each week. I've had to instigate a wait list, and RSVPs are essential. It is, without a doubt, the most popular Wednesday afternoon, library-based book club in the whole of Leeds. I do not exaggerate.

That's how we come to be gathered here this afternoon, at the long table in the conference room, with the lights dimly lit – for ambience – and polite chatter bouncing amongst the members as they wait for me to start proceedings.

As a known people-hater, having twenty people in a room whom I'm supposed to oversee is my idea of hell. I clear my throat nervously, and Elle assists with a 'shush', followed by a teacher glare and a purse of her lips. It does the job, and a hush falls over the group. All eyes turn on me. I turn bright red, I'm sure, since my skin is basically translucent, and all of the blood has drained from the rest of my body to my face.

'Thank you all for coming. This week, we were to read Chapters 10 through to 15 of *Cloaked Lust*, paying particular attention to how the author has used similes, metaphors and analogies in her writing.'

There is a silence while everyone waits for me to steer this ship in some direction or another. Thankfully, Elle knows that I am disorientated and takes the helm. She provides not only the social lubricant, but also, she would argue, asks the hard-hitting questions.

'I'll go first, if you don't mind Meg?' she asks politely. I nod and smile gratefully at her. She pushes her reading glasses up on her nose and opens her book to where she has placed a sticky note. 'In chapter twelve, paragraph four ...' she says, and pauses for a moment while everyone else finds the spot, '... the author describes Patrick's cock as, "as long as it is wide."' A snicker travels around the group. Elle acknowledges it with a quirk of her lips, then continues. 'Do you think the author wanted to convey that Patrick's appendage was short and stubby, or impressive in both length and width?'

I don't know what I am expecting – probably some sort of sensible redirection from someone in the group with more dignity and self-respect than Elle. That's not what I get.

'It would make most sense if it was the latter,' pipes up a voice from the far end of the table. 'He is the Male Main Character, and the feats he is able to achieve with it would require both length, and girth.'

'Indeed,' agrees Elle, 'but we are talking about dimensions like those of a square; all four sides equal in length? Don't you think it would be more realistic if it were short and stout, rather than both long and wide? I just can't picture it.'

'Short and stubby can be just as effective if a man knows how to use it,' says a middle-aged woman with bright red lipstick and a bleach blonde bob, 'and we're talking about a man who comes in, masked and cloaked, through women's open bedroom windows. He's already considerably ahead of the game. By the time The Chosen One is tied up to the bedhead, she's not going to worry if he's a 2 x 2, or an 8 x 8.'

Let me explain something briefly, to allay any concerns that may have arisen. *Cloaked Lust* is a consensual-non-consensual novel, or CNC for short. The 'Chosen Ones', who have heard about Patrick, the lusty cloaked crusader, on the news, volunteer themselves to him by leaving their bedroom windows open, and an LED candle on the windowsill. In other words, the women are into it. Oh, and Patrick uses condoms, so it's practically G-rated. Educational, even. That will be my only saving grace if my boss finds out about the change in tone that Book Club has recently undertaken under my tutelage, or a complaint is made to Council. Or both.

All eyes suddenly turn to the diminutive 100-year-old lady, wearing a cotton dress that resembles a nightie, with her velvet night gown over the top.

'What I can't understand,' says Margy, her eyes twinkling as she surveys her prey, 'is why in the dickens a burglar would bring his rooster with him on his errands. Surely it would be more of a hindrance than a help, regardless of its size.'

There is a confused silence for a moment as we all simultaneously try to fathom what on earth Margy is talking about, before Elle applies the social lubricant I mentioned.

'I totally agree, Margy,' she says congenially. 'Anyone would think he wished to be caught in the act.'

'That's right,' says Margy, encouraged. 'And another thing. Why does he only burgle homes with cats? Unless he's a fool, he should know that a cock is going to clash with pussies and cause a kerfuffle.' She narrows her eyes, and brings a finger up, pointing it indiscriminately at other attendees. 'Something else is going on with this burglar, and I'm going to get to the bottom of it.'

Bravo, Margy. Artfully convincing a room full of women that she thinks she has been reading a detective novel, and not dark erotica. I dip my eyebrows at her in a sign of disapproval. She shrugs and presses her lips together to stop herself from smiling.

It is all too much for Elle. She has now turned bright red with the effort of not bursting into laughter. Tears are welling in the corner of her eyes, and if I don't say something fast, she is going to implode.

'I rather think that by describing Patrick's member in the way she has, the author is giving us one of the first hints that the story is being told by an unreliable narrator.' Now *I* am the focus of the confused looks. 'We're not meant to understand what she means. We're just meant to realise that not everything she tells us is to be taken at face value. His rooster is unrealistic, because she isn't giving us the reality – only her version of it.'

'Ah, Meg, that's why you are our gallant leader,' says Elle, who has managed to compose herself. 'I'm sure you are right. Look at us, girls. Taking everything so literally,' she says with an engaging smile and a scan around the group, which garners a few sheepish smiles in return. 'What a kerfuffle we'd be in without you,' she adds. She couldn't help herself. I know. But that's done it. Everyone is now in a fit of side-splitting laughter, except for me, the ultimate professional.

It takes a good fifteen minutes for everyone to settle down enough to return to the book, but somehow, I just know that every mention of Patrick's cock from here on in will be met with sniggers of laughter and poultry-related side comments. But it's my own fault for choosing such a fowl-mouthed book.

***

The day after Book Club – Thursdays – I start work late, to make up for the overtime I do on a Wednesday. If I leave home an hour later though, I'll be stuck in the traffic, so I make my way towards work at the usual time and take up my favourite spot at the coffee shop beneath the library. The library is on the first floor of one of the oldest buildings in Leeds, and the coffee shop is one of the most popular in this part of town, so it's always busy at this time of the morning. I walk in and I'm instantly hit with the tantalising aroma of good-quality coffee and freshly baked muffins.

My spot is by the front window, in the far corner. I love it, because I can sit and read without feeling like I'm in the way, and when I want to, I can gaze out the window and people watch. Sometimes, I'll try to match a person walking by to a character in the book I'm reading. And in Leeds, there isn't a character *anyone* could write who won't walk past at some stage.

I order a flat white, and then head for my table. I pull *Cloaked Lust* out of the reusable shopping bag I carry for work, and I'm about to settle in to read when a familiar face walks in. It's 'the one'. Elle's 'one', that is: Joe. He's not usually someone I'd see in this part of town at this time in the morning, which makes me suspect it's me he's looking for.

Sure enough, he notices me, and raises his hand in greeting, then makes his way over. I place *Cloaked Lust* down and stand up to greet him with a kiss on the cheek.

'You all right, Joe?'

'How do, Meg?'

Joe is quite possibly the sweetest man on earth, and handsome too. He is tall and lean, with blonde hair, baby-blue eyes and the sort of face that holds not a speck of malice. He couldn't smirk or scowl even if he wanted to, and when he smiles, I find I can't help but smile back. He has a gentle, softly spoken nature, tending more towards serious, than jovial. I used to think that was what made him such a good match for Elle – she brought out the lighter side of Joe, and he was a steadying influence on Elle. But lately, I worry.

'What are you doing in Leeds?' Joe has a sheep farm in the Dales that he inherited after his father passed a few years ago. He always knew it would be his one day, but his father's death from a heart attack was sudden, and Joe wound up a farmer long before he planned. He took it all in his stride, but he has been on a steep learning curve.

'Need to see the accountant.'

'Oh. Is that all?'

'Also, wanted to talk to you.' Oh dear. What was it that Elle had been saying about gout, and was it… possible consumption? 'Have you been speaking to Elle?'

'I saw her at Book Club last night.' Joe knits his brows, and I realise I've said the wrong thing. 'She said she had a headache. She left early,' I add. Joe looks more concerned, than annoyed.

'Aye, bit goin' on at work, she says.'

'Is something worrying you, Joe?' How can I not ask? He's come out of his way to see me, hoping to find out what's going on with Elle. I can't help him with that, because she's a puzzle to me as well, but

I can offer him a chance to get it off his chest. He is isolated on the farm. It's just him and his mum, and they are a good hour from Leeds. I wonder if that's one of the reasons he proposed to Elle while they are still so young. It would be a hard life on his own.

'Aye,' he says. He rubs his hand across his chin. 'I think she's avoiding me. Always busy when I want to see her, but still out and about.'

'How about I ask them to make my coffee a takeaway, and we go for a walk?' I suggest, and Joe nods.

I have half an hour before work. In that time, we mooch around town, coffees in hand. Joe tells me his Elle-related woes, and I provide what I hope are suitable Elle-related excuses on her behalf. When we part ways, Joe seems appeased, and I am five minutes late for work.

I rush up the stairs to the first floor, not wanting to lose any more precious seconds waiting for the lift. I burst into the staff room and hastily pull out my lunch, shove it in the fridge, secure my name tag to the front of my black t-shirt and head out onto the library floor. It is at this exact moment that I realise what I have left downstairs, on my favourite table in the coffee shop.

***

Cloaked Lust is neither present, nor accounted for. My stomach drops. It's not the sort of book one would want to fall into the wrong hands. Not only is it fowl-mouthed, but it is also one of the library's copies, and to not return a library book is a most heinous crime to those of my profession.

If my boss hasn't noticed I was late, then perhaps, I could explain that I need to pop downstairs for something I've forgotten. Or perhaps I could make up an excuse to go to the newsagent across the road, and detour via the coffee shop. But if she has noticed, she is going to be riding me like a fairground pony for the next seven hours.

A voice behind me makes me cringe. 'Nice of you to join us, Meg.' Fairground pony it is, then. I don't know if there is a better way of pointing out that someone is late, but I can't help but feel my boss has chosen the most patronising way possible.

'Morning, Pip. Sorry I'm late. I got caught up,' I say, as I turn towards her. She raises her eyebrows but doesn't speak. I think she's waiting for further explanation. That won't be forthcoming, as there isn't one. 'I'll get onto the re-shelving,' I say, mainly to make her go away.

'Yes, and then you can take over the Toddler Time session from Yvonne. I need her on customer service.' For fuck's sake. My least favourite job, and she knows it.

There seems to be two extremes when it comes to toddlers. There are the ones who cry as soon as they see me, even when I attempt the friendliest, least threatening demeanour at my disposal. Maybe it's my tattoos, or maybe it's that I dress like the grim reaper, I don't know, but I frighten them, and they frighten me. Then there are the ones who frighten me even more – those who have absolutely no concept of personal space. The ones who want to sit on my lap, and play with my hair, and lick me and bite me, all beneath the facade of listening to a story.

Surely, my monotone, expressionless reading voice would be enough to prevent a responsible library manager from putting me on Toddler Time. I make even the most carefully crafted, entertaining children's literature sound like the stock market report. But when Pip is displeased, she will stop at nothing to reap her revenge.

And she's not quite done.

'An impressive turn out for Book Club yesterday,' she says. Her tone conveys this isn't intended as the pat on the back I feel I deserve. 'I'll have to make it along to a session. I'd love to know what arts you've employed to make it such a raging success.'

Oh, for the love of God, don't do that, Pip. If that happens, Toddler Time will be the least of my worries, and finding new employment will be the most pertinent. Maybe she knows, and she's just biding her time to make the killer blow, content with using Toddler Time as a form of torture until then.

Pip goes back to her office, and I am about to turn for the re-shelving trolleys in the Large Print section, when I'm stopped in my tracks. Quite literally, I cannot move.

A man has just walked through the automatic glass sliding doors into the library. That might not sound like too much of an odd occurrence. Statistically, it is a rarity. Ninety-five percent of our patrons are female. But I can hand on heart tell you that men of the type of this one make up exactly zero point zero, zero, zero percent of our patronage.

He has dark brown wavy hair, pulled back in a messy man bun at the nape of his neck, except for one lock that sits loose across his thick dark brows. Neat, dark facial hair covers his upper lip and his chin, and he has a stretcher earring in his left earlobe. He is wearing a black motorcycle jacket over a white t-shirt, black jeans, and heavy boots. He is solidly built, and tall. Really tall. He could easily have eight inches on me, and from the look of the bulge in his jeans, he could be packing 8 x 8 down there as well. And he is drop. Dead. Gorgeous.

I think my mouth might be hanging open, and I know I have to move, or look away, or something, but I genuinely can't. And then, my life flashes before my eyes, because in the palm of one of his gigantic, tattooed hands is a copy of *Cloaked Lust*.

Chapter Three

My mind whirrs. I quickly recount the timeline of the morning. I sat down at 8:15am in the coffee shop. Joe entered shortly afterwards. We spoke for maybe five minutes before we left. It's now 9:20am. That leaves… oh dear God, approximately one hour of *Cloaked Lust's* time unaccounted for. It could have been anywhere during that hour, including in the enormous hands of this man before me.

He has stopped just inside the library entrance, and he's looking around, as though assessing for signs of threat in this unfamiliar habitat. Then he looks at me. Straight at me. First at my face, and then, to my surprise and discomfort, his eyes travel down my body. Slowly they traverse past my t-shirt, down my black skinny jeans, to my black high-top boots, then they make their way back up just as slowly. I have never been appraised in quite this manner before, and I don't know what to do. I'd love to dive behind something to hide, but there's nothing nearby, and my feet still seem to be nailed to the ground. I feel the heat rising in my cheeks, and I know I must now look like a member of the Addams family who has caught the sun.

He steps towards me, and I take the only evasive measure I seem capable of right now. I divert my eyes and become keenly interested in a suspect spot on the carpet about a metre in front of me. That is, until the spot is replaced by the top of his boots.

I'm going to have to speak to him. I've racked my brains for any other possible solution to this social conundrum, and there isn't one. I pull my eyes up from his boots to the top of his shoulder, which seems slightly less intimidating than meeting his eyes.

'Can I help you, sir?'

Sir? Really, Meg?

A deep, gravelly voice emerges from what I can only imagine must be his strapping vocal cords.

'Are you Meg Drury?'

Fuck. He knows my name. How does he know my name? And how did he know where to find me? I don't know what to say, and I'm not thinking clearly. Clearly. Because I say, 'N-no.'

I just can't. It's too embarrassing. If he has opened to any random page of *Cloaked Lust*, then he will know I was sitting in that coffee shop reading literary porn, and not the sweet, innocent, boy meets girl, boy shags girl in many varied ways, boy marries girl, literary porn. No, no. This is cloaked psychopath meets girl, shags girl while tied to her bed head, proceeds to shag many other girls in a similar fashion, literary porn. The hard stuff.

'You're wearing a name badge.'

Shit. I forgot about that. In that case, 'Yes, I'm Meg Drury,' I concede.

'Is this your book?'

You know what? You know it is, you bastard. Just hand it over. We don't need to discuss it. You're a fish out of water here. I am clearly floundering. Let's get this over with.

'Yes, thank-you.' I hold out my hand. He doesn't hand it over. Instead, he pulls out the unopened letter from my car insurer from between the pages, where it had been holding my place as a bookmark. Another heinous crime. He's either unaware of this fact, or a complete sicko. At least I know now how he knew my name. He turns the envelope over to the back, where it is covered in felt pen drawings. I draw on everything. Patterns, objects, faces. Tattoos. I love to draw tattoos. All my ink I have designed myself. None of it means anything, it's simply creative expression. When I draw something I particularly enjoy the look of, I get it tattooed on my body somewhere. I almost have a full sleeve on my right arm, and the rest are scattered over my body, wherever I feel the urge to get one that day. There's no rhyme or reason, just a feel.

'Did you draw these?' he asks.

'Yes.'

He nods, and to my horror, he folds the envelope, and places it in the inside pocket of his jacket. It has my home address on it. I want to say something, but I can't. Or I don't, I'm not sure which. Finally, he hands me the book.

'H-how did you know where to find me?' I ask, because it seems the responsible thing to do, with the stalker vibes now hitting strong.

'It's a library book, isn't it?' he says. 'This is a library. Don't they lock you up if you don't return your books?'

That might have been a joke. I risk a look up at his face, and his lips twitch slightly as I meet his eyes. His eyes are hard, though, scrutinising me with an intensity that makes me blush again.

'First time offenders generally get no worse than a slap on the wrists. But thank-you, anyway. I couldn't afford a lawyer.'

He gives a single, deep chuckle. Surely, he is going to leave now that *Cloaked Lust* has been repatriated. He looks around again. 'How does this place work?'

'Sorry?'

'Say I wanted a book. What do I have to do to get one?'

I blink several times before I can respond.

'Well… it's quite straightforward. You find what you want on the shelves, and then you bring it to the counter. The rest is my area of speciality.'

He raises an eyebrow. 'What else do you specialise in?'

God, I think he's flirting with me. He can't be, can he? He's waiting for an answer. I've got to say something. Self-deprecation usually works to parlay the advances of male suitors. I'll try that.

'Sadly, I have few other talents.'

He seems to accept that response. Perhaps it's worked.

'I need a book about bikes. Got any of those?'

I think I know the answer without asking, but I ask anyway. 'Push bikes or motorbikes?'

His lips twitch again. 'Motorbikes.'

I find it hard to believe that this man really wants a book about motorbikes from the local library in Leeds. But being the ultimate professional, I can't refuse his request.

'You'll want the non-fiction section. Aisle 22, about mid-way along, bottom shelf. I gesture towards the section to his right.

'Lead the way.' It's not a suggestion. It's an order.

I wriggle my toes. There is movement. Perhaps I can walk now. I send a determined message from my brain to my feet, and yes, there we go, they are now moving in a reciprocal motion towards the automotive section in Aisle 22. He follows behind me, and when we reach the target shelf, I stand back and allow him to look.

He crouches down and gives the spines a cursory glance before pulling one out. *A History of British Motorcycles.*

'This is the one,' he says. I'm sure it can't be.

'Fine. This way. I lead him towards the front counter. He walks in step beside me, and as we walk, I pluck up the courage to ask the question that has been relentlessly drumming in my brain. 'You didn't... read any of my book, did you?'

Two deep chuckles this time. That bodes ill. I look at him, and I know there is panic in my eyes. We've reached the counter, and I walk around to the staff side. He places the motorcycle book on the counter and slides it towards me.

'I don't read.' Unaware of the irony, or being ironic? I can't tell. I always have trouble reading people, but this man is truly confounding me.

'I'll need to sign you up as a member. May I see some ID?'

His self-assuredness slips, and he becomes defensive. 'What do you need that for?'

'I need to enter a home address and a phone number. The system will send you a text message with a reminder when the book is due back. And if you don't return it, we will know where to send the bobby.'

I notice him tense, but he takes out his wallet and hands me a business card. The card reads, 'R.J. Ink' and beneath, Reed Johnson, Owner Manager, the address and phone number of the shop. I shouldn't really accept this as ID, but I'm not going to argue.

I'm surprised to note that I'm not familiar with the shop. I thought I was up to speed with what was available in town, but then, I do have my favourite place, and I haven't had the need to shop around for a while.

I enter the details into the system, all the while aware of his eyes trained on me. He is leaning slightly on the desk, and I can smell his aftershave. It's a crisp, clean smell. I place the business card, along with Reed's new library card on top of the book, and I slide it across towards him.

'All done,' I say, and offer the polite, professional smile I produce for all borrowers once the process is complete.

'Dinner tonight.'

'S-sorry?'

'You and me. Dinner. Tonight,' he says. 'I'll pick you up at seven.'

Oh God. He just asked me out.

'Ah, I... thank-you but, no, I can't.'

Somehow, I don't think he gets turned down too often. He stands up straight, and pulls out his wallet, placing the library card inside, but his eyes haven't budged from me.

'Why not?'

Fuck. Because you frighten me, and there is just no way I could get even halfway through dinner with you without a sedative of some sort.

'I play netball on Thursday nights.' It's true, I do. I know it seems unlikely, but I was five foot nine when I was twelve years old, and that really left me with no choice. All I had to do to get picked for representative teams was stand on court and occasionally raise my arms in the air. I'm not the sporty type, but apparently you don't have to be to play Goal Keeper. Anyway, playing netball is how I met Elle and Gabby, and Elle then adopted me as a friend, so it all worked out the way it was meant to.

Reed doesn't seem to think my excuse is plausible. He raises an eyebrow at me, and there is a slight smirk on his face. 'Netball, hey?'

'Yes.' Suddenly, I feel defensive. 'I'm actually quite good.'

The smirk widens to a lopsided smile. 'I don't doubt you're good at many things.' He couldn't be more wrong, but I'm not going to correct him. He picks up a pen from the spares we have on the desk for people to sign the back of their library card with. He takes his business card and crosses out 'Reed Johnson'. Below it, he writes, all in capitals, 'JOHNNO', and beside it, a mobile number – I assume, his. He slides the card across the desk towards me.

'In case you change your mind. He picks up *A History of British Motorcycles* and strives for the exit, my peace of mind leaving with him.

Chapter Four

I have thought about nothing but Reed 'Johnno' Johnson all day. By the time I arrive at netball, I am practically bursting to tell Elle about it, and simultaneously horrified at the thought of telling Gabby about it.

Elle and Gabby are passing a ball back and forwards between them when I get there. Gabby is our Goal Defence, which means I'm stuck down one end of the court with her for the entire game. Not a nice place to be for someone with minimal commitment and motivation for the cause, because Gabby is elite, and expects the rest of us to match her. Gabby will play for England one day. She's on the verge. I can't wait for her to make it. She might be too busy for the Leeds Lightning then.

'You look constipated, Meg. What's wrong with you?' *Ah, Gabby. So intuitive.* I dump my bag down and join them on court.

'Not that.' I throw Elle a look that I hope conveys I have something to tell her. She gives me a curious look in return, and then gasps.

'Has Margy died?'

How is there any similarity between my, 'I need to tell you about a guy who asked me out face', and my 'someone has just died' face?

'Margy is alive and well,' I say. 'At least, as far as I know.'

Elle furrows her brow, and I give her another speaking look that I hope has more of the romantic entwinement about it and less of the recently bereaved. Perhaps it has worked, because she grabs me by the elbow and says, 'Let me warm you up,' and drags me to the far end of the court. Thankfully, Gabby doesn't follow.

Elle was our team's starting Goal Attack, and an absolute weapon, until last year when she was involved in a car accident. She suffered a head injury that left her with altered vision, and she hasn't been able to shoot the same since. She is devastated about it, but at the same time, extremely fortunate. Not everyone in the car made it, and I sure as hell would prefer Elle alive with poor vision, and some unresolved, deeply suppressed emotional trauma than the alternative.

Remarkably, she has managed to improve enough to still make the bench, but her shooting percentage is down around 70 percent, rather than her previous 85, and that isn't good enough to earn her place back in the starting side. Elle is convinced all she has to do is 're-calibrate'. She says shooting is more about feel and perception than it is about vision, and once she adjusts to how she sees things now, her accuracy will improve. I hope she is right, because it means a lot to her. She takes her place in the circle, and puts up shots while I attempt to block, and then turn to challenge her for rebounds.

'Spill the tea, Meg. If that look you were giving me wasn't due to a lack of fibre in your diet, then what was it?' Elle asks with a cheeky smile.

I take a rebound, pass the ball back to her and then flick my hair, that I have swept back and secured in a high ponytail, over my shoulder with a purse of my lips to dismiss the tease.

'I've had an interesting day today.' I'll build the intrigue. Elle will like that.

'Ooh, if *you* think it was interesting, then it must have been!'

'I saw Joe this morning.'

The smug grin she was giving me disappears. 'What was he doing in town?'

'Visiting his accountant and trying to determine for how long you'll be in Bath on your healing sojourn.'

'Oh dear,' says Elle, dismayed. 'What did you tell him?'

'I told him you'd be in touch on your return, and not to worry, you're not having an affair, or planning to cry off.'

Elle, who was lining up a shot, lowers her arms and suddenly looks pale. 'Is that what he thinks?'

'I think he's starting to have concerns, Elle. He knows you're avoiding him. Knowing Joe, he's giving you the benefit of the doubt, but for how much longer? He went out of his way to question me about it.'

Elle stares at me for a moment, before saying, 'Fuck,' and putting up another shot. She misses by a mile, and the ball bounces away towards the stands. I jog over to get it, and then pass it back to her. She's still frowning, so I decide I'll change the subject. Plus, I desperately want to tell her about Johnno. I just don't want her to *know* how desperately I want to tell her.

'Joe's visit did trigger a chain of events that led to a guy asking me out.'

Elle's face instantly brightens. She is a hopeless romantic, and I get the feeling she is living vicariously through me while she's not relishing the prospect of marrying Joe.

'At work? A library guy? Oh, Meg, I bet he will be perfect for you! What's he like? Is he good looking?'

Drop dead gorgeous. 'Not half bad, I suppose.'

'Details!' she demands.

'He's got the bad-boy aesthetic going on. Nice ink.'

'A bad boy library guy? I didn't know there was such a thing!'

'There isn't.'

'How did this come about? What charms did you employ, my dear Meg, to ensnare him in your web?'

'As you know very well, I have no charms. It all came about because when Joe caught me, I left my copy of *Cloaked Lust* behind by accident at the coffee shop downstairs from work, and he returned it to me. I don't think he's ever set foot in a library prior to that.'

'Oh Meg! It's so romantic!' Elle says, conveniently ignoring the part where I told her he isn't really a bad boy library guy. 'When are you going out?'

Here's the part I'm not looking forward to telling her, because she is going to give me hell.

'I said no.'

Here it comes.

'Meg Drury! Are you completely daft? You said no, to a not half bad library bad boy who asked you out, without you even needing to try??' She shakes her head at me, with her hand on her hip, and the netball under her other arm. 'I'm very disappointed in you.'

Now I think I'm a bit disappointed in myself. 'I *couldn't* say yes. He was intimidating. I'm sure I wouldn't get through a whole date with him, and if I did, he would realise within the first half hour that he was badly mistaken about the whole thing and would probably end up with a sudden attack of the gout.'

'Rubbish, Meg! God, you frustrate me with this lack of confidence. I want to shake you. When will you realise what a catch you are?'

I shrug my shoulders, but Elle's reprimand has made me feel suitably repentant. I'll never see myself as a catch. Not from where I started, as the pale, awkward, gangly teen who couldn't talk to anyone, let alone boys. I have come a way since then, sure. Netball has helped, as has growing into my height, getting ink, and meeting friends who are almost as weird as I am. But inside, I'll always be that book nerd who hid in the shadows, and cowered from attention like a vampire would from the light.

Coach blows her whistle, and we're going to have to join the team, but as we jog over, Elle says, 'I want to know how you're going to fix this,' and if I know Elle, she's not going to let this go until I give her an answer.

***

As I ready myself for work the next morning, after a solid win against the side from Hull, Elle's words are ringing in my mind. How *am* I going to fix this? One thing is clear to me after sleeping on it— I want to see that man again. He is living rent free in my mind, and this never happens to me. Ever. I was so nervous yesterday I didn't even really take him in. What colour were his eyes? How long would his hair be if it wasn't tied up? Did he have all of his teeth? How can I fantasise about him for the rest of my life without knowing those details? I can't go out with him, but God, I'd love to spend another two minutes in his company. That would be enough to keep me going.

Maybe it's that thought that makes me put in just a little extra effort with my appearance this morning. I wear my hair down, parting it just off to the side so that it falls over my shoulder on the right, add some red-tinted lip gloss and mascara, and put my nose stud back in that I had to take out for netball. I still wear my skinny jeans and black high tops, but instead of my usual t-shirt, I opt for a black satin button-up blouse that I half tuck-in at my waist.

I don't usually buy a coffee on Friday mornings, because I have to be at work early to open up for 8am, but this morning, I leave extra early so I can grab one to go, on the off chance he might be there. No luck, but the coffee is good.

I open, and as always, business is slow for the first couple of hours. While a couple of regulars browse the shelves, and a young mother who looks desperate for a half hour of respite from her child lets the kid run riot through the children's section, I think about what I might be able to do to see Johnno again.

He has to come back, right? He borrowed a book. Loans are two weeks. At some point, he must return it or suffer the consequence of increasingly persistent text reminders until he does. But two weeks—that's a long time, and even then, what if I'm not here when he comes? I log in to the computer system and see if there might be a way of activating the return reminder text early. I never told him he could keep the book for two weeks. He won't know if the loan time is two days, or two weeks, will he? If I can send the text, he'll have to come back. After fifteen minutes taking a deep dive into the back end of the text reminder system, I find that there is a way to manually enter a date.

That's all well and good, but what if he comes back out of hours and uses the after-hours returns chute? I'll have to do something about that too. It should be easy enough. I just have to block up the chute somehow, and it can't look like deliberate sabotage. I'll have to wedge a book half-way down. That will jam it, and it will automatically switch to out-of-order mode and lock down.

It's decided. I'll send the text at midday, then block the chute before I lock up for the weekend. As I start the task of re-shelving the books in the Geography and Travel section, I make a mental note to keep an eye out for a book of the perfect size to block the chute. I can't wait to tell Elle I've thought of a way to fix the prob—

'How was netball?' a deep, gravelly voice asks from behind me.

I drop the book I'm holding and let out a high-pitched scream, then clap my hand over my mouth to smother it. I glance left and right, and see the disapproving looks directed my way from the regulars, and from a few rows over, I hear an irritated, 'Shh' hiss in my direction through the shelves.

Slowly I turn around to face Johnno.

'Fuck, what was that?' he asks.

'You startled me. What are you doing here?'

'Borrowed a book, remember? Came to return it.'

'Loans are for two weeks. I'm sorry, I should have told you yesterday.'

'You could've texted me. I gave you my number.'

Ah, yes. A text. But that would have been far too simple.

I seem to be coping better with my second exposure to Johnno. I can look at him a little more easily today, and God, it's a pleasure to do so. He's even more gorgeous than I remember. I notice the firm set of his jaw, and the way his facial hair fades as it approaches his ear and connects to his sideburns. I can't look at his eyes yet, but his jaw is nice.

My gaze falls on his chest. He isn't wearing a jacket today, and his tight black V-neck t-shirt hugs the curves of his pecs and allows a glimpse of the tattoo at the top of his neck that continues on beneath it. I want to take that t-shirt off him right here, right now, and examine every inch of him. I've never had that urge before. Usually when I feel compelled to take a man's shirt off it's by the voice in my head that says, 'Do it, Meg. That's what you're supposed to do in this situation, and the sooner you do it, the sooner this whole charade will be over.'

'Well, how was it?'

I have no idea what he's talking about. I'm still staring at his chest. I reef my eyes up to his face. His eyes are green. I don't know how I didn't notice yesterday, because they are the nicest thing about him. They don't seem like they should be green, because they are hard, but they are green, and it makes him seem kind of...magical. 'What?'

'Netball.'

'Fine. We won.'

'I know. 32-12.'

Fuck. How the hell does he know that? 'How do you know?'

'Googled you. You play in the county comp.'

'I stand on court and a game takes place around me, yes.'

'I thought you said you were quite good.'

'I exaggerated because you piqued me.'

'Forgive me,' he says, with a courtesy that seems out of place. 'You didn't strike me as an athlete. I thought you were trying to get out of dinner.'

I don't say anything, even though he waits, as though he expects me to admit that I was, in fact, trying to get out of dinner. Eventually, he gives up on getting a confession out of me.

'What do I do with this?' He holds up *A History of British Motor-cycles*.

'Finished already?'

'I only wanted to look at the pictures.' The hard look is still there in his eyes, but that twitch of a smile is on his face as well. He's... funny?

'I see. Follow me.'

I lead him to the returns chute, and show him how to slide his book through the opening with the barcode up so it automatically scans back in.

'Thanks.'

'No problem. It's my speciality.'

I smile my professional smile, and as he doesn't say anything more, I start to walk back over to Aisle 25 to continue re-shelving.

'Got any books about netball?'

I stop and turn back. It's my lips that twitch this time.

'Yes. Follow me.' On the way to the sports section, I ask, 'Is your interest in netball longstanding?'

'Started yesterday,' he replies. A pleasant wave of sensation washes over my body. He is flirting. With *me*. Meg Drury. Librarian and people-repeller extraordinaire. If only I wasn't so deathly afraid of him, I might be enjoying this.

We reach the section with books about all things netball. There aren't that many— five or six.

'Are you looking for skills focused, facts, or history?'

'What do you recommend?'

'Is it the pictures you're interested in?'

'Correct.'

I pull out *Everything You Need to Know About Netball* from the *Everything You Need to Know About Stuff* series. 'I think you'll find this very informative,' I say, and hand it to Johnno. He takes it and flips it open to the first couple of pages, studies them for a moment, and then looks at me.

'Do you wear one of these little dresses when you play?'

I blush so hard I get a head spin. 'They're compulsory.'

He closes the book, and holds it in his left hand, and then his eyes scan my body the way they did yesterday, but even more deliberately—or at least it seems that way, perhaps because he is closer, and there is a faint smile on his lips, as though he is quite unashamedly enjoying it. As he reaches my chest, where the top of my shirt buttons together, his eyes rest on the floral tattoo visible in black ink at the top of my right breast. It continues down my sternum, on its way to finishing beneath my left breast. If I'm being honest, it's why I wore this shirt. He can't see all of it, obviously, but I assume he must like what he can see, because he licks his bottom lip, and when he fixes his eyes on mine, there is a heat there that I almost can't take. I think I am going to pass out.

'Colour?'

'Blue and white.'

'I'd like to see that.' Whether he means me in a netball dress, or the rest of my tattoo, I don't care. I want him to see it too. 'Have dinner with me. You choose the night.'

Fuck. I want to but... I can't. Fantasising about him is one thing. Exchanging brief statements, largely about books, for no longer than ten minutes at a time, in my comfort zone of the library, I can just about cope with. Dinner? No.

'I-I really can't.' Even as I say it, I feel the regret swelling in my chest. But the words are out. I see his jaw clench, and he raises his hand towards me. For a terrifying moment I think he's going to touch me. But then he puts it back down and shoves it in his pocket.

'Is that blonde thing you were with in the coffee shop your boyfriend?' he asks gruffly.

Poor Joe. I'm sure he wouldn't be happy with that description. 'No. Just a friend.'

'He lives then. Who *do* I have to kill?'

I can't help but smile a little. No one has ever threatened to murder someone in their quest to date me before. It feels surprisingly good. Even though it's very hard to determine if this guy is joking, or completely serious.

'I don't have a boyfriend.'

Johnno doesn't seem too placated by that. 'Just can't then, hey?'

I nod.

He stares at me, as though willing me to crack, and then he turns and strides towards the customer service counter where Pip is now on duty. He places *Everything You Need to Know About Netball* down on the counter with enough force that I'm sure Pip will be questioning his suitability to borrow, then pulls his library card out of his wallet, and tosses it on the desk. It is the sexiest thing I've ever seen in my life. It's going to keep me up at night. As Pip scans his card, and his book, he looks back over his shoulder at me. He looks pissed off, and I hope he interprets the look I give him back as, 'I'm sorry, you're just way too hot for me, and I'll regret turning you down for the rest of my life, but if you ask me out a hundred times, I will do the same, because that's who I am and I'm destined to be alone.'

I'll be surprised if he got all that.

He turns back to Pip as she hands him back his card and tries to encourage him to take a free re-usable hessian bag to protect his loan. He declines with a shake of his head, and as he leaves, he doesn't look back.

Chapter Five

I am blessed with a large family. Two younger brothers whom I adore, an older sister whom I despise, and my parents whom I try to remember to refer to as Mum and Dad now that I am twenty-one, instead of Mummy and Daddy. I do still slip up occasionally.

My sister has moved out of home— thankfully, because when she was at home we had to share a bedroom. My brothers have always had separate rooms, but Mum thought making me and Sophie share would bring us closer together. It didn't. We hate each other even more due to the prolonged close proximity we were forced to endure.

On Sundays, Mum prepares the traditional Sunday roast lunch, and we all gather to eat together. Sophie almost always comes home for the event, and sometimes surrogate family members, like Elle and Joe, join us as well.

On this particular Sunday, I am not in the mood, but bailing out is not an option. It's important to Mum that we're all there. She gets very hurt if any of us skive off, and I would never do it to her.

I manage to drag myself out of bed around half nine, and I am absent-mindedly peeling potatoes when Mum commences her weekly interrogation about my love life.

'How *are* you, Meggy?' she asks, the same way she does every Sunday.

'Fine.'

'How is your book club going?'

'Well.'

'Will Elle be joining us today?'

'No.'

'What is she up to this weekend?'

'She's in Bath.'

I'm not being deliberately difficult. I just don't want to talk, and I know she's just building up to asking what she really wants to ask.

'How is that nice young man who took you out last week? Have you seen him again?'

'Who?'

'The one who picked you up in his car and took you to dinner. Italian, wasn't it?'

'Oh. Him.' I can't even remember his name. Poor form, since I slept with him. 'I won't be seeing him again.'

'Why not?' How can she seem disappointed? She didn't know him. I introduced him, only because he came to the front door before I could get out to meet him quickly enough to prevent that very thing.

'He's not "the one."'

'You know, for someone to be "the one", they don't have to be perfect,' Mum says. 'It's the eighty-twenty rule.'

Now, Mum has piqued by interest. Of course, I know what the eighty-twenty rule is. Every good librarian does. The rule dictates that eighty percent of library borrowing comes from twenty percent of members. You keep the twenty percent happy; you remain on Council payroll. But Mum is no mathematical genius, unless we are talking the quickest in the room to calculate an additional twenty percent off sale items. 'What on earth does the Pareto principle have to do with dating?' I wait with baited, if slightly dubious, breath for her response.

'Dating has nothing to do with parrots, Meg.' She scoffs lightly. 'What I mean is, if you find someone who is eighty percent suitable, then you accept and learn to love the other twenty percent.' She smiles at me encouragingly, as though cajoling me to admit that Mr Italian might be eighty percent lovable, and a meagre twenty percent unbearable.

'Oh, I see. So, you don't mean twenty percent of my failed dating exploits are eighty percent of the reason for my inability to make a bloke stick?' I receive a look of acute confusion from Professor Drury, but I am curious now whether this rule applies only to the desperate, or whether it also applies to the happiest couple I know. 'What about Dad? Was he only eighty percent right for you?'

'Dad and I are probably closer to ninety percent,' she admits, with a goofy smile on her face. 'We were lucky. But if you keep on looking for perfection, you will end up disappointed, my love.'

'Alone, you mean.'

'Meg,' Mum says, taking the peeler out of my hand and placing it gently down. I'm getting intervention vibes. 'You're moping. What's the matter?'

'Nothing, Mum.' She doesn't believe me. 'Work. I had to do Toddler Time again this week. I think I'm still recovering.'

For the first time in recent memory, I'm happy to see my sister barge into the room, only because all attention will now be turned to her and remain on her for as long as she is here, thus freeing me from scrutiny.

'You all right, Mummy?' she says brightly, and comes over to give Mum a kiss.

'Yes, all right, Soph,' says Mum, and squeezes her.

Sophie sits down at one of the bench seats on the other side of the counter, far away from any of the work-related tasks.

'What's wrong with you, Meg? Having a sulk?' she asks, as she decides I'm worthy of acknowledgement.

'This is my normal face. You know that.'

Sophie smiles smugly and flicks her long blonde hair over her shoulder. 'Have you told Mummy about Thursday's game?'

'No, it hasn't come up.' I pick up a knife and start to chop the potatoes, hoping if I look busy enough, I might avoid being included in this Sophie-focused conversation.

'We won, against Hull. 32-12. Their Centre is one of the best in the comp, but I shut her down quite effectively, didn't I Meg?'

Actually, Gabby completely decimated their Goal Attack, and that's why we won, but saying that will only set Sophie off. Sophie is the Centre for Leeds Lightning. She is a typical Centre. Energetic and annoying, with just a hint of obnoxious 'I-can-go-anywhere-I-want-on-the-court-except-in-the-circles-can-you?' about them. All netball positions have their personality types. Goal Shooters are confident and disciplined. Goal Attacks, like Elle, are bubbly and charismatic. Goal Defences, like Gabby, are serious and cutthroat. Wing Attacks are reckless and impulsive. Wing Defences are shy and retiring. And Goal Keepers are moody and indifferent— on a good day.

'Quite.'

Sophie and I really couldn't be more different. She has mum's blonde hair and is what one might call fashionably tall. It's a similar concept to being fashionably late. There is a certain degree of lateness that is acceptable. In fact, one even wants to be a little late, so as not to appear too eager. It's the same with height. To a point, being tall is desirable. But then a certain point is reached where it is no longer fashionable, and one is considered too tall. Sophie stopped growing just a smidgen below that point. I, however, continued long past the point of fashionable, and Sophie has always loved to be the first one to bring that to people's attention. When I finally got my boobs, and she was twenty years old with still no sign of puberty, she had to accept that I had bested her in that category at least. It is the one and only advantage I can claim to have over her.

The only similarity between Sophie and I is that we both have Mum's blue eyes. Other than that, I take after Dad in every way. He used to have pitch black hair like mine, but his has since turned silvery grey. He, too, is beyond fashionably tall. In fact, there is nothing at all fashionable about Dad. He is shy, and quite nervy around people he doesn't know, but he is the kindest, most brilliant man in the world. I adore him, and quietly, I know he loves me more than Sophie. He's never said it, it's just a vibe.

'What do you think Coach is going to do about Elle? She can't keep playing her on the bench when her percentage is so dreadful.'

I stiffen and pause from my potato chopping to glare at Sophie. Mum notices, and says in a warning tone, 'Meg'.

'Elle is improving all the time. Anyway, she only played a quarter, and we still won comfortably, and you know as well as I do that Goal Attack is about more than just shooting percentage. She contributes right through the middle.'

'We can't keep carrying her.'

Now Mum says, 'Soph' in a warning tone.

'Who would you bring in instead, Sophie?' I ask, my blood thoroughly boiling now. I point the knife at her as I speak, which I know is concerning Mum. 'There's no one better in Reserves. Elle is—' I stop, because I've noticed the smirk spreading across Sophie's face, and I realise, as I always do too late, that I am doing exactly what she wants me to do. She simply loves to stir me. She finds it hilarious when I react, probably because she knows that she is one of the very few people who can push me to it. 'Sorry, Mum.' I place down the knife and step away from the potatoes. 'I'll be in my room.'

***

I slam my bedroom door shut and collapse face down onto my bed. The last thing I feel like doing today is sparring with Sophie. All I want to do is stay in my room and read, and draw, and sleep.

With that comfortable aim in mind, I open my bedside drawer and take out my sketch book. I flick through the pages to my last drawing, and stare at it. It's good. Probably won't be a tattoo any time soon, but still. It's Johnno. His profile, looking down, with a single lock of hair hanging down over his eyes. I've drawn his jaw just right, strong and angular, and the likeness is clear. I turn back another page. There he is again, this time from front on, with a slight smile on his lips. I love this one. As I drew it, I imagined what sorts of things might make him smile like that. I came up with motorbikes, and naked women. There are a few more drawings of him in my book, with various facial expressions. This has been my therapy. My way of accepting it's over and commemorating my loss.

I turn to a fresh page, and take a deep breath, blowing it out slowly. I'm ready. The time is now. I've been wanting to do this for a while, but somehow, drawing his tatts has felt too personal. Too voyeuristic. I take my pencil and carefully sketch the outline of a muscular male torso with arms. I stop it just below where the hip bones would be. I close my eyes and try to recall every detail I can of the ink that covered his body. There were tatts visible on his neck, and down each of his arms. Some I can remember, and some I will need to improvise. Both will be fun. I start to draw intricate patterns over every inch of his body. I completely lose myself in drawing. When my bedroom door bursts open, I squeal, and quickly tuck my sketch book beneath my pillow, right as James, the older of my two younger brothers, comes into the room and crashes down on the bed beside me.

'How do?' he asks, borrowing the Yorkshire greeting he has picked up from school.

'How do to you too, sir?' He giggles. I love that he still giggles, even though he is thirteen. James is a gorgeous boy. Tall for his age, as we all are, with sandy brown hair, like none of us, and the sweetest of smiles.

'Mum said to come and grab you for lunch. What you doing in here on your own?'

'Drawing. And I love to be alone.'

'Can I see?'

'Huh! No, you may not, lad. Now take yourself off. I'll be out in a minute.'

He stays, lazing beside me with his hands behind his head, gently swaying his ankles from side to side. 'Is Elle coming today?'

'Why?' I ask, narrowing my eyes at him. He blushes, bright red. He has my same, treacherous skin that won't let even the slightest blush go by undetected.

'No reason,' he says quickly. Now, he jumps up. 'Tell her I said hi, when you see her.' I smile, but my heart breaks a little. My little boy is growing up.

'I will.'

James heads out of my room, narrowly avoiding a collision with my youngest brother, Harry, who is racing through the house at break-neck speed, to be first to the roast potatoes. For looks, Harry is the male, ten-year-old equivalent of me. But for personality, he is the total opposite. Harry is always giggling, always running, and always looking for ways to make other people laugh. Not only will he be the first to fill his plate on this occasion, he will also be the first one finished his meal, with not a sign of indigestion to hamper him.

I sidle out of my room after James, hoping I can sneak into the dining room without crossing paths with Sophie. When I get there, everyone is already seated in their usual spots at our rectangular wooden dining table— the same one we've sat at since James was a baby in a highchair. Mum sits at one end, and Dad at the other. I sit down at Dad's end, next to James, and across from Harry. Sophie sits opposite James, at Mum's end.

Mum has laid out all the food in the centre of the table. As well as her speciality, roast potatoes cooked in duck fat, there are peas, honey carrots, parsnips, pumpkin, Yorkshire puddings, and the roast. Today it is pork, with the perfect crunchy crackling.

We pile our plates with food, and when Dad gives the nod, we start eating. When I say he gives the nod, he literally gives a slight nod of his head. He doesn't say a word, but we are all watching and waiting for it. He commands respect, without demanding it.

As we eat, Dad does the rounds of asking everyone how their week has been. He works long hours as a business lawyer, so he doesn't get to chat to us much during the week. The boys love to entertain with stories from school, and Sophie likes to counter everything they say with a more impressive anecdote of her own. I like to listen, and hope everyone just leaves me alone. Dad knows that, and he tends to let me off the hook. He knows we will catch up later, as we always do, with a cup of tea and biscuits in the front room, or when it's warm enough, outside in the back garden.

We all sit together for about a quarter of an hour before the boys are itching to go. James asks if he may be excused, closely followed by Harry. Mum, Dad, Sophie and I stay. Without the youthful exuberance of the boys, conversation grinds to a halt. There is still a lot of self-indulgent prose coming out of Sophie, but that isn't conversation, is it? There is a little thing called turn taking she hasn't yet mastered.

My thoughts turn to how I can extricate myself without causing offence to Mum, who has spent hours preparing a meal that is all over in less than thirty minutes, but I am interrupted by the emergence back into the dining room of Harry. And what do I see in his sticky little paws? My sketch book.

I jump out of my seat. 'What are you doing with that?' I shriek. He is giggling, and when he realises I'm about to murder him, he starts dancing from foot to foot, on the opposite side of the table, confounding me with indecision about which direction to come at him from. 'Give it to me right now, Harry. It's not funny!'

'Meg's been drawing pictures of fellas!' Harry cries, and giggles even harder, turning red in the face with a combination of glee at the discomfort he knows he is causing me, and fear of the fate that awaits him once I get my hands on him.

Enough is enough. I set off anticlockwise around the table towards him. He gives a squeal, and runs in the same direction, so that I am now chasing him around the dining table.

'Give us a look,' says Sophie, her eyes lighting up with the promise of embarrassing me further. Harry throws her the book just before I can catch up with him and grab his arm.

'No!' I shout, but to no avail. Sophie opens the book and turns straight to the pages of my pictures of Johnno.

'Well, well, well,' she says, with a smirk. 'Who do we 'ave 'ere?' She turns the book around, and flicks through the pages, so that Mum and Dad can both see the efforts of my perverted labour.

'Nobody.'

'Nobody? He's lush, Meg. Anyone we know?'

'No! It's just someone I made up. An imaginary man. A bad boy library guy. Non-existent. Now, give it to me!'

'Ooh, a fantasy man, hey? But Meg, don't you think you should invent fantasy boyfriends whose type you might be?'

What. The. Hell? 'What is that supposed to mean?' I'm sure my eyes are flashing dangerously at her, and if my blood pressure doesn't settle, I'll burst an aneurysm.

'Girls, calm down,' says Dad. One statement I am sure, in the history of all time, has never calmed anyone down.

'Go on, Sophie. Tell me. What makes my mythical boyfriend not my type?' *And who the bleeding hell made you the judge?*

'Sophie, love, give Meg the book.' That was Mum's lame attempt at intervening. Never going to work, when Sophie knows she is pounding a hammer on a nerve right now.

Sophie laughs, a fake, forced laugh. 'This is a manly man. He would want a woman with, you know, sex appeal.'

'FUCK YOU, SOPHIE!' I scream, and I lunge across the table at her, grabbing my book before she knows what has happened. Mum and Dad have both risen to their feet, and Mum is scolding me wildly for my language. Dad is quiet, but his face is stony, full of disappointment. He hates it when we fight. I want to slap that girl so badly, but I won't do it. Swearing at her over Sunday family lunch is the lowest I will stoop today.

Harry is now standing very meekly in the doorway. I can't be cross with him. For one thing, it will have been James who told him to take the book. He was the one who saw me tuck it under my pillow in such a guilty fashion that his curiosity would have been thoroughly piqued. And Harry wouldn't have known what a mischief he was doing me by showing it to Sophie. I push past Harry on my way out of the dining room and give him a glare, as feedback on his behaviour. If I see James, I will wring his neck. James knows that, and so I don't see him, at least not on my way to my bedroom, where I slam my door, throw my book down on the bed, and bury my face in my pillow to cry.

***

I don't come out for a long while. In fact, I'm planning on never coming out again, but then there is a gentle knock on my bedroom door, and it cautiously opens. I turn my face towards it, still laying sprawled in prone on my bed. It's Dad.

'Is she gone?' I ask.

'Yes. Tea?'

I roll over and sit up. 'Yes, please.'

I follow Dad out of my room, and to the kitchen, where the kettle is already boiling, and two mugs are set out on the bench with tea bags in them, waiting to be filled. Dad does the honours once the kettle boils, and I add the milk and sugar.

'It's a beautiful afternoon. Let's sit outside, Meggy.'

We head outside to where we have a cushioned wicker outdoor settee on the patio that overlooks our back garden. Dad has some vegetables growing in raised beds along the fence on either side. In one back corner is a small garden shed, and a greenhouse. In the other is the boys' cubby house, sitting elevated on four thick wooden posts.

We sit down on either end of the settee. It is a beautiful afternoon. The temperature is warm, with just a gentle breeze blowing. It's still bright from the afternoon sunshine, but it's a soft brightness. I feel my mood lifting slightly.

'How's your week?' Dad asks.

'Fine.' When most people ask me that question, that is the answer they get, and no more. But this is Dad. I like to talk to Dad. 'Book club is thriving. We had a good turn out again.' Dad doesn't know about the X-rated turn Book Club has taken, so his pride in my success is uninhibited by knowledge of the truth.

'Well done, Meggy. I knew you'd be just what they needed there.'

'How's your week been?'

'Busy. Two new bankruptcy claims this week. Times are tough in business, it seems.'

'Except for those in business law,' I say. 'And librarians are immune, thankfully.'

'Yes,' Dad says with a slight chuckle.

We lapse into silence, sipping our teas and listening to the sounds of the birds, contrasting against the steady whir of traffic on the busy street a few blocks over. I know Dad is going to want to talk about what happened with Sophie. He's thinking about how to bring it up. I decide to put him out of his misery and bring it up myself.

'Sorry, Dad. About lunch. I shouldn't have sworn at Sophie. She just—'

'I know.'

'She knows just what to say to hurt me.'

'She does.'

'It's like she gets off on making me feel small and inferior.'

Dad is quiet, and then says gently, 'You give her that power, Meg.'

'Me? I just want to be left alone,' I say defensively.

'You're not a little girl anymore, Meg. You're a woman. A capable, brilliant woman. There is nothing anyone can say that should make you feel less than what you are, my love.'

Aaawww, Dad.

'Thanks Dad. I'll try to remember that.'

I wonder if he is going to ask about the pictures. Bit awkward, talking to one's daughter about her fantasy boyfriend she obsessively draws in her free time, I would imagine.

'Who is the man?'

He went there. 'No one.' I sigh. I wish I could lie to Dad. 'Someone I met at the library a little while ago.' Just your standard borrower. 'His look appealed to me. He has a lot of ink. I like to draw him.'

'You're very good, you know.'

'Thanks, Dad.'

'Not just at drawing. There's not a man alive who wouldn't be lucky to have you, my girl.'

Yes. Being with me is like winning sixth division lottery. Exciting at first, until you see you've only won five quid. 'Perhaps.'

Dad softly chuckles. 'I heard you took a nice intercept in the fourth quarter against Hull.'

I did. 'Yes. I seemed to be in the right place at the right time. Who told you?'

'Sophie. She was proud of you.'

I resist the urge to roll my eyes. 'How nice,' I say sweetly. Dad smiles wryly and says no more.

Chapter Six

It should be against the law for anyone to have to have to start work before 8am on a Monday, let alone librarians. But alas, Pip thinks we need a whole hour before the doors open to prepare for the week, and I am forced to drag myself to work for 7:30am. What she thinks has happened over the weekend, when the library is closed, to require such an outrageous amount of time for preparation is beyond me.

This Monday is even worse than usual, because as soon as I get there, I'm told Yvonne is sick, so I'll have to cover Toddler Time at 9am. Then, when I open the bin at the back of the afterhours returns chute, the first book I see is *Everything You Need to Know About Netball*. Damn it. I forgot to jam the chute before I left on Friday. Or was I complacent? Did I really think I could continue to turn him down, and he would just keep coming back for more? Do I consider myself that irresistible? No. I forgot.

I sort the books from the chute onto their trolleys for re-shelving, and by the time I've done that, and set up for Toddler Time, the place is swarming with mini humans. I make eye contact with one by accident, and he cowers behind his mother, even though I've traded my usual black-on-black look for black high-waisted skinny jeans, paired with a white cropped t-shirt with a magnificent blue dragon adorning it. My outfit screams approachability. It must be, as I have long suspected, my face that is the problem.

As it approaches nine, I pile my hair on top of my head and secure it into a bun— a safety measure I take before I bring myself down to their level. One thing I have learned is that toddlers have a penchant for hair pulling. I swap my usual lanyard for my Emergency Toddler Time lanyard. On it is several squishy, pliable and chewable objects that I can offer to children who seem inclined to use my facial features as playthings.

At one minute past nine, I sit down cross-legged on the colourful rug in the children's section that displays the letters of the alphabet. I can't sit on this rug without wondering when the last time was that it was properly cleaned. I mean, not just vacuumed, but sanitised. It has a scent. It's not pure rug. There are elements of rug smell, but there are also elements of... other things. Depending on where I sit, the aroma changes. Sometimes off milk. Sometimes a farmyard. But never pure rug.

Over the course of the next twenty minutes, we sing a welcome song, walk around in a circle like a derailed choo-choo train, hurtling its passengers towards certain death, make a lot of indiscriminate animal noises, and then settle back in our circle for story time.

Children's stories rely on the reader to make them interesting. It's a bit of a cheat, really. The authors can write practically anything, and as long as there is an enthusiastic adult on the other end to bring it alive, they are home and hosed. The expectation is that the reader will add mystery and intrigue to each page with comments like, 'Ooh, I wonder where the naughty teddy bear is now?' and 'Uh oh, that's a big puddle. I wonder what will happen?'

I am not one of those adults, but fortunately, adults who own toddlers are well trained in their role. So, as I turn each page, I simply read the words out stock-market-report style, pause, and wait for a parent to provide the necessary commentary. I'm butchering a classic piece of children's literature in just this way when the automatic doors at the front of the library open, and Johnno walks in.

His timing could not be worse.

He stops, and the doors close behind him. He looks around, and sees me, surrounded by children, one of whom has just planted himself in my lap, and the corners of his mouth turn up. If this doesn't scare the children, then it just isn't fair. I am in no way as intimidating as this man. He is wearing black cargo trousers, heavy boots, and a black hoodie with the sleeves rolled up to his elbows, so the tattoos that cover both of his forearms and the backs of his hands are visible. He saunters over towards the group and sits down at a booth table at the edge of the children's section. He rests back, drapes his arm across the back of the bench seat, and fixes his eyes on me, his enjoyment of my current situation obvious from the smirk still on his face. A few of the mothers exchange looks, and hushed comments and I seriously want to climb beneath this rug and allow the radioactive contamination within its fibres to gradually break down my body until not a trace is left.

I can't do that though, because the worst is yet to come. The good-bye song. I have skipped the good-bye song before, and I learned my lesson the hard way. Apparently, toddlers love routine. Mess with their routine, and it leads to meltdowns. On that day, I was held responsible for the meltdowns of several attendees. The feedback was scathing. Was it worth risking that again to prevent Johnno from hearing me sing? Hell yes.

I close the book and place it down on the ground beside me.

'What a lively session we have had today.' I smile— professionally. 'That's all we have time for. Yvonne will be back next week. Bye for now.'

I stand, but no one stands with me.

'What about the good-bye song?' says one of the mothers, glancing nervously at her daughter, who looks like a real piece of work. The child has her thumb in her mouth, and she is staring at me so threateningly that if my own mother was there, I would be cowering behind her.

'It's only 9:28am. Doesn't the session go until half nine?' another mother pipes up. I have to wonder how she is so oriented to time when she has forgotten to change out of her pyjama bottoms, and she has used a rubber band to secure her hair.

I glance at Johnno, only to receive confirmation that I am still the focus of his attention. He has the nerve to nod at me in silent encouragement.

Reluctantly, I sit back down. 'Fine.'

I start to clap my hands in the required rhythm, and recite the farewell incantation, summoning the spirits to quell the rising emotional dysregulation of the toddlers before me.

'Our Mums and Dads brought us along,
To play our games and sing our songs.
We've had a lot of fun today,
But now's the time to go away.
Miss Meg will miss you all a bunch,
But go home now and have some lunch.
Now that we have said our rhyme,

It's bye bye now to Toddler Time.'

The children are all coaxed to give each other high fives by their well-meaning parents, who fear that their child's social development will be severely impacted upon if they don't learn this essential bonding skill early in life. I am the recipient of many greasy-fingered high fives myself, and then, finally, I can escape their clutches without fear of retribution. I make my way over to where Johnno is sitting, and as I approach, he breaks into a broad smile that makes my heart quicken. He has all his teeth, just as I was hoping.

'Is there something I can help you with, or did you come here to revel in my misery?'

'I don't know what you're talking about, Miss Meg. You're a natural.'

I want to slap him.

'How did you enjoy your book? You didn't keep it for long.'

'I enjoyed it more than it has ever been enjoyed before.' *Oh, good God. That's creepy. So why did my clit just send a message to my brain conveying quite the opposite?* 'You're wearing blue and white today.'

'Coincidence.' It's not.

'It brings out your eyes.'

He has noticed my eyes. 'Are you in need of some fresh ...er... reading material? If not, I should really start tidying up.'

'Not for me today.' His demeanour becomes more serious, and the flirtatiousness leaves his tone. 'What would a thirteen-year-old girl want to read if she had nothing much to do for two weeks?'

This was not what I was expecting him to ask. I take him in for a moment. Maybe it's because I am still standing, and he is sitting, so he seems a little less intimidating, but this is the first time I've felt brave enough to really see him, and to my surprise, he looks away, as though my scrutiny is too much. Of course, I am curious about who he wants the books for, but I'm not going to ask. I barely know him.

'What is she in to?'

'I don't really know,' he says, and he stands up and steps out from the booth. 'Forget it.' He starts to leave, and without thinking about it, I reach out and take a light hold of his wrist. He looks at where I am touching him, and then at me. I quickly let go, and he stays.

'*Dragon Chicks* is a safe place to start,' I suggest. 'Come with me.'

I head towards Junior Fiction, and Johnno follows with his hands in his pockets. He seems self-conscious, and I suppose it is reasonable. He looks completely out of place in this section, even next to me. I locate the series and hand him the first three books.

'Thanks,' he says quietly, appraising the covers. 'Is this what you read?' He nods at my t-shirt.

I almost smile. 'I read them when I was younger. Now I read adult dragon stories.'

'That's a thing?'

'Indeed.'

He taps the books lightly with one knuckle. 'I need them for longer than two weeks. She's not here yet.'

'Fine. We can renew them, as long as no one has reserved them in the meantime.'

'People do that?'

I blink. 'Yes.' He makes a face of reluctant acceptance of that truth. 'Is there anything else?'

'Yeah. Dinner.'

Not this again. We've talked about this. Not in detail, of course. But I said no. And no means no. Doesn't it? But then, I did wear a blue and white t-shirt to work today— the first time I have donned colours since I started here a year ago— just because he indicated that he may want to see me in those colours. Perhaps it isn't unreasonable that he thinks it's worth another shot.

I want to say yes. 'I can't. Sorry.' *Fuck. That came out wrong.*

He growls, and his eyes penetrate me. My heart quickens again, but it's not in the same way it did when he smiled. A few times I have wondered if he isn't as intimidating as I've built him up to be, but in this moment, he seems all that and more.

'Why not?'

'I haven't got a good reason.' I can see he is fuming. 'I'm frustrating you. I think you should go.' I retreat half a step, because without realising it, I had ended up close enough to him to hear his breathing.

'I'm not frustrated.'

'Your knuckles are white.'

He looks at his hand that has a death grip around books 1-3 of *Dragon Chicks*, and relaxes it enough that the colour runs back into his joints.

'You're the most frustrating woman I've ever met.'

'I know. I can assure you that *being* me is also a very frustrating experience, so I can relate.'

For a moment, he seems like he's going to explode, and then he laughs and shakes his head. 'It doesn't have to be dinner. Anything you want. A drink.'

'No.' Adding alcohol to this equation would not be a good idea, mainly because my clit has just sent a message to my brain that it thinks it would be a fantastic idea.

'Ten pin bowling.'

'God no.'

'The movies.' I hesitate.

'You hesitated.'

'I didn't.'

I've got to get away from him. He is wearing me down. Before he can say anything more, I walk away from him with determination, back towards the children's section that is now abandoned. A stray sippy cup and the toys, books and musical instruments we used for the session are the only remnants of the joyful time we had. I pick up a handful of toys and carry them to the storage cupboard at the back of the section. I know Johnno is following me, but if I pretend he isn't there, surely, he will go away. No self-respecting man could possibly continue to pursue me when I'm being such an arsehole. Surely.

I step inside the cupboard to put the toys on the shelf, and realise too late the position I've put myself in. His large frame blocks the doorway, and I can't get out without going through him. Fool. How could I be so careless? I don't know this man. I don't know if I can trust him, and I've just let him corner me in a cupboard, with no one else around. If I scream, someone will probably hear me, but if he doesn't want me to scream, he would be able to stop me quite easily. He pulls the door partially shut behind him, and I draw in a sharp breath.

'Don't scream,' he says firmly, but softly. He places the *Dragon Chicks* books down on a shelf. 'I'm not going to hurt you.'

I have no reason to believe him, but for some reason, I do. He comes a step closer. I can smell his aftershave, or whatever smelly stuff he uses, and I can feel the warmth of his body. Then he raises his hand, and he takes a hold of the side of my face. His touch is hot against my skin, even though my cheeks are already burning.

'Let me kiss you. If you still don't want anything to do with me, then I'll leave you alone.' He has drawn me closer, and his hand on my jaw tilts my chin towards him. I feel powerless, but not controlled. I know I am not resisting. I am bending to his will, willingly.

I feel his breath on my lips, and then his lips brush mine. My lips part, and that must have been what he was waiting for, because as soon as they do, he lays claim to them, his coarse facial hair pressing against my chin as he draws my bottom lip into his mouth. In the heat of the moment, I lose track of where my limbs are, and as I am me, my elbow lands hard on a squeaky animal toy on one of the shelves behind me. The noise startles us both, and Johnno pulls away. I obviously wasn't ready for him to do that, because my wayward limb then finds its way around Johnno's neck and pulls him back to me, and now I am unmistakably kissing him like my life depends on it. He groans and presses his body against me, which presses me against the shelves, and I will probably set off more toys, but I'm too into this to care. I can feel his rooster, proudly standing at full attention, pressing against my inner thigh and my clit is now screaming at my brain that this is the good stuff, and we need more of it. If we don't stop there's going to be quite the kerfuffle in here.

'I could fuck you right here if you want me to,' he says, as his lips start to make their way down the side of my neck. My back arches at the sensation, but my brain is still online enough that I know that can't happen. I am a librarian. There are certain standards I hold myself to, and not fucking a random guy in the toy cupboard is one of them.

'No,' I choke out. 'I'm at work. That can't happen.' His lips pause against my collarbone, and then he pulls away.

'Movies. Tonight. I don't care what we see. I won't be watching anyway.'

Just say yes, Meg, you moron. 'Why?'

He is taken aback. He is breathing heavily, and he grabs his cock through his trousers, I can only assume in some discomfort.

'Why?' I nod. 'Because you're fucking hot. Because I can't stop thinking about you.'

I don't know what answer I wanted, or expected, but that wasn't it. He doesn't know me. Once he does, he will know I'm not for him, and

I don't think I can bear rejection from this man. I don't think I've ever cared before, but I care now.

'I can't.'

His head drops for a moment, and when he lifts it, his face is steely. 'I'm not going to beg you any more than I already have. If it's a no, then I'm done. I'm not coming back.'

I nod, and silently cuss myself out, but I just don't seem to be able to do anything else.

He picks up the Dragon Chicks books, pushes the door back, and leaves me alone in the cupboard of shame, to think about what I've done.

Chapter Seven

I t hit me as soon as he left me, stranded and horny in the cupboard, that I really didn't want him to leave. I stayed in there for a good while, replaying what had happened. I have never been kissed the way he kissed me. Not even close. And I sure as hell have never wanted to kiss someone back like I did. I know next to nothing about him. Only that he owns a tattoo studio and has a thirteen-year-old...something...in his life. That's not nothing. But God, I fancy him.

It's been three days and nine hours since that moment in the cupboard, and I'm pining just as hard as I was for the rest of the day Monday, when I refused to even rally myself to partake in birthday cupcakes for one of the other librarians. I've got it bad for him, and it's my own stupid fault I don't have it.

We've just had another win in an away game, against Bradford, so Gabby and Elle are in a good mood as we drive back together from netball in Elle's car. That means my fit of the sulks stands out even more than my usual set point of disinterested melancholy in comparison. I'm sitting in the back, and so far, they've been ignoring me, but that won't last forever. I notice Elle looking back in the rear view mirror every now and then, trying to catch my eye. She knows something's up.

'Have you seen the not-half-bad library bad boy again Meg?' she asks.

Fuck. I really don't want to talk about this with Gabby. I don't want to talk about it at all, but especially not with Gabby.

I make a guttural sound that attempts to convey, 'Yes, it went very, very well, and then very, very badly and I don't want to talk about it.'

'Sweetie, you need to use your words. I can't understand you when you grunt at me.'

I meet her eyes in the rear view mirror and give her a pleading look.

'Oooh,' she says. Good. We understand each other.

'What?' Gabby demands. 'What's this about a not-half-bad library bad boy? Have you had a shag, Meg?'

I groan.

'I don't think Meg wants to talk about it right now, Gabby,' says Elle.

'Why not? I have as much right to know as you do,' Gabby argues.

'I think it's because your personality is so abrasive,' Elle so helpfully explains. 'That's just a guess. Correct me if I'm wrong, Meg.'

Thanks Elle.

'Fuck off,' says Gabby.

'There's nothing to tell anyway. It's over,' I say. My words come out slightly warbled as my chin is resting on my hand as I stare out the window.

'Over? How can it be over, Meg? It's barely even begun, and from everything you've told me so far, I just know he is "the one!"' She obviously hasn't been listening, has she? 'What happened to your plan? The text reminder and blocking the chute?'

'It didn't work out.' That's all I can bring myself to say.

Elle is frowning at me. 'Let's get rid of Gabby, and then we'll talk,' she says, with a glance to her left.

Gabby crosses her arms and scowls. 'Next time I get laid, neither of you are going to hear about it.'

'I will hear about it, Gabby. I always hear it. The walls are thin, and you are loud, girlfriend,' says Elle with a giggle. We've just pulled up outside their flat. 'Now, get out. I'll see you when I see you.' Gabby rolls her eyes, grabs her bag and gets out, slamming the car door behind her. Elle giggles again. 'She's good value, isn't she?'

'I suppose.' I get out of the back seat and climb in the front next to Elle. She immediately reaches across and pulls me into a hug, and it is just what I need. A take a deep breath to stop myself from bursting into tears.

'Now, tell me everything, you goose.'

***

By the time Elle pulls up outside my place, she is up to speed with the cupboard tryst, and she's used a few harsher adjectives than, 'you goose' to describe me.

When I get out of the car she gets out as well and follows me inside to my bedroom. I guess she doesn't think I'm ready to be alone yet. Maybe she's right, because I do feel better than I have all week. I need to remember that. Sometimes, talking does help, and what felt huge now just feels kind of silly.

Elle lies down on my bed and I lie down beside her. She's toying with her hair, and she seems lost in thought, which gives me time to gather my thoughts as well. There's been something I've been wanting to ask her about.

'Where did you get your tatt done?' Elle only has one— a small Virgo glyph on her left buttock.

'A place in town. Can't think what it was called. It was a few years ago, but it's on the main street. Why?'

I take Johnno's business card out from my wallet and hand it to her. 'Have you heard of this place?'

Elle studies the card. 'No,' she says, and then she turns a look on me that makes me shrink. 'Meg Drury, are you completely dicked in the nob?'

That's regency romance talk for am I completely insane.

'Perhaps, but why do you ask?'

'Is this, or is this not, Johnno's phone number?'

'It...is, I assume.'

'You are telling me that you hatched an elaborate plan to message him through the text-reminder system at work and then block the after-hours chute, when all along you had his phone number in your wallet on this card??'

'Perhaps.'

'For heaven's sake, Meg! What am I going to do with you?' She seems genuinely annoyed with me. She pouts. 'I was going to stay at Joe's tonight, but I'm going to tell him I need to be with you instead. This is more serious than even I realised.' She pulls out her phone. 'You're sick, Meg,' she says as she scrolls. 'My bag is in the car. Would you go and grab it while I call Joe?' The way she flutters her eyelids at me frightens me. 'And bring me a snack, if you would be so kind?'

'What do you want?'

'Whatever is going in the Drury household will do nicely.'

I sigh and go off to do her bidding. This sudden adjustment of her plans has more to do with avoiding Joe than it does providing emotional support to me, but I'm not going to complain. I love the girl, as daft as she is.

When I come back to the bedroom ten minutes later with Elle's bag, and a toasted cheese sandwich, since there really wasn't much 'going' in the Drury household, Elle is still lying on the bed. Johnno's business card is on the bedside table, so I put it away back in my wallet. Elle gets up and changes into her pyjamas, then climbs back into bed, beneath the covers, to eat her sandwich. She's going to leave crumbs, I know it.

'How did Joe take it?'

'Joe?'

'Joe.'

'Oh, yes, he was fine. You know Joe.'

I get changed into my pyjamas as well and climb in beside her. My bed is a double, so not exactly spacious for two taller-than-average adults.

'What do you make of the thirteen-year-old?' Elle asks between bites. 'Do you think it's a daughter?'

'Perhaps. Though he said he doesn't know what she's in to, so it didn't sound like he knows her well.'

'Kids that age are tricky.' Elle would know. She's a primary teacher. I would know too. I have a thirteen-year-old brother, but he's like an open book. We can't shut the kid up. 'How old do you think he is?'

'I would have guessed late twenties, but that makes him young to have a thirteen-year-old.'

'Yes.' Elle finishes the sandwich and puts the plate down on the bedside table.

'You should take that out. It will attract roaches.'

'Yes,' she says again, as she lays down, and makes herself comfortable, bringing the blankets up tightly under her chin. 'I will in the morning.'

I shake my head with disapproval, but she doesn't notice. I lie down as well, with my back to her and she wraps an arm around my waist. Weird, I know, but we've done it ever since we started having sleepovers, so it feels normal.

In that moment, I feel I can ask her what I need to ask. 'Elle, are you and Joe OK?'

She is quiet. Too quiet. Then she sighs. 'I love Joe. He is my best friend. He is the best sort of man. It will be OK.' I haven't heard her sound so sad since the accident.

'Are you OK?'

She doesn't answer but just squeezes me a little tighter around the waist. I take that as a 'no'.

***

Elle leaves for work before I do the next morning, but she leaves her things behind, which makes me think she's planning on coming back later. Sure enough, when I get home from work, she's already in my bedroom. Last night's toasted sandwich plate is still on the bedside table, and an empty teacup has joined it. She really is making herself at home.

'Meg, my love, how was your day?' she asks brightly as I sit down on the edge of the bed. She's on her laptop, probably still working, but she shuts it and puts it into her bag.

'Fine.'

'No Toddler Time today?'

'No. Yvonne is back, thank God.'

'What are your plans for this evening?'

'Reading. Drawing. Sleeping.'

Elle looks quickly at her phone. Checking the time?

'Why don't we go out tonight? It's been a while. We could grab dinner and a movie?' She smiles at me in such a way that it arouses suspicion in my breast.

'Sounds... fine.' I narrow my eyes in the hope I might be able to see through her ruse.

'Brill. It's half five now. Shall we get ready and go at, say, seven?' She pulls a bottle of white wine out of her bag. 'Pre-drinks?'

'Really?'

She makes this little, 'himph' sound and gives a pretty shrug of her shoulders. It's her trademark. It means, 'yes, and?'

'I'll grab some glasses.' I stand and walk around to her side of the bed to collect her plate and cup, and make my way to the kitchen, returning a short time later with two wine glasses.

Elle fills them both, offers a cheers, and takes a generous gulp. 'Now, what are you going to wear?'

'For dinner and a movie with you?'

'Yes.'

I look myself up and down. 'Probably this.'

'That won't do at all!' She jumps up and heads into my walk-in robe. 'Stay there, I will handle it.'

***

By five to seven, I am feeling quite tipsy, and very confused. Somehow, I have ended up dressed to the nines in a black corset top, a black leather A-line skirt that stops above my knees, with patterned black tights beneath, my black high tops and a faded black denim jacket. Elle made me wash and dry my hair, and she straightened it for me— a job that takes me over an hour, but she can somehow achieve much more quickly. She even chose my underwear for me, and she's insisted I wear proper make-up, even foundation and red lippy.

She, meanwhile, still hasn't changed out of the clothes she wore to work. She keeps on looking furtively out the front window, and I just know she is up to no good. This goes on for a further ten minutes, before the sound of a motorbike engine out the front of my place makes her jump up and rush to the window.

'He's here.'

My stomach drops. Did I just hear correctly? Elle is now before me, and she has both of my hands in hers.

'Meg, don't be mad. Last night, when I asked you to get my bag from the car, I sent a message to Johnno using your phone. He's here to take you out.'

'Elle!' I say in a high-pitched squeal. 'How could you?!' I start to hyperventilate.

'I know, it seems like I've been very naughty Meg, but I'm sure you won't regret giving him a chance. He must really like you, because he agreed straight away, no questions asked, *and* he's only five minutes late. I know how much you value punctuality.'

I look out the window and see he has just dismounted. If I don't get out there quickly, he will come to the front door, and my parents might answer it.

'Fuck, Elle. I've never ridden on a motorbike.' It's not my biggest concern about this whole thing, but it's up there.

'You'll be fine. He will look after you.' Elle looks out the window again, and I'm assuming it's the first time she's seen him without the helmet on, because she immediately turns back to me with her eyes blazing. 'Meg Drury! You are the most unreliable of narrators! You told me he was 'not half bad'! That man is fit as fit can be!' She grabs me by both of my arms and gives me a shake. 'You and him, together— my god Meg, you have to let me watch.' I must look horrified as I shake her off, because she adds, 'Not right away, obviously. Get comfortable first.'

'That won't be happening, Elle.'

'Meg, please, just relax. What will be, will be. You are an amazing woman. The more you let him get to know you— the real you— the more he will love you.'

I feel like crying. 'Will you stay here tonight? I want you to be here when I come back.'

Elle looks reluctant. 'What if you want to bring him back here, though? I wasn't serious about watching.'

I shake my head. 'I don't want to sleep with him tonight. I'm not ready.' Elle still doesn't look convinced. I have to be honest. 'He frightens me.'

She is serious now. 'What do you mean, Meg? Do you mean you don't feel safe with him? If that's the case, I will go out and tell him that I sent the message, and he needs to go away.'

'No. I don't feel unsafe. Just intimidated.'

'In that case, I'll stay only to give you confidence that you don't have to do anything you're not ready for, and I promise I will check on you throughout. But if you want me to go, just say.'

'Fine.' I let her give me a final hug, and then I pick up my phone and wallet and head to the door. 'Thanks Elle.'

Chapter Eight

I meet Johnno halfway down the drive, greet him, and steer him quickly back in the direction of his bike. He looks so sexy. He's wearing the same black jeans I've seen him in before, and a black t-shirt, with a leather jacket over the top. Simple, but it suits him perfectly. He smells extra nice too. I think he's washed his hair. It seems slightly lighter and wavier where it sits in a low bun at the back of his neck.

'I was surprised to get your text,' he says, as we walk.

'Yes. I was surprised I sent it,' I say, and then realise that was the wrong thing to say, because he stops and looks at me with his brows knitted.

'Do you want to do this, or not?'

'Yes,' I say quickly. 'That came out wrong. What I mean is, it's out of character for me to ask someone out. So, you should feel special.'

He relaxes. 'I do. Even though you made me beg before we got to this point.' He throws me a helmet, and I hold it, looking at it, betraying that I have no idea what to do with it. He looks at me, and one corner of his mouth turns up. 'Haven't ridden a bike before?'

'No.'

He takes the helmet back off me, gently brushes my hair away from my face and tucks it behind my ears. 'You look hot.' Palpitations. 'Gorgeous, actually. I want to kiss you.'

'If you kiss me now, you'll have red lipstick on your lips all night.' I see his tongue touch his lower lip, and God, I want to kiss him too.

'Later.'

'Where are we going?' I ask.

'The movies.'

'Because I hesitated?'

'I'm glad you're ready to admit that now.' He lowers the helmet over my head before I have time to counter with something witty and tightens the strap beneath my chin. 'Hold on tight round my waist. That's all you have to do.' He grabs the handlebars and swings his leg over, and then looks back at me, waiting for me to do the same. I place my hand on his shoulder and climb over. I wrap my arms around his waist, and he pulls them around tighter before starting the bike.

Riding through Leeds with my arms around Johnno feels like a full-circle moment for me. Gangly, bookish Meg from high school could never have even dreamed this moment would happen. But here I am, a cool motorcycle-riding bad ass girl, with my bad ass date... whom my best friend had to text on my behalf because I was too afraid to do it myself. Sometimes, I wish I could arrest my trains of thought a fraction earlier.

We pull up at the cinemas, and it's busy. I haven't been to a movie in ages, and I didn't think anyone else went anymore either, but apparently tonight, they do.

We head inside and look at the options on the electronic screens behind the counter. There are three theatres, so three movies playing at peak times.

'What do you want to watch?' Johnno asks.

I look around. There is safety in numbers. A comment he made when he asked me out rattles around in my nervous brain. 'I won't be watching it anyway,' he had said. If he wouldn't be watching it, I assume that meant he intended to be doing... other things...I assume, to me.

There is clearly one movie more popular than the others. Judging by the many young people, some with parents and some without, mingling outside that theatre with frozen drinks, popcorn and a range of emo outfits, I quickly deduce it is the latest PG-13 tween block-buster, *Full Blood Moon*, based on the novel of the same name. It's a modern-day vampire love story. That's my jam right there, and if Johnno thinks he'll be getting frisky with me amongst a throng of tweens, he's going to be sadly disappointed. I am resolute about that. Almost.

'That one,' I say, pointing to the poster.

He sighs, and briefly closes his eyes. 'I was afraid you were going to say that.' He approaches the counter and when I pull out my wallet to pay for my ticket, he pushes my hand away, and pays for both. Chivalry isn't dead, I guess?

'Want something to eat?'

'Yes.' We are early, and there is a cafe attached to the complex that sells light meals like sandwiches and muffins, for extortionate prices. We each choose a sandwich and sit down to wait. This is the part where I'm going to have to make conversation, or at least try not to shut down any attempts Johnno makes with my reflex one-word answers. I'm nervous. So nervous.

Johnno isn't saying anything, and this is definitely the first time I've been on a date and cared if there was silence. I don't want to fail this time. I want him to like me. *Fuck. That makes it even harder.*

'How long have you been in Yorkshire? You don't have the accent.' I cringe as the words leave my mouth. I know how many times I have rolled my eyes at that same question on a date.

'I come and go.'

'Where are you from?'

'London, originally.'

'Me too.' Standard social skills would dictate that the conversation partner should throw in a, 'Which part of London are you from?' But I get nothing from Johnno. It's difficult having to do all the work, I now realise. 'Where do you come and go from?'

He doesn't answer for a moment. 'I'm fairly nomadic.'

Nomadic? 'Is that a polite way of saying you're homeless?'

'In a way.'

If Elle hadn't insisted I wear rouge, I would be turning pale. 'I shouldn't have let you buy my ticket,' I say meekly.

He chuckles. 'I've got money, don't worry about that.'

'Are you staying for long in Leeds?'

'Depends.'

'On?'

'Whether I've got any reason to stick around.'

I wonder how nosy I can get before he will shut me down. He was touchy about giving me his address for his library card application, but I want to know more.

'Where do you stay when you're here?'

'Above the shop.'

'R.J. Ink?'

'Yeah.' He leans in and lowers his voice. 'Speaking of ink, I have a question for *you*, now.' With the back of his index finger, he traces the top part of the floral tattoo that starts on my right breast and continues down my sternum, visible above the top edge of my corset top. The move is discreet, with my jacket obscuring the view of the people around us. I catch my breath at his touch. 'Is this your design?'

'Yes.'

'It's very intricate. You're talented.'

'Thank-you.'

He lowers his voice further and leans in so he is speaking into my ear. 'Where does it finish?'

I bite my lip as his mouth brushes my neck. How obviously turned on he is by a part of my body is incredibly arousing for me, too, and it's making me feel bold. I take his hand in mine, and interlace our fingers, so that I can guide the back of his index finger along the path of the tattoo, down my sternum and beneath my left breast. He likes that. A smile spreads across his face.

'Nice. I'm fucking dying to see it.' I must look startled, because he gives a short laugh. 'Not here. Later.'

This is purely about sex for him, which bodes ill for the longevity of this relationship. Once he realises I'm pathetic in bed, we'll be over. My only chance of survival is to delay that inevitability for as long as possible. And I get the feeling patience is not one of Johnno's virtues.

***

We have joined the throng of vampire-loving tweens, and are man-
aging to blend in, as adults who are still rocking the emo aesthetic.
Not that Johnno blends in too well anywhere, I would imagine, thanks
to his size and eye-catching good looks. They open the doors, and we
find our seats, in the middle of one of the rows in the centre section.
Johnno is on my right. On his right is a young couple, probably around
my age. On my left is a kid— possibly ten or eleven, and on his left is
his mother. Johnno's displeasure at the situation is obvious. He glares
at the kid, then at the kid's mother, who has quickly summed us up
as the sort of riff raff who shouldn't be at a PG-13 movie on a Friday
night. Johnno gives an audible huff and crosses his arms. The mother
glares back and then switches seats with the kid, positioning herself
as a human riff raff shield. I stifle a smile. In the safety of this public
environment, I can see the funny side of things. If I was alone with
Johnno and he looked this pissed off, it might be a different story.

The lights dim, and the advertisements start to roll. No change to
his demeanor. Luckily, his profile is a pleasure to look at, because that's
all I'm getting at this point. *Full Blood Moon* eventually starts, and
when we are confronted with the first pale-skinned, pointy-toothed
teen vampire, he audibly groans.

'You said you didn't care what we watched,' I whisper.

He turns his head quickly and shoots me a thunderous look. 'That
was when I didn't think I'd be watching it,' he whispers back.

I feel slightly offended now. Surely, he can put up with a crappy
movie for a couple of hours for the benefit of my crappy company,
considering how badly he apparently wants to get in my pants.

'If this isn't meeting your expectations, perhaps you should go,' I
say, with a petty lift of my chin up and away from him.

In an instant, his hand is on my left cheek, and he forces my eyes
back to him.

'My expectation was that I'd be on my knees in front of you by now. So no, it's not meeting my expectation. Doesn't mean I want to leave.' Before he lets go of my face, he adds, with a dark look in his eyes, which I can't look away from because I am captive, 'Behave.'

I need a moment to catch my breath. I am a hundred percent sure that he is a hundred and ten percent serious that it was his intention to go down on me in the cinema, had I not chosen a theatre packed with people. Horny bastard. While I am still caught up in imagining my possible fate had I, as a grown woman of twenty-one, *not* chosen a children's movie to watch on a first date with the hottest man alive, he shrugs out of his jacket, and the next thing I notice is it falling across my lap, over my crossed legs.

The mother of the kid next to me notices it too, and shoots a reproving look our way. *She* has obviously had some fun at the cinemas at some stage in her life, because she seems to have her...finger... on the pulse of what is happening. Johnno meets her reproving look with a 'fuck off' glare of his own, and then I feel his hand on my thigh beneath the jacket. I give Mum an apologetic look, and check that the kid is thoroughly engrossed in the movie. I take a breath and let it out slowly, and then uncross my legs.

Johnno approves. He kisses my neck, just below my ear, gently at first, and then open-mouthed, as his hand slides slowly up the inside of my thigh across the fabric of my tights, and underneath the hem of my skirt. Thank God I wore tights.

Johnno confirms my suspicion that had I not, my modesty would be in shreds right now, when he whispers into my ear, 'You wore too many clothes tonight.'

I turn my face towards him and his lips meet mine. At the same time, his fingers find their target, and he strokes my clit as he teases my lips with his tongue, until I open my mouth and let him play with my tongue as well. I am in heaven, but I know what he is going to want to happen, and I'm sure I can't get there with this many people around, especially since Mum beside me knows exactly what's going on.

Sure enough, after a while, he whispers, 'Come for me.'

'I can't,' I whisper back breathlessly.

He growls softly. 'Two words I'm sick to death of hearing out of your mouth.'

I must want to please him, because I kiss his lips, and say, 'Later.'

Chapter Nine

At this point, with his fingers drawing lazy circles around my clit until I can barely catch my breath, and my toes clenching so hard I've lost circulation, my earlier vow to hold out for as long as possible on sleeping with Johnno has been forgotten, and I have every intention of following through.

Finally, he concedes defeat, having had no joy on his quest to make me come in a cinema full of people. He's a quitter. There's something else I now know about him.

I stare at my phone, willing myself to message Elle. I know she will disappear in an instant if I ask her to. She's that sort of friend.

I scroll through my contacts, but when I come to Elle's name, I baulk. I continue scrolling. I reach Johnno's name and open a message.

Meg

> I know I said 'later', but I have a friend staying with me tonight. I can't invite you in. Sorry.

Elle will be fuming with me if I tell her I used her as an excuse. I turn my phone face-down in my lap, and wait, nervously drumming my fingers on my leg, as Johnno's phone buzzes in his pocket. He pulls it out and reads the message. He looks at me, his face glowering. I give him an apologetic smile. He doesn't smile. He starts to type.

Johnno

> Don't see what difference that makes. You've got a spare room, don't you?

Ah, not exactly. See, the thing is Johnno, I still live at home with my parents, and my two younger brothers, and therefore, there are no spare rooms, and when Elle stays over, she sleeps in my bed with me.

Meg

> She sleeps in my bed.

He reads the message, then shoots me another look, this time, with raised eyebrows. I message again.

Meg

> Not like 'that'. It's just what we do.

I receive another disbelieving look, and then he types.

Johnno

> Don't need a bed. A cupboard will do.

Meg

> Is cupboard sex a fetish of yours?

Johnno

> My fetish is you. I'll have you anywhere.

Ah Johnno, so naive, bless your cotton socks. I hate to tell you this via text, but your fetish is, in fact, an enthusiastic proponent of the starfish position, and only the starfish position.

Meg

> You don't know me.

Johnno

> I don't have to know you to want you.

It would be nice if you wanted to know me, and not just fuck me. I put my phone away and cross my arms. I'm a little stung. Almost immediately, my phone buzzes, and I pull it back out.

Johnno

> Doesn't mean I don't want to know you as well. I'm just desperate to fuck you.

I'm a little mollified by that eloquent display of affection, but I'm not willing to show it.

Meg

> No means no.

Johnno

> Except when both people agree it doesn't.

This startles me. *Cloaked Lust.* He is talking about CNC — tell me you want it, then pretend that you don't. Straight out of Patrick's playbook. I type a message and then look at him with my eyes narrowed as he reads it.

Meg

> Did you read my book??

He smiles.

That really doesn't answer the question though, does it? An uneasy feeling permeates my being. If he's into that, and he thinks I'm into that because I read about it... then I have no business sleeping with Johnno. Sure, I love to read about it. The darker and kinkier the better. Some twisted part of my mind enjoys it. But to take part in it? No way. That's not me at all. I like one flavour, and that's vanilla. And up to this point, I haven't even particularly enjoyed that.

And now, my insecurity really kicks in. What am I doing on a date with this man, who is clearly on an entirely different planet than me when it comes to sexual appetite, and the way all the signs are pointing, prowess? I shouldn't be here, and this is going to all come horribly undone when he realises it.

My phone buzzes again, but this time it's Elle.

***

By the time we pull up out the front of my place it's after 10pm. Johnno cuts the engine and takes off his helmet, then swings his leg over the bike, but instead of standing, he swivels around and throws his leg back over so he is facing me. He unbuckles my helmet and takes it off me, hooking it over the handlebar, then puts his hands on both of my thighs.

'You good?' he asks.

It's a strange question, and I'm not exactly sure what he means. But I *am* good. Despite the varying degrees of stress I've been under during the evening, I am good.

'Fine.'

'Are you ever better than fine?'

'Rarely. What about you? Did you really hate the movie as much as you seemed to?'

'Yeah,' he says, but there is a slight smile on his face. 'At least I'll be able to talk to Shaelea about it next week. She'll be into it, I'd say.' I don't say anything, but I tilt my head slightly in silent question and wonder if he will answer. 'My daughter.'

I nod. 'It certainly seems to be a hit with the young ones.' I know I'm being annoying, and he acknowledges it with a wry laugh. 'Where is Shaelea when she isn't with you?'

'With her mother in London. I only get two weeks in the holidays.'

'Two weeks...'

'A year.'

'Oh,' I say. My tone betrays my surprise. That seems very limited compared to other custody agreements I know of. But what would I know. I want to ask his age, but I'm sure that would be rude.

'She wasn't planned. We were sixteen. We were together. She was on the pill. Didn't take it properly.' I don't say anything. He seems to say more when I just keep my mouth shut. 'It was equally my fault,' he adds. 'I'm more careful now.'

'What is she like?'

He stiffens slightly, and I think I've caused offence, but then he responds. 'Last time I saw her she was smart, beautiful, sassy. All she wanted to talk about was some boy band she liked. That's probably all changed now.'

'I have a younger brother who is thirteen,' I say, risking him asking me where the lad is located, and then having to either tell him he is inside the property we are currently sitting outside, or make up an elaborate lie about his whereabouts. 'It's an awkward age, but my brother, at least, is still very childlike, underneath the hormones.'

'Is he into vampire movies?'

'Yes. Loves them.'

'If he's thirteen, how old does that make you?'

'Twenty-one. Mum and Dad had a long break after me. Make of that what you will.'

I thought he might laugh, but he frowns. 'You put yourself down too much. It pisses me off.' He reaches up behind my neck and pulls me towards him, then he kisses me in a way that takes my breath away, holding me in place until he is done. He pulls back slightly, and with his lips hovering just above mine, he says, 'Guess what time it is, Meg.' I can't guess. I make a sound, but it isn't words. 'Later.'

***

'Look at you,' he says, his voice a deep, husky growl. 'You're so fucking hot on my bike.'

He has switched places with me, and with clear directions I felt compelled to follow, has positioned me so that I am resting back on the engine of his bike, with my knees bent and my feet resting on part of the bike on either side. My heart is racing and my chest is heaving with each breath I take. Johnno's eyes are drawn there, and he fixates on my tattoo. His lips part and I see his tongue just touch his bottom lip. He catches my eye quickly. It's the sort of look a child would give their mother before they are about to do something they know is naughty. A look to judge how much they might get away with. He leans forward, and braces his arms on the handlebars, and then brings his mouth to the top of my right breast. He starts with just a kiss, and then another, and then his lips and his tongue are exploring my tattoo, all the way to the top of my corset where it disappears beneath. He groans, and his teeth close on the fabric. He nips at it, and pushes his tongue beneath it, where there is a gap between my breasts.

'This fucking thing has to come off,' he says.

Johnno seems to have a way of bringing me at least part of the way around to his ideas. However, there is one significant barrier standing in the way of me agreeing to this one— the chance that my parents have heard his bike pull up and are currently peeking through the blinds to see who is on a motorbike outside their house at this hour. Therefore, I will not be getting topless on this bike, however much the idea is starting to appeal to me. I am, though, extremely reluctant to tell him I live with my parents. That piece of information will need to be dragged from me kicking and screaming. Thankfully, Elle comes to my rescue. I look at my bedroom window, which is at the front of the house, and see her face looking past the edge of my blind. She quickly darts away when she sees me look, but the cheeky git is back again a few seconds later, with a grin on her face.

As Johnno's fingers curl over the top of my corset and make to pull it down, I protest. 'I will remain clothed if you don't mind.' He stops and looks up at me, his eyes is wild. 'We have a spectator.' I nod towards my bedroom window. He turns his head to look, and spots Elle. She waves.

Johnno turns back to me. At least he knows I'm not lying about my house guest, I suppose. 'Weird.'

'Oh, yes. Very,' I agree.

He is breathing heavily, and I realise quickly, that he is undeterred. I may be wrong about the fetish. I don't think it's cupboards. I think it's being caught. A devilish smile comes onto his face.

'If she wants to watch, she can.'

Yes, she wants to. But my parents, Johnno.

His left hand remains on the handlebar of the bike. His eyes hold mine, and his right hand slips beneath the waistband of my tights, and inside my knickers. I feel his warm, slightly rough fingers against my clit, which is already on edge. My breath catches sharply. His middle finger slides down to my entrance, and he is about to know that he is not the only desperate one. He groans as though he is in deep agony as he slides it inside me.

'Fuck, Meg,' he says, sitting back and watching his hand start to move in and out of me, 'you are so wet. So wet for me, baby. You want me like I want you.'

I couldn't speak if I wanted to. He keeps going, driving his finger in and out of me, gradually quickening his pace, but never stopping. I have lost all sense of where I am, and I can't even bring myself to care that Elle is watching.

'I want to taste you.' As though the idea excites him even more, his fingers move even quicker. I'm having sensations down there that are new to me. Pressure and intensity building that I don't know what to do with. I want to come, but it doesn't feel like it does when I touch myself. 'I could lick my fingers, but I want to taste your juices on your skin. I want to taste all of you. Now that I know how wet I make you, I know you can't hold out on me forever, Meg.'

A whimper escapes from me – a sound that I don't even recognise, as I know I'm close to something. I feel so out of control, it's terrifying, but he's not stopping. He just goes faster.

'You're going to come for me now. You're ready. Show me baby.'

I don't have a choice. My legs start to shake, and I am convulsing around his hand in wave after wave. I reach down and grip tightly onto his hand. I need him to stop, I'm at my limit, and mercifully, he does, so I can gradually come back down. His finger is still inside me as I settle around him, and my hand is probably keeping it there. Now that he has stopped moving, it feels good. I think I'd keep him there, especially if he would keep looking at me the way he is. Like I'm the one who has just blown his mind, not the other way around.

'Get rid of your friend,' he says, his voice low and menacing. I trust it isn't a threat.

'I can't.'

He lets out a primal growl of frustration, and I quickly cover his mouth with my free hand. The last thing I need is that sound waking up my parents, if by some miracle they haven't just witnessed their daughter come on the back of a motorcycle.

I release his hand that is still between my legs, and he slowly takes his finger from me, sliding it up over my clit as he does and making my hips jerk.

'Why are you holding out on me?'

'I'm not.' I totally am. 'It's just the circumstances.'

Gingerly, I swing my leg over the bike, and he doesn't try to stop me. My legs are still weak. I straighten my skirt and smooth down my hair. 'Thank you for a pleasant evening.'

'You're driving me crazy.'

My lips twitch. I turn and start walking up the drive.

'When can I see you again?'

I stop. I turn and come back to him, and push all of my fears and misgivings to the back of my mind so I can grab him around the neck and pull him to me. I kiss him with conviction, then say, 'I'll text you.'

***

Elle jumps up from her spot by the window as I come into the room.

'Meg, that was so hot. Did he get you off?' she asks urgently, taking me by the hands.

'Perhaps.'

'Meg!'

'Shh,' I say, since she is practically shouting at me. 'Yes, but you shouldn't have been watching. It's weird, Elle.'

'I know, I'm sorry, I couldn't resist.' She lets go of my hands, only to grab me by the face, one hand on each cheek. 'Was it amazing? He is so hot for you, Meg.'

'It was fine.' Her face drops. 'I need to change my knickers.' Instantly, she brightens.

'That good?'

'It was amazing. But that's all it is to him. Sex. He likes my body. My tatts. He wants to fuck me. That's it.'

'Is there anything wrong with that, honey?'

'I don't know, perhaps not.' I'm going to tell her the truth, even though I know saying it out loud will suck. 'I want to be loved, Elle. Not fucked.'

Tears spring to my eyes, and almost immediately, they spring to Elle's eyes as well. She pulls me into a tight hug. 'I get that, Meg. You deserve that.' After a while, she pulls back, and I dry her eyes with my thumbs.

'What are your tears?'

'All I want,' she says, her voice wavering, 'is to be wanted like that.'

Chapter Ten

The weekend has felt like two years rather than two days. I haven't heard from Johnno, and I haven't messaged him. Not because I don't want to, but because I don't know what to say, and I don't know where it would lead. I have simply obsessed over him every second since we said goodbye.

It's Monday morning now, and I am yet to get out of bed. My feelings have come to a point, and I have to make a choice. There are two options. The first is to let this magical, slightly surreal experience die a natural death by never texting him as I had promised to do, and I keep the memories of the time we've had, and the best orgasm of my life, alive through my drawings. It's either a tragic romance, right up there with Shakespeare's best work, or completely pathetic, the stuff of weekly therapy sessions.

The second option is to take a sickie from work and text him while my family is out, invite him over and sleep with him. This, too, will bring the relationship to a natural death, as he isn't going to want to do it twice, so the outcome is essentially the same, whichever option I choose. But with the latter, I get to have what will likely be the best sex of my life before we meet our tragic end. That way, when I am an old lady, sad and alone, I will have a tale to tell my great-nieces and nephews of the time their Great Aunt Meg shagged the hottest man alive. By that stage of my life, I'm sure I will derive a lot of pleasure from that.

I am not one to take sickies. I've never done it before. I have Dad's work ethic. How to achieve it successfully, I'm not sure. I will myself to actually feel sick, but I can't even manifest the slightest headache.

I decide to ask for advice. It's half six in the morning. Elle will be up. I reach for my phone on the bedside table and send her a text.

Meg

> Morning. I want to pull a sickie today. How do I go about it? xx

I wait, and she responds quickly.

Elle

> Morning. Tell Pip that your house was broken into last night by a masked and cloaked intruder, which has triggered a fit of the vapours, and it will take you the day to recover xx

How could I forget? Elle can't tell a lie to save her life. Her lies are always so elaborate that one can see through them straight away. Except for Joe, it seems. I'll have to ask Gabby.

Meg

> Morning. I want to pull a sickie today. How do I go about it? xx

Gabby takes a little longer to reply. She's probably still in bed. She is a high school teacher, but she only works casually. She doesn't want the responsibility of a full-time job, since she's so close to making the England netball team. I look nervously at the time. I have to make the call soon, or I'll end up just having to go in. Finally, she responds.

Gabby

> Is this a serious question, you muppet? How long do you want off? x

I text back quickly, hoping to keep her attention on the conversation.

Meg

> Just today x

I don't have to wait long.

Gabby

> D and V is the way to go. That will get you tomorrow as well. 24 hours post symptoms. No questions will be asked, no one will want details. For best effect, flush the toilet during the phone call x

Thanks Gabby, but I'm not doing that. However, her logic is sound for the tummy bug. I'll go with that. Pip insists we call her when sick— no text messages. I phone her mobile and leave what I hope is a suitably loose-bowelled voice message. Now for my next challenge: what to say to Johnno.

***

I procrastinate on exactly that for the rest of the morning, and into the afternoon, until half one, when I finally send a carefully worded text, employing the full arts of seduction.

> Hi. What are you up to? x

If that doesn't scream booty call, I don't know what does, and Johnno is picking up what I'm putting down.

> Free in an hour. Where are u? x

> At home x

Who says I don't have charms?

***

It's half two now. I've spent the last hour trying to conceal any evidence that anyone else lives with me. Not an easy task, when this is a family home of five, previously six until Sophie moved out, and we've lived here for ten years. There are family photos everywhere, copious amounts of shoes in every size and style you can imagine, and everything in this place screams family home, not bachelorette pad. I do my best to push the most obvious signs out of sight, like Dad's finance magazines that live beside the sofa. I shut all the bedroom doors, and hope I can steer Johnno straight to my room without him noticing too much. My brothers have football after school, which means they've taken all their gear with them from the entryway and won't be home until after five.

I shower and dress in ripped black denim jeans and a white cut-off singlet top, and I leave my hair down.

By a quarter to three, I'm starting to feel like a goose, because I don't think he's going to come. I read the text message exchange again, and realise with a sinking heart that I didn't invite him, did I? I asked him what he was up to, and told him where I was, but I gave no indication that I wanted him to relocate to my address. Fuck.

I'm about to pull out my phone and clarify that I want him to come over, when I hear his motorbike pull up out the front. He reads between the lines. An essential skill for anyone who wants, or can't avoid, communicating with me.

He brings his helmet with him to the front door, and I meet him there. As I open the door he smiles a crooked smile at me, and my knees threaten to buckle.

'I thought you weren't going to text,' he says, as he enters, and I shut the door behind him. He puts his helmet down, and before I know it's happening, my back is against the door, and his mouth is crushing mine. He pulls away. 'Any house guests today?'

'No. We're alone.' I remember my plan to conceal the existence of my family, and take his hand, leading him out of the foyer and down the hallway to my room. He stops at a photo hanging on the wall— all six of us on the day of Sophie's high school graduation.

'Is this your family?'

'Yes.'

He looks at it for a while, taking in each face. I wonder what he's thinking. Then he says, 'Cute,' and we keep going.

We enter my bedroom, and as I cross the threshold, I realise for the first time how childish my room looks. It looks that way because it's been my bedroom since I was eleven, but that isn't a defence I can use right now. My bookcase still has the books in it I used to read as a teen, mixed in with the adult fantasy and romance I read now. My duvet is black, with a large skull and red roses across it. I chose it when I was fifteen, and I still loved it right up until twenty seconds ago, when I decided it is completely cringe. I don't even have throw cushions. Adults should have throw cushions. In the corner— Mum's doing— is a cabinet containing my netball trophies and medallions. Why she couldn't put that in her own room I don't know, but alas, it's there, and it's too late to do anything about it now. Johnno stops and looks around, with a slight smile, and I want to die. He moves to my bed and lays down, and then, I realise my biggest mistake of all. *Cloaked Lust* is in pride of place on my bedside table.

He picks it up and turns to my bookmark. He glances up at me, where I am still standing just inside the doorway, and his smile grows a little. Then he turns his attention to the book. There's not much I can do now. I walk around to the other side of the bed and lie down beside him. Just simply lying next to him on the bed has my body fully awake and certain parts screaming at me, but he is thoroughly preoccupied.

'I thought you said you don't read.'

'I don't.' He doesn't look at me. His attention is still fixed on *Cloaked Lust*.

My discomfort is made worse by the fact that I know exactly where he is up to. Patrick the cloaked crusader has chosen his favourite victim, and decided he can't stay away. I had stopped reading and put my bookmark in right after he had climbed in the window, and, having found his Chosen One in bed with her husband, tied the unfortunate spouse to a chair in the corner of the room. Not to say that *Cloaked Lust* is predictable and formulaic, but I'm sure a kerfuffle ensues.

Johnno finishes the chapter before he places the book back down on my bedside table, this time with my bookmark still in place— his etiquette is improving— and he rolls over on top of me. He is straining against his jeans as he kisses me. I wrap my arm around his neck and separate my legs to let him press against me, and he accepts that invitation willingly. His hands slide beneath my singlet, and he pulls it up and over my head in one movement, leaving me in a black lacy bra. He props himself up on his arms. His eyes roam my body, and I want his mouth all over me. His eyes are hungry as he fixes on my breasts, and he traces a finger over the tattoo on my sternum, then brings his mouth to my neck, trailing his mouth and tongue across my collar bone, and then working his way down. My back arches in anticipation as he pulls down on the strap on my right shoulder and bares my nipple. He groans quietly as he pulls it into his mouth. I have never felt so desired. I have never felt so turned on. I'm so ready to have this man. I am at his mercy, until—

He stops and climbs off the bed. His breath is ragged, his eyes are wild. A feral smile spreads across his face, and suddenly, I am nervous. He shrugs out of his jacket and takes off the black t-shirt he was wearing underneath, and finally I can see all of his ink. I want to just stare at him and memorise every piece, but he walks away, over to my cupboard and opens it, looking for something— I'm not sure what, until he finds it. The satin belt from my dressing gown. He wraps it around his hands as he comes back to the bed and sits down.

'Ready to have some fun, baby?' he asks, huskily.

Oh, fuck. This was all heading in a wonderful, non-threatening direction that I was thoroughly enjoying, but we seem to be taking a detour down a path I have not, and was planning to never, tread. I have no idea how to direct this back on course.

He tests the strength of my metal bedhead by attempting to wobble it back and forwards. He seems satisfied when it doesn't move, and he sets to work, threading the belt through the rungs.

'Arms up,' he says firmly. I am about to comply, because I don't know what else to do, when my phone on the bedside table lights up. He notices it too and looks from it to me. I meet his eyes, then quickly sit up and reach for the phone.

'Sorry, this is important,' I say. I jump up and flee from the room, shutting the door behind me. I hurry down the hallway and decide on James's room as the best place to hide.

I shut myself in and sit down on his bed. I am so mortified. I'm in my bra, sitting on my little brother's bed, hiding from the hottest man alive, whom I invited over with the intention of sleeping with. And I am staring at an 'important' spam text message from the department store downtown advising me they have 30% off on manchester this week, only for loyalty shoppers. This is a new low.

It's after three. Elle will be finished in class. I need help. I call, and thank God, she picks up.

'You all right? How are you feeling?' she asks.

'Believe it or not, I think I am actually having a fit of the vapours.'

'That's not like you! What's happening?'

'Johnno's here.'

'Ooh, is that why you wanted to take a sickie? Did you invite him over? Have you shagged?'

'Yes, I invited him, and no, we haven't. He wants to tie me up.' Elle giggles. She seems to be confused. This really isn't funny. 'I need your help.'

'What do you mean? Don't you want him to tie you up?'

'No!'

'Why not? You like him. And I would have thought being tied up would suit you perfectly. You don't have to worry about performing—the onus is on him.'

'Yes, but he will expect moaning, and writhing, and things of that nature. That's not me, Elle. I can't do it.'

'Don't be ridiculous! Just go and enjoy yourself.'

'You're not listening,' I squeal, and I hear my voice break. 'I don't want to do it. I don't want to be tied up. I just want normal, boring, vanilla sex. I want to look at his tatts and do my starfish routine. Not this.'

'OK, OK,' Elle says. 'I will help, Meg. Don't worry. Of course I will help.' She pauses. 'What exactly do you want me to do?'

It's a good question. 'I don't know. Get me out of this situation. I can't go back in there.'

'Where are you?'

'James's room.' Elle giggles again. 'Elle!'

'Sorry, my love. It just sounds a little... comical. This is what we will do. I will come over. I haven't left school yet, I'm only a couple of minutes away.'

'Yes.'

'I will go to your bedroom. I assume that's where he is?'

'Yes.'

'I will talk to Johnno.'

'Yes.'

'And ask him is if it's all right if I take your place.'

'Elle!'

The irrepressible giggles return. 'It was just a suggestion. I will talk to Johnno and tell him that you aren't into BDSM and could you please reschedule to another day.'

'No! You can't tell him that.'

'Why not? It's the truth, isn't it?'

Well isn't this rich. 'You're very quick to want to tell the truth, the whole truth and nothing but the truth when it involves *me*, aren't you? But when it involves you and Joe, you hide behind headaches and gout —'

'Hey! This isn't about me and Joe,' Elle says. She sounds a little hurt, and I realise in my stressed state, I've overstepped.

'Sorry, Elle. I just don't want to tell him that. Can you get me out of it another way, that doesn't involve the truth?'

'Of course.' I have some concerns about what she might come up with, but this is a desperate situation. 'When I arrive, you will go out and wait in my car, and once I have seen Johnno off, we will make our escape.'

'Thanks, Elle. See you soon.'

I breathe a little easier knowing she is on her way. She might be daft, but I know for sure she won't let me down. I am going to need a shirt, though. I open James's cupboard and pull out his Leeds United football jersey. It's a generous size. It will fit. I put it on and wait nervously until I hear the front door open. Elle comes straight to James's room, opens the door and gives me a tight hug. Then breaks into the Leeds United song.

'Shush,' I say, and cover her mouth with my hand. 'Are you ready?' When I'm sure she's stopped singing, I release her.

'Yes. Will he be mad?'

'Perhaps. What are you going to tell him?'

'I've thought carefully about it,' says Elle sombrely, 'and I think it will be best if I don't tell you until afterwards.' She hands me her car keys. 'I've parked in the street. Go and wait in the car. It will all be over before you know it.'

Why doesn't that feel reassuring? She gives me a comforting smile, tightens her ponytail, and heads down the hallway to my room. I slink, like a complete coward, out of the house, and to her car to wait.

***

It's only a few minutes before, from my position crouched low in her passenger seat, I see Johnno come out of the house with his helmet, fully clothed and with a scowl on his face. He glares in the direction of Elle's car, and then storms to his bike, climbs on, does a U-turn and rides away, fast, in the opposite direction.

Right behind him, Elle comes out and pulls the door shut, then makes her way to the car. She gets in and shuts the door without looking at me.

'How did it go?' I ask, dreading the answer.

Elle shakes her head sadly. 'Not well, I'm afraid.'

'Fuck. Was he fuming?'

'No,' she says, but she sounds uncertain. 'Not mad. He seemed... disappointed.'

I think that's worse. 'What did you tell him?'

Elle takes a deep breath, and let's it out in a puff. She starts the car and pulls out in the direction of her place. 'I told him your second cousin needed you urgently, as she has been detained by police on suspicion of treason. You are the only one who holds the evidence that can free her.'

For fuck's sake. It's like she has tried to think of the worst possible lie she could, and then added in the second cousin just for good measure. Treason, fine, I can swallow that. But the second cousin is just too much.

'Elle! Second cousin? Why?' I say, unable to keep the frustration from my voice.

'I couldn't choose someone who existed! What if he met them and asked them about it?'

'You couldn't have just made it an unspecified friend? He is very unlikely at this point to meet anyone associated with me. And even then, who casually discusses alleged treason with a passing acquaintance?'

'I'm sorry, Meg,' she says, pettishly. 'I thought I was doing the right thing. Next time, perhaps you should extricate yourself if I've not done it to your satisfaction.'

I sigh. 'No, Elle. I'm sorry. I owe you. Anyway, what did he say?'

'He said ...,' she makes her voice low and gruff in a very poor impersonation of Johnno..., 'She invited *me* here,', then a few other things under his breath that I couldn't clearly interpret.'

'Is that all?'

'No.' She seems reluctant to go on. She takes another deep breath, then continues. 'He said it would have been nice if you could have lied to his face, instead of sending your weird girlfriend to do it for you.' I groan, a prolonged, forlorn sound, followed by several sobs. 'I know, right? He called me weird!'

'He's not wrong.'

Elle gasps. 'Well, I never,' she says, only reinforcing that she *is* weird.

'I'm sorry, Elle, but this is just the worst possible outcome to what was meant to be the best sex of my life, followed by a forever of solitude. Now I have the solitude, without the sex, and a whole lot of shame and embarrassment to carry around as baggage.'

'And *I'm* the weird one,' she says, and I can't help but think she has
a point.

Chapter Eleven

I stayed at Elle's on Monday night, for moral support. I spent the day on Tuesday, while I continued to fake my recovery from gastro, comfort eating in my pyjamas, and biting the head off anyone who came near me. In an effort to escape my painful thoughts, I slept during the day, which meant I didn't sleep on Tuesday night.

Now, it's Wednesday morning, and I have to rally myself to resume my normal life. It is a struggle. The only thing that encourages me out of bed is the knowledge that Book Club is on tonight. I dress in black tights and a black fitted singlet top and tie a brown and grey flannel checked shirt around my waist. I can't be bothered with my hair, so I throw it up in a bun on top of my head.

My day at the library passes uneventfully. I have no expectation of ever seeing Johnno again. I'm sure he is as embarrassed as I am, if not more, and I'm certain he wants to be as far away from me as possible. As does Pip, it seems. Even she must be able to tell that I am not to be messed with right now, and she thinks better of inflicting me on the toddlers, even when Yvonne calls in sick. She takes Toddler Time herself, and let's me brood in peace in re-shelving.

At half three, I am desperately tired, and I need a coffee if I'm going to get through the social interactions necessary for Book Club. I ask Yvonne if I can go downstairs to get one, and to my surprise, she agrees. I take the lift down to the ground floor and turn to enter the coffee shop. I have my head down looking at my phone when I find myself rebounding off a solid male body.

I stumble, and strong hands reach out to steady me. One of them, I recognise by the tattoo on the back of it. I look up and meet Johnno's hard, green eyes.

'I-I'm so sorry, I wasn't looking.' This is excruciating. My cheeks are burning hot, and after the initial look up to confirm it was him, I have fixed my eyes on my own feet. I will him to keep walking, but it seems he isn't going to, because I can still see his shoes in front of me.

'It's OK.'

'I'm working. Just grabbing a coffee before Book Club starts.'

'Book Club?'

He seems to want an explanation. I can't keep talking to my shoes. I lift my eyes and look at him again. His eyes have softened a little. He doesn't look mad. But he is unsmiling.

'It's a group I run. We all read the same book, and then chat about it each week.' He doesn't say anything, which makes me feel like I need to keep talking. 'It's very popular.'

'Some people really like books, hey?'

I stifle a smile. 'They do.'

We lapse into silence, but he's still standing here, and I still need to buy a coffee and get back to work. I don't have the social skills necessary to bring this about. 'I should—'

'—Right,' he says, cutting me off. 'Me too.'

Great. I'm glad that's sorted. But for some reason, I don't move, and neither does he.

I clear my throat nervously. 'Johnno, about the other day. I'm so sorry. I really fucked up.'

'Interesting,' he says.

What does that mean? 'What is?'

'I thought it was me who fucked up.'

'No,' I say quickly, with a shake of my head. Oh God, if he apologises to me, I will die. 'You— you did nothing wrong. I was... God, I can't even... I was a twat.'

His eyes crinkle, and the slightest smile start at the corner of his mouth. 'How's your second cousin?' I drop my eyes again in shame. I'm blushing so hard, I think I've changed species. His finger lifts my chin. 'Pretty serious charges, treason.'

'I shouldn't have sent Elle. She's a terrible liar.'

'Why did you?'

'I'm a coward.'

'Why did you feel like you had to lie?'

'I lost my nerve.'

He looks at me, and I can't be sure it's not concern in his eyes. 'Have I been reading this wrong? I thought you were into it.'

'You weren't wrong,' I practically whisper. I check the time. 'I'm sorry, I have to grab a coffee and get back to work.'

Johnno looks back inside the coffee shop, where he has just come from. There are only a couple of people waiting. 'Can I wait with you?'

I nod, and we go inside. I stand in the line, and he stands beside me, close, but we are not touching. His hands are in his pockets. He doesn't say anything, but I can sense he wants to. I make it to the front of the line and order, and then we stand off to the side of the counter to wait. It's so awkward. Of course it is. How could it not be after what happened? If only I could think of something— anything— to say. But I've got absolutely nothing. I look around, hoping something to talk about will jump out at me. I am so focused on my efforts to produce some small talk, that when Johnno says my name, I jump.

He shakes his head at me, and I smile sheepishly. 'Yes?'

'Your friend— what's her name?'

'Elle.'

'Is there something going on there?'

I look at him blankly. Is he asking if she's the full quid? If so, what do I tell him? 'She's a teacher. She's actually very intelligent.'

Now *he's* looking at *me* blankly. 'That's... not what I meant. You said you don't have a boyfriend, but are you two... involved?'

'What?!' I squeal. 'No!'

'OK,' he says, using his hands to signal me to calm down. 'Just asking. Thought that might be why you're so...'

'What?'

'Hot and cold. One minute you're into it, the next you're not. It's confusing. Just thought that might explain it.'

I shake my head. 'No. That's not it. Elle is engaged to the blonde thing you saw me with here the day I met you.'

He still isn't convinced. 'And you don't have feelings for her?'

'No. I'm into men,' I say firmly, and then with out of character bravery, I add, 'Specifically, you.'

He frowns, and looks like he wants to say more, but my coffee is ready, and I step forward to take it from the barista.

I walk in the direction of the exit, and Johnno walks alongside me.

'I'm into you too. So, what am I getting wrong?' I push the button for the lift, and it opens straight away. I step in, and he follows me. He wants an answer. The doors close, entrapping me with my interrogator. I can't tell him. I can't tell him I just want plain, boring sex. He might be into me *now*, but he won't be into me once I tell him that. It's no coincidence he read *Cloaked Lust* and then went all caped crusader on me. He thinks that's my jam, and it's obviously his.

'You're not getting anything wrong. It's me.'

It's not a long ride, and we're already at the first floor. The doors open. We step out together.

'It's not you, it's me? We've made our way through the lies, only to arrive at the cliches?'

Ouch. That was catty. Clever, but catty. I didn't expect that. We enter the library, and we're standing outside the conference room, where I've set up the sign for Book Club, and attendees are starting to filter in.

'I'm sorry, I can't talk about this now. All I can say is you did nothing wrong. And I'm sorry. I really am.' I try to make that sound final, and I make a move towards the conference room, but Johnno takes my elbow. I turn back to him.

'You apologise too much,' he says gruffly.

'Meg, look out!' a voice shouts from near the entrance to the library. Oh God, it's Margy, and doesn't she just have that look in her eye. 'Unhand her this instant! Security!' she shrieks.

'Margy, please, can we not do this,' I try to say, but she screams again and waves her cane in the air.

'SECURITY!'

Johnno looks thoroughly embarrassed, and I feel awful. 'There is no security,' I say quietly to him. Margy starts hobbling towards us, and I am worried about what she's planning to do. How far will she take this? Thankfully, Elle comes through the entrance just behind her, right in the nick of time. I shoot her a pleading look and stand between Margy and Johnno.

Margy isn't slowing down. Still, she isn't very fast. I'm not concerned about Johnno's ability to defend himself, but just the scene this is causing. The Book Club crowd are casting glances in our direction— some curious, some concerned.

Elle realises what is happening, and God bless her, she intervenes. 'Margy, my love, why don't you come into Book Club and sit by me? Meg is fine, I promise you. That man is her... her...'

Oh no.

'Father!' Elle says, with a triumphant smile at me and Johnno. She thinks she's done well. 'That's right. I bet he just bought her that coffee to see her through the afternoon.'

I look at Johnno apologetically, and thankfully, he is fighting a smile. 'I don't really look like your dad, do I?' he asks quietly.

I choke back a giggle, which is very unlike me. Margy shoots a grin at me over her shoulder, seemingly pleased with the commotion she has caused, as Elle ushers her into the conference room, elaborating further on her lie as she goes. 'He and Meg's mother had Meg at a very young age, you see...'

How young? Eight? 'Thank God for Elle,' I say, with a stifled smile. I check the time. It's four. 'I need to grab my book.' I walk over to the front counter and lean over for my copy of *Cloaked Lust* and return with it in-hand.

'Is *that* the book for Book Club?' he asks with surprise.

'Yes.'

'You and a bunch of women sit around and talk about *that*?'

'Yes.'

'Hardcore porn.'

'Sshh,' I say urgently. 'It is not!' I know my denial is fruitless, because it absolutely is.

Right at that moment, Pip emerges. She does a double take when she sees Johnno. He is distinctive. She would remember him from his earlier visits. She is clearly surprised to see him speaking with me. Her eyes narrow.

'What is the commotion out here? This is a library, not a night club. I heard someone calling for security.'

'Misunderstanding,' I say quickly. 'Margy was...confused. There's no issue.'

Pip is standing a few metres away from us, looking from me, to Johnno, and back again, with a hand on her hip. 'I think I'll attend Book Club this afternoon,' she says. 'Make a start, I'll be in shortly.'

She strides away. Panic completely overwhelms me. I open and close my mouth several times, to no avail. No suitable reason for Pip not to attend Book Club is forthcoming.

'Are you OK?' Johnno asks me, his concern evident.

'No.' I say. 'She can't come.'

'Does she know what you're reading?'

'No.'

He nods his understanding. 'I'll sort it.' I like this man. I really like this man. I look up at him gratefully, and even though I have no idea how he intends to 'sort it', I believe him. I reach out and take his hand, squeeze it quickly, and let it go. He smiles, and I enter the conference room.

I remain near the doorway, with my back to it. I'm too curious to know what he is going to do. The group settles down into their seats. Elle looks at me, and she must sense that I need more time, because she starts making chit chat with the group, while I listen intently to what is happening just outside.

'Excuse me,' I hear Johnno say in his deep, oh so sexy voice. 'Are you the guvnor?'

I stifle a smile. Pip wouldn't get that often. 'Yes,' she confirms. 'What can I do for you?'

'About the automotive section in Aisle 22.'

'I see. I'm a little busy. If you need some help to find a book—'

'—No. It's not that. I want to make a complaint,' he says. He is doing a really good job of sounding pissed off. 'Do you realise you've only got eight books about motorbikes?'

'Only eight? Well, perhaps that's all that's needed to cover—'

'—Eight. Eight books.' His tone is indignant. 'I pay council taxes, and I'm telling you, that's not enough. Come and see for yourself, and I'll explain what's missing.'

I sneak a look out, and see Pip following him to Aisle 22, and I know without a doubt that this is the moment that I have fallen, head over heels, in love with Johnno.

Chapter Twelve

After a revelation like that one, it is fitting that the discussion at Book Club this afternoon is to centre around the age-old debate of lust versus love.

I take my seat at the table, and as usual, Elle gains the attention of the room, and then throws to me.

'Good afternoon, everyone. Thank-you for coming. We are nearing the end of *Cloaked Lust*. In Chapter 25, we learned that Patrick has decided that Bella is his one true love, and, though she is married, he has to have her.

'My question for you is, are you, the reader, convinced that Patrick is in love with Bella? Or is it a case of, as the title perhaps cleverly foreshadows, nothing but cloaked lust? Lust disguised as love.'

'Well, all he's done is fucked her. Bit rich to call that love, innit?' says a woman with long brown hair and a chipped front tooth from the end of the table. 'And she's been gagged most of the time at that!'

Elle takes over as chief facilitator of discussion, and I sit back, more than willing to let her. This conversation interests me greatly, considering I have just mentally declared my love for a man who I have yet to have a proper conversation with— at least, not one that wasn't about sex in some way. The collective life experience of the women in this room with, I estimate, an average age of around 35 (Margy pushing that number up considerably) would be approximately 600 years. That equates to quite a healthy amount of wisdom.

'Yes, but don't you think it is possible he just *knows*?' asks Elle. The girl is a romance author's dream. She will look for the happily ever after wherever she can, even against the toughest of odds. Patrick, for example, is a psychopath. But Elle still just wants him to find 'the one'.

The woman with the blonde bob and red lipstick, who was willing to give Patrick's short, stubby member the benefit of the doubt back in Chapter 15, responds. 'Honey, I've been married twice, and let me tell you this. There is a big difference between the man whose clothes you want to tear off, and the man you marry. Never the twain shall meet.'

We all look at her a little confused, so she adds, 'What I mean is, I strongly recommend that the two never meet. It causes all manner of problems when they do,' and then she throws her head back in raucous laughter. I guess she is implying she took a lover during her marriage, and it was his clothes she wanted to tear off, not her husband's.

Elle is frowning, which is rare. I look more closely. She is not just frowning. Her cheeks are very red, and she looks proper distressed. 'Yes, but isn't it true that for a relationship to work long term, there must be a degree of lust there in the beginning, at least? How, if things are lukewarm the entire time, does one keep an interest in the relationship? Wouldn't the mind start to wander? Patrick might currently be mainly about the clothes tearing, but if there is a spark there, and they are compatible, wouldn't it be an ideal basis for a long-term relationship?'

Never mind that Bella is married to someone else, and Patrick has been slutting around the neighbourhood with anyone who leaves their window open. Have some standards, Elle.

'I agree entirely with Janice,' says the woman beside the one with the blonde hair, who I assume is Janice. I really should know by now, but I have never gotten around to instigating name tags. 'The man you marry is the one who will do as he is told and keep out of mischief. The one whose clothes you want to tear off will be a temporary pleasure at best. One day, you'll come home and find a torn pair of knickers you don't recognise, and you'll be sorry you didn't marry the nice young man who felt you up politely in the car before sending you inside to wait until you were both ready.'

I'm almost certain they've both been drinking.

I'm going to have to intervene, but I don't know how to steer the discussion in a different direction. Elle looks like she is going to burst into tears.

'You must be wrong. True love ticks both boxes. I'm sure of it,' she says. She scans the faces of everyone in the room. 'Surely there is someone in this room who can attest to being both strongly attracted to, and in love with their partner?'

Perhaps the book club crowd is the wrong focus group for what Elle wants. She meets with a lot of sympathetic smiles, and subtle shakes of the head. 'Why the fuck do you think we're here, reading *Cloaked Lust* with a bunch of other women, love?' says the woman with the brown hair and chipped tooth. That comment is followed by knowing laughter amongst the group.

'Oh dear,' Elle says quietly, and slumps back in her chair.

Margy has been quietly whispering to her carer beside her, but suddenly, she sits forward.

'Have I got this right?' she asks. 'Does the girl want to know if lust is just as important as love in a marriage?'

Everyone falls silent and turns their attention to Margy.

'Yes,' I say, with a quick sideways glance at Elle. 'That's what she wants to know, Margy.'

Margy, as sober as I have ever seen her, carefully pushes her chair back and stands up. 'Let me tell you, lass. I was happily married for fifty years before my husband passed away. There were times I didn't want to touch him with barge pole. But until the day he died, there was never another man I would have looked sideways at. He was the love, and the lust of my life. If you find that, marry the geezer straight away.'

The room is truly stunned into silence. Margy slowly sits back down, and quiet murmurs start. I look at Elle. Her bottom lip is quivering, and she quickly excuses herself from the room. I want to follow, but I have to stay.

'Well, then,' I say, 'perhaps there is hope for Patrick and Bella after all.'

***

By the time Book Club wraps, and I leave the conference room, Johnno is gone. I spot Elle, sitting at a booth, resting forward with her chin on her arm. She sits up as I approach and manages a smile.

'You all right?' I ask, as I sit down beside her.

She sighs, a heavy sigh. 'Yes.'

'Did you see Johnno leave?' Self-centred, but I have to ask.

'Yes, he hung around for a bit but left about fifteen minutes ago.'

'Did you speak to him?' I ask, slightly worried.

'No. He gave me a wide berth.' The slight giggle that follows is a relief to me. Maybe she is OK. 'Did you two talk?'

'Yes. I ran into him— literally— downstairs at the coffee shop. We had a very stilted conversation about what happened.'

'And?'

'He asked if you and I are a thing.'

'What?!' Elle squeals. 'What gave him that idea?'

'I don't know, Elle. Possibly the fact that you sleep in my bed with me, you watched through the window while he fingered me, and I sent you in to rescue me from sex with him.'

'Oh,' says Elle with a proper giggle this time. 'When you put it like that, I suppose it's not unreasonable. What happens now? Are you going to go out again?'

'I don't know. I told him I'm into him. He says that, against all odds, he's still into me—'

'He said *that*?'

'No. I added the "against all odds" part.'

'Meg!'

'Sorry.'

'Are you going to message him?' Her eyes are pleading with me to say yes, so invested in this is she.

'Perhaps.'

'Meg!' she growls at me. 'What do you mean, "perhaps"? What more does that man have to do to fix his interest with you?'

'It's just that the same thing will happen again, won't it? I can't sleep with him. He's into stuff I'm not, and unless I tell him that, these misunderstandings will be repeated. And I don't want to tell him. He has this image of me as some sort of tattooed freak in the sheets. I don't want to see his face when that comes crashing down. It doesn't matter how I feel about him. It's just not me.'

Elle was looking deflated, but at something I have said, she perks up. 'How *do* you feel about him?' she asks. 'You haven't mentioned feelings before. Only the need for fresh underwear.'

I feel so silly to say it out loud. How can it be love? I don't know him, and he doesn't know me. But if I can't say it to Elle, I can't say it to anyone, and I think I want to say it. 'I think I'm in love with him.'

Elle's eyes widen, and she opens her mouth wide as she gasps. I shush her. We're not totally alone yet. There are still a few stragglers from Book Club. 'Meg! That's wonderful.'

'No, it isn't! Be realistic, Elle. I know barely anything about him. I'm sure I'm being foolish.'

'What makes you say it then? I've never known you to ever be even close to in love before. There must be a reason you're feeling this way now.'

She is looking at me so eagerly. I get the feeling what I tell her will have ramifications beyond this conversation. 'I just...I feel that if we never spoke two words to each other, it wouldn't matter, as long as I was with him. In his presence. It's just a sense. It's not logical.'

She just stares at me, and as she does, tears start to well in her eyes. With her lips quivering, she says, 'I can't marry Joe.'

***

I pack up Book Club as quickly as I can and get ready to close up, while Elle sits with her head in her hands in the booth. She hasn't stopped crying since she said those words, and I almost feel like joining her. This is bad. Really bad. She has to marry Joe. They are engaged. He is the sweetest man alive. He adores her. He will make her happy. Won't he?

Once I'm ready to set the alarm, I take her by the elbow and lead her outside. I punch in the code to turn on the alarm, and then I turn my attention back to her. Her tear-stained face kills me to look at. She is the happiest, bubbliest person I know, despite what she has been through with the accident. This should be the most exciting time of her life. She shouldn't be standing here in front of me in despair. I pull her close and hold her, which sets off a fresh round of tears.

'Let's go downstairs and get something to eat. We can talk about it there,' I say. I take her by the hand, and we make our way down in the lift. I grab a couple of menus from the counter of the coffee shop, and we establish ourselves at my favourite table by the window. Now that we are comfortable, we can talk.

'Elle, I'm sure this is just cold feet, my love. You're faced with the prospect of forever, and it's a frightening thought. I'm sure I'd be the same. But Joe is your best friend, and he is so devoted to you. You are really good together.'

'Yes, we are. We are great as friends. He is the very best of men. I know that. But I don't only not want to tear his clothes off. I don't want to take his clothes off at all. I want him to remain clothed at all times. I don't want to sleep with him anymore. At all. Ever again. I feel sick saying it, Meg, but it's the truth.'

Fuck.

'There is more to a marriage than hot sex. When you and Joe are together, you talk, and laugh. You're affectionate. He sees all your craziness, and he loves you anyway. And he is loyal. You would never have to worry about Joe straying.'

'But I don't have the feeling you've just described for Joe, and I never have. Joe has always been my best friend, from the beginning. We were each other's first time. I thought things would improve with time. That it was just a little lacklustre because we were both inexperienced. But it hasn't. There's no heat, Meg. None.'

I'm struck by inspiration, as I think back to the conversation with Mum in the kitchen. 'The eighty-twenty rule!'

'The what?' Elle asks.

'The eighty-twenty rule. Mum told me about it. If the person you are with is eighty percent right, they are "the one" and the other twenty percent you learn to love.'

'I don't think that's a thing, Meg. Do you think Johnno is only eighty percent right? You are crazy about him.'

Oh, God. It makes sense now. She is comparing her and Joe to me and Johnno, but there really is no comparison. Johnno wants to bed me. Joe wants to be her forever. And while she has doubts that the sex will last her a lifetime, I doubt there is even the potential for a next week, let alone a lifetime, for me and Johnno. She can't throw this away over something that doesn't even exist.

'Elle, forget what I said about Johnno. I have no idea what percentage he is! I'm being ridiculous, can't you see that? How can I be in love with a man I don't even know? I'm sure what I'm experiencing is pure lust. Hormones. Dopamine flooding my brain because of the novelty of a man paying me some attention. What you and Joe have is so much more than that.'

Elle shakes her head sadly. 'I've been through this entire conversation with myself, in my head, a thousand times over the past few months. I've made the exact same arguments with myself. I've thought about what a wonderful father he would be, and how pleasant he would be to sit in a rocking chair beside while we wait to die. But it all comes back to the same thing. I want to feel more than this. I want to feel desperation. I want to feel like my life can't go on if I don't have that person. It exists, I'm sure of it. And I haven't found it with Joe.'

I don't know what else to say. I had no idea she had been feeling this way for so long. There were hints she was having doubts, but not to this extent. 'What are you going to do?'

'I don't know. I can't break his heart. But I know for sure, I cannot marry him.'

***

After counselling Elle for the rest of the evening, I finally arrive home at half eight. I jump straight in the shower, and then climb into bed. Elle's significant problem has pushed my own more trivial situation to the back of my mind, and I fall to sleep still thinking over everything we discussed, and all the ways this might pan out. There is still a chance it will be OK. They will get married and live happily ever after— if a little sexually frustrated. By the time I left Elle, she wasn't so adamant that it couldn't be done.

I am startled awake a few hours later by a loud thud on my bedroom floor. I sit bolt upright in bed, and as a large figure looms over me, I let out an almighty, ear-splitting scream.

'Meg,' the figure says. I scream again. I can't help it. My entire body is flooded with adrenaline. 'It's just me.'

I have no time to process who, 'just me' might be, before my bedroom door bursts open, and there is my mum and dad. Dad switches on the light, and I see the fear in both of my parents' faces as they are confronted by the tattooed hulk of a man that is Johnno.

'What the hell is going on?' Dad manages to say, which is very brave, because he must be terrified. I'm sure in his mind, the only reasonable explanation for this man being in my bedroom, and my screaming my head off, is that he is an intruder who has come to do us a serious mischief.

Before I can answer, my brothers both arrive on the scene. James pushes past Mum into the room, holding his cricket bat. That shows impressive forethought. I'll have to tell him how proud I am tomorrow. Harry is next, and the second he lays eyes on Johnno, he lets out a blood-curdling scream of his own, and then runs away back down the hall.

'Your brother?' Johnno asks. I nod meekly. 'You scream the same.' I guess he now knows I live with my parents. Johnno puts his hands up in the air to show he is unarmed, as James raises the cricket bat and takes a step forward, and I know I have to speak.

'Dad, James, it's fine,' I say, clutching my chest as my heart feels like it is going to burst through my rib cage. 'I know him. He's a friend. I was just startled.'

'A friend?' Dad says, his eyes wide. He looks closely at Johnno, and then I see the recognition dawn on his face. The man from the drawings. Only Dad knows I was drawing a real person. 'I see.' Dad pushes on James's arm, encouraging him to lower the cricket bat.

'What the fuck are you doing in Meg's bedroom?' James asks. His voice is shaky, and though it hasn't broken yet, he pushes it low.

'Language, James,' says Dad. James turns to him with a look of utter confusion, as if to say, 'what the hell are you doing scolding me for my language when there is a serial killer in Meg's bedroom'?

'It's all right. I'll show myself out,' says Johnno, and with a dark look at me, he climbs back out the window, and he is gone.

'Meg Drury, you have some explaining to do,' says Mum, who has just regained her power of speech.

'I know. I'm sorry, truly.' And they are not the only ones who I owe an explanation to. Johnno wouldn't have come in through my window if he'd known in advance that I live with my family. I can only imagine how pissed off he must be. Speaking of my family, they are still all staring at me. 'Oh, you want me to explain now?'

'No time like the present, my love,' says Dad. And I suppose he is right.

Chapter Thirteen

I didn't tell my parents everything. I told them Johnno is the man from the drawings, and that we've been seeing each other. I didn't tell them that he thought of climbing in through my bedroom window because of the hardcore porn I've been reading. I said he sent me a message, but I fell asleep and missed it. Dad said I should strongly encourage him to use the front door next time. Fair. Though I don't think there will be a next time.

I arrive at our netball game at half five. Elle, Gabby and Sophie are already warming up, and it doesn't take me long to realise that someone— most likely the treacherous fiend I used to call Mummy— has told Sophie all about it. Sophie has a grin like the Cheshire cat, and as soon as a put down my bag and join them on court, she catches the ball they have been passing and holds it under one arm.

'Meg! I wasn't sure we would see you after what happened last night.'

Sophie absolutely does not think that a man coming through my bedroom window would stop me from playing netball the following night. She simply wants to bring it up, in front of Gabby and Elle, to embarrass me.

'All right, Soph. As you can see, I'm in fine fettle. Pass the ball.'

Sophie fires a pass at me, and I catch it and throw a lob up for Elle. Gabby leaps across and intercepts it before Elle can take it, and Elle gives her a push in the back in retaliation.

I expect things to be a little awkward between me and Elle after last night. What she disclosed was heavy stuff. She is looking at me curiously but doesn't say anything. She knows what Sophie is like, even if she is too nice to ever show it, and she will give people the benefit of the doubt long after she should. What she won't do is bite if she thinks Sophie is throwing out bait to hurt me.

Gabby, on the other hand, is a blunt instrument. She isn't intentionally mean or cruel. She just cuts straight to the chase, without bothering with the subtle nuances of social interaction.

'Go on then, Meg. What happened last night? Put us out of our misery.'

'I'd rather not,' I say, as Gabby fires the ball back at me.

'It was a very eventful evening, from what I've heard,' says Sophie, clapping her hands at me to request a pass. I pass to Gabby. 'Who was he? The "friend" who came in through your bedroom window at midnight?'

Elle gasps. 'Not Patrick!'

I can't help it. I roll my eyes at her. 'No Elle. Patrick is a fictional character.'

She breathes a sigh of relief. 'Thank God for that.' Then, I see the penny drop. 'Oooh,' she says, and then squeezes her lips tightly shut. Yes, oooh indeed.

'Sophie, it's really none of your business who visits me in the night. So if you don't mind, let's talk about something else.'

Now Gabby has her hands on her hips. 'Nighttime visitors coming in through bedroom windows? This might not be Sophie's business, but it sure as hell is mine. Now, Meg, I want details, and I want them now.'

Oh God. I'm just going to tell them to get them off my back and take the wind out of Sophie's obnoxious sails. 'There are no details to tell. Someone I've been seeing came through the window, I screamed blue murder, everyone woke up and came to my room, all involved were seriously mortified, he left the way he came, and I'll never see him again.'

'Meg!' Elle says despairingly. 'Surely, my love, you should have known it would be him, and you could have kept your composure! Especially after... you know... the feelings.'

I could throttle her.

'Feelings?' Gabby parrots. 'What feelings? Have you caught feelings Meg?'

I groan. 'I don't want to talk about it. It's irrelevant.'

Fortunately, we can't talk any more about it, because Coach calls us over at that moment to start our proper warm-up. I glance at Elle as we make our way over. She looks at me as though deeply offended.

We spend the next half an hour warming up, and then take on the team from York. We win, but when we come from the court, I can see Elle is upset. She didn't get any time on court, and it is getting to her. As soon as the court is clear, she picks up the ball she brought with her, her drink bottle and a soft measuring tape, and heads to the circle. She measures two feet out from the post, puts her drink bottle down to mark the spot, and starts practising. She will be at it for a while. She will take fifty shots from that distance, on five different angles, then move back another foot and do the same, until she is at least three quarters of the way out from the hoop. I decide to wait for her. She needs the moral support.

I go into the change rooms, shower and dress in a pair of short tight shorts and a crop top. I pull a fleece sweater on over the top, then I sit down in the front row of seats at the goal end and take out my phone to mindlessly scroll while I wait. I should have known better than to think Elle would let me off the hook that easily. She doesn't pause in her routine but scolds me simultaneously.

'Meg, I'm sorry I called you out in front of the other girls, but really! Johnno came to see you and you *screamed*? When you had just gotten back on track.'

'Be fair, Elle. It was the middle of the night. It was a reflex. I couldn't help it.'

'I hate seeing you self-sabotage like this.'

'That's not what I'm doing!' I say defensively. It's not, is it? It really was a reflex. I didn't mean to do it. But then, I could have just told him earlier that I live with my parents. Perhaps that's what Elle is referring to.

'I think it's time you are honest with him, Meg. You need to take a risk. Tell him what it is you want, and let things unfold from there. If he really wants nothing to do with you after that, well, you're no worse off than you are now.'

'It's too late. There's been too many... incidents now. I'm sure I won't get another—'

I stop talking, because Johnno has just walked in through the entrance at the middle of the court. I stand up automatically and move towards Elle. He has his bike helmet in his hands, and his hair is down. I've never seen it down before. It reaches his shoulders in soft waves, and my God, he is even more gorgeous than when he has it up. I look at Elle, and she has a mischievous smile on her face.

'Elle! Did you do this?'

She catches her ball and turns around. 'You all right, Johnno?' she says with a smile, as he walks towards us. She picks up her tape measure, and her drink bottle. 'I kept his number the first time I texted him from your phone,' she says quietly, so that only I can hear her. 'I thought it was the responsible thing to do, since I was sending you off with him— in case the police needed it to help find your body.' She touches my arm and gives me a reassuring smile. 'I will be down the other end for as long as you want me to stay,' she says to me. Then she turns to Johnno. 'And if you want to murder Meg and chop her body up into pieces, I won't stand for it,' she says firmly, 'though I would understand.' Then she beams at us both, before turning and walking to the opposite end of the court to continue her practice.

I sit back down in the front row, and Johnno sits down beside me. Neither of us speaks for what feels like half an hour, but I guess is probably two minutes.

'I would also understand if you wanted to chop me up,' I eventually say.

'I do, but I'm afraid of her,' he says, with a nod towards Elle. I bite my lip. 'What is she doing?'

'Re-calibrating. She had an accident about a year ago. It affected her vision. She practises like this because she believes she will be able to get the feel for every spot in the circle, and she won't be so reliant on her vision.'

Johnno nods. 'She's pretty good.'

'Yes. She was even better before.'

He sighs. 'So, you live with your parents, hey?'

'I should have told you.'

'Might've been helpful.'

'Why are you here? After everything, I don't know how you can possibly want anything to do with me.'

He turns to look at me, and I don't look away. 'I don't seem to be able to stay away.'

My heart is beating a million miles an hour. Is it possible I have another chance? If I do, then Elle is right. I have to be honest. Totally honest.

'What else do I need to know about you, Meg?' he asks. His eyes are so intense, so searching. I think he knows. He knows he has been misled. That I'm not who he thought.

I take a deep breath and let it out slowly. 'There is something else. I think that, perhaps, you may have the wrong idea about who I am... sexually.' I practically whisper that last word, and I am cringing so hard, I might implode.

'What do you mean?' I knew he'd ask that.

'I mean, I'm really just into plain...ordinary...vanilla sex. And even then, I can't claim to be anything special.'

'I see.'

'I can understand why you might've thought I'd be into... other things... since you found my book, and clearly, you *do* read, but that stuff is just that to me— reading material. I'm not interested in doing those things in real life.' The more I speak, the less I like myself. I wish I could stop talking. But he isn't saying anything, and it's making me feel like I have to keep going. 'I totally get if that's what attracted you to me, and you know now it was all a facade, you will want to wrap this up. I won't try to stop y—'

'—Can you be quiet?'

'Yes. Sorry.'

He doesn't say anything. He's watching Elle. His jaw is tense. 'Please tell me what you are thinking,' I say quietly.

'I'm re-calibrating.' That wasn't the answer I was expecting. Eventually, he looks back at me. 'You're right. The day I saw you in the coffee shop, I thought you were the hottest thing I'd ever seen. Then, you left your book. I picked it up, read a bit, and I got a certain idea in my head of what you would be like, and I don't have to tell you, it excited the hell out of me. Then, things didn't really go the way I was expecting. For some reason, I couldn't get you out of my head, even though my life's complicated right now and this wasn't in my plans. But here I am, chasing a hot librarian who lives with her parents, and is apparently young enough to be my daughter, trying to figure out what I need to say to you to make this right.'

'You don't have to say anything to make it right, Johnno. You haven't done anything wrong.'

'I'm a dad, Meg. I have a daughter. I'm disgusted with myself if you've ever felt unsafe with me.'

'I've never felt unsafe,' I insist. 'Everything we've done, I've enjoyed, a lot. Whenever I've been uncomfortable, you've stopped.'

He is studying me, as though trying to determine if I am telling the truth, and I have to admit that I don't blame him. I have thrown out so many red herrings, it's no surprise he can't take what I say at face value.

'If I could give you what you want, would you want it from me?' he asks gently. I can hardly believe it, but he actually seems vulnerable right now.

'Do you mean vanilla sex?'

He cracks the subtlest of smiles. 'Come here,' he says, and he leans back, inviting me onto his lap. I am going to accept, but first, it's time to get rid of Elle. I place my hand on his thigh to let him know I am willing, and then I call out. 'Elle.' She catches her ball and turns around. I nod my head in the direction of the exit. She smiles, picks up her drink bottle, and her tape measure, and grabs her bag on the way out. She really is a great friend.

I stand up, and Johnno takes me around my waist, pulling me down to him so my back is against his chest. His hands are on my thighs, and he slowly moves them down towards my knees and then back up.

'These legs, Meg. I've thought about them a lot. They're even better than I imagined,' he says huskily into my ear. 'Now, about this so-called vanilla sex.' His lips brush my neck. 'How does this sound? What if I take you out somewhere nice— or to a kid's movie of your choice, if you prefer.'

'I like it so far.'

'When it's done, I bring you home. We go inside, I shake your dad's hand, kiss your mum on the cheek, and ruffle both of your brothers' hair.'

'Mhmm.'

'We go to your bedroom, and we lie down together. I kiss you and cuddle you for a bit, and then if that's going well, I might slip my hand inside your pants.' As he says it, his hand inches higher, until his fingers brush against my centre. 'If you seem to like that, I might take your pants off, get down between your legs, and fuck you with my mouth until you come. You might even say my name if I'm lucky.'

I swallow. 'Yes,' I whisper.

'And then, if things are still going well, I might pull myself up over you, and fuck you nice and slowly, in missionary, until you are fully satisfied. And if I do something you don't like, you tell me, and I re-calibrate.' I reach my arm up and take him behind the neck. 'Would that be vanilla enough for you, baby?'

Oh, hell yes. This man is now speaking my kind of sweet nothings.

'Yes, but I don't— '

'Don't what?'

'Want to wait. Come home with me.'

***

I surprise myself sometimes.

By the time we arrive at my place after netball, both of my brothers are in their rooms, and Mum and Dad are in the front room watching telly. After a very quick introduction, which goes better than the impromptu midnight version, we make our way straight for my room, skipping the hair ruffling.

Johnno is a little affronted to find out there isn't a lock on my bedroom door, but he soon solves the problem by jamming my make-up chair beneath the doorknob. He takes off his leather jacket and slings it down on the bed, and then his hands find my hips and draw me close. My eye is drawn to the top of his neck, where his v-neck t-shirt dips, giving just a glimpse of the ink beneath. I trace my finger along his collarbone, and my gaze follows it. I know if I lift them, they will meet his intense green eyes. He is studying me, probably wondering if he can trust me this time. That I mean what I say. Finally, I look up. He smiles gently and brings a hand up to stroke my cheek.

'Still with me?'

'Yes.' *Be honest.* 'But I am nervous.'

His brows furrow slightly. 'Why?'

'Because...because I start to think about all the times I've... done it wrong.' My cheeks heat at the admission. 'Moved wrong. Been too quiet. Too awkward. Not performed. Not...been enough.'

'Meg.' My name comes out as a growl, and his fingers tighten where they now rest behind my neck. 'Who the fuck have you been sleeping with to have made you feel that way?' He kisses my lips, lingering only for a second. 'I want names, and addresses.' His tone is so serious that I glance at my phone on my nightstand. Only then does a subtle smile touch his lips. 'Not now, sweetheart.' He takes me by the hand and leads me to the bed. I sit, but with strong hands on my hips, Johnno shifts me back until my head hits my pillow and he props himself over me. He watches me carefully as his hand slides up beneath my sweater and stops in the centre of my chest. I feel my heart racing against his warm palm. 'If you're ever with a man and he has the nerve to tell you you're doing something wrong, then he is focused on the wrong thing, Meg. If he's worried about his own satisfaction, then I can guarantee he isn't fucking you right.' He touches his lips to mine. 'But you don't have to worry about that anymore. I'm going to fuck you right. I know how you kissed me in that cupboard. I know how you responded to me on my bike. God, Meg. The sound you made when you came for me is etched in my memory. I can't think about any damn thing else.' His voice becomes a low, breathless rumble as his lips move to my neck. 'I know how to treat you sweetheart.'

My back arches beneath him as his lips caress my skin, and his words caress my mind, slowly but surely lowering my inhibitions. His fingers grip the top of my crop top and he pulls it down, while his other hand slides my sweater up. My breasts are bare to him, and his hand closes over one, while his lips close around the other. He takes his time, sucking me until I squeeze my legs together to quell the sensation there. Perceptive as he is, he smiles, with his teeth resting gently on my nipple, and then swaps sides. When I squirm beneath him again, he releases my breasts and travels lower, trailing kisses across my stomach. He glances up briefly, before yanking my shorts and my knickers down to my knees. His gaze falls between my legs, and then his mouth closes over me. My breath hitches as his tongue meets my clit, as awake as it already was, and he starts a rhythm that feels like it is just for me. Like he speaks a language that only my body understands, a combination of pressure and pace that has me meeting his every move. But right as I think he is going to get me there quicker than anyone has ever achieved it before, the rhythm changes. Now, when I search for more, he pulls back, eluding me. Teasing me. When I retreat, he draws me back in, making me think that finally, I will get what I need. Like this, he continues, until I am desperate to come. And then, he stops. He rests back on his knees, straddling me. A lazy smile spreads across his face.

He knows I haven't come yet, doesn't he? Oh, God. He must know. What if he doesn't? What if he leaves me like this, teetering on the edge? What if –

'Don't worry. I'm not done with you yet.' His smile broadens, before he puts his index finger between his lips. 'I just think you need to be a little closer to the edge before I push you over.' He slides one long, thick finger inside me. His eyes rake over my body, drinking me in as he draws it back, and then forwards again, stroking my wall, slowly, deliberately— frustratingly.

'Johnno—,' I choke out.

'What sweetheart?' he asks. His finger continues a steady pace. He brings his brows together, as though concerned. The bastard isn't. 'What is it? Do you want another one?'

'I want...' I know what I want. I want this torture to stop, because as fucking delicious as it feels, it isn't enough. It will never get me there. I need faster. Rougher. More. 'Yes. I want another one.' My voice comes out rough and demanding. I don't even recognise it.

Johnno chuckles, and the next time his finger withdraws, a second one joins it. Stretching me. Filling me. But still too fucking slow. 'Faster.'

'I don't know what you mean,' he says with a smirk. 'You'd better show me.'

I think he does know. I reach behind me to grab the bedhead for leverage and dig my heels into the mattress. As though anticipating what I intend to do, he lifts his weight just slightly so I can move. With my free hand, I grip onto his, and I show him. I fuck his fingers, searching for what I want. His hand is strong and unmoving, until he whispers, 'Fuck' beneath his breath, and then he joins in, pumping his fingers faster and harder until I am right on the verge. And he stops. His chest heaves, and beneath his rough stubble his cheeks are flushed. His eyes, always intense, are wild and animalistic. 'What do you think, Meg? Do you want to come on my mouth?'

I don't answer him. I just take him behind the neck, grip his hair with my fingers, and pull him down to me. And finally, I get what I want. His tongue takes me there within seconds, and my hips gyrate against him as I come harder than I ever have before. His name chokes from my throat and he groans against me in response. Only when I can't possibly come for any longer, do I let him go. And no sooner do I do that, then he tears his shirt off over his head, exposing rippling muscles and intricate artwork that pulls my whole focus. As I stare at him, soaking him in, he removes his jeans and his underwear, then pulls mine the rest of the way off and discards it all on the floor. I raise my arms, and he pulls off my sweater and crop, and there we are, completely naked. He is as drawn to my ink as I am to his. He trails is fingers over my arms, my torso and my thighs, then brings his hand to his cock.

'There's a condom in my wallet.' He nods to where it sits on my nightstand, next to my phone.

Fuck. My insecurities rush back in. Not this. If I pull it out, he is going to expect me to put it on him, isn't he? I feel my anxiety rise. I reach for his wallet, because he hasn't, and I know he is waiting for me. My fingers fumble with the openings as I look through. Why can't I find the damn thing? How am I going to put it on if I can't even locate it? I start to panic. All this has been amazing. So good, I would do it again, every day, for the foreseeable future, if it was an option. But this...this is going to bring me undone.

I freeze when Johnno's hand closes over mine. 'Hey, what's wrong? You're shaking.' I hazard a glance at him and see concern on his face.

'I can't find it. Perhaps you should look.'

'OK.' He takes his wallet from me and pulls a condom out of one of the compartments I had already checked. He tosses his wallet aside and then leans over me. He kisses me gently. 'Where did you go, sweetheart?'

God. I don't want to explain. But if I don't, he might think he has done something wrong. 'I...I just got nervous.'

'About fucking?'

'No. About the condom.' I suck in a breath. 'I've put one on wrong before. It was embarrassing. I don't want to do it. I don't want to fuck up now. This has been fun.'

I expect him to laugh in my face. To embarrass me, just like I was that night. But instead, he frowns.

'Listen to me. You can't fuck this up. I'm into you, Meg. You and me, this is safe, and you can trust me.' His eyes dart away briefly before coming back to mine. 'At least, about this, you can.'

My stomach dips for a moment at those words. Is he implying there are things I *can't* trust him about? But he kisses me, softly, and then more deeply, and I feel his hard length touch on my thigh. I abandon my concerns, and kiss him back, until he pulls away, puts on the condom, and brings himself between my legs.

'Do you want me, Meg?' he asks, barely above a whisper.

'Yes.' I wrap my legs around his hips, and draw him closer, and he presses inside me. His body moves with strength, and confidence, but he is mindful, attentive. I realise I have never been fucked like this. As though my enjoyment was important. As though my experience mattered, and my body was more than just a gateway to someone else's pleasure. And I realise all those times I said, 'fine', I should have said 'no'.

I wrap an arm around his hips, encouraging him deeper, and he responds by lifting my thigh and driving into me a little harder and faster. 'More,' I whisper. His head goes back, and he gives me more, until I am shaking beneath him with a second, record-breaking orgasm, and finally, Johnno's body shudders, and he releases. He gently lowers my leg, and collapses to the bed beside me. I am shattered. My body is limp, and Johnno doesn't seem to have fared much better. We stay like that, both of us staring at the ceiling, breathing heavily, until he turns his head to look at me, and I do the same.

'I...that was... I haven't ever—,' I try to say, but whatever incoherent sentence I am trying to form escapes me.

'I know. I told you, baby. They weren't fucking you right.'

***

Johnno goes to the bathroom, and I pull the bed sheet over myself. It's then my mind returns to Johnno's earlier admission. 'You can trust me. At least, about this you can.' A sentence intended to allay my concerns but has managed to introduce some fresh ones.

He returns from the bathroom, and his lazy smile appears as he sits down beside me, leans over and kisses my lips. 'You are so beautiful, and you have no idea, do you?'

My instinct is to make a self-deprecating joke, but it is starting to sink in that he doesn't like it when I do that, so instead, I say, 'You make me feel beautiful.'

'I'm getting something right then.' He is getting an awful lot right. I hope he knows that. But...

'Johnno.'

'Baby.'

'Are there circumstances under which I shouldn't trust you?'

Johnno's face drops instantly, and a hand runs over his hair. 'You can never be too careful,' he says dismissively. He stands and reaches for his wallet. Then his jacket. He's leaving. Is it because I asked? He zips his jacket with his back to me, and then stands there for a moment, still. Slowly, he turns around. His face is grave. 'I told you my life is complicated right now. If it wasn't...I'd want every piece of you, Meg. But it is. And you need to be careful.'

My heart suddenly feels like lead. 'I can trust you with my body, but nothing else?' He doesn't answer. 'I don't think trust can be divvied up like that,' I say quietly.

He leans over me and kisses my lips. 'You can trust the way I feel about you. That's what's important.'

He straightens. 'I have to go down to London tomorrow to pick Shaelea up. I'll be back Saturday. When can I see you again?'

I am incapable of self-preservation right now. Completely defence-less. 'You know where to find me.' And with that, the man I am already in love with, who has just warned me not to trust him, disappears through my bedroom window.

Chapter Fourteen

The days have passed slowly since I last saw Johnno. He travelled to London on Friday to be there to pick Shaelea up from school, and then brought her back to Leeds on Saturday. Sunday, he spent with her, and I spent with my family, as per Drury family protocols. Dad and I shared our customary cup of tea on Sunday afternoon, and to my surprise, Dad said nothing about Johnno. But as we finished our cuppas and prepared to return inside, he did pull me into an unusually tight and prolonged hug. I take it he has concerns.

Johnno messaged me regularly, and aside from one request for a nude, which I politely declined to provide— he accepted the rebuff without question— he has been the perfect gentleman. I'm not expecting to see much of him over the next two weeks while Shaelea is in town, and I don't begrudge that. Two weeks a year is not enough to spend with one's daughter, and I would not want to take up any of that precious time.

It's now Monday, and I have been forced back to work by the need to pay my keep at home, but all I can think about is Johnno. I am obsessed. I haunt the aisles of the library floor, moving through them like a ghostly apparition. Able to be seen, but not touched or spoken to, as I am a million miles away. I'm like a zombified version of myself, but instead of being fixated on eating brains, I'm fixated on Johnno eating me. I really am just being crude now, but I'm trying to make a point. I've changed. I don't even recognise myself in the sex-crazed individual I have become.

After an initial rush in the morning, Monday afternoons are usually quiet, and this one is no different, even though it is the summer holidays. The youth of today have better things to do than hang out at their local library. I'm about to go into the back office and laminate some fresh signage for the aisles, when a very welcome sight greets my eyes. Johnno has just walked in, followed closely by a slender, pretty teen with blonde hair up in a ponytail. She is wearing a black singlet top, shorts and a pair of black high tops, with a red hoodie tied around her waist. Emo chic. Fancy that. My mind instantly wanders to what Johnno's ex must look like for them to have produced such a gorgeous offspring.

Johnno smiles as he sees me, and relieved things seems to be OK between us, I grin back like a fool. As he approaches me, I give a quick scan for Pip, and then back myself between the aisles of the romantic fiction section, where we will be out of sight to most of the library, except for anyone who enters this aisle directly. I notice the pile of *Dragon Chicks* books in Shaelea's hands, but she doesn't stick around, and heads straight to Junior Fiction without a word to Johnno. He throws a glance in her direction, and then returns his attention to me. In no time at all, he has pinned me to the wall at the end of the aisle, and he takes a hold of my face and kisses me.

'Meg,' he says huskily, in the way of greeting. 'God, I've missed you.'

My cheeks become hot. 'It's only been three days.'

'You haven't missed me?'

'Terribly.' He smiles and kisses me again. 'How is Shaelea?'

'Surlier than I remember.'

'Still into boy bands?'

'No. As far as I can tell, she isn't into anything. Everything's cringe. At least anything I try to talk to her about. What are you smiling about?'

'Sorry. She just sounds exactly like me at that age.'

'What do you mean, at that age?' A dig at my sunny personality.

'Excuse me, I am positively bubbly compared to what I was like when I was thirteen.' I receive a smirk in response. 'Has she finished the books?'

'No. They're cringe, apparently. She wants different ones.' He leans in close to me and his hand sneaks beneath my shirt to cup my breast over the top of my bra. 'I want—'

'Reed,' a youthful voice, tinged with impatience, says from behind him. Johnno closes his eyes, and I can sense frustration as he quickly withdraws his hand and turns to Shaelea.

'Got what you need, sweetheart?'

Shaelea visibly shudders. Wow. Cold. 'I suppose.'

Johnno shifts to the side, which brings me face to face with Shaelea. 'This is Meg.'

She lifts her chin at me.

'All right? Lovely to meet you,' I say, in my friendliest tone, which Shaelea should know is only reserved for Very Important People. 'I'm sorry about the *Dragon Chicks*. They were my recommendation. A safe choice, I thought.'

Shaelea looks me up and down, and I'm reminded of the last time I felt this heavily scrutinised— the first time I met her father. 'Do you read dragon books?' she asks.

'Yes. Adult ones.'

'What about vampire books?'

'Love them.'

'Have you read *Full Blood Moon*?'

'No. I'm sure I would like it though. I've seen the movie.' I give Johnno a glance and see that he is stifling a smile. 'Have you read it?'

Shaelea nods. 'It's good.'

I'm going to take a risk here. A risk that will either thoroughly de-cringeify myself, or plummet me to the depths of cringe, with no hope of escape, ever. 'I wonder if you might enjoy the *Eventide* series. Have you heard of it?'

'Heard of it,' she says warily.

'It is a little... vintage now, but I loved it when I was your age. We have a set under 'L' in Junior Fiction. If you're interested, I can show you.'

'I'll find it,' she says, and lifts her chin as if to say, 'I don't need your help, old lady.'

I nod, and she turns and walks back over to Junior Fiction.

'She's calling me Reed. It's pissing me off, and she knows it,' Johnno says, explaining the frustration I had picked up on.

'It must be difficult to re-establish a relationship each year. How long has it been like this?' I ask, cautiously, unsure of whether this is territory I am welcome in.

Johnno watches her, and I think he isn't going to answer, but then he says, 'Her mum and I stayed together until she was four. Then some stuff happened, and I didn't see her at all for a while. The two-week thing has only been the last couple of years.' He looks at me. 'Do you have any time off during the week?'

'No. I'm 8 until 4, or thereabouts, every day. I finish late on Wednesdays and start late on Thursdays.'

'She doesn't want much to do with me during the day. She goes out on her own. But I can't leave her on her own at the shop at night. The bloke who works for me lives there too.'

He kisses me again, pushing his tongue between my lips. 'I want to be alone with you. That toy cupboard seems like a better idea by the second, don't you think?'

Maybe I wasn't wrong about the cupboard fetish. 'I might have a better idea,' I say, deftly removing the large paw that is working its way down the back of my jeans, and holding it captive. 'I wonder if Shaelea would get along with my brother, James. If I start at my normal time on Thursday, I could ask Pip if I can leave early on Friday afternoon instead. You could both come to my place, and if Shaelea and James hit it off, we might be able to disappear for a bit.'

'Friday?' Johnno looks at me with just a hint of insanity in his eyes. 'I haven't eaten since last Friday. You want me to wait a whole week?' Yes. He is insane. It's a turn on, I have to admit. 'I'll starve,' he adds huskily. I gulp.

'It's the best I can do.'

'Fine,' he says curtly. 'But I hope I can trust your brother with my daughter.'

'There's nothing to worry about there. James is a complete innocent. Still a babe. He's only just noticed that Elle is attractive, and he's known her for years.'

'Mr Johnson.'

Johnno whips around. 'What?' he asks gruffly.

Pip looks taken aback, and then highly suspicious. She narrows her eyes at me, and then speaks to Johnno. 'I'm glad I caught you. It's about the automotive section. I've checked the budget, and I think I can allocate some funds to some more items. Do you have a moment to discuss the options?'

I expect him to growl, but he doesn't. 'I've got a moment,' he says. As he follows Pip, he looks back over his shoulder at me with a scowl, and I fight the urge to giggle. Perhaps not-half-bad library bad boys do exist.

I decide to go and see if Shaelea has found the *Eventide* series. I locate her in Junior Fiction, and she is flicking through the first book in the series.

'How do I borrow these?' she asks as I approach. 'Can I use my London card?'

'No, sorry, you will need a Leeds one. Your dad has one. Shall we ask him for it?'

'He's not my dad,' Shaelae spits out. 'He's just some guy I'm forced to live with for two weeks a year.' Then, in a clear sign the conversation is over, she walks away.

***

It is the final Book Club for *Cloaked Lust*. The entire book has been read, and Patrick has ended up in prison, put there by his Chosen One's husband who laid a careful trap, and had the police in the wings waiting to swoop in to arrest the most wanted villain in all of England.

Patrick's penchant for LCD candles in windows was his undoing in the end.

In keeping with that theme, Elle had the idea of spicing up tonight's Book Club with the addition of a complimentary glass of champagne, LCD candles along the length of the table, and attendees coming dressed in cloaks and masks. I took some convincing to go along with the plan, but Elle hasn't been quite herself since last week when she spilled her guts about not wanting to marry Joe, and when I saw the sparkle return to her eyes at the idea of drinking and dressing up, I couldn't say no.

Pip, thank God, left early today, so the Book Club members teeming into the library in cloaks and masks will go unnoticed. It would have taken some explaining had she been witness to it. Most of the women have gone for a simple black strip of fabric across their eyes with holes cut in it so they can see. Margy, on the other hand, must have been thinking 'night at the masquerade ball', rather than 'night-time prowler', because she is proudly wearing a fancy silver number, with feather plumes and a large rosette at the side. She is in her dressing gown, which tonight, for the first time, is appropriate attire.

The group takes a while to settle. There is much excitement. Many didn't see the twist at the end coming. Most of us, perhaps egged on by Elle's faith in Patrick and Bella's love story, were expecting them to end up together against all odds— perhaps flee to Russia, out of reach of Bella's husband and the UK authorities.

'Welcome to the final Book Club session for *Cloaked Lust*. I'm sure you will all agree, it has been quite the journey,' I say to open proceedings. There are enthusiastic murmurs and nodding heads, a few poultry jokes, and ensuing giggles. 'The question tonight for your consideration is, did the author nail the morally grey hero trope with

Patrick, and is the fact he has ended up in prison a tragedy, or was he actually a fully-fledged villain who has met his deserved fate?'

Janice, the woman with blonde hair and red lipstick who never fails to disappoint, pipes up first. 'He gave a lot of women a lot of satisfaction before he was stitched up. There's got to be something heroic about that.'

'Yes, it was only the stuffy husbands who took issue with it. The 'Chosen Ones' were always willing. Was he really doing anything wrong? I think it was an injustice,' adds Janice's friend beside her.

'Can anyone play devil's advocate?' I ask. 'Does anyone think he was truly the villain?'

'I, for one, think I was wrong about Patrick.' The voice of the devil's advocate was not the one I was expecting. All eyes turn on Elle, the former head of Patrick's fan club. 'I think he was a bad man, who didn't really love Bella. The real love story is between Bella and her husband, who was brave enough to grass on Patrick to the police, even though there is zero chance he won't be un-alive by Patrick the instant he gets out of prison.'

Now, I am seriously worried about Elle. Where has the hopeless romantic gone?

'But weren't you of the opinion that Patrick's unyielding attraction to Bella was a sign that she was "the one"?' I ask, hoping that the real Elle will resurface if prompted.

'Yes, I was. But now I think Bella made the right choice, staying with her dependable, if unexciting, husband. She would have been better off not knowing that cocks could come in 8 x 8, and enjoying the mundane sex life she was accustomed to, until death do they part.'

Fuck. I'm not sure if she's being serious, or sarcastic. I steal a glance at her, and she looks serious. No one is sure what to say. I am the only person in the group who is privy to Elle's personal circumstances, but everyone seems to recognise that this is either an Elle imposter, or she has lost her mind.

Not surprisingly, it is Margy who comes to the rescue, just when I think I am going to have to say something to break the strange, awkward silence that has descended. 'I knew Detective Martin would get his man.' She waggles her finger as she adds, 'He always does in the end.' Yes. In the one and only book that Detective Martin appears in, and even then, with only one mention by name.

'Yes, if there is anyone who can put a stop to a kerfuffle right in the nick of time, it is Detective Martin,' says Elle enthusiastically. She raises her champagne glass. 'To Detective Martin.' We all drink to that.

***

Elle waits with me as I pack up and secure the library. We walk together to our cars, which are parked in our usual spot together, so we don't have to make our way there on our own in the dark after Book Club. We make idle chit chat, and she seems fine, but I have to ask.

'How are things with Joe?'

'Joe is well,' she says lightly.

'That's not what I meant.'

'Oh. You mean am I still having doubts?'

'Yes.'

She sighs. 'There are still moments I wish for more, Meg. But then I remember how lucky I really am to have Joe. Think about Bella— even if Patrick hadn't been arrested, how could she ever be comfortable, with his past being what it is? With Joe, things are unexciting, but they are uncomplicated.' *My life is complicated.* 'I know I can trust him.' *You can trust me. At least, about this you can.* 'How can I hold that against him?'

I have some thinking to do.

Chapter Fifteen

The netball season is drawing to a close. We have at most only two games left. The semi-final is tonight, against the Hull team we beat earlier in the season, but we are playing away from home, in York, since it is a final. If we win this game, we are in to the grand final, and after that, the team to represent Yorkshire in the national competition will be announced. Gabby is a certainty to be in the team. Elle, before her injury would have been as well, but now has no chance at all, since she still can't get consistent court time. The rest of us have a chance, but not a strong one, so I for one am not too fussed about it. What I would like is for it to be Friday already.

Elle is driving us to York. It's about a fifty-minute drive at this time of night. Gabby is in the front passenger seat, and I am condemned to being in the back with Sophie. She has been prattling on for the past half hour about who will make the Yorkshire side, and who won't. She rates herself a very good chance, and she's probably right. Of course, she has already stated the bleeding obvious that Elle won't be chosen, dripping with fake sympathy, and has then proceeded to list off all the Goal Attacks in the county who she feels are now ahead of Elle in the pecking order. Elle has taken it in good grace, as she takes most things, but I know it would be hurting. I've told Sophie to pull her head in, to no avail. She has also written me off, of course, just because it's me. I don't care. I can't wait to have a break from netball. Plus, I'm hoping to have other pursuits for my Thursday evenings once Shaelea goes back home. Not that I'm counting down the days. I'm not. That would be selfish.

Eventually, Gabby breaks through Sophie's narcissistic drivel, which would be a relief, if she had chosen any other topic than my love life.

'Meg, Elle tells me things are back on with the midnight intruder. Any recent break-ins to report?' she asks, turning around from the front to scrutinise my face.

'No, he's been busy. And he uses the door now.'

'What could he possibly be too busy doing, to not be doing a hot thing like you, Meg Drury?' Well, that's a compliment coming from Gabby.

'Remember I told you he has a daughter? He has her for two weeks in the school holidays,' Elle says. It's so nice to know my life is discussed, in detail, between these two behind my back. 'Do you think you will meet her, Meg?'

Beside me, Sophie's eyes have lit up. Not with joy for her younger sister's happiness. No. She knows what Elle does not. That Johnno's teenage daughter will be unwelcome news to my parents. As I've said, Elle gives people the benefit of the doubt for far too long, and here she has assumed that Sophie, being a loving, supportive sister, can be privy to this information without cause for concern. Elle is very wrong.

'Yes. I've met her. They came to the library.'

'Really?' Elle says excitedly. 'What is she like?'

'Gorgeous. Emo. Surly. Think me, but less bubbly.'

Elle giggles. 'Not very bubbly then, my love.'

Sophie hasn't spoken yet, and I know why. She's building ammunition. She's waiting to see how much more Elle will reveal, or I will be forced to reveal by Elle, before she unmasks herself as the traitor I already know her to be.

'Johnno must be quite serious about you to have brought her in, Meg, don't you think?' Elle muses.

'I don't know. I think she needed different books. She wasn't interested in *Dragon Chicks.*'

'Huh! That man will find any excuse to visit the library since he's realised how sexy the librarian is. Did he try to get you into the toy cupboard again?'

'Can we stop?' I say, wincing.

'Did he?' Gabby demands.

'He suggested it, to no avail.'

'My, my, little Meg. So much you haven't been telling me,' says Sophie finally. I'm sure the hairs on the back of Elle's neck will have just stood up. 'Do Mummy and Daddy know about Johnno's daughter?'

Elle meets my eyes in the rear-view mirror and gives me an apologetic look.

'I'm sure they will in ten minutes from now, won't they? And I'm bigger than you, and don't you forget it Sophie,' I retort, because she brings out the best in me.

Sophie laughs. 'Oh no, I won't say a word. I think it will be fun for them to discover it themselves, don't you?'

***

By Friday afternoon, I haven't received any panicked phone calls or texts from Mum or Dad, demanding an immediate explanation as to why I'm dating a midnight intruder who owns a teenager, so Sophie has been true to her word. The mature thing to do would be to tell them myself, but it seems a little too soon to do that. I've introduced Johnno to them only as my friend, and as I really have no clue what it is we have ventured into together, other than vanilla sex and conditional trust, I don't feel ready to disclose any more than that to my parents. On the topic of trust, I have thought long and hard since my conversation with Elle, when she pointed out the benefits of uncomplicated, trustworthy suitors. I have decided that this afternoon, I will attempt to uncover a little more about Johnno, and perhaps, the nature of the 'complication'.

I leave work at 3pm on Friday and make my way home as quickly as possible, leaving myself fifteen minutes to get ready for Johnno and Shaelea to arrive at half three. Since it is warm, I change into a short red and black tartan skirt and a black singlet top. I put my hair down and run the straightener through it and refresh my make-up.

I've briefed James on what is to occur this afternoon. He is to be friendly, welcoming and polite, and win Shaelea over so they can pass an enjoyable afternoon together, while Johnno and I do the same. I may have dropped in a mention of how pretty Shaelea is, for extra motivation. I'm sure Johnno wouldn't approve of that, but I trust James won't know what to do with that information, and it will make little difference.

Harry is around too. He is infinitely friendly, and very likeable, so that will only help, if there isn't any residual Johnno-related trauma from the night he came in through the window.

Shaelea and Johnno arrive right on half three. Johnno hasn't worn black, for the first time since I met him. He is wearing a white t-shirt, with a blue button up shirt over the top that he has left undone, and blue jeans. Perhaps an attempt to appear non-threatening. As I greet him at the door, he gives my legs an appreciative look up and down, and I see his tongue touch on his bottom lip, before his eyes give me a speaking look that I'm confident I am interpreting correctly. I send a prayer to my God, James, that he is able to keep Shaelea occupied for long enough for me to find out exactly what it means. In detail.

The boys are in the front room playing console games, and they look up as we come in. James's face betrays him instantly. Shaelea *is* pretty, and though he has no idea what to do with that information, he knows there must be *something* he is meant to do with it.

Harry is oblivious. He offers a friendly, 'hi', and then turns his attention back to the game. 'You can have a go after me,' he adds. Shaelea sits down next to James, asks what they are playing, and reaches for the popcorn beside him. A good sign. Johnno gives a tug on my arm in the direction of my room. I tug him in the opposite direction, towards the sofa, and sit down. He sits down, reluctantly, beside me.

They are playing some sort of fantasy game, with a strapping character with swords, and bows and arrows, taking on all manner of beasts in a quest for something important, I'm sure. We watch as Harry, then Shaelea, then James, fall victim to a spiky tailed black dragon. Johnno is becoming increasingly frustrated beside me. As Harry tries to take the controller back, Johnno stands up and plants himself between Harry and James. 'My turn. Give it here,' he says gruffly. Harry promptly hands over the controller and looks up in awe at Johnno.

As casually as you like, he rests one of his forearms on his knee, and a thrilling battle ensues between Johnno and the spiky tailed dragon, ending with the great beast's downfall, and enthusiastic celebrations from James and Harry, a withering eye roll from Shaelea, and my usual neutral expression undisturbed. It's not that I'm unaffected by my not-half-bad library bad boy slaying a fearsome dragon on behalf of my little brothers. Nothing could be hotter. It just takes a lot for it to show on my face.

Johnno gets back up, and with a determined nod in the direction of my bedroom, he summons me to follow.

Chapter Sixteen

It takes about half a second from my bedroom door closing behind me for Johnno to prop the chair beneath the doorknob and begin his new quest— to disrobe me.

I catch his hands as they grasp at the edge of my singlet top. 'Wait.'

Johnno's eyes flash. I let go of his hands and move swiftly out of his reach, to my make-up table, where I avoid eye contact and fidget with my foundation brush as I speak. 'I thought, you know, since we have this time together, we could... get to know each other a little more.'

Johnno gives a short, dark laugh. 'Getting to know you better was exactly what I had planned.'

I glance at him and purse my lips. 'I'm sure it was. But I'd like to *talk* with you. I know so little about you.'

Johnno gives a sigh, plants himself heavily on the side of my bed and swings his legs up, placing his hands behind his head. 'Fine. It's not like I've been dying to have you naked for over a week, or that I've been obsessing over what you've got on under that skirt since I've been here,' he grumbles. I lie down beside him, and roll onto my side, propping my head up with my hand so I can look at him. Even surly, he is still gorgeous. He turns his head slightly, and I get the hint of a smile. 'I don't think you appreciate how quickly I slayed that dragon so I could get you alone.'

'I'm sure the boys appreciate it. They've been working on that for ages.'

Johnno glares at me, then picks up *Cloaked Lust* from my bedside table. I haven't returned it yet, even though Book Club is finished with it. Perhaps I have some sentimental attachment, since it brought Johnno and I together, then apart, then together, then apart, and then finally, together again.

'No paper in it. Finished?'

He's learning. 'Book folk refer to the paper as a bookmark. And yes, finished.'

'What happens at the end?'

I have to smile. I wonder if *he* recognises himself in the man *he* has become. 'The caped crusader falls victim to his inability to keep it in his pants and ends up in prison.'

He had been flicking nonchalantly through the pages, I assume looking for the spicy parts, but he quickly puts it back down on the bedside table, as though it suddenly became radioactive.

'Doesn't sound like a happy ending.'

'No. And he was no Prince Charming.'

Johnno seems bothered by Patrick's downfall. 'Seems a bit harsh,' he mutters. 'Fucking cops.'

I throw him a quizzical look. He ignores it. I decide to change the subject. 'How is Shaelea enjoying the *Eventide* saga?'

Johnno looks confused for a moment, before a look of recognition dawns.

'The books? She likes them. She thinks you're cool now.'

'Cool? Are you sure?'

Johnno thinks for a moment. 'Nah, probably not cool. Probably 'fire' or 'lit' or something. I, on the other hand, still can't do any God damn thing right.'

'Teenage angst is real. I remember it well.'

'Because it was, what? Last week?'

I lift my chin defiantly at the jibe from my father figure. 'People have always said I'm very mature for my age.'

'Makes sense why we're so good together then,' says Johnno, flicking his finger against my cheek, 'because people have always said I need to grow the fuck up eventually.'

He has given me an 'in' without even realising it. Now my own quest begins— to find out as much as I can about this 'complicated' man.

'Where *did* you grow up?'

'Told you before. London.' He frowns and tuts his disapproval. 'You need to listen.'

'London is a big place. Could you narrow it down?'

He sighs. 'You're not going to let up, are you?'

I shake my head. 'I want your origin story.'

'Fine. I was born in Croydon. Lived there until I was eight.'

'And then?' I prompt, when it seems he thinks he is finished.

'Then Mum got sick,' he says stiffly. 'Dad stopped work to look after her. We couldn't afford to live in our own place anymore. We moved to a council flat in Peckham.' He appears lost in thought for a moment, and I don't know where to go next with my enquiries. But then, he brings his right arm down from behind his head and holds it out to me, with his palm facing up. I'm not sure what I'm looking at, but then I notice a subtle detail on the tattoo on his forearm. It's a snail, about the size of a 50 pence coin, with a swirly trail running behind it. In numbers so small I have to squint to make them out is a date range, following the snail's trail. A date range that would often indicate... I run my finger along it, then look at Johnno. 'Did your mum...'

'Yeah. She was sick for a long time. Breast cancer. She almost got better a few times, but it kept coming back.' He falls quiet, and I don't press. 'I was obsessed with ink from...I don't even know when it started. Young. When she was too sick to be up, I'd sit at her bedside and ask her to draw things on me. The snail was her favourite.' He chuckles gently. 'She was no artist. See the little smile?'

I nod. 'It's cute.'

'Yeah. She died when I was sixteen. This was my first tattoo. I got it the year after.'

He would have been only seventeen. 'Did your dad help you get it? You would have been too young.'

He scoffs. 'Dad wanted nothing to do with me by then.'

I want to ask more about that, but Johnno rolls onto his side, so he is facing me, and brushes my hair back from my face, tucking it behind my ear. 'There. Now it's my turn.'

'You want to know my origin story? It's rather dull, I'm afraid.'

'No.' His hand moves down to massage my neck. My eyes drift closed beneath his strong fingers. 'I want to know about your first time.'

My eyes snap back open. 'You *what*?'

'Hey, I've earned a disclosure.'

'Yes, but...' I feel my cheeks get hot, and my mouth feels dry. 'It's very embarrassing.'

He looks at me, his eyes kind, and then leans in to kiss my lips. 'Too bad.'

I press my lips together, but I know I am going to have to tell him, after what he has just told me.

I groan. Johnno kisses me again. I begin. 'It was my last year of high school. I was friends with a boy in my year. He was awkward, like me. A bit of an outcast. We got along, but it was nothing romantic.' Johnno listens attentively, gently twirling my hair between his fingers. 'One day, we got talking about sex. Both of us rated our chances of ever sleeping with anyone, ever, pretty low.' He emits a low growl— I ignore it and continue. 'So, we agreed to sleep with each other. Just once. For the experience. I thought it was... safe, you know, since we were friends. I was nervous, and of course, it wasn't great. OK, it was terrible, but that was to be expected, I thought.' My throat constricts as the memories return. 'Afterwards we agreed to leave it in the past. But I guess the temptation to get some...notoriety was too strong.'

Johnno's fingers stop dead. 'What did he do?'

'He told everyone... or at least enough people that once it spread, everyone knew that we'd slept together, and it was terrible. And that became who I was for the rest of high school.'

Johnno doesn't say anything. His eyes glaze over, his jaw is tight, and his fingers that had been toying with my hair so gently, tighten at the base of my neck. 'Johnno?'

He looks at me. 'Is this bloke in Leeds?'

I swallow. 'I-I don't know. We're not in contact.'

'I need you to promise me something.'

'OK,' I say cautiously.

'If we are ever together, and we run into him, do not tell me who he is.'

'Ah...OK.'

'Because I will shred him.' I choke on a laugh, but Johnno is completely serious. 'No, Meg. To have you, and disrespect you like that... I would need to sort that out. He isn't the same bloke who laughed about the condom?'

'No. No, I've been with other guys. But I guess since then, I've never been able to...relax. To enjoy it. Until you.'

His face softens a little at that. 'It does make sense now, why you baulked with me. But Meg,' his hand moves to my cheek, and he brushes his thumb across it, 'I loved unravelling you. Fuck, you were gorgeous when you let loose. Your body responds to me, baby.'

Hell yes, it does.

His hand moves from my cheek, down my front, until it reaches my thigh, then slides beneath my skirt to cup my butt. He kisses me, nipping at my bottom lip. 'And we are just getting started, sweetheart. You say you like vanilla, but I think,' his fingers move lower, right to my centre, where my body is responding, and his lips curl up, 'I think there are a lot of things you will like, if you give them a chance. You are a sensual woman, Meg. Sexy as hell.' He kisses me again. His voice is a purr. 'And so, so wet.' I bite my lip. *Guilty as charged.* His fingers rub against the fabric between my legs, making my breath come fast and shallow. 'How long have we got?'

'Dad won't be home until six.'

'Good,' he says with a smirk. He takes his hand away, and a complaintive 'oh' escapes my lips.

'Stand up.'

I do as he asks, and stand by the bed, waiting for further instruction. I take him in, sprawled on my bed. All muscles, and ink. One hand still rests behind his head. The other, he brings to his cock, that strains against his jeans, and he unashamedly grips it.

'Lift up your skirt.'

'What? Just…lift it up?'

'That's what I said.'

Tentatively, I reach for the front of my skirt, and bunch it just above my red lace g-string as my heart races. The intensity of him has me feeling self-conscious, despite how intimately he already knows me.

'Fuck,' Johnno growls, and his hand squeezes again. Then he sits up and swings his legs over the side of the bed. He reaches for me and pulls me close by the hips. 'Turn around.'

I pivot in his arms, and his hands move beneath my skirt, grasping the sides of my g-string and lowering it. I step out and turn back around in time to see it disappear into the pocket of his jeans. 'Fucking perfect,' he says with satisfaction.

'Johnno! 'What are you…you aren't thinking of *keeping* those, are you?'

He gives a dirty laugh. 'Oh, baby. I'm thinking of *collecting* these.'

I swallow. 'You are going to wash them, aren't you?'

He looks affronted. 'What I do in the privacy of my own home is my business, thank-you. Mind your own, sweetheart.' I make to protest, but he pulls me forwards onto his lap so I am straddling him, and the words die on my lips. 'Now what's say I bend you over—,'

My blood suddenly turns cold in my veins, and he and I both freeze. I've just heard the jangling of my dad's keys. A distinctive sound I have listened out for since I was a little girl, waiting for Daddy to come in from work to race towards him and be hoisted into his arms. On this occasion, to put it lightly, the sound is less welcome.

'What the fuck?' I whisper. 'He's home early. He never comes home early.' I look at Johnno, whose eyes are wide with concern, and add, for emphasis, 'Never.'

Johnno jumps up and is at the door before me, moving the chair away from the doorknob, and I am right behind.

'Wait! My knickers,' I plead.

'Not up for negotiation,' Johnno, says firmly, and I can't argue any further, as he opens the door and strides down the hallway to the front room. I hear Dad's voice speaking to the kids.

'Who is your friend, boys?' he asks.

'I don't know nothing about it,' says Harry, quickly jumping to his feet and shaking his head. He will make an excellent alibi for someone, one day.

'James?' Dad asks sternly.

James looks nervously at Dad, then at me at the doorway, where I have just arrived. He will be shitting himself that he will be on trial for having a girl over. He *should* know that it is I, Meg Drury, who will be facing the judge.

James begins his defence. 'This is Shaelea. She's Johnno's—'

'I'm with Reed,' Shaelea cuts in, and nods her head towards us, and then a sinister smirk spreads across her face. 'The guy who's fucking your daughter.'

I let out a squeal, more piglet than human, and then cover my mouth with my hand, as though that will prevent another from escaping. James sniggers, and Harry is standing open mouthed, as though he can't believe anyone would dare say such a word in front of Dad.

'Shaelea! Outside, now,' Johnno orders. Shaelea stands up, the smirk still in place, and walks from the room. I hear the front door open and close as she exits. 'I'm sorry about that, Mr Drury,' Johnno says. *Mr Drury. Bless his heart.*

'Teenagers,' Dad says philosophically, and I don't miss the pointed glance he sends my way. 'Please, call me Dave.'

Johnno nods. 'We should get going.' He kisses my cheek. 'See you later, boys,' he says with a wave at my brothers. He holds his hand out to Dad, who shakes it, and then he follows Shaelea from the house.

Sophie's words ring in my ears.

'Well, this has been fun,' I say, and beat a hasty retreat to my room.

***

I am laying on my stomach, thinking, when I hear the light tap on my door, and it then opens.

'May I come in?' Dad asks.

'You may,' I reply, and sit up against my pillows. There is no point trying to avoid the conversation. It has to be had. Dad sits down on the end of the bed. His face is tense, and his hands are clasped on his knees.

'This man...' he starts. Instantly I can sense how deeply his disapproval runs.

'Johnno.'

'Johnno. He has a teenage daughter?'

'Yes.' Dad nods, just a single nod, and doesn't say anything. I see it now, so clearly. This is how he makes me talk. By saying nothing, even when there is so much to be said. 'She isn't with him often. Only two weeks a year. The rest of the time she is in London, with her mother.'

I thought Dad would be placated by that. Shaelea doesn't need a mother figure. Just the occasional book recommendation. But he turns to look at me with such concern, I almost can't meet his eyes.

'Two weeks a year?'

'Yes.' I'm unsure of the significance.

'That's not a common arrangement.'

'Is it not?' I ask nervously, but I know he is right. Even Gabby, who was raised by a single mum and hated her dad, had to see him once a fortnight.

'No. The courts will usually only restrict access to that degree with good reason.'

Dad would know. He is a lawyer. I don't know what to say, so I say, 'I see.'

Dad sighs. 'Is this relationship becoming serious, Meg?'

So old-school Dad. I want to scoff, but it wouldn't go down well. Relationship? Who does that anymore. These days, young people just fly by the seat of our pants, completely carefree, with no need to know the intentions of the other, even when we have been performing the most intimate of acts with one another. Right?

'I don't know.'

'Serious enough for him to introduce you to his daughter.' Dad stands. 'Bring him to lunch on Sunday.'

'What?!' I squeal, then clear my throat. 'I mean, I don't know, Dad. Shaelea will still be here. I'm sure they will be busy.'

'She should come as well. I'd like to get to know them better.'

How I am going to get Johnno to agree to this, I have no idea. 'Fine,' I mutter. 'Thanks Dad.'

Dad walks to the bedroom door, before turning back to me. I know he is going to say something profound. People always walk away a bit and then turn back when they're about to say something profound.

'Meggy.'

'Yes?'

'Be careful, my love.'

That's what he *said.*

***

There is an awkward silence over dinner. I eat quickly, and then retreat to my room, where I lay back down on my stomach, to continue thinking.

Is it so bad that he has a teenage daughter? He was young, and since then, he hasn't had any more accidental children, that I know of. He seems to take reasonable care of Shaelea when she is with him. He brought her to the library. That rates as top-notch parenting, if you ask me.

I have been curious about what he has done to draw so much of her ire. Of course, I have been largely putting it down to teenage angst. But is it just convenient for me to do that, so I don't need to consider what other reasons there might be? Surely, if he had ever done anything to hurt her, he wouldn't be allowed to take her at all, even for two weeks. But still, what Dad has said has unnerved me. Whatever Johnno has done in the past to have his access to Shaelea so heavily restricted must have been... serious.

This leads me to think about how much I really don't know about the man I've fallen for. I know a little about his family. I know vaguely where he lives, though he doesn't live there all the time. I know vaguely what he does— manages tattoo parlours— but he never speaks about it.

My phone buzzes beside me, and I pick it up to read the message.

Johnno

How has the old man taken the news? x

Meg

Mr Drury has taken it as well as can be expected x

Johnno

Pissed off? x

Meg

Not pissed off. Philosophical x

There is a longer pause, before I receive a reply.

Johnno

I had to look that up, and I still don't know what it means x

Meg

Never mind. He wants you and Shaelea to come to lunch on Sunday xx

An even longer pause. He's not going to reply. I write again.

Meg

Mum does a roast. The potatoes are quite something xx

Finally, a reply.

Johnno

Shae wants to know if your brothers will be there, and can she play the console x

I can't believe he is considering this.

Meg

Yes for console. Yes for brothers. It's compulsory for all Drurys xx

Johnno

She says she'll come for the potatoes, and she'll stay for the games. But I can't promise either of us will behave x

I smile. I'm sure she didn't say that, but regardless, they're going to come. This might mean something.

Meg

I'm almost certain you're as afraid of my dad as I am xx

Johnno

The only thing I'm afraid of is him coming in between me and your sweet pussy, my darling x

Well, I know what *that* means.

Chapter Seventeen

Having a date for Sunday lunch is so not me. I would be thrilled about it, if I didn't know that Johnno is about to be cross-examined by one of the highest profile lawyers in Leeds.

The weather is warm, so I wear short, ripped blue denim shorts, and a button up red flannel shirt. I bunch my hair on top of my head and roll up a bandana to tie around as a head band. I look cute, but for the life of me, I can't find my high tops. They should be by the door, where I always leave them, but they're not. I mentally scroll through all the places I might have left them. Work? No, I never take them off there. Netball? No, I remember bringing them home on Thursday night. The gym? No, I'm not a member of a gym. I give up and settle on a pair of black sneakers as a poor second, and then at the sound of Johnno's motorbike pulling up, I rush to meet him.

He greets me with a smile that makes my heart race and pulls me to him to kiss me. Shaelea takes off her helmet and gives me a curt greeting, but then she adds, 'I like your outfit.' I think we are friends.

'Let me take you in and introduce you to my mum, then you can join the boys on the console.' Shaelea and Johnno follow me into the house.

I find Mum in the kitchen. She throws a warm, friendly smile in Shaelea and Johnno's direction, and puts down the knife she has been using to score the pork. 'Johnno, nice to see you again.' She approaches him with her hands outstretched. This is terrifying. I'm unsure if she is going in for a hug, or the cheek-grab-and-kiss she is most fond of. It's the latter. Johnno accepts it, but shoots me a look that says, 'How much more of this can I expect?' I don't know what to tell him. Probably quite a lot.

'And you must be Shaelea.' Thankfully, she refrains from performing the same manoeuvre on her.

'That's right,' says Shaelea, with unexpected civility. Mum radiates so much pure loveliness that even Shaelea can't resist defrosting a little.

'I hope you like roast pork, and I'm quite proud of my potatoes, aren't I Meggy?'

'Yes Mum, they're quite something.' Out of the corner of my eye I catch Johnno smiling.

'The boys are playing games in the front room, lovey. Go on in and join them,' Mum says, and Shaelea does just that. 'Now, Meggy, you can peel the potatoes and Johnno, you can chop the carrots.'

Mum beams at us, and then turns back to the pork. Johnno gives me a startled look, and I suppress a giggle.

'Do you cook?' I ask quietly, as we take up position shoulder to shoulder at the kitchen bench.

'Not if I can avoid it,' Johnno replies. 'I suppose I can butcher some carrots though.'

We work in silence, until Mum steps out of the kitchen. I then seize the opportunity to impart a warning. 'There's something I need to tell you. It's about my sister.'

'Mhmm,' says Johnno, cautiously.

'She's... well... the devil incarnate.'

Johnno puts down his knife and wraps his arms around me. That, I like. 'Sounds like we'll have a lot in common then, baby.' That, I don't. I stiffen, and with my hand that isn't holding the peeler, I brush his hands off me. Nothing could set my back up more than suggesting he will like my sister.

'You don't understand,' I say through clenched teeth.

'Did I say something wrong?' His hand moves to the back of my neck, and he massages it, until I close my eyes and lean back into him.

'Yes. It's just—,' I stop, as I hear footsteps enter the kitchen. Familiar footsteps. Familiar because— 'Are they my fucking high tops?' I spin around, foisting Johnno out of the way to confront the she-devil herself.

'Meg! How nice to see you too! Yes, I borrowed them. I hope you don't mind,' Sophie says with a smug smile. She flicks her hair over her shoulder and looks my— whatever he is— up and down. 'Well, hello. You must be Meg's new love interest.' Love interest. There we go. 'I'm Sophie.' She holds out her hand towards Johnno. He seems unsure what to do with it, but awkwardly shakes it, and then puts both of his hands in his pockets.

One would have to see it to believe it. Sophie, my prim and preppy sister, is dressed in black skinny jeans, a black singlet top, and my black high tops. She has come to family lunch, to meet my— "love interest" —for the first time. Dressed as me.

Johnno looks at me, and I can only assume there must be steam coming out of my ears, because he looks afraid.

'Actually, I do mind. I was looking for them,' I say, but I don't know if it is intelligible because my teeth are clenched so tightly together. 'Why the fuck are you dressed like me?'

'Mind your language, Meg,' Sophie scolds. 'And I'm not dressed like you. These are *my* clothes. Except for the boots, of course.'

Johnno carefully removes the potato peeler from my hand, and places it on the bench. I turn on him. 'I can't kill her with that, can I?' I shout. He flinches.

'In this mood you could inflict some damage,' he mutters.

'It's not a mood!'

Sophie laughs. 'Ah Meggy, this is going to be fun. I can feel it.' And before I can retort with anything but a growl, she heads for the door, in my boots, and goes out into the back garden.

'Wow,' says Johnno.

I am still seething, but now that she's out of my face, I return to some level of sanity.

'Sorry. She pushes my buttons.'

'I can see that.' Johnno presses my back to the counter, and his hands slide around to cup my butt. 'I need to find those buttons. You're fucking sexy when you're fired up, baby.'

My hostility melts away as he kisses me deeply. 'Perhaps we could hurry up here, and then—' I begin, but I'm interrupted by a throat clearing somewhere behind Johnno. He turns quickly around to face my dad.

'Mr Drury,' Johnno says, quickly stuffing his hands in his pockets.

'Dave,' Dad says. 'How are you, Johnno?'

'Fine, thanks.'

'Emily has put you to work, I see. Nothing too strenuous I hope.'

Good one, Dad.

'Nothing I can't handle.'

'Why don't you leave Meggy to do the vegetables, and join me for a beer in the garden?'

Oh no. A big, red, flashing warning sign is going off in my mind right now, but how to communicate to Johnno that he should, under no circumstances, allow himself to be unchaperoned with my father?

'Sure.'

Too late. He kisses my cheek, and follows Dad out to the back garden, with a nervous glance over his shoulder at me on his way out. It's been nice knowing Johnno. It really has.

***

'You warned me about your sister, but didn't think to warn me that your dad's a fucking lawyer, Meg?' Johnno finds me laying down on my bed in my room a half hour later. He lands heavily on the side of the bed.

'It didn't come up.' The excuse sounds weak, even to my ears, but then, I'm not entirely sure why I need one.

'What sort of lawyer?' he demands.

'Business.'

'A *business* lawyer?' He rubs his hands over his face. 'Fuck.'

An odd reaction, requiring further investigation.

'Is that a problem?'

Johnno laughs wryly. 'No. Not yet.' Interesting response. 'But that's the sort of intel you need to be leading with in future, OK?'

'OK. Sorry.'

Johnno looks at me and softens. He leans over and kisses me. 'Hiding any cops from me? Any second cousins in the force?'

I stifle a guilty smile. 'I don't think any of my cousins even have children yet.'

Johnno growls and buries his face in my chest, which makes me giggle out loud. When he looks up at me, he is smiling slightly as well. 'If I'm going to keep seeing you, I'm going to have to sort my shit out.' I have no idea what to make of that, but I like the thought that he wants to keep seeing me.

'On that...'

He anticipates what is coming. 'Oh, no.'

'I just wondered...when you said your life is complicated, what exactly did you mean?' Johnno doesn't answer. 'Did you mean Shae, or something else?'

Still, he is quiet, and I think he is just going to ignore me, but then he says quietly. 'Have you ever made a mistake, and you've tried to make up for it, but it wasn't enough? It still hangs over you?'

'Yes,' I say confidently. 'Once, Elle let me borrow a white blouse of hers. It was new, she'd barely worn it herself. Wouldn't you know it, I spilt gravy all down the front. I said sorry, and paid for a new one, but she's never let me borrow her clothes since.'

A slight smile touches Johnno's lips, but his eyes look...sad. 'It's a bit like that for me, Meg. I made mistakes. Too many. And now, even though I've done my time...they still follow me.'

'What kind of mistakes?' What could be so bad that he can't make up for it?

'I can't tell you that, sweetheart. You'll have to trust me that you're better off not knowing.'

'Johnno—'

We are interrupted by James, bellowing, 'Lunch is ready,' down the hallway. We get up together from the bed, and start towards the door, but I stop, and grab Johnno's hand.

'Wait.' He stops and turns to me. 'Whatever happens out there—'.

'Meg,'

'Yes?'

'We're not going to war. It's just lunch.'

So naive, Johnno.

'I just want you to know, I've enjoyed our time together.' I really mean it.

'So, it's been fine?'

He's getting rather cheeky.

'Yes. Fine. I'd almost say, good.'

He pulls me to him and kisses me. 'What have I got to do to you to get you to great, baby?' he asks, with his sexy lopsided grin that kills me every time.

'That would be unprecedented,' I reply, 'but I'm sure if anyone can do it, it will be you.'

***

Mum has outdone herself with lunch. In addition to the usual roast lunch inclusions, she has added roasted brussel sprouts, stuffing, homemade apple sauce and caramelised onions. To fit two extra guests in, we all need to sit a little closer together, but it is manageable. Johnno sits in between me and James, and Shaelea sits at Mum's end, beside Sophie.

Shaelea seems nervous, and who can blame her? It must be daunting, being at your dad's love interest's family lunch. She keeps looking across at James, and he is trying hard to act cool. Or fire, or lit, or something.

Dad gives the nod, and James in turn gives the nod to Shaelea, and there is little chatter while everyone fills their plates, aside from Dad scolding Harry for taking more than his fair share of potatoes and making him give some to Sophie.

The situation calls for someone who is skilled at small talk. That counts out me, Dad, Harry, James, Johnno and, as far as I can tell, Shaelea. If anyone is going to act as social lubricant here, it will be Mum.

'Shaelea, tell us about home. I hear you live in London most of the time?'

Very diplomatic Emily. It's so nice to know there are social skills buried deeply somewhere in my DNA.

'Yes. I live with my mum and her partner.'

'We used to live in London. In Bromley. Which part of London are you from?'

Textbook lubrication, Mum.

'Camden.'

'Do you enjoy visiting Leeds?'

'No.' Uh oh. 'First time I've ever been here, and if I have a choice I'll never come back,' Shaelea says, with a glare across the table at Johnno. 'Wouldn't have come this time if the court didn't say I had to.' Johnno doesn't react, but he chews a little more slowly.

'It must be hard to be away from your mum,' Mum offers as a possible explanation for Shaelea's hatred of Leeds.

'No. It's hard to be with Reed, because I hate him.'

'Shae!' Johnno says gruffly. Shae smirks, and annoyingly, so does Sophie.

'You are a sassy thing, aren't you?' Sophie says to Shaelea, and Shaelea smiles the brightest I have seen since I've known her. Sophie turns her attention to Johnno. With an ally in Shaelea, the shit stirring is going to start in earnest.

'Johnno, tell us, I've heard about the first time you met the rest of the family, but how *did* you meet Meg?'

Johnno looks at me out of the corner of his eye, my earlier warning about Sophie now ringing in his ears, I am sure.

'Meg left her book behind at the coffee shop beneath the library. I returned it to her.'

Sophie throws her head back in laughter. No one else seems to understand what is funny.

'How sweet! Who would have thought Meg would meet someone at the *library*, of all places. Isn't that where spinster book nerds go to die?' Now, Shaelea laughs.

Mum offers her usual, 'Soph,' in a weak attempt at behaviour management.

I roll my eyes. It's such a stupid thing to say. I'm twenty-one for God's sake, and it's such an obvious attempt to get at me, that even I don't fall for it this time. Johnno bristles beside me, however. 'I didn't notice any spinsters, but then I was probably too busy looking at your gorgeous sister.'

My insides have instantly turned to mush, but the only thing dimming my joy at Johnno's brave declaration of support in front of my whole family, is the dangerous look that has come into Sophie's eyes. She doesn't like to be slighted.

'She must enjoy looking at you too,' she says sweetly. 'She draws you, you know, in her little book.'

Oh. No. She. Didn't. I jump to my feet. I am mortified, but I barely acknowledge that emotion, because I'm completely overcome by another. Pure rage. It's as though twenty-one years of being bullied, put down, and embarrassed by this person has culminated in this moment. If she had any love for me, she could never do what she has just done. She dies now.

Seconds later, I am around her side of the table. She sees me coming and stands as well, but I am fast, and I am seeing red. My only thought is to pull every pretty blonde hair from her head. I grab her ponytail in one hand, and I wrap my other arm around her neck. She screams and cusses, and I just don't care. The blood is rushing so fast in my head that I don't even know what's happening around me anymore. I know others have stood up, and people are fruitlessly shouting both of our names. She stomps down, hard, on my foot, wearing my high tops, which only makes me madder. Strong arms take a hold of me from behind, but still, I don't let go.

'I fucking hate you Sophie. I will kill you—'.

'—Open her hand,' Johnno's voice says firmly, I'm not sure to whom, but it is James who attempts to pry open my hand that is in her hair. He is successful, and before I can latch back on, I feel Sophie's teeth sink into the bicep of my arm that is around her throat, through my shirt sleeve. I scream, my hold breaks, and as soon as it does, I'm lifted off my feet, and carried, like I'm not a six-foot-tall giant of a woman, straight to my bedroom.

Johnno only puts me down once we are in my room, then he shuts the door, and jams it with the chair. I am completely embarrassed, but the adrenaline is pumping so hard through my veins I can't even attempt to speak, to explain myself, to—.

Johnno grabs my face and crushes his mouth to mine. He deftly takes the bandana from my hair and lets it down, and then both of his hands are in my hair, keeping me in place while he thrusts his tongue into my mouth. The buttons of my shirt are insignificant as he tears the two sides apart with brute strength and pulls it off my arms. He stops kissing me to look at the place on my arm where Sophie bit me. There is a red mark, but the skin isn't broken. Then his lips are back on mine, and he reaches around to remove my bra.

I need to say something, to explain the drawings and my rage, but I can't, so I cling onto him for dear life and kiss him back, while he deals summarily with my shorts and knickers, and I am naked in his arms. He knows I'm a perverted creep with anger issues, but he seems to be overlooking it for now, and I have to just go with it, because I don't see any other choice.

He lets go of my hair and pushes me towards the edge of the bed until it hits the back of my legs and I sit. There is a crazed look in his eyes as he stands in front of me. He is rock hard, and as he undoes the button on his jeans and pulls down his zipper with one hand, he brings his other thumb to my bottom lip and strokes it. My mind goes instantly to wrapping my mouth around him. I reach for him, pull his boxer briefs down, and slide my lips down his shaft. He groans, and as I suck him, he pulls a condom from his pocket and opens it. He stops me by taking my chin in his hands and drawing back.

'Hold on, baby,' he says, and as he rolls the condom on, he fixes his eyes on mine, and says, 'You're going to take this rage, and you're going to angry-fuck me with it.' He pulls me to my feet and watches my face as he pushes two fingers inside me, making me gasp, and as he starts to pump them in and out, he says the most dreaded words imaginable. 'And then, you're going to show me the drawings.'

'Johnno, I can't—' I say breathlessly, as I grip his shoulders to remain standing.

'—Shut your mouth, and ride my cock,' he growls, but he has the laziest, sexiest smile on his face to go with his wild eyes, and I am feeling extremely obedient. He wraps his arms around me, drawing me onto the bed with him. His hands on my hips bring me into position on top of him, and I sink gratefully down on to him, and do as I am told. I throw my head back as he fills me and he reaches for my breasts. He isn't gentle, he is desperate. His hips move beneath me, and even though it's not me, and I don't do this, I surrender fully. I take all of the hatred I have for Sophie in this moment, and I channel it into fucking him— fast, and hard. He lets me be in control for a while, and he rubs my clit with his thumb as I ride him. When he wants more, he wraps an arm around my hips and thrusts into me from beneath, driving deep as he works my clit, and I come completely undone around him. Only then does he let go himself.

I lift off him, and fall to the bed beside him, absolutely spent. I am breathless, shaking, but so fucking satisfied. As my heart settles, I realise I have never felt better in my life than in this moment, beside this man, even though less than half an hour ago, I attempted cold-blooded murder.

I turn my head to look at him and find him already looking at me. He smiles his crooked smile at me.

'You good, baby?' he asks.

'Yes.'

'Just good?'

'No. Great.'

He leans over and kisses me, then, abruptly, he gets to his feet.

'Good. I'm going to the bathroom, then I'm seeing these drawings.'

Chapter Eighteen

'I honestly don't know where my sketch book is.' I am beneath the sheets, still naked and Johnno is lying beside me, fully clothed. He opens my bedside table. I didn't think he would be so bold.

'Is this it?' he asks, pulling it out.

'No.' Before he has a chance to flick it open, I snatch it from his hands and clutch it to my chest. I give him my most determined look. He smiles.

'Why are you so shy about this?'

'How could I not be? Don't you think it's creepy?'

'No. I'm flattered.'

'Flattered?!' I ask, disbelieving. 'You won't be when you see them.'

'Why? No good?'

'No, they're...I mean, they look like you. But there's just a lot—hey!' I cry, as he snatches the sketch book from my hands. 'Johnno, please. Don't look at them,' I beg. He opens the book at the beginning, and starts looking through, page by page. Dozens of drawings, of all manner of things. He stops and looks for a while at a picture I drew of a dragon with a female rider, inspired by a book I read a few months ago.

'Nice,' he mutters. The next drawing he pauses on is a male fae, with pointed ears and sharp eye teeth. 'Who's this?'

'It's a book character, from a fantasy novel. I like to draw the characters, and the settings. Bring them to life.' He nods slowly and keeps going. I am literally sweating as he gets closer and closer to the first picture I drew of him. 'I really wish you would stop. I'm deeply uncomfortable with you looking at this,' I say, trying my best to sound dignified, when I am dying inside.

He pauses, looks at me, and then flicks the page over. His eyebrows raise immediately, and I close my eyes so I don't have to see him get the ick. I can hear the pages turning over and know that he is realising just how many times I drew him.

'Wow,' he says quietly. Cautiously, I open one eye. He is on the page where his naked torso is on display, covered in the tattoos I imagined for him, before I'd seen him with his shirt off. When he looks at me, he is smiling. 'These are fucking good, Meg. Really good.'

I open both eyes. 'You really don't mind?'

'Don't mind what?'

'That I was drawing you before we were even... I mean, I was picturing you with your shirt off before we'd ever...'

Johnno laughs, a deep, filthy laugh. 'You wouldn't be asking me that if you knew the things I've been imagining since I met you, baby. I can guarantee, they're not even close to as wholesome as this.' *Wholesome?* He keeps the book open on that page, and studies it closely. 'Why did this set you off like it did? With your sister? I don't get it.'

'Her intention was to embarrass me, by telling you about the drawings. She wanted to make you think I'm desperate.' I feel my blood start to boil again, but then the anger seems to transform. A lump forms in my throat and I think I'm going to cry. 'When she saw them, how hot you are, she said...,' my voice catches and I don't think I can say it out loud.

'What, baby? To make you react like that it must have been bad.'

'She said I wouldn't be your type. That a man like you would want a woman with...,' I practically mouth the last words, '...sex appeal.'

Johnno stares at me. Just stares, for what feels like forever. His jaw is tense, and I think I might be in trouble. Eventually, he speaks, in a low, sinister voice.

'What the fuck?'

Perhaps he thinks I'm lying. 'She meant I'm not in your league,' I say nervously. 'I'm the geeky kid who couldn't talk to anyone, let alone someone like you. She likes to remind me of that. That I'll always be inferior to her.'

Johnno frowns, and he says with a sneer, 'Inferior? Are you serious?' I nod.

'I've dealt with it my whole life. I know.'

He shakes his head slowly. 'She's jealous.'

I do something I never do. I laugh. It's not funny, it's utterly ridiculous. 'No way.'

'Yes, she is. You're gorgeous, smart, talented. If she needs to bring you down, it's because you make *her* feel inferior.'

I shake my head. 'Sophie is conventionally attractive. She is better at everything than I am, except for drawing. She has more friends, more boyfriends, more charisma. She's just... more.'

Johnno shuts the book, and places it down, then turns onto his side to look at me.

'Sophie is attractive,' he says darkly. 'You, Meg, are fucking torture.' My cheeks are burning hot, and I must be bright red. I can't look at him. But then, I have to, because he takes me by the chin and turns my face to him. 'The morning you walked into the coffee shop, I couldn't take my eyes off you. That's not surprising, because you *are* my type of woman. My fantasy. But you know what? Every single person in that place stopped and stared at you when you walked in. You wouldn't have noticed, because you had your eyes down the whole time, until you got to the front of the line and had to order. You don't realise.'

'Of course, people look at me. I'm six foot and covered in tatts,' I say quietly. 'That's why I look at my feet. I hate the way people stare.'

'I can't tell you how frustrating it is that you don't know how beautiful you are,' he growls. God, I'm back to frustrating him. 'And so fucking adorable at the same time. But I'm not going to have any woman of mine going around thinking she's inferior to anyone.' He kisses me so, dare I say, lovingly. And I think my heart is about to explode.

'This is what you're going to do.' He pulls the bedsheet down to my waist, and automatically, I bring my arm across my chest. I feel so exposed, with him fully clothed beside me. His eyes flash at me. 'Put your arms up. Above your head.' I tentatively do as he asks. In a move I don't see coming, he gently takes my hair and brings it forwards over my shoulder. He runs his fingers through it, and then smooths it down. 'I want you to draw me something,' he says gently. 'You. Exactly like this.'

'Oh, J-Johnno, I can't—'

'You don't say those words to me. You can, and you will.' He sits up, and turns his body around to face me, then he picks up my phone from the bedside table. With his index finger, he pushes my cheek away. 'Look back at me.' I do as he asks, and he uses my phone to take a photo of me. I feel so self-conscious. I start to bring my arms down, but I'm stopped, as he leans over me and takes a hold of both of my wrists, pinning them in place above my head. 'Not yet.'

He tosses my phone back onto the bedside table, his grasp on my wrists unbroken. He brings his mouth to the tattoo between my breasts. He caresses it with his tongue, and his lips, and then he releases my wrists. His mouth travels further down my body, until he reaches another tattoo that sits on the right side of my pelvis, and angles down towards my groin. It's a dagger, with a jewelled hilt. The one that hurt the most to have done. He explores it with his tongue as well, and then as I lay there, feeling more beautiful than I ever have before, he explores my sex, until I release in a shuddering, breathtaking orgasm.

Finally, I am free to cover myself, and I find I don't even want to anymore. He lays down beside me and strokes my hair, and I draw him to me to kiss his lips.

'We have to go back out there,' he says softly.

'I know.'

'Are you going to be OK?'

'Yes. I am now.'

We get up, I dress, and put my hair back up, as though that might make it less obvious to my family what we've been doing in my room for the past hour, and then we start down the hallway towards the front room. I hear Sophie's laugh. I shudder. Johnno grabs me by the waist from behind, halting me, and says into my ear by far the most romantic thing anyone has ever said to me.

'I'll handle your sister, but if you still want to kill her, baby, you know I'll help you hide the body.'

***

You could cut the silence with a potato peeler as we come into the front room, and Johnno pulls me down onto the long sofa, beside him. I can't look at Sophie. She is sitting on the individual sofa with her legs curled up. Her feet are bare, so somewhere along the line, my boots have been discarded, deemed unnecessary since her aim has been achieved.

Johnno wraps his arm around me and pulls me close, the kids turn their attention back to the game, and Sophie provides commentary as they play, showering Shaelea in compliments, and teasing the boys, until Mum comes in from the dining room with an offer of ice-creams. Harry, James and Shaelea quickly abandon the game and follow Mum from the room, leaving Johnno and I alone with Sophie. I am determined not to speak to her, but she is looking at me expectantly. Expectant of what, I wonder. An apology? *She'll be waiting a damn while for that.*

I try to stand, but Johnno squeezes me around the waist, keeping me where I am. I get the feeling he is about to handle Sophie.

'Sophie, I wanted to thank you for telling me about Meg's drawings.'

'Of course,' Sophie says stiffly.

'She wouldn't have showed me herself. She's too modest. But I love finding out about her…,' a kiss to my neck, '…hidden talents.'

It's working. Sophie is glowering.

'Indeed,' she says haughtily.

'She's a very talented girl.' A curt nod from Sophie. A sly smirk from Johnno. 'She rides cock like a pro, too.'

Sophie jumps to her feet as I gasp, and then bite my lip, and a deliciously evil smile spreads across Johnno's face.

'I did not need to know that,' Sophie says, and with a flick of her hair, she leaves the room.

Johnno laughs. 'Yes, she did.'

***

We sit together on the sofa for a while, listening to the chatter coming from the dining room, and resisting the call to join the others, until I am surprised to see Shaelea come back to the front room, ice-cream cone in hand.

'All right sweetheart?' Johnno asks.

Ignoring Johnno, she addresses me. 'Meg, can I speak to you for a moment. In private.' Johnno says nothing, but just presses his lips together in a thin line, and releases his arms from around my waist to allow me to stand.

'Of course. Come to my room.'

I lead the way down the corridor, wondering what on earth Shaelea would want to talk to me about, in private. I'm nervous as I shut the bedroom door behind us, and Shaelea clearly is too. She moves to the side of my bed and sits down. I say nothing as she looks around. Her attention is drawn to my bookcase, but she doesn't get up. Eventually, she says, 'The drawings.'

Oh, good God. Where is this going?

'Yes?'

'Of Reed. Can I see them?' Right where I was hoping it *wasn't* going.

'Ah…why?'

She shrugs. 'I'd like to see them.' I stand with my hands behind my back. My eyes keep flicking to the sketch book on my bedside table, as much as I try to stop it from happening. I know it's a dead giveaway. I must be blushing, or seem embarrassed, because Shaelea adds, 'I won't take the piss.'

I suppose it *is* her dad. Maybe she has a right to see them? Wholesome as they are.

'Fine.' I pick up the sketch book and sit down beside her. I flick to the pages of the first pictures I drew, of his face from different angles, and hand it to Shaelea. She looks at it for what feels like forever, then slowly turns the pages. 'You may not want to see the next one,' I warn, when she reaches the last page before the one of him shirtless. She glances at me out of the corner of her eye, carefully turns the page, then quickly turns it back.

'Got a thing for tatts, hey?' The slightest of smiles hits her lips.

'Yes.' No point denying it.

'Can I have one of these?'

'Oh,' I say, betraying my surprise. 'One of the drawings?'

'Yeah.'

'Sure,' I say, cautiously. 'Why?'

Shaelea shrugs. 'I don't have any recent photos of Reed, and it's too weird to ask, since I barely know him. Anything could happen in a year. He could die, or…. anything. I might want to remember what he looks like one day.'

'I… well, I mean, I'm sure he won't die, but of course, you may have one. Pick whichever one you like, and I'll tear it out.'

Shaelea studies the book again, and eventually settles on one I have drawn with his eyes straight ahead, as though he was looking into the lens of a camera.

She points to it, and says, 'This one,' as she hands me the book.

As she does, a thought occurs to me. I could completely put my foot in it, but I decide to risk it. 'I could draw a picture of the two of you together, if you like. It wouldn't take me long.'

Shaelea turns to me, and she almost looks startled. But then she says, 'Really? What, not like all lovey dovey?'

'No, no. Just side by side.'

'You could really draw *me*, like this?' She gestures to the sketch book.

'Yes, I'm sure I could.'

She considers it. 'OK. Do I need to sit here?'

'No, I can work from memory.'

'That's lit.'

'Oh, thank-you.' I am in slight disbelief that this conversation is happening, and in the interests of not stuffing it up, I decide to bring it to a close.

'Give me half an hour. I'll bring it out.'

'Thanks.' Shaelea stands up. 'Just, don't tell Reed. Please. I don't want him to know. It's weird.'

'I'm sure he wouldn't think so.' Shaelea looks suddenly like she is going to change her mind, so I quickly add, 'But I won't tell him. Of course. Just between us.'

***

I find Dad, later that afternoon, once Sophie, Johnno and Shaelea have gone home, pottering in the back garden. I must be in disgrace, since he didn't come looking for me, but when I approach, he looks up from the broad beans growing in one of the planter boxes, and smiles. It's a little wistful, but it's a smile.

'Tea, Dad?'

'Yes. Let's have it out here.'

I go back inside and return a few moments later with two cups of tea. I hand one to Dad and sit down on the settee with my own. Neither of us speaks for quite some time. Not unusual for us, but this is a pregnant silence. Something is brewing. Who will be first to break?

'Is there anything you want to talk about, Meg? From lunch?'

Not particularly, Dad.

'I wish I had acted a little differently.'

'Mhmm,' Dad says, clearly expecting some further explanation.

'I was embarrassed. She was trying to embarrass me. I thought Johnno would hate that I'd been drawing him. She was trying to mess things up for me.' Dad says nothing. 'But if I had my time again, I would have tried to kill her later, when we were alone. Not in front of everyone.'

Dad doesn't approve. 'You're twenty-one Meg. You need to stop reacting this way to everything Sophie says and does.'

'She bit me!'

'You had her in a headlock.' I stand up. I have never, ever walked away from Dad mid-conversation. But he has never provoked me like this. Why is it all my responsibility to react differently to Sophie? Why can't Sophie *behave* differently towards me? 'Sit down, Meggy.'

My emotions are getting the better of me, again. I don't sit. 'What if he had broken up with me because of what she did, Dad? Would you still be telling me I have to 'react' differently?'

'I have spoken to Sophie as well—'

'—Really, Dad? Because you know damn well she has done this my whole life, and you and Mum do little to nothing about it. She has been putting me down for as long as I can remember, and you sit back and watch, and then tell *me* to *react* differently?'

'Meg—'

I think of the photo. The one that will be the first I see when I finally have the courage to open my gallery.

'Johnno is the first person who has made me see myself in a different light. To accept myself. She could have ruined that for me. I'm not going to apologise for being hurt by that, Dad.'

I have tears now, streaming down my face. I try to wipe them away, but they just keep coming. Dad stands, and I don't resist as he wraps me in his arms and holds me while I cry.

'I'm sorry, my love,' he says gently. 'Perhaps I have failed you.'

God damn it. Instantly, I feel guilty. I pull away. 'No, you haven't. I'm sorry. You've always been here for me. I'm just emotional, it's been a long day.'

'It has.' Dad gestures to the settee, and we sit back down. All is quiet again, but I am deep in thought, until Dad says, 'Meggy, there is something I need to speak to you about. About Johnno.'

Fuck. Not words I wanted to hear.

'I know he's probably not quite what you expected. He's older, and there's Shae, but he's good to me.'

'I'm glad,' Dad says, but he sounds as glad as he would if he'd just been told our house is being repossessed. 'Those are not my main... concerns.'

So, there are concerns.

'Go on then,' I say meekly.

'Johnno is in business, I understand.'

Where is this going? 'Yes. He owns a tattoo studio downtown.'

'He says he owns a couple.'

Dad knows more than I do then. It would explain the nomadic lifestyle, perhaps.

'I only knew about the one in Leeds.'

Dad nods. 'For someone with a chain of small businesses, he seems to know very little about... business.'

'Perhaps he just didn't want to chat about it,' I say defensively. 'It's Sunday lunch. Who wants to talk about work?'

'You could be right, love.' I know that isn't the end of this. 'But most people I have met who have a small business *love* to talk about it. The numbers. The details. He didn't just seem like he didn't want to talk about it. He seemed like he didn't know those things.'

My heart is beating a little faster. I don't know what Dad is imply-ing, but it sure as hell isn't anything good.

'What is your concern exactly? That he might be in debt? He paid for my movie ticket on a date. He says he has money.'

'No. That's not my concern.'

'What then?' I ask, my impatience colouring my tone.

'My concern is that he isn't in the business of tattoos, Meggy,' Dad says gently.

'That's ridiculous,' I say quickly. 'He has a business card.' Dad says nothing. 'If it isn't tattoos then what would it be?'

Dad still says nothing, until eventually he says, 'What's his name, Meg? Reed who?'

No. I am not going to let Dad investigate him. That is going too far. Johnno has done nothing to deserve this.

I stand. 'I think your imagination is running away with you. You're judging him on how he looks. There is no reason to suspect his business is anything but what he says it is.'

'If that's the case, you'll give me his name, and I will be able to put my qualms aside, once I have looked into it.'

I stand. 'No,' I say stubbornly. 'I am happy, Dad. Please stay out of it.'

Chapter Nineteen

You can trust me. At least, about this you can.

There is this annoying feeling that takes hold sometimes. When a thought— an anxiety, a worry, or, shall I say, a concern— sits at the back of one's mind, and loiters there, like a seagull around a person eating chips at the beachfront. Such a feeling is plaguing me now. My father is an intelligent man, and I have the utmost trust and respect for him. Therefore, despite my initial unwillingness to consider that he might be right about Johnno— that there could be more than meets the eye— I just can't shake the doubt that has crept into my mind. It's that, and also possibly the slight feeling of disbelief that this whole situation could be real. That a man like Johnno could really want me like he seems to, and that there may actually be nothing wrong with him. If the eighty-twenty rule runs true, there has to be something wrong with him. It's too perfect right now.

This is what brings me here, on my lunch break, to the threshold of R.J. Ink, on a sunny Thursday afternoon. I stand on the footpath, looking at the entrance, but so far, too nervous to go in. The sign above the door is black, with the shop name written in green. It screams kid's horror series to me, as though the paint is going to start dripping like slime to the pavement. But perhaps that's only me.

I can't see in. The windows are tinted. I assume whoever is inside can see out though, so I can't stand here for long just staring at the front door. If I am seen, then I can't possibly leave. That would be weird, and when we have made such progress, I don't want to go back to the strange behaviours I displayed earlier in our courtship. I am going to have to go in. In all likelihood, he will be happy to see me. If he isn't, I will simply lift up my shirt and flash him my bra, and then I'm sure he will be happy to see me. He seems to be a simple man like that.

I take a deep breath, let it out slowly, and then step forward to push on the door. As I do, a bell tinkles, and it makes me jump a mile, and starts my heart racing as I step inside. It isn't what I was expecting. The room is dimly lit, and it seems as though the entire tattooing process must take place in this one room. There is shelving along all three walls of the shop, aside from the glass windows of the shop frontage, packed with equipment— needles in their packaging, gloves, hand sanitiser— all the usual stuff. Studios I have been to in the past usually have a reception room, and the chair, or plinth they do the work in is in another room. It makes sense, from a privacy perspective, as people will often want tattoos in sensitive areas. Here, the vinyl-covered adjustable plinth is sitting off to the left of the reception desk, where Johnno is standing, leaning over the desk, deep in discussion with a man on the other side.

He stops talking abruptly, and his head turns quickly as the bell sounds. As he sees it is me, he straightens, and immediately, his brows crease. He doesn't look happy. Now would be the time to lift up my shirt, but alas, I don't have the courage.

'All right?' I ask nervously.

'Meg, what are you doing here?'

The other man, who looks in his mid-twenties, covered in tatts, smiles a gap-toothed smile, and suddenly I feel very self-conscious.

'All right, love?' he says. My skin crawls.

'Go on a break,' Johnno says gruffly to the man. The man doesn't move, he just stands there smiling. 'Get out, Miller.' Johnno says more firmly. The man laughs, and with his eyes on me the entire way, moves out from behind the desk, and walks from the store, the bell tinkling again as he exits.

'Sorry about him.' Johnno approaches me and kisses me lightly on the lips. 'He doesn't get out much.'

'OK.'

'What are you doing here?' he asks me again.

'I'm on my lunch break. I wanted to see you,' I say tentatively. 'I thought you would be happy to see me, since, you know... you said you wanted to keep seeing me. I'm sorry, I'll text next time,' I say, proper flustered now. 'Shall I go?'

'No— I mean, yes, of course you can come, any time you like. I just wasn't expecting you.' Finally, his face relaxes, and he smiles. 'I am happy to see you, baby. Come here.' He takes my hand and leads me to the plinth, and then puts his hands on my hips and lifts me up onto it. I wrap my arms around his neck. He wraps his arms around my waist and leans in to kiss me. My anxiety melts away as his tongue seeks mine out, and his hands slip beneath my t-shirt to caress my back.

Eventually, I pull back and look around again. It seems strange that everything is so... tidy. The rubbish bin is empty. The small metal trolley I assume holds the equipment in use holds nothing at all. There are no open gloves, or wipes or paper towel. Just rows of very neatly packed supplies that look like they haven't been disturbed in a while.

'How is business?' Not the sort of question I would usually ask, and it doesn't exactly roll off my tongue.

Johnno smiles and kisses my neck. 'Slow.'

'Is it not doing well?' Johnno laughs, with his mouth still against my neck. It tickles and makes me squirm. 'You sound like your— hold on...,' Johnno pulls back now, and his brows knit. 'What has he said to you?'

I study the ceiling. 'Nothing,' I say, evasively.

Johnno takes my chin beneath his fingers and lowers my gaze to meet his. I bite my lip. 'Meg,' he says warningly. 'You're not telling me the truth.'

Well, I can't tell him the bloody truth, can I?

'I'm simply asking because there are no clients here, and everything looks very...orderly. It doesn't look like you've been very busy. I'm sorry. I didn't mean to offend you.'

Johnno smirks. 'You haven't,' he says, politely. I'm starting to realise he speaks politely to me when he knows I'm full of shit. 'Please, don't be concerned. Business is fine. And if Dad wants to see the books, he's more than welcome.'

I colour ferociously. 'I-I'm sure that won't be necessary,' I stammer. The smile I receive in return is sinister, but those gorgeous green eyes are soft, and I think we're OK.

'What are your plans this evening, Detective Drury?'

Perhaps I'm still in a wee bit of trouble.

'Netball. It's the grand final tonight.'

'Really? Last game for the season?'

'Yes.'

'I haven't seen you in that little dress yet. Maybe Shae and I should come along.' A swift pull of my hips towards the edge of the plinth accompanies that statement, and his hard length is now pressing between my legs. 'If Mr Drury will be there, we can talk business some more.'

Fuck. The last thing I need during a grand final, that I'm only semi-committed to at best, is Johnno sitting beside my dad, talking business.

'Perhaps you should sit separately,' I suggest, my voice becoming unsteady as he grinds his hips against me.

'Perhaps you should know that I can hold my own with anyone, including your dad,' he says, his own voice becoming husky as his state of arousal increases.

'I believe you.'

His hands slide up my sides, pulling my t-shirt up as they go and exposing my black lacy bra. His mouth moves to my cleavage, and he kisses the tops my breasts. I wrap my legs around him, holding his cock against my centre, and lean back to enjoy it.

'Have you finished my drawing yet?' he says between kisses.

'No.'

'You've got until Sunday. Family lunch. If it's not done by then, there will be consequences.'

I swallow nervously. 'You're coming to lunch again?'

He stops kissing me, and straightens, fixing his eyes on mine. 'Do you want me to?'

'Yes,' I say quickly. 'I just thought you may prefer not to, after last time. You know, the near homicide you witnessed. And the carrot chopping.'

'You'll have to do worse than that to scare me off,' he says, with a lopsided grin. Then he stops smiling, and his expression becomes serious. 'Mr Drury thinks I'm up to no good. What do you think, Meg?'

God, what do I think? I think there is so much more to him than meets the eye. How can there not be? Whether I am in denial, or not, I really can't tell. Love is a form of madness, I am sure. But somehow, I just believe he is good. 'I trust you.'

He keeps looking at me for a moment, but then his eyes dart away, and he steps back, releasing me.

'Miller will be back soon. You'd better go.'

I pull my shirt down and slide off the plinth. There has been a sudden change in his demeanour. He doesn't want to look at me. I touch his cheek, gently. He places his hand over the top, and brings my hand to his lips.

'See you tonight, baby,' he says, and I take that as my cue to leave.

***

I look up to the stands from my position down one end of the court, and my stomach does a somersault at the sight of Johnno, with Shaelea on his other side, sitting next to my mum, who is likely to be a very permeable buffer between him and my dad. I am surprised he came. Even more surprised he is sitting with my parents.

I'm so preoccupied with watching him, that I miss Gabby calling my name the first time, and so I receive a curt, 'Drury!' the second time.

'What?' I force my attention back to the court.

'We've got this. Just for fuck's sake, look alive, woman!' Gabby scolds. It's good advice. This is a grand final after all. She gives my butt a slap of camaraderie, and then heads to the transverse line for the starting buzzer.

We're playing the team from Sheffield. They've only lost one game this season— to us. We have only lost one game as well— to them. It's bound to be a tough game. The girl I am up against in Goal Shooter is a strong holding player. Not as tall as I am, but heavily built. My advantage will be my mobility. If their passes are pinpoint, I will have no chance. I won't out-jostle her for position. But if they are off by a fraction, I need to be ready to move more quickly than her, and intercept or deflect.

The buzzer sounds, and the game begins. It is such a fast-paced game that I barely have a chance to think about what might be happening up in the stands. We lead 27-29 at half time, and a quick look at the opposition bench tells me they are changing things up. They are bringing on their bench shooter, who I have less experience playing against.

I quickly realise, once we head back out, that she is a great match up against me. She is fast as well, and she has excellent shooting range. By three-quarter time and having Gabby and Sophie up my ribs for the last fifteen minutes, we are down 32- 38. Six goals behind, heading into the final quarter. I'm about to suggest to coach that she bench me, when instead, she throws a curve ball. She decides to bring Elle on in Goal Attack. Elle, who has been watching with animation from the sidelines, shouting encouragement and tactical advice throughout the game, looks like she can't believe it. To be honest, I am surprised. But Coach explains that with Elle being our best defensive Goal Attack, she is our best chance of turning this around. Smart. Elle is known for being relentless in both attack, and defence, which not all Goal Attacks are. She also takes a statistically high number of intercepts in mid-court for a Goal Attack, and that, surprisingly, hasn't been affected by her vision problems. She must be right when she says it's more about feel, than vision.

We take the court for the final quarter, and I don't know what it is, but just having Elle on court lifts us. The doubt she puts in the minds of our opponents means the attacking passes coming our way take a fraction longer to make it, giving us more time to read them. Gabby makes a couple of great intercepts, and we get back within four. An error from Sheffield gives us another goal against the centre pass, and momentum has completed shifted to us. When the final buzzer goes, we have managed to scrape through with the win— 40-41. The team goes absolutely crazy, and even I perform an awkward celebratory fist pump, before I wrap Elle up in the biggest hug, because she absolutely blitzed it. She missed only one goal, which was rebounded by our shooter, and slotted through anyway, and she was the difference between the two teams. I couldn't be more proud of her, and as Coach comes up and steals her from my arms to wrap her in her own, I see tears start to stream from her eyes. Finally, I look up to the stands, and see my family, and Johnno and Shaelea, on their feet, clapping and cheering. This, I have to admit, is fucking amazing. Never thought I'd say that about sport.

***

The trophy presentation is complete. Gabby, as team captain, took centre stage. She enjoyed that, and her victory speech will be remembered for a long time, because she cussed right in the middle of it. While we have been having photos taken with the trophy, the stadium staff have brought out seating for all of us, along with players from the other Yorkshire clubs, for the announcement of the Yorkshire team to play in the national competition.

The seats fill up fast as the players pile on to the court, and the coach of the Yorkshire side is handed a microphone to address us. I grab a hold of Elle's hand, and we find a place to stand at the back. We both know we won't be called upon, so there is no need for us to be near the front. Sophie is feeling confident. She has planted herself front and centre, next to Gabby, who will be the first name called.

I give Elle's hand a squeeze, and she gives me a smile. This is going to be hard for her. 'It's OK,' she whispers. 'Tonight has been amazing.'

As expected, Gabby is the first name called, along with her season stats, and she is named as captain of the side. Several players from other sides, including the Goal Attack from Sheffield we have just played against, are called, before Sophie is named. She gives a performance that I'm sure she has practised in front of a mirror, bringing her hands to her mouth to feign shock, and then giving a double-handed wave as she takes her place next to Gabby at the front. Eleven players have been called. The squad will be twelve in total. That leaves only one place. They have called a Goal Keeper already. A girl from Hull.

'Finally, with 16 intercepts—'

That's funny.

'25 deflections—'

Those numbers are the same as—

'19 of those with gain—'

Mine.

'Meg Drury, Leeds Lightning.'

'What the fuck?' As luck would have it, a shocked silence had just fallen over the crowd as I made my exclamation. A few girls around me start to giggle, and I think even the coach heard me. I feel a push in the back. It's Elle.

'Go,' she whispers. I look at her, and she is smiling at me with unbridled excitement and encouragement. The crowd are cheering now, and I glance up to see Mum and Dad clapping and smiling, and Johnno doing the same, but with a look on his face that says he can see the absurdity of the situation. I mean, my stats are fine, but my attitude stinks.

I cautiously make my way to the front, still in some disbelief. Surely, at some moment, the coach will check her notes again and realise she has read the wrong name. She actually meant to call Deg Mury, or someone of that nature. But no. I get there without being waylaid, and here I am, standing in front of a room full of high-class netballers, feeling like a complete fraud. Not to mention, guilty as hell that my best friend, who is ten times the player I am, and one hundred times more committed, is not up here.

As soon as the formalities are over, I attempt an escape. I rush to the change rooms with the intention of a quick shower, so I can catch up with Elle before she leaves with Joe. I whip off my dress, but before I get any further, I hear my name, spoken in that most unwelcome, familiar voice.

'Quite the achievement, Meg. Making the county side.'

Sophie dumps her bag down and comes towards me, spoiling for a fight.

'Not now, Sophie. I want to catch Elle.' I start removing my shoes and socks, hoping she will get the message to leave it alone.

'She is bound to be disappointed,' Sophie says, dripping in fake sympathy. 'It must be hard on her— seeing her best friend who doesn't give a shit make the team, when she is stuck on the sidelines.'

She has hit a nerve with pinpoint accuracy, as usual. It *would* hurt. It may not be directly my fault, but it kills me that I might be causing my friend pain. As usual, Sophie has me on the hook. I stop what I'm doing and engage. But rather than take her bait, and bite back about Elle, something deeper rises within me. This isn't about Elle. This is about us. And it's gone on long enough.

'Why do you do it? Why do you always have to provoke me?'

'I just state facts, Meg. It isn't my fault you are so sensitive.'

My hands ball into fists at my sides, and my heart thumps at my ribs. Unlike at lunch, there is no one here to tear me off Sophie, should I get my hands on her. 'You know exactly what you do, Sophie. I want to know why. Why do you do everything in your power to provoke me?'

Sophie's eyes narrow. For a moment, I think she won't answer, but then words blurt from her mouth in a rush. 'Because you are so frustrating! You are completely apathetic about everything, but it all just falls in your lap. It always has.'

'What are you talking about?' I shout back at her. 'Why can't you be happy for me when things go right? You are my sister, for God's sake.' I choke on the words as they leave my throat. Because for all she does— for all she has always done— that's who she is. And as much as I hate her, I love her too.

Her face is on fire, and her chest heaves before she shouts back at me. 'God, Meg! Admit it. Life just happens to you, and you stand by, like a helpless spectator. You don't give a toss about netball, but you just happen to be six foot tall with arms like fucking tentacles. Meanwhile, I, shortest on court, have had to work twice as hard as you for something you don't even care about! Your job at the library fell in your lap. You didn't even have to apply; you were gifted it the minute you finished school. I have had to fight and claw my way to even get to the bottom rung in marketing. Friends fall in your lap, and you act like it means nothing. And now you've got yourself a man. But do you even care about any of it?'

I don't know what to say. What Sophie is accusing me of is…well, fuck. Maybe it's true. 'Is this why you tried to mess things up for me with Johnno? Why you dressed like me at lunch, and told him about the drawings? To punish me?'

Sophie laughs bitterly. 'I knew he was going to fall in your lap, just like everything else has. I just thought for once I'd make things harder for you. Make you fight a bit.'

I take a moment to process what Sophie is saying. Has my life really been that easy? Have I really had the blessed experience she describes? I think back on high school. How awkward I felt. How much trouble I had speaking to people. How lonely I was. That was why I spent long hours at the library after school. It was my safe place. That's how Pip got to know me and offered me a job when I graduated.

Sophie's eyes blaze at me, and to my surprise, they also glisten as though tears could fall at any moment. For all the hurt her words have caused, I can see she is hurting too. 'As your *sister*, I just wish you could see how good you have it,' she says, her tone laced with acid.

When I speak next, the edge has left my voice, but I take a step closer. I want her to *feel* what I have to say next. To really understand how I have hurt. To feel the wounds she constantly picks at to stop me from fully healing. 'Do you ever question if you are good enough, Soph?'

'For what?' she snaps.

'To just be. Good enough to be spoken to. Noticed. Good enough to be in a room. Good enough to be loved. Or is that something you take for granted?' Sophie doesn't answer, but the fire goes out of her eyes. '*That* is the one thing that hasn't fallen in my lap.'

We look at each other for what feels like a long time. I have nothing more to say. It seems neither does Sophie. Finally, I abandon my plan for a shower, and throw my dress back on. Sophie's eyes burn my back as I leave.

***

I see Joe and Elle crossing the carpark as I exit the stadium. I also see Johnno standing by his bike with Shaelea, off to my right. I put my hand up and motion for him to wait, and then I chase after Elle.

'Elle,' I call, and she, and Joe, turn around. She smiles broadly at me, but her cheeks are tear stained.

'How do, Meg?' Joe says politely, and I give him a quick kiss on the cheek, before pulling Elle into a hug.

'You should have been up there, not me.'

'Don't be so ridiculous,' Elle says. 'You deserve it, Meg. You've been consistent all season. I've even questioned at times whether you quite like netball.'

'I don't.'

Elle smiles. 'I'm proud of you. And I don't want you to worry about me. It's just not meant to be. I'll be OK.' Joe places a comforting hand on her back, and she turns her smile to him.

'You'll have another chance, my love, next year,' he says.

'No. It's best I let it go. I'll be content to support Meg from the sidelines, and chastise Gabby, to keep her ego in check. I'll focus on writing my first novel. *The Adventures of Verity Harbinger, A 19th Century Girl Stuck in A Modern World.'*

'Fairly autobiographical then,' I say, and Elle gives a shrug. I want to say something encouraging, but I can't think of anything. She is being so brave, but this is her dream, going up in smoke.

'You should go, Meg. Johnno is waiting.' She gives him a quick wave. I look over my shoulder to see him casually return it.

I turn back to Elle. 'Are you coming on Sunday?'

'Yes, of course. Have I got it right? It is lamb this week, isn't it?'

'Yes.'

'We wouldn't miss it, would we, my love?' she says, and gives Joe's hand a squeeze.

'Tell me all about Verity then,' I say.

We say good-bye, and I make my way over to Johnno and Shaelea. He opens his arms as I approach, and I fall gladly into them. He kisses my head, before releasing me, but keeps one hand on the small of my back.

I open with, 'Sorry, I stink.'

Johnno, being a deviant, leans down to my armpits and breaths in deeply. Shaelea gives him a disgusted look, and I can't say I blame her. 'You do, baby. It's good.' My face is mirroring Shaelea's. He smiles, the look of satisfaction on his face disturbing. 'You weren't lying when you said you were quite good,' he says. 'Even Shae was impressed, weren't you kiddo?'

'Well done, Meg,' Shaelea says, ignoring Johnno.

'So, what does this Yorkshire team mean?' Johnno asks.

I groan. 'It means I have to keep training and playing over the off-season, which is usually when I try to avoid physical activity at all costs. And I'll have to gallivant all over the country to play games against elite players, who will obliterate...wait,' I say, as a cheerful thought strikes me. 'Perhaps Pip won't let me play. I'd have to miss some Fridays for travel. She won't like that.' Resolutely, I add, 'I'll have to pull out. I can't let the library patrons down.'

'Don't do anything too hasty. I don't know anything about netball, except for what I learned from the pictures in *Everything You Need to Know About Netball*, but as far as I can tell, you should be proud of yourself. You smashed it tonight.'

I smile at the memory of him borrowing that book. 'Thank-you,' I mumble. 'I'm glad I got to see you before you leave, Shaelea. It's been great to meet you.' Johnno will have to take her back to London tomorrow. His two weeks are up.

'You too,' Shaelea offers in response. I will have to be content with that, as nothing else seems to be forthcoming. Then, to my surprise, she adds, 'Your family are nice. Except for your sister. She's a cow.'

Though our argument is still raw, I stifle a laugh, as Johnno half-heartedly scolds her. I see Mum, Dad and Sophie coming out of the stadium. I give Johnno a quick kiss, and before I go to join them, Johnno whispers in my ear, 'Don't forget my drawing.'

Somehow, I don't think he is going to let me forget.

Chapter Twenty

It isn't until Sunday morning that I finally bring myself around to looking at the photo of myself, and only because Johnno will be here in a couple of hours, and then I imagine I won't have a choice.

I lie down on the bed with my sketch book. I've put the chair beneath the door handle. Can't believe I never thought to do that myself, it has been life-changing in securing privacy when I need it. Because the last thing I want is to be caught drawing a half-naked picture of myself. Even the thought makes me cringe. I can't believe I'm doing this.

I open my phone gallery, and there it is. I can't keep my eyes on it at first. It seems far too taboo. But gradually, I convince myself to look for a little longer. I have to look in detail to be able to draw it. I need to take in each contour, and where the light and shade falls. And the more I look at it, the more I start to think it isn't so bad. Actually, it is beautiful. It feels an arrogant thought, but I think *I* am beautiful in this photo. It takes me a little longer to finish it than I normally would. Breasts are harder to draw than I realised, however, I am satisfied with the final product. Before Johnno arrives, I have one more picture I want to draw. I am just finishing that one when I hear his motorbike. I complete the finishing touches, close the book, and go out the front to meet him.

I wonder if he will be feeling sad, since he had to take Shaelea home, but he greets me with a smile and a kiss and he seems fine.

'How was your trip?'

'Good. The bike's got a rattle I need to look into, but it went all right.'

'And Shaelea?'

'Glad to see the back of me.'

God, I'd love to tell him about the picture. Though she didn't make a big song and dance, as I expected she wouldn't, she was happy with what I drew.

We won't have long together before Elle and Joe arrive, so after taking Johnno into the kitchen to greet Mum and Dad, I take him straight to my bedroom. He seems to be on a slightly different wavelength to me, because the second the door is shut behind us, and the chair propped beneath the handle, he attempts to undress me.

I take hold of his hands as they reach for the button on my jeans. 'Wait. Can I speak to you about something first?'

'Fuck now, talk later, baby. I've missed you.'

He easily breaks my hold on his hands and tries pulling my t-shirt off instead, but I push his arms away and move out of his reach.

'I have something you want.'

'Hell yes, you do.' *One track mind.*

'The drawing.'

Finally, he stops, and a smile spreads across his face. 'Go on, then.'

I sit down on the side of the bed, and he sits beside me. I take my sketch book from the bedside table, and open to the picture of myself. I am surprised to find I'm not even nervous to give it to him. I know it is a good reproduction of the photo, and honestly, I like it. From the look on Johnno's face, he likes it too. As he looks at it, his tongue touches his bottom lip.

'Meg. Fucking gorgeous.' He tears it swiftly from the book, folds it, and places it in the inside pocket of his motorbike jacket, that he had taken off and placed on the end of the bed. 'I know exactly where that's going.'

'Somewhere safe, I hope,' I say, nervously.

Johnno laughs. 'That's not what I mean.' I raise my eyebrows at him in question. 'I mean, I know where I'm having it.' He lifts the back of his shirt up. 'That spot right there, on the middle of my back.' My eyes widen as I understand his meaning. There is a space there, just between his shoulder blades, about the size of my hand.

'Y-you can't be serious.'

'Fuck yes. If I want to get a tattoo of my hot local librarian, I will. No one can stop me.' He pulls his shirt back down, and the smile on his face is pure trouble. 'Might get one of Pip, as well.'

'Johnno, you're mad! I'm topless in that picture,' I say, quietly panicking.

'No one's going to see it, unless they see me with my shirt off. Which will only be you, baby.'

'God. If I knew that's what you wanted it for—'

'—What? You wouldn't have done it?'

I think he knows he has me. If I'd known, I think I still would have done it. Because truth be told, as terrifying as it is, I am mighty flattered. But what if we break up? I mean, we have never even discussed that we are together, as such. He has called me his 'woman', and offered to hide a body with me, but other than that…

'I hope Pip won't be topless as well,' I say, to avoid a more meaningful response.

Johnno laughs, and rather than answer me, he kisses me. 'I like the picture, a lot.'

'I drew something else for you.' This one, I *am* nervous to give him. I take the book back from his hands, and flick over a couple of pages. If he takes this the wrong way, then I may not be immortalised in tattoo form after all. I tear out the picture of him and Shaelea that I finished before he arrived, and tentatively hand it to him. 'I thought you might not have many photos together.'

He takes it, and stares at it, without saying anything. He looks at me, then back at the picture, then clears his throat. 'I'm glad you drew it like that.'

'Like what?' I ask gently.

'Like…we're just there together. I'm glad you didn't make it look like…,' before he finishes the sentences, he folds the picture, but keeps it in his hands, then he sighs. 'Like she doesn't hate me.'

Does that mean he thinks I've drawn it like she *does* hate him? I thought it was fairly neutral. Maybe I've fucked up. He looks so sad. Now I desperately want to tell him about the drawing I did for Shaelea, but I promised her I wouldn't, and I know I can't.

'Of course she doesn't hate you. She's just a teenager. I'm sure every second parent goes through the same thing.' I reach for his hand and hold it.

He shakes his head. 'Did you ever hate your dad?'

'I said every *second* parent.'

His brows knit. 'She has her reasons for hating me. I can't blame it on her being a teenager. I wasn't there when I should've been.' He unfolds the paper and looks at it again. 'You've got the eyes just right.' He folds it again, and places it with the picture of me, in his jacket pocket.

'Have I stuffed up?' I ask nervously.

He turns to me and brings his arm round my waist. 'No. I love it. Thank you.'

***

A quiet tension simmers between Sophie and I over lunch, but it doesn't result in the warfare the family has come to expect. I put it down to Elle's presence, and that social lubricant she is famous for. And today, Sophie seems quite...tame. She has come dressed as herself, in a summery dress, with her hair down around her shoulders. She has returned my boots, and she even passes up the opportunity to make fun of me when Elle brings up Book Club. The library is usually her favourite ammunition.

With the addition of Elle and Joe, Mum and Dad's attention is spread so thinly there isn't enough for Sophie to bask in, so she leaves shortly after lunch. The rest of us, after helping Mum clean up, move outside to sit in the back garden. The weather is perfect. Dad brings out some extra chairs from the garage, and the boys climb up in the cubby.

Mum asks Joe about the farm, and Dad shows interest in that conversation with polite non-verbals, while Elle sits on the settee with me and Johnno. She talks animatedly, but in a hushed tone, with frequent furtive glances at Joe, about her plans for Verity Harbinger. Verity, she has decided, will be a primary teacher (not surprising), who flees to Australia to escape an arranged marriage to a wealthy duke (somewhat surprising). There are mentions of magnificent cocks, whiteboard cleaning solutions and quizzing glasses, sometimes within the same sentence, and I'm struggling to see how it will all come together. But knowing Elle, it will. Johnno seems quite fascinated, more by how daft Elle is, than by her story pitch, but either way, the time is passing pleasantly.

Things take a turn when something over behind us catches Elle's eye. Something she has been eagerly anticipating. Elle has known my brothers for a few years now, since she moved up to Yorkshire with Gabby. Harry was only seven then, and James was ten. Young boys. Elle, being a primary school teacher and having two older twin brothers, is very good with boys. She has always played with my brothers, especially games of pretend. Even though they are now ten and thirteen, when they are around Elle, they revert to those young boys they were when they first met her. I follow Elle's eyes, and see James, with Harry pinned to the ground, roughhousing on the grass at the foot of the cubby.

'Ooh! A mill!' With a grin, Elle springs to her feet. She takes off her glasses, uses the hair tie around her wrist to tie her hair up in a ponytail, tightens it, and then heads towards my brothers. James looks up as she approaches, with a grin on his face to match her own.

'Unhand that poor lad at once, scoundrel!' Elle cries, and next minute, she is in the thick of it, trying to wrestle James off Harry. James, being now thirteen, and quickly gaining on both of us for size, is not quite the easy opponent he was when he was ten, and Elle was eighteen. Elle has a few good moves. Apparently, you don't grow up with twin brothers four years your senior without acquiring some handy self-defence skills. But James quickly shifts his target from

Harry to Elle, and has Elle pinned in quick time. Harry has his arms around James's neck, trying in vain to rescue Elle. There is a lot of giggling happening from all parties, but between giggles, Elle is calling desperately for help from Joe.

Joe shifts nervously in his place.

'You should go, Joe. You know what she's like. She'll be disappointed if you don't play along,' I say encouragingly.

Joe sighs and as though resigned to his fate, takes his phone and wallet from his pocket and goes to the assistance of his fair maiden.

Things don't go as planned for Joe. As soon as Joe is in reach, James launches off Elle, and takes Joe around the ankles, bringing him to the ground. Harry then decides that instead of rescuing Elle, which is now all too easy, he is going to help James to defeat Joe. Joe cries out in protest as James deploys a forceful body slam on him, and Harry wraps himself around both of Joe's legs and holds on for dear life. Joe is completely helpless. Elle, who has now been released, stands and surveys this, with her arms folded, and her lips pursed.

'Help, my love,' Joe begs from beneath my brothers.

Elle rolls her eyes. 'For Heaven's sake, Joseph! You were meant to be rescuing me!' Elle tightens her ponytail again, and then pounces on James, who is still leaning on Joe, pinning him to the ground, and unleashes her most effective, and feared, weapon. Tickling. Within seconds, she has James in a crumpled mess on the floor, weeping from relentless tickling, and Harry, who sees the condition that James is in, surrenders.

Joe gets gingerly to his feet. 'Quick Joe, to the castle tower, and stay there until I have this situation under control,' Elle orders Joe, who decides it is very good advice, and climbs up onto the cubby platform to watch what unfolds.

With Joe out of the picture, Harry regains his courage, and decides to rescue his brother, and that means fighting fire with fire. So next minute, Elle is also in tears, as Harry tickles *her* mercilessly. She has no choice but to let James up and beg for mercy. It is not forthcoming. She is pinned to the ground once more, and I can barely watch as James and Harry both tickle her to actual death. Not really, but you would think so from the sounds coming from her. Mum and Dad are considering intervening, but before they can, Johnno's voice rumbles from beside me.

'I've seen enough.'

'What are you going to—'

As I watch on in disbelief, he strides over and picks James up like a baby. Cradling him in his arms, he carries him to the green house, opens the door, and puts him inside. He shuts the door and goes back for Harry. The greenhouse isn't lockable, and James could get out, but he plays the role of captive, calling out to Harry for rescue. Harry has frozen in place, watching his older brother be man-handled, and therefore is easy pickings for Johnno, who gives him the same treatment.

Elle sits up, dishevelled and out of breath. As Johnno walks over to sit back down with me, and my brothers come sheepishly out of the greenhouse, Elle gets to her feet and dusts herself off. Arms crossed, she shoots a filthy look up at Joe, who remains in the treehouse.

'I'm sorry, my love, they had me. You saw.'

'You didn't even try to come to my aid, Joseph! You just sat there and watched as I was assaulted by two assailants!'

'Aye, but—'

'What sort of mortal peril would I have to be in to activate any sort of chivalry in you, may I ask?' Elle continues. This should be funny, but Elle isn't joking. Her cheeks are bright red, her chest is heaving, and she looks like she is about to burst into tears.

'You know if I really thought you were in danger, I would've called the bobby, my love. Without delay.'

Oh Joe. Not the police. Not that. I know exactly where Elle's thoughts are going to go. To Bella's cowardly beau, who couldn't deal with Patrick without the aid of the capable, but truly unromantic, Detective Martin.

'The *police*?' Elle cries. 'Oh, now I've heard it all.'

Joe looks terribly confused, for which he can't be blamed. With one last look of hurt and reproach thrown back over her shoulder at him, Elle storms inside.

No one knows quite what to say. Except for Johnno. Casually, he leans back, places his arm behind my shoulder, and with a smile says, 'Never a dull moment at the Drury's.'

*****

I find Elle in my room, pacing back and forward with a stormy look on her face.

'Can you believe him, Meg?' she cries, as soon as I enter the room and shut the door behind me. 'The police! He would rather watch me suffer a horrific fate, than intervene himself. He's- he's- he's- a coward.' The second the words leave her mouth; she bursts into tears. Proper, hysterical tears. I am almost too shocked to do anything, but then something in the back of my brain says, *tissues, Meg. When someone cries, offer them tissues,* so that's what I do. Elle takes them and buries her face in one.

When she resurfaces, she says, 'I can't do it, Meg.'

'What?'

'Marry him. I can't marry Joe.' I knew this hadn't really gone away since Book Club, when she pronounced her allegiance to the safe, dependable, unexciting option. 'I thought I could suppress it. I thought I could go ahead with it, in the interests of not hurting him, and loyalty, and being a Good Catholic Girl. But Meg, I just can't.'

'OK, Elle, please try to calm down and talk to me rationally about this,' I say, trying to keep the panic from my own voice. 'What has this got to do with wrestling my brothers?'

'Nothing, and everything.' A very Elle response. 'Of course it seems silly, Meg, but it also perfectly demonstrates the problem I have.'

'Which is?'

'I don't want to sleep with Joe anymore. I just don't. There is no heat. No passion. No desire. No longing. None. He is sweet, and kind, and all things good, but he doesn't even light a match under me, let alone a fire. There's no, 'Come here Elle, I need to have you, right now, on the seat of this tractor.' It's always, 'Can we make love please, it's been two weeks.' Elle gives a shudder, and I have to admit, I kind of get it.

I have to resign myself to the fact that my best friend is going to break up with another one of my best friends, and that feels really shit. But there is no way back from this.

'OK.' I sit down on the edge of the bed. 'So what are you going to do? Break up with him? Today? Here?'

'Of course not,' Elle snaps. 'Don't be daft, Meg. I can't break up with him.'

Now I'm confused. 'Sorry?'

'He is the sweetest man alive. It would ruin him. I may not want to sleep with him, but I still love him as a friend, and I could never hurt him.'

'Fine,' I say cautiously, but really, nothing is fine about this. 'What are you planning to do then?'

'I'm going to move to Australia,' Elle says triumphantly.

'What?!' I know this sounds dramatic, but my world just stopped for a moment. This can't be happening. This has to be just an Elle whim.

'Not forever. Just for two years. I'm going to get a working holiday visa. I will tell Joe I just need some time away. I'll say missing the netball team has affected me more than I realised, and I need to get away, to process it.'

My head is spinning. She sounds serious. She sounds like she has thought this through.

'Isn't that effectively breaking up with him, Elle?'

'No, I won't break up with him. I will tell him I want him to come.'

'But you know he can't come. He has the farm.'

'Exactly,' Elle says, and she sounds way too satisfied about it. 'He can't come. That's what makes it so perfect. He will think it is nothing to do with him, and that I just need to get away for a bit. He will have to stay home. We will do long distance for a while, and gradually over time, he will forget all about me, and we will be over. Like applying a small amount of apple cider vinegar to a wart daily, and eventually it just falls off. No hurt feelings. It will be completely painless. He'll barely even notice it happening.'

How do I explain to Elle that losing her from his life— and mine— will be nothing like that? Elle is the sort of person whose absence, once one has had her in one's life, will be like missing a fucking limb.

'Please don't do this. It's a horrible idea. There must be another solution.'

'Can you think of one?' she asks expectantly. She waits. I think. 'Didn't think so.'

'Just don't say anything to Joe yet. Sleep on it, at least.'

Elle looks at me, and there is hurt in her eyes. 'You, Meg, of all people, I thought would understand.'

'*Me?*'

'Yes, you. Gabby, I know will struggle when I tell her. But you, Meg. You are in love. Surely, you must understand how hard it is for me to be engaged to someone who I just don't feel that for anymore, if I ever did at all?'

'In *love?* Elle, that involves the feelings of two people, not just one. What I feel might be completely one-sided for all I know! You can't compare me and Johnno, to you and Joe. It is totally different.'

Elle's nose goes in the air. We are at odds. 'I can't believe you, Meg Drury. That man is out there right now, schmoozing your parents, and you have the audacity to say he is not in love with you.'

'You don't know that's what he's doing,' I say pettishly.

'I refuse to take relationship advice from a woman with the most satisfied pussy I know. This conversation is done,' she says, and with that, she flounces from my room, shutting the door behind her as she leaves.

Chapter Twenty-One

I am still sitting on my bed, processing my conversation with Elle, when the door opens, and Johnno comes in. He must know straight away that something is seriously wrong, because he sits down quietly beside me, and puts his arm around my shoulders, without even attempting to undress me.

'Where is Elle?' I ask.

'Gone home.'

'Did she go with Joe?'

'Yes.'

I groan. God, I hope she doesn't say anything yet. I need more time to make her see sense.

'Did you argue?'

'Yes.'

'Talk to me. What happened?'

I can barely bring myself to say it out loud. 'She doesn't want to marry Joe. She says she doesn't want to sleep with him anymore, and she can't go through with it.' And then, possibly the worst part of all. The part I can't even begin to accept. 'She says she's going to move to Australia.'

Johnno nods, and lays back on the bed, with his hands behind his head. 'Makes sense.'

'What?!' I exclaim, turning on him with a look of fury.

'Not the Australia part. I thought that was Charity, or Verity, or whoever she was on about. But the part about Joe makes sense. The guy's a pussy.'

'Johnno! Joe is the loveliest man alive. He is kind, and gentle-natured. That doesn't make him a pussy! And that term is very misogynistic.'

Johnno shrugs. 'Sorry. I just can't see it.'

'See what?'

'Him and Elle together.'

'That's ridiculous! They've been together for almost three years.' Johnno doesn't say anything, but he's looking back at me like he knows he's in the right. About *my* best friend, and another one of *my* best friends. 'Explain yourself.'

'Elle is... energetic. Joe doesn't match her energy. She wants someone who will join her on this other planet she seems to live on. He's not on that level.'

'Don't you think he grounds her? If she was with someone as mad as her, it wouldn't work at all.'

He shrugs. 'Maybe not. But if she's not turned on by him, she's got no business marrying him.'

I am starting to feel flustered, and I can feel this becoming personal— less about Joe and Elle, and more about me and Johnno.

'There has to be more to a relationship than that. It can't just all be about sex. What about friendship, and emotional connection, and conversation? Shared values? Loyalty?'

'All important too. But I've stayed in a relationship before once the sex died, and it wasn't good. I'd never do it again.' I growl with frustration. Talk about a one-track mind. I stand up, keeping my back to him. I hear him sit up behind me, but I can't look at him. 'It would come out one way or another, eventually.'

'What would?' I ask, without turning around.

'The dissatisfaction. The frustration. It'll come out in picking fights, or drinking. Or cheating.'

Now, I jerk my head around.

'Elle would never cheat. She's very loyal.'

'I didn't think I would either. I thought I could stay with Shae's Mum because it was the right thing to do. No one ever thinks they'll cheat, until they do.'

I'm not sure I've heard correctly. God, I hope I haven't. But if I have, it might explain the way Shaelea feels towards him.

'You cheated?'

Johnno nods. 'Not proud of it, obviously.'

'F-for how long?' I ask, even while knowing there is no good answer.

'Not long. I told her pretty much straight away and that was it. We were over.'

I feel like I'm going to cry. It has been obvious from the beginning that Johnno couldn't be perfect. I've ignored blatant red flags because of how I feel about him. But this... I didn't expect. He stands up, and steps closer to me. I still have my back to him. His hands land on my hips.

'Is this why you warned me not to trust you?' My voice wavers, so close to breaking.

'No,' he says adamantly. 'I'm not the same person I was then. I learned a lot from it, Meg. We were kids, and we *had* a kid. She and I were nothing like you and me.' He kisses my neck, and I close my eyes. 'I will never commit myself to someone again unless I know I can be faithful.' His arms wrap more closely around me. I'm ready to give in, and let this conversation be over. But then, he says softly, 'Don't you want your friend to have this? What we have?'

My eyes spring open, and I spin around in his arms.

'What *we* have?' Johnno looks taken aback, like he doesn't understand what he has said wrong, but my blood is boiling. 'Johnno, Joe loves Elle. Adores her. He wants to marry her. He wants to have a family with her. They are best friends. What *we* have? Sex? You think she should give all of that up, for *this*?'

Johnno's hands fall to his sides, and he takes a step back, and I see it straight away. He is hurt. His jaw tightens, he grabs at his hair like he's going to tear it out, then decides against it. 'Seriously, Meg? That's where you're at?'

Instantly, I want to back track. This is not what I expected at all. I thought he would laugh, and make some sexually laced comment, like, 'It's great sex though, isn't it, baby?' I didn't expect him to look like he is going to fucking cry. But that's exactly what it looks like.

He shakes his head, glares at me, then grabs his jacket from the end of my bed and heads for the window. He pushes it up and climbs through.

'Johnno, wait.' He doesn't. I have to follow him. I can't lose him. Not now, after having had him like I have. But God, I wish he'd use the door.

I swing my legs out the window and run after him. He's at his bike before I catch him.

'Stop,' I say, my own voice cracking. He puts his helmet on. I put myself between him and the bike, and grip onto the front of his jacket as tightly as I can. 'Johnno, I don't want you to go. I've said the wrong thing. Whatever it was, I'm sorry.'

His hands cover mine, and his fingers curl around my palms, and I think he's going to open my hands and push me away. But then he lets go and takes his helmet back off. He throws it down on the grass, and with one hand, he grips the back of my neck.

'It's not something you should be sorry for.' It's terrifying, because I have never seen him look so intense, and he is an intense kind of guy.

'How do I fix this then?' I hope he can feel how much I need to make things OK between us.

His fingers tighten at the back of my neck, and his voice is strained as he speaks. 'I've just had Sunday lunch with your whole family. I didn't fuck off the second I found out your dad's a lawyer. I've introduced you to my daughter. I joined the library just so I could see you. I want a tattoo of you over the place where my fucking heart beats, for God's sake, Meg. And to you, this is just sex?'

'N-no,' I stammer. I am being completely swamped with emotion that I don't even recognise, and I am terrible at expressing it. 'But you told me not to trust you. You told me to be careful.'

'Because I didn't want to make you promises that I can't keep. Because until—,' he cuts himself off, breathing heavily. 'Until I know I will be here for you in the long term, and I can give you everything you deserve, and I'm not going to hurt you, you *do* need to be careful. It doesn't mean I'm not fucking crazy about you. I've been in love with you since the first time I kissed you in that toy cupboard. And you...' he shakes his head at me. He's still holding my neck. My bottom lip is wavering. I have to speak. 'If you're not feeling this, then I have to get the fuck out of here.' He drops his hand from my neck.

I. Have. To. Speak. Speak Meg. Do it. It's now or never, because he is bending down to pick up his helmet and—

'I love you too.'

He stops, and slowly stands back up. 'Really?'

'Yes. I love you. I've known since you used your status as a council taxpayer to save my book club. Perhaps I didn't dare to believe you would feel the same way.'

His face doesn't relax, but the slightest smile touches his lips, and then he pulls me into his arms and crushes his lips to mine. When he takes his lips away, he keeps me close, and says,

'Let me ask you again, then, Meg. Don't you want your friend to have what we have?'

***

'Is this really necessary?' I ask, as I stand in my bedroom in my blue and white Leeds Lightning netball dress, and Johnno sits on the side of the bed, ogling me. After declaring our love for each other, and then climbing back inside through my bedroom window, we have quickly decided it's time for our first ever make-up sex. I didn't think it would involve dress-ups. Apparently, I was wrong.

'Absolutely. If I hadn't had Shae with me on Thursday night, I would've come home with you and fucked you in that dress. Not an experience I'm willing to wait until next season for.'

'Fine.' I attempt to climb onto his lap, but he holds me off with firm hands around my ribs.

'Wait. Hair up. In a ponytail, like you had it on Thursday night.'

'Really?'

'Yes.'

Begrudgingly, I walk over to my dresser and draw my hair up in a smooth, high ponytail, securing it with a band. Then I attempt the straddle again. This time, Johnno draws me onto his lap, kisses me, and then immediately pulls out the hair band I have just put around my ponytail, letting my hair fall down around my shoulders. He runs his hands through it, as he laughs, and I purse my lips to stop myself from smiling as well.

'Are you looking for those buttons you thought might be fun to press?' I ask.

'Maybe I am. Now, what have you got on underneath this little number?' he asks, sliding his hands beneath the dress, up the outside of my thighs and over my bare buttocks. Only the g-string I had on before, beneath my jeans. A dirty smile spreads across his face, and his fingers hook beneath the thin strip of lace around my waist.

'Very nice. This will be perfect for when you sit on my face. Come on.'

We seem to be straying further and further from the vanilla sex of old. I don't mind, but with each new… frontier… I still find myself a little nervous. 'You want me to—'

'—Hell yes. Stop talking and do it.' Bossy. He lifts me off him, and shuffles onto the bed so he can lie down on my pillow and then pulls me towards him with an arm around my waist, and I kneel on the bed. I think I'm just going to do it. I like the things he does with his mouth, and he certainly seems to enjoy it. What could go wrong?

I start to throw my leg over him, but he stops me, and says, 'No, the other way. Turn around.' I do as he asks and he draws my hips back towards the head of the bed, so I am positioned over the top of his face. He pushes my dress up, and his lips leave a trail of kisses across each of my buttocks, before he pulls my g-string to the side, and brings me down to him with a firm arm around my waist. I moan at the first touch of his warm, wet lips on my sex, and before long, I am thoroughly enjoying myself as he pleasures me. His cock is right in front of me, so hard that it is calling me to stroke it. I undo the button and zipper on his jeans, and run my hand along his length, while my other holds on for dear life to his thigh as I feel myself getting close. But then, he pauses, and when his tongue touches me again, it's... not in the place I expected.

I squirm and pull slightly away. 'I think you may have lost your way there.'

Johnno chuckles, low and deep. 'I know where I am, baby.'

His tongue touches me there again. No. He must be disorientated. I squirm away again. 'I don't think you do.'

'I do. You don't like it?' I don't know how to answer. It's not that I don't like it. If I was sure that he wanted to do it, then perhaps... 'I don't want to make you uncomfortable. I promised you I wouldn't. How about you let me do it for five seconds, and if you hate it, I won't do it again.'

'D-do you like to do it?'

'I love it.'

That's what I needed to hear. 'Fine. Five seconds.'

I count to five slowly in my head as he runs his tongue around my...well, I'm not going to say it...and as I get used to the sensation, I find I really don't want him to stop, except that it's frustrating other parts of me that are crying out for the same treatment. He must count a little more slowly than me, but shortly after I get to five, he stops. 'What do you think?'

'I don't hate it.'

'Good. Because what I really want to do is that, and this...,' he slides two fingers inside me, and curls his fingers to stroke the spot that took me to heaven on his bike the first time we went out. His tongue resumes, and his fingers work me, until I am on the verge of something I don't know what to do with. I cuss under my breath at the pressure building, that I know is just going to have to release, because it's that, or I will die. I don't even know if it's pleasure, or torture I'm experiencing, until I can't hold out any longer, and I come apart in a gush. Johnno takes his fingers from me right at that moment, and reaches forward for my clit, but I just can't, because what the fuck just happened? I mean, I know what happened, but I didn't expect it, and now I feel— God— mortified. I jump up, on the verge of hyperventilating, and cover my mouth with my hand to stop myself from swearing.

Johnno props himself up, and I look away as he wipes his face. 'Meg, are you OK?'

I'm not. 'Fuck, I didn't know that would— I'm so sorry.'

Johnno gets quickly to his feet, and tries to hold me, but I turn away. I'm so embarrassed, I can't look at him.

'Baby, what? Don't be sorry. Hey...,' he wraps his arms around me, and cups my face so that I have to look at him. 'I knew, sweetheart. I touched you like that on purpose. I knew. It's OK.'

I can see that he means it, and he is looking at me with such concern, that finally, I calm a little and relax in his arms. 'You like it?'

'Yeah,' he says with a gentle laugh. 'Fuck, I love it. It happened when I touched you on my bike, but you had your tights on. Maybe you couldn't tell.' He kisses me tenderly just beneath my ear. 'There's nothing you can do wrong with me, baby. Nothing. I love everything about you, Meg. Every inch of you. Right down to your pretty—,'

'Don't say it—'

'—little—'

'—No, really.'

'—arsehole.'

'Oh, dear God. You said it.'

He laughs his dirty laugh, and kisses my lips, but then he is serious. 'I rushed you to there. I'm sorry. I didn't mean to freak you out.' He brushes my hair back from my face, in a way which is so tender, and so loving, and then his eyes darken, and a slight smirk comes onto his face. 'Did it feel good?'

It felt fucking amazing, if I'd let myself enjoy it.

'Fine,' I say, but my own smile, and my burning hot cheeks, betray me, even as I try to hide it by burying my face against his chest.

His smirk widens. 'Just fine, hey? I'll have to do better then, next time.'

Chapter Twenty-Two

I wake up on Monday a new woman. A woman in love. Not just with any man, but with a man I would never have imagined would even look at me, let alone be in love with me back. It has certainly given me a new perspective on Elle's situation. Yes, I want her to have what I'm having. She deserves it, and she's not getting it with Joe. But I absolutely do not want her to move to Australia. Can't happen. Uh-uh.

I drive over to her place straight after work, hoping to catch her there. I knock on the door of her flat, test the doorknob, and enter, since it's unlocked. I find not just Elle, but also Gabby and Joe. They are all sitting on the settee, and they immediately stop talking as I walk in. Not even a hi. Just silent stares in my direction. Couldn't be more bleeding obvious that they have just been talking about me.

'All right, what have I been up to now?' I ask. Joe, being the gentleman that he is, stands from the settee, and takes up position on the floor, leaning against the wall, so I can sit down. 'Bless you, Joe,' I say, as I sit in between Elle and Gabby in the spot Joe has vacated.

'Tea?' Elle asks quickly and jumps to her feet.

'Please. Then you can tell me what you've just been saying about me, you cow.'

Still silence. Even from Gabby. Now I'm worried.

'How's things with Johnno?' Gabby finally asks, with a broad, fake smile. Elle makes a strange spluttering sound from the kitchen.

'Fine,' I say, turning around to see her quickly focus back on the teas.

'Details!' Gabby cries. I've got to give her something. She'll like this.

'He says he loves me, right down to my pretty little arsehole.' Gabby squeals with delight, Elle proclaims her joy from the kitchen while simultaneously crossing herself, and Joe turns beetroot red and mutters something about his intention to leave.

'Did you say you love him back?' Elle asks, so desperate for me to say yes, she is practically bursting.

I pause, just a little longer than necessary, to build the anticipation. 'Yes.'

'Oh Meg! I'm so proud of you!'

'What about his arsehole?' Gabby asks.

'No. I left that out of the declaration.'

'Booo!' she cries.

'Why do you ask about me and Johnno, anyway?'

'I like to know these things. Your happiness is important to me,' Gabby claims.

'Thanks, Gabby. Now what's the real reason?'

Gabby laughs, then straightens her face. 'Fine, I'll tell you. Joe has tea about Johnno.'

'*Joe* has tea?' I look at Joe. He looks up towards the ceiling, and his lips form a whistling shape, but no sound comes out. 'Joe?' His head snaps back down, as though I've startled him from a daze.

'How do, Meg? Didn't see you come in.'

I cross my arms and give him the most withering look I can manage. 'Taking lessons in lying from Elle?'

'Elle? You don't lie, do you my sweet?' he asks, as Elle places a tea down in front of me on the coffee table, and then sits down beside Joe on the carpet.

'Not when I can avoid it, my love,' she replies. They exchange a smile, and God I wish that Joe would just grow a pair and fuck her right, because they are so damn cute together. And because he is wrapped so damn tightly around her finger that he is going to completely unravel when things finally hit the fan.

'If there is something I should know about Johnno, I suggest you spill it, Joe. I'm sure it's nothing I don't already know anyway,' I say defensively.

'You won't know this,' Joe says. We all look at him. He looks at Elle. 'I'm going to tell her.' Elle and Gabby exchange foreboding looks.

'Tell me what?'

'I had a chat with Johnno on Sunday, when you were in your room talking with Elle about your second cousin and the treason charges. How's that going anyway?'

I shoot daggers at Elle. She gives me an encouraging thumbs up. Cheeky git.

'It will be difficult for the charges to stick.' *To an imaginary person.*

'Good to hear,' Joe says, with far more relief than necessary. 'Anyway, Johnno. Turns out I went to boarding school with the bloke who works for him at the tattoo studio, Peter Wentworth. He was a couple of grades higher up.'

Joe has been in the area his entire life, and he seems to know everyone. If he doesn't know them, he knows someone who knows a friend of someone who knows them. He probably even knows my second cousin.

'How on earth did you work that out, Joe?'

'He referred to him as Miller. That was his nickname back in high school. I asked a few more questions, and it's the same bloke. He is distinctive, with the missing teeth and all.'

'And?' I'm losing patience.

'Well, Miller...we called him Miller because of that actor.'

'Joe, if you don't get to your point soon, I'm going to strangle it out of you,' I say, and immediately feel bad, because poor Joe cowers.

'You will do no such thing, you bully,' Elle says, and Joe's courage is restored.

'You know the one. From that show where they try to get out of prison,' he says. Still, I have nothing but a blank look for Joe. 'Peter went to juvie in Year 10. Never came back to school. He's been in and out of the slammer since.' Finally, I understand, but Joe feels the need to drive home his point. 'Peter Wentworth. Miller. Aye?'

'Aye,' I say, resignedly.

Johnno is employing a seasoned criminal to work for him. In a tattoo parlour that doesn't seem to perform very many tattoos. That my dad has concerns may be conducting 'other business'. This could explain Johnno's distaste for those in the legal profession. My head is starting to spin. I don't know how long I stare into space before I hear my name called by Gabby.

'Meg, what are you going to do?'

'I-I'm not sure. What— I mean, what am I meant to do? Ask him about it? Does it matter if he's employing a jail bird?' They all stare at me. 'What crimes are we talking about, Joe?'

'Stealing cars, break and enter, that sort of thing,' Joe says. 'But I don't know the whole,' he adds evasively.

'I must admit, I am somewhat…curious…Meg, about how Johnno came to know Mr Wentworth,' Elle says, and I can't help but feel grateful that she added the 'Mr'. Miller, all of sudden, seems dignified and respectable. What she is implying, however, is anything but respectable. 'I don't think he would have dropped in a resume at the shop, do you?' she asks gently.

'Spell it out, Elle,' I say.

'It just makes me wonder if, perhaps— I could be wrong, of course, and I pray that I am. Johnno may have encountered Miller in p-r-i-s-o-n.' She presses her lips together after she says it, and I know it was hard for her to make the accusation. Still, she's pushed my buttons.

'Excuse me, Elle Adams! You think that Johnno would have been to p-r-i-s-o-n and not *told* me that little detail?'

'Of course, you're right, my love,' she says, quickly back tracking. 'I just wondered, that's all. But you know me, I have an active imagination. I have you and Johnno already fleeing to Russia together on the back of his motorbike.'

I can't bring myself to smile. Because if I'm honest, I have no confidence whatsoever that she isn't right. I know barely anything about what Johnno has been doing for the past, well— I know barely anything about his past. What I do know is that he has a strong distaste for lawyers, he has very limited access to his daughter, he wasn't there when he needed to be when she was growing up, and he seems quite confident he could hide a body. Is it the detective novel we've been reading at Book Club, or does this all mean something? And am I kidding myself that I know nothing about his past? Maybe I know a lot more than I'm willing to admit.

'Wouldn't work, my love,' says Joe to Elle.

'What wouldn't?' she asks.

'Russia. They'd have to cross the English Channel. Can't do it on a motorbike.'

'I'm sure they can, Joe. Johnno would find a way.'

Joe shrugs. 'That's not all. They don't speak Russian.'

'For Heaven's sake, Joe! They'd learn fast enough. And they'd have each other, so what would it matter?' Elle says with frustration.

'Seems a bit daft to me.'

'Of course it would,' Elle mumbles, and gets a pettish look on her face. Joe reaches over and gives her a peck on the lips, and he receives a coy smile in return. Then he gets slowly to his feet. 'I've got to get going, my love. Farm tomorrow?'

'Yes, I'll see you then,' she says. Joe pulls her to her feet, then gives each of us a peck on the cheek, before taking his leave. Gabby also decides she's had enough of us, and goes to her room, and Elle sits down on the opposite end of the settee to me.

Finally, I can return to the original aim of my visit. I push Johnno to the back of my mind.

Elle, in a blatantly obvious attempt to avoid the conversation she must know is coming, says, 'Telly?' and switches it on.

I ignore the question, and ask, 'Does Gabby know?'

'About Russia?'

'Elle.'

Elle sighs. 'Yes. I told her this morning.'

'And?'

'She wasn't happy.'

I feel vindicated.

'Neither am I, Elle.'

'I know. You made that clear on Sunday. But I haven't changed my mind. It's the only way.'

'It is absolutely not the only way. You can talk to Joe. You can kindly and gently break it to him that you love him as a friend, you don't want to lose him, but you don't want to marry him.'

'No can do,' says Elle stubbornly. 'Besides, I *want* to go to Australia. It will be fun. Sun, sand, diverse wildlife—'

'—You're scared of *cats*.'

Elle ignores me and continues. 'I'm thinking Queensland for a start. Did you know they call it the sunshine state? It's even on their number plates. Doesn't that sound just wonderful? And on the tourism website they claim the weather is beautiful one day; the next, perfect. Such confidence in their meteorological superiority—'

'Elle, please. I don't want you to go. I love you. What will I do without you? You're my only friend.'

'Rubbish, Meg. You'll have Gabby, and Joe, and Johnno. You don't need me. I'm practically cramping your style these days.'

'You're not.'

'And you know, with netball not working out, there really is nothing keeping me here—'

'I'm *nothing* to you now?'

Elle looks at me, then reaches across and places her hand over mine. 'Of course not. I love you dearly, Meg. You know that. But I need to do this. For me, and for Joe.'

I growl. 'Elle! You have the nerve to call Joe a coward, but you—' I stop suddenly, because, inspired by Elle's cowardice, an equally cowardly plan has just formed in my own mind, to address my own problem without meeting it front on.

'Meg?' I look at Elle. 'You were about to call me some names, I believe.'

'That can wait. I know what I'm going to do.'

'About?'

'Johnno.'

***

'Let me get this straight. You're going to go to R.J. Ink and ask for a tattoo, to test whether it is an actual tattoo studio?'

'Yes.'

'And you assume that if the business isn't legitimate, Johnno won't let a man nicknamed Miller, because of that prison show, come at you with a needle?'

'Correct.'

'And if he *does*?'

'Then it must be a legitimate tattoo studio, and I will have some fun new ink to prove it.'

'And if it *isn't* a legitimate studio, and Johnno still lets Miller tattoo you, and it's a complete disaster...'

I gulp. 'I'll cross that bridge when I come to it. But I'm sure it won't come to it, because Johnno won't do that, and everything will be perfectly above board.'

'Of course,' Elle says, and gives me a supportive smile. 'What will you ask for?'

I consider the question for a moment. I have a fae character I've drawn that I am favouring for my next tattoo, but it is quite intricate. I want to test Miller, but I also don't want my design to be cocked up. Something simple would be better. But nothing too personal.

'I've been wanting an owl. Just the face. I think I'll ask for that.'

'Do you want me to come with you, my love?'

Bless her heart. 'No. I'll do this alone. But be ready for the debrief.'

Chapter Twenty-Three

I have kept my cards close to my chest all week. When I've seen Johnno, I've made no mention of wanting a new tattoo, or of the intel I have received about Miller. Johnno surely must have realised that Joe's knowledge about Miller would make its way to me, but he hasn't said a word. I find it reassuring that he isn't concerned. Perhaps he has nothing to hide.

I have decided on Saturday morning to go to the shop. I couldn't bring myself to pull another sickie, and then risk being seen downtown. I get dressed in jeans and a singlet top, and I'm just about to pull a sweater on over the top when my bedroom door opens, and Elle comes in.

'All right?'

'What are you doing here?' I ask and accept a kiss on the cheek.

'I know you said you didn't want me to come—'

'—That's how I remember it.'

'—but I thought I should. Just in case. I won't come in with you, but I will wait outside, and if it seems like things are taking too long, or you signal for help, I will come to your aid.'

From her handbag, she pulls a small red object on a key chain and hands it to me.

'Don't pull the chain. It will set off an alarm. But if you get into trouble, I will hear it.'

'Isn't this going a little overboard, Elle?'

'I hope so, my love. But in case you are about to uncover a major underground criminal operation, and Johnno decides he has to un-alive you to keep his secrets safe, I think you should take it. Better safe than sorry.'

'Quite,' I say meekly. 'If that *is* the case though, I may need a rescuer who can withstand a harsher attack than ferocious tickling.'

Elle giggles. 'If they tickle me, we are both done for, my love.'

I purse my lips, and then give Elle a hug. 'Let's hope it doesn't come to that then.'

***

The bell tinkles as I walk through the door of R.J. Ink. I've instructed Elle to wait just down the street, on a bench seat, and I have her alarm in my pocket— just in case. No one is in the studio, but a moment later, Miller comes through a doorway that must conceal the steps to the upper level, where Johnno said he and Miller live.

I receive a welcoming smile from Miller that makes my insides curdle.

'All right?' he says. 'I'll call the guvnor.' He goes back out the back, and I hear him call out, and then the sound of heavy footsteps descending from upstairs.

Johnno comes through the doorway, and his eyes soften as he sees me.

'Meg, what are you doing here?' he asks, as he comes towards me. I meet him halfway and reach my arms around his neck as he wraps his arms around me. 'Miller, go out for a bit,' he says, as Miller comes back through the door as well and stands, watching us.

'Actually, perhaps Miller should stay.' Nervously, I take the folded piece of paper from my pocket with the owl design on it. I try to still my shaking hands and manage to do so well enough that it is barely perceptible. 'I was wondering if you could help me with this?'

Johnno takes the paper from me and unfolds it. He looks at me.

'What do you want me to do?'

'I'd like a tattoo, on my arm. Here.' I roll up the right sleeve of my sweater and point to a space about the size of a bottle top. 'Just a small one. I know I should have booked, but I was hoping you could squeeze me in.'

Johnno doesn't say anything. He looks at the picture, then at Miller, who is smiling broadly.

'Come here,' he says gruffly to Miller. Miller comes over. He hands him the picture. 'Can you do this?'

'Aye, guvnor.'

Johnno narrows his eyes at Miller, and Miller's smile broadens a little further. 'You sure?'

'Aye, piece o' cake.'

Johnno continues to stare at Miller, then drags his eyes away and back to me. He nods his head at the plinth.

'Sit down.'

I move to the plinth and sit down on the edge, and Johnno pulls Miller over to the reception desk, where he speaks to him quietly. I can't hear what is said. None of this is filling me with confidence, and I have half a mind to back out. But if I do that, my question remains unanswered. I won't know if Johnno would have let me go through with it, and I won't know if Miller is really a tattoo artist.

The conversation finishes, and Johnno comes over to me. 'Are you sure about this baby? There's better places you can get this done.'

Better places? 'Yes, but you're my…love interest.'

'So that's what I am.'

'Yes. And given that, I would feel disloyal to go anywhere else.'

'Disloyal,' Johnno repeats, more to himself than to me. Miller approaches with a clipboard and some forms. Standard practice. Probably medical details and a disclaimer. 'Put that away,' Johnno says curtly.

'But you say they always need to sign the—'

'—Not needed for Meg,' Johnno says.

Miller raises his eyebrows.

'Because if you fuck this up, I'm going away for a long time. For your fucking murder. Put it away.'

Miller laughs. 'I won't fuck it up. Nowt to worry about. I've done hundreds of 'em. Never fucked one up in my life.'

Miller starts to gather supplies and put them onto the small metal trolley on wheels that sits nearby. I notice he takes out a pair of medium size gloves first, then takes them off, puts them in the bin, and takes out a large pair from the next box. I can't help but think it bodes ill that he doesn't know his glove size.

Finally, he is ready. Everything is gathered, and as Miller sits down on a wheeled stool, and rolls himself towards me, I know I can't go ahead with it. I have zero confidence that this man knows what he is doing. Johnno is standing beside me with his hands in his pockets, but he can't stand still. He is rocking from foot to foot, and every now and then, he turns around in a circle, as though he wants to walk away, and then brings himself back.

Miller picks up a razor, and a piece of gauze, and grins at me. How much further will I allow this to go? And more to the point, how much further will Johnno allow it to go?

'Do you mind if I do it, Miller?' I ask.

'Go on then.' He hands me the razor.

'Do you have any lotion?'

Miller picks up a bottle from the trolley and hands it to me. I apply some lotion to my arm and shave the area. Still, Johnno says nothing. I hand the razor back to Miller. He wipes my arm with the gauze. The alcohol stings as he pats the area down.

Miller picks up the tattoo machine and, looking at me with that same grin on his face that has been there since he found out he was going to be allowed to maim me, pulls the trigger, making it buzz. No more terrifying sight have I ever seen, nor even imagined.

I'm about to put an end to it, but before I can, Johnno says, 'Stop.' I look at him. His cheeks are red. He runs a hand through his hair. 'Miller, take off for fifteen.'

'What?!' Miller says, his face dropping. 'I was about to get started.'

'It's not happening,' Johnno says.

'Aargh,' Miller says, and drops the machine back down in disgust. He pulls off his gloves, tosses them in the bin, and with a scowl at Johnno, he walks out, mumbling under his breath.

I don't say anything for a moment. I pull my sleeve down. I'm sure Johnno knows. He knows that I know. But still, he says nothing. It is me who eventually breaks the silence.

'Miller isn't qualified, is he?'

Johnno shakes his head, and perches on the plinth beside me. 'He knows what he's doing though.'

'Where did he learn to give tattoos?'

'Self-taught.'

'I see,' I say quietly. I'm disappointed. I had hoped for the truth. As much as I am glad he didn't let me go through with it, I feel I deserve better than this.

But then Johnno surprises me. 'He learned in prison.' My heart quickly stirs at the fact that he has admitted that much, at least, but then quickly falls again as I realise he has just confirmed my fears. Without a legitimate tattoo artist, his business can not be legitimate.

'How is it that he comes to be working for you?'

'I encountered him when I was setting up the shops. He said he could do tattoos. I asked him to do one for me. He didn't fuck it up, so I employed him. He had no chance of getting a job anywhere else with his record.'

I am shaking again, and I don't even know why, but my hand goes into my pocket, and I clutch the alarm Elle gave me.

'When you say you encountered him,' I ask tentatively, 'how did that come about?'

Johnno's jaw tenses. He stands up, his hands go in his pockets, and he walks away from me. When he turns around, his green eyes are hard, and cold.

'Don't you encounter people Meg?'

He is between me and the doorway, and that fucking frightens me right now. I slide my feet to the ground and start to move towards the door. I resolve that if he tries to stop me, I will press the alarm. I keep my eyes on him. I don't want to turn my back, so I end up side-stepping.

'Meg,' he says. He takes a step towards me, and I try to pull the cord on the alarm, but it's difficult one handed and my fingers fumble. In that moment, his eyes soften, and he reaches for me. I let go of the alarm and fall into his arms. 'I'm sorry. I should've told you straight up.'

'Yes.' I look up at him, and stroke the side of his face, feeling his rough stubble beneath my fingers. 'You can trust me.'

'I know.' He bends to kiss me. 'But some things, it's better you don't know.'

I frown and search his eyes. 'I want to know everything about you.'

He kisses me again. 'Once I've sorted my shit out, you will, sweetheart.'

I let Johnno kiss me some more, and I secure a promise that I will see him tonight. Then I leave the store, deeply troubled.

Elle jumps up as I walk down the footpath towards her. I can see the concern on her face as she tries to read mine.

'What happened? I saw Miller come out, and I knew you mustn't have gone through with it.'

I fill Elle in on what happened, and what I now know about Miller. Which isn't a whole lot more than we already suspected. When I'm finished Elle looks sober, which is unusual for her.

'Are you and Johnno OK?' she asks.

'Yes. For now. But there is more he isn't telling me. I need to know it all.'

Elle furrows her brow. 'What would Detective Martin do?' I roll my eyes, but Elle is undeterred. 'I know! He would seek collateral information, from others known to the suspect. Who else do you know who might know something about Johnno?'

'You know that's a pointless question, Elle,' I say testily. 'The only person I know who knew Johnno before me is Shaelea, and I can't speak to her.'

We walk in silence back to where Elle has parked her car at the end of the block. We are about to get in, when Elle stops.

'Of course!'

'Of course, what?'

'You can't talk to Shaelea, but what about James? They spent a lot of time together when she was here. Perhaps she told him something.'

God, she's right. Why didn't I think of that? 'Perhaps. With a bribe, I might get something out of him.'

'We'll stop at the shop on the way back to your place,' says Elle, and she smiles at me in a way that makes me think it will all be OK.

***

James isn't at home when we get there, but we manage to locate him at the park just down the road. He has his football, and he is juggling it on his feet as we pull up. When he sees Elle's car, he quickly catches it, straightens up and swipes his hand back through his hair.

'All right, James?' Elle says brightly as we get out of the car.

'How do?' he says with a smile, and a blush.

'I do very nicely, thank you. Fancy a packet of crisps and a Jaffa cake?'

James's face lights up. He doesn't know what he's done to secure this good fortune. Nothing yet.

'Go on, then.'

Elle's face transforms, and suddenly, she is Detective Elle Adams, relentless in her pursuit of the truth.

'Well, young man, tell us everything you know about Mr Reed 'Johnno' Johnson, and it shall be yours.'

James looks startled. Elle's transformation to detective has triggered James's transformation into unwilling informant with much to hide. He shakes his head.

'I don't know nuffink about nuffink,' he says. Elle stalks closer to him. 'I swear,' he adds, which only confirms that he knows something.

'We can do this the easy way,' says Elle, 'or the hard way.'

'W-what does the hard way involve?' James asks, backing away.

'Let me tell you about the easy way first. You give us the knowledge we seek, and we give you the snacks.' She tries to circle James, but he continues to back away, so they are doing some strange sort of dance together. 'The hard way— well— if death by tickle is the way you want to go, then that can be arranged.'

James shakes his head quickly. 'N-no. That's not the way I want to go.'

'Wise choice—' says Elle, but I interrupt.

'I'll take it from here, Detective Adams.'

Elle looks at me, disappointed, but submits to her superior. 'Fine, Detective Drury. But if tickling is required, I'm your girl.' She throws a warning glance at James, who giggles nervously, and then she takes up position behind my left shoulder, with her arms crossed.

What the hell. I might as well get in character as well. I fold my arms and start to pace back and forwards as I speak.

'I understand you are acquainted with a Miss Shaelea...' Fuck, I don't know her surname. 'With Miss Shaelea.'

'Maybe,' says James, with a defiant lift of his chin. 'Who's asking?'

'Never you mind. Did Miss Shaelea ever mention her father's line of work?'

'He's in the tattoo business.'

'I see. And before that?'

'I don't know,' says James. 'Shaelea said she barely knows him.'

I stamp my foot. 'She must have told you *something*, James.' James squirms, and his eyes look up and to the right. As a reluctant reader of detective novels, I recognise this as a sign of withholding information.

'She said I can't tell you. She said if I do, Johnno will kill her.'

'I'm sure she didn't mean literally.' But I don't think even I'm a hundred percent convinced. James doesn't look like he is going to budge. He drops his football down to his feet and starts to juggle it from foot to foot again.

'James!' I say, my impatience getting the better of me. 'If you know something— anything— about Johnno's past, I have to know. *Especially* if it's something bad.'

James keeps kicking until he loses control of the ball. He lets it roll away.

'Fine. Shaelea barely knows Johnno because he wasn't around when she was growing up.'

'Yes, and?'

'Because he was in jail. That's why she hates him.'

Inside, my world comes crashing down, but I won't let it show in front of my brother. I feel Elle's hand on my shoulder. I manage to say, 'Fine,' then I turn and head quickly towards Elle's car.

'Sorry, Meg,' James calls after me, but I can't respond, and I can't look back. I get into the car, and as soon as I'm there, I lean forward on the dash and burst into tears. I feel so betrayed. How could he keep something this big from me? Elle gets into the driver's seat and wraps her arms around me. I sink into her hug, and let my tears soak into her t-shirt.

'There were opportunities to tell me.' My voice breaks with sobs.

'I know,' Elle says gently. She strokes my hair. 'He should have told you.'

'He said he loves me.'

'I'm sure he does.'

'I don't even know him. I don't know what he's done. It could be anything.'

'You need to ask him, my love,' Elle says.

'I never want to see him again,' though, I know even as I say it that it isn't true.

'Shh, it hurts, I know.'

'Dad tried to warn me. I feel like such a fool.'

'You haven't heard his side. You love him. You're not a fool for trusting someone you love, Meg. You need to give him the chance to explain.' I pull back and look at Elle, then wish I hadn't. Her eyes, so soft, so compassionate, make me start sobbing again. 'I see the way he looks at you. And I know you wouldn't fall in love with a bad man, Meg.'

She knows exactly what to say. Her faith in me settles me. 'I'll talk to him. Tonight.'

Chapter Twenty-Four

Elle stayed for the rest of the day. She went home at five, and I expect Johnno at around seven. She left the alarm with me. I don't think I will need to use it in my own home, but I think Elle felt better with me having it.

I am nervous as hell about the conversation we need to have. I have been teary all day, and I can't bring myself to dress in anything better than a pair of black tracksuit bottoms and a sweater.

I meet Johnno out the front. I can't bear him speaking to my family until I know what he has done. I feel guilty enough that he has been around to dinner, played with my younger brothers, been in our home, before I even knew who he was.

When he arrives, he is tense. He gives me a gentle kiss on the lips in greeting, then follows me into the house and to my room. I sit down on my bed, with my pillow propped against the bed head, and hug my knees to my chest. Johnno sits down on the side of the bed. He has left his hair down. It softens his appearance. He, too, has worn tracksuit bottoms, and I can't help but think about how nice it would be to snuggle in the bed together all night, and run my hands through his hair while he does all the wonderful things he is so good at doing to my body. And my heart. My heart is heavily involved here.

I can't afford to get too attached to these thoughts.

'Things weren't right with us when you left this morning,' Johnno says. He bends his knee and rests it on the bed and turns his body to me. 'You were upset with me.'

'I was.' *Be honest.* 'I am.' Johnno lowers his head. I reach for his hand and bring it to my lips. I kiss it, allowing my lips to linger on his skin for just a moment, while I try to embed the memory in my mind. It might be the last time I feel it. 'I don't want to be. But I need you to start being honest with me. About your past.'

'The past isn't important. The future is what matters. That's you and me.'

I shake my head. 'I need to know who you are. We have no future without that.'

The tension in his body, and his face is obvious. I want to relieve it, at the same time as I want to tear him to pieces for still holding out on me.

'I never meant to keep it from you.' His eyes come up to meet mine, and they are sincere. 'I didn't expect to fall in love with you as quickly as I did. Once I did, I just...I couldn't tell you. I didn't want to lose you.'

Still, he doesn't tell me. 'Tell me what?' I ask gently. My eyes close as I wait for the answer.

'The longest was five years. That was when I met Miller. Moorland Prison. I was in and out for years before that. A bit longer each time.'

Five years. OK. You don't get five years for murder. Or manslaughter. That is, if one gets caught, one would certainly get longer. But one who is skilled at hiding bodies...

'What did you do?' I ask through the tears that have started again, against my will. If it has anything to do with women or children, we are over. I brace myself, and hope his crimes are somewhat palatable.

'Not important,' Johnno says shortly.

Wrong answer, Johnno. 'I disagree.' Johnno says nothing. He just looks at me, stubbornly. I want to wring his neck. 'Fine. I was hoping you would tell me. I was hoping you might finally choose to be honest. But if not, you should leave.'

'Meg—'

'—I can't trust you if I don't know what you've done.'

He doesn't move. As I consider my options for his removal, he says, 'Fine.' He sighs and rubs his hands across his face. 'It started when Mum was sick. We had no money. Life was shit. I started shop lifting so I could give Mum things, to cheer her up. She thought Dad was giving me the money. I hid it all from Dad. It started small, but I guess the more I did it the bolder I got. Mum died, and I got mixed up in something with a few lads I went to school with. Didn't realise until too late what they were up to. Ended up being charged with looting. I had a couple of minor offences already, so I got a few months.'

'How old were you?'

'Seventeen.'

So, he got his first tattoo in prison.

'After that, I stole a car. Got a year. Met some people inside who I ended up selling drugs for when I got out. Got caught doing that. Couple of years there. Shortly after I got out that time, I got into an argument with some guys about some...stuff. I set a car on fire. Got five years for arson. I was released three years ago. I've stayed out of trouble since then.'

Arson. Theft. Drugs. Stuff. It is a real moment of personal discovery when you find yourself weighing whether your love interest's crimes are palatable or not. All I know so far is, I can't look at him. I can't look at those magical green eyes that so recently made me so happy. I can't associate them with what I now know.

'No women?' I choke out.

'I've never laid a finger on a woman who didn't want me to,' he growls.

'You are in my home. I have a right to ask.'

Johnno stands up and starts to pace with agitation. He puts his hands behind his head, then drops them again. Then before I know anything about it, he sits down beside me and takes my face between his hands, forcing me to look at him. I close my eyes tightly to avoid it.

'Meg, look at me.' When I refuse, he says it again, with urgency. I open them, and I know straight away what I was afraid of. As soon as I look into his eyes, I know I still love him, despite everything he has told me. It would be simpler if I didn't. If I could just end it and be done. Instead, I have to choose between what my heart is telling me it wants, and what my head is telling me to do. 'Do you love me?'

Fuck. I don't want to answer right now.

'Meg!' he almost shouts. 'I'm the same man I was before you knew all of this. I've made mistakes. I *make* mistakes. But nothing has changed.' He repeats the question. 'Do you love me?'

'Yes,' I whisper.

He exhales, and I realise he had been holding his breath waiting for the answer. 'Then you need to know everything.'

***

Somehow, I let him kiss me. I let him turn off the light, take his shirt off and get into bed beside me. I lie down beside him, and I let his legs intertwine with mine. I let my fingers lace through his hair, and I enjoy it as his hand moves to the back of my neck and kneads my tense muscles. How easy it would be to bring him closer. To let his centre meet mine, to feel him harden, and let him inside me. But I need to know everything.

His hands continue to rub my neck, as he starts to talk.

'When I came out, I had nothing. No money. No prospects of making money. No home. Dad wanted nothing to do with me.

'I couch-surfed for a while with friends. Acquaintances. Anyone who would have me. I ended up staying with some guys who I'd met on the inside. They put a proposition to me— if I would be willing to open some shop fronts, they would finance it.

'I knew Miller was due to come out soon too, and if he didn't have a place to stay, and a way to make money, he'd be back inside within a week. That was the pattern he was in. I wanted to give him a chance. So I agreed to open the shop up here in Leeds, and employ Miller.'

Alarm bells are sounding. I am totally out of my depth in attempting to understand what Johnno is telling me. But this, I know. If the shops were financed by people he met on the inside, there is a very high chance they are not avid tattoo studio investors.

'They didn't care what the business was, as long as they could handle the books.'

The alarm bells stop, and are replaced by emergency sirens, rapidly closing in. I feel like I can't even breath.

'My intention was to get the tattoo side of the business thriving, so I didn't have to rely on those guys anymore. I could pay them back the start-up costs and take it all over. Make it legit. But with Miller not being properly qualified...it hasn't worked out. The franchise in London is the same. I've got an ex-inmate working down there too. Talented guy, but business is slow.

'I went into it with my eyes open. I know whatever they're using the business for is shady as fuck. But I got into it just wanting to survive and do something to help other guys when they came out. It wasn't meant to be forever. Guys like Miller just don't know what to do on the outside, so they keep on fucking up. The same way I was. They need a chance, but no one will employ them once they've been inside. I'm all too aware of that. I thought if I had a successful business, in something they were good at, I could help even a few of the guys who get stuck like that. But now, *I'm* stuck. I can't get out. I can't turn a profit, except with the stuff I don't even want to know about. The stuff that pays my wage and keeps a roof over my head.'

'Johnno,' I whisper, because I don't know what else to say. 'This isn't good.'

'I know. But Meg, listen. I want to sort it out. I'd give anything to sort it out. I don't want to bail completely, and I can't anyway. I'd be dead, because I can't pay them back. I only have money because they pay me.

'Right before I met you, I was starting to seriously think about running. Just leaving it all behind. I decided that after my two weeks with Shae, I'd go. I knew I'd never be able to see her again, but I was feeling that hopeless...but then I met you, and I saw your drawings, on the envelope. I felt so drawn to you. I forgot about running. This morning, after you left, I pulled that envelope out— your premium's gone up by the way— and I thought of something. You.'

'What about me?'

'You can help.'

I am dumbfounded. Surely, he must know I won't be touching this train wreck with a ten-foot pole.

'Sorry?'

'Your drawings. You're so talented, Meg. Your designs are unique, and beautiful. They would bring people in. I can afford to get Miller trained, but he'll never have your creativity. He's got a steady hand though, and he could work off a stencil.'

'Johnno, surely you must know I can't get involved in this.'

'I would keep you safe. I'd never let anything happen to you. We just display your designs, and you get a cut for any that get taken up.'

I shake my head. 'This is crazy. How could I do this without being implicated? I know too much already, with what you've just told me.'

'There's no proof you know anything. It's all verbal. You deny it.'

Simple as that. Silly Meg. You're totally overreacting. It's all verbal. That means it doesn't really exist. My love interest *isn't* the face of an illegal money laundering operation. Because it's all verbal.

'I'm sorry, Johnno. I would do it for free if I thought there was a way it could be done without ending up in disaster. But there's just no way. I can't help you.' And that's not all. *But how the hell do I say this?* How do I tell the man I love that I can't be with him anymore? That the percentage has just dropped well below the eighty required for a successful relationship. I have to make a decision fast, because the lump that had temporarily subsided from my throat is returning. 'I can't help you, and I can't be with you anymore. I'm sorry. I love you, but this...I just can't.'

'Meg, please. Don't do this.'

The desperation in his voice almost breaks me. Almost.

'This conversation never happened. But you need to go. Now.' Johnno stands, puts his shirt on, and grabs his things. He heads for the door. 'No,' I say. He looks back at me, with hope. 'Through the window. Not past Mum and Dad.' The hope disappears, and Johnno disappears, through my bedroom window. I cry myself to sleep.

Chapter Twenty-Five

I wake Sunday morning and don't bother to look at myself in the mirror. I know my eyes will be bloodshot, and my cheeks will be tear-stained. I will be pure misery in human form. I pull on a pair of tracksuit pants and a sweater and throw my hair up in a messy ponytail. It's past 9am. My stomach is hollow, but I barely have an appetite. I know I need to eat something though, so I hope to sneak into the kitchen unseen.

As my luck would have it, Mum, Dad, James and Harry are all in the kitchen when I arrive. Mum greets me with a sunny smile and a kiss on the cheek and then, immediately, I see the worry come into her eyes.

'Breakfast, my love?' she asks.

My mouth is dry when I try to speak. 'I'll take some cereal and eat in my room.'

'I'll fix it for you. A bowl for Johnno as well?'

'No,' is all I can bring myself to say.

'Will we see him later, for lunch?'

Mum is just being nosy now. 'No.'

'I see.'

Everyone is staring at me. I don't have the energy to care. I take a glass down from the cabinet above the stove and fill it from the water dispenser in the fridge door while Mum prepares a bowl of cornflakes for me. I thank her and disappear with it to my room.

I do nothing with the morning. Just lie on my bed and think. There is no indecision in my mind. There was only one choice I could make. But it hurts and hurts and hurts, and my mind wants nothing but to revel in that pain, as though it's a way of making me believe it was all real, and for a brief time, it was beautiful. I wonder how long I will cling to this pain. It hasn't been 24 hours yet, but I can't envisage it ending any time soon.

I drift off to sleep around 11am. A self-defence mechanism, so I don't have to think about my family out there together at lunch, talking about my misfortune. James will probably tell them what he knows. They will discuss how they all could see it coming. Dad will shake his head, full of disappointment. Mum will say I should have stuck to the nice, nameless young man who took me out for Greek, or was it Italian? Harry will say, 'Can I have Meg's potatoes?' and they will all laugh, and playfully scold him, and life will move on, bleak and Johnno-less.

When I wake up, it's after three, and it is Dad who knocks quietly and opens the door, as I knew he would around this time.

'Tea, Meggy?'

'No, thank-you.'

He comes in, cautiously, and sits down on the bed. The pillow is damp with fresh tears. I'm sure he notices. 'You and Johnno aren't seeing each other anymore?'

'That's right.'

'I'm sorry.' He's so sombre, but I feel nothing but resentment.

'Don't be. You were right about him.' And I turn my back on my lifeline. The one who has been there since I was a little girl, standing by my shoulder, picking up pieces and putting them back together when necessary, with calm, measured support and love. Because I can't stand the fact that he was right about this.

Dad stands. 'If you need to talk, you know I'm always here.'

My tears start to flow again, and I can't respond. I let him leave.

***

Somehow, I force myself through Monday. If once I was a horny ghost, haunting the aisles of the library, levitating with lust, now I am a corpse in chains. Heavy, iron chains, dragging behind my body so every step is effortful, and my eyes convey a death so gruesome that everyone who encounters me cowers in fright.

I seem to have some divine control over the weather, because the skies are drizzly, and it is cooler than it has been in weeks. The cold, dreary weather tends to lower overall traffic at the library. Most people aren't motivated enough by fresh reading material to leave the comfort of their home. However, we see an increase in toddlers, whose mothers, desperate to leave the confines of their house, and not having the option of the parks and playgrounds, take refuge in the library, and our odoriferous alphabet rug.

Hour by hour limps by, until four, when I am finally unshackled, and I can go and see Elle. I drive straight to her flat after work. The door is unlocked when I get there, so I walk right in. Elle looks up quickly from where she is sitting at the dining table, with her glasses on and papers spread all around her. Hurriedly, she closes her laptop and places a book on top of some of the papers, in a lame attempt at concealing that she is doing something she feels guilty about.

'All right, Meg?' she says brightly, but her face drops as she takes me in. 'Oh, my love.' She gets to her feet and wraps me in her arms. That's it. Any semblance of composure is gone, and I crumble as she holds me. 'Tell me everything.'

She drags me to the sofa, we sit, and I tell her every detail. Every word that passed between us. There is no point hiding anything from Elle. She has been by my side through it all. I even tell her about the business but swear her to take it to her grave. She revels in the dramatic nature of the vow. By the time I'm done, my tears have dried, and in their place is just a hollow, dry-eyed nothingness. Elle doesn't say a lot, just listens, and offers consoling touch.

Finally, she asks, 'Are you sure, Meg?'

I can do nothing but stare at her in disbelief.

'Am I *sure*? That I can't be with a man whose criminal record is longer than my overdue loans history?'

'He hasn't *hurt* anyone...as such.'

'Your faith in humanity is disturbing, Elle.'

'No. My faith isn't in humanity. It's in you, Meg. You believed in him, so I do too.'

'I didn't know him!' I protest. 'And he is in so deep, it's only a matter of time before...' I can't say it. He's going back in. How can he not?

'But it was for survival, and to provide a lifeline to those who needed it.'

'Boo-fucking-hoo.'

'Meg! I don't believe you,' Elle says. I can't believe she is scolding me about this. Common sense has completely deserted her in the name of hopeless— no, senseless— romanticism.

We are interrupted by the door opening, and Gabby entering the flat. I give Elle a warning look, and mouth, 'to your grave,' and she nods her understanding.

Gabby doesn't bother with a greeting, but just frowns, and says, 'God Meg, when's the Armageddon?'

'Shush, Gabby,' says Elle, and distorts her face to convey that John-no and I are no more.

'I don't know what you're trying to tell me, Elle, but if the wind changes you will be horribly disfigured.' Gabby walks to the dining table and picks the book up that Elle had placed over her paperwork. As she absent-mindedly looks at the cover, Elle jumps to her feet, and the guilty expression is back.

'What are you doing?' she asks.

Gabby looks up. 'Nothing.' As she notices Elle's anxiety, her eyes narrow. She looks back at the book, then at the table. She picks up the top sheet of paper.

'What's this?' It's not a question. It's an accusation.

'Nothing,' Elle says. It's clearly something. Elle is flustered.

'417 Visa?'

'I had to start the process. It takes time and I need it sorted so I can secure a job for next year.'

'What the fuck?' Gabby shouts. 'We've talked about this. You're not going.'

'We have talked about it Gabby, but you're not listening. I'm going. I'm not getting married. It's my life, and this is what I'm doing with it.'

'No,' Gabby says, shaking her head. Her jaw is stubbornly set, and she is completely uncompromising. She holds up the sheet between two hands, and for a moment I think she is going to tear it, but Elle vaults over the back of the sofa and snatches it from her hands before she can.

'Gabby, enough! You must see you can't stop me.'

'Meg! Speak to her!' Gabby orders. All the while I have been watching them go at it, my blood has been quietly boiling. The last 48 hours are coming at me in a rush. The pain of losing someone I love, compounded now by the prospect of losing another. I'm not thinking straight, I know, but I have no capacity to act rationally right now. Gabby is staring at me, willing me to speak. Willing me to change Elle's mind like she hasn't been able to. I see her desperation, and internally, I am mirroring it. But externally...

I stand. I feel my eyes blaze as I look at Elle. When I speak, my tone is cold. It sounds controlled. It isn't. It is unbridled desperation. But ice cold.

'How can you be so selfish?'

Elle's face changes from stubborn petulance to wide-eyed shock.

'Excuse me?'

'You. You pushed me towards Johnno. When I was reluctant, you interfered. You've championed him when a rational person, with my best interests at heart, would have told me to walk away. And now, now, you are going to hurt a perfectly kind, loving partner, who can give you everything you want and more, and for what?' I can see I'm breaking her. She's breathing heavily. Her face is flushed. I am too. 'For sex. You fool. Because you can't bring yourself to make love with a gentle, kind soul, because he doesn't "light your fucking fire". He can offer you a home, a family, security, loyalty. A future. And you are turning your back on that, and on us. For sex. Selfish fool.'

Gabby is stunned. Elle is stunned. She looks at Gabby. Gabby clears her throat, glances at me, turns back to Elle, and as tentatively as I have ever heard her speak, she says, 'She's right. You're being selfish.' With even less certainty, but a defiant lift of her chin, she adds, 'You should do something about that.'

Elle's lip quivers, and she runs the few steps to her bedroom door, slamming it behind her. Gabby stands staring at Elle's bedroom door for a moment, then looks at me. I am still too flooded to even cry.

'Well said, Meg. That might have just done the trick,' Gabby says, and she smiles, but even I can see she knows I've gone too far. And if Gabby thinks I've gone too far, I've gone well past the point of too far. I leave, and when I get home, I cry myself to sleep again.

Chapter Twenty-Six

Days start to blend into each other. Tuesday after work, I drag myself to netball training in York, for the godforsaken Yorkshire side. I see Gabby. She has metamorphosised into an even fiercer competitor, and she is relentless at training. She passes harder, and faster in drills than she ever did for Leeds. She doesn't let up, even when I argue that catching is a skill I rarely need to utilise as the last line of defence. When we have brief breaks between drills, she says nothing about Elle, and I don't ask.

It is on Wednesday morning, as I once more drag myself into work, that I am taught one of life's harshest lessons— right when you think things can't get any worse, they often do. Pip intersects me on my way from the staff room to the service desk with the face of a head teacher, and a folded piece of paper in hand.

'Meg. A word in my office,' she says sternly. I follow her towards the rear of the library, and she closes the door of her office behind me but doesn't sit down. She is as stoney-faced as I have ever seen her, and she isn't exactly a ray of sunshine at the best of times.

'I will cut to the chase. I know you haven't been at your best lately, but I am unable to ignore the seriousness of what has come to my attention.'

She hands me the folded piece of paper, and with hands that tremble, betraying my nerves, I unfold it. It's an email, addressed 'to whom it may concern', from a 'janice_the_menace@hotmail.com. Subject line: Book Club.

To Whom it May Concern,

I am writing to express my disappointment at recent changes to the Leeds Library Book Club; an event I, until recently, looked forward to with gusto. I was drawn to the group by the daring title choice, Cloaked Lust, *and the stimulating (no pun intended) conversation it provoked. Few book clubs are bold enough to embrace the dark romance genre. So impressed was I, that I invited along my friends, and Wednesday evenings became the highlight of our week, replacing Contract Bridge, which was dull in comparison.*

Unfortunately, in recent weeks, Book Club has reverted to the same old boring tripe most book clubs are renowned for. I implore you to please speak to the nice young lady with the black hair, who always looks like she's come straight from a funeral and set her back on the right course before I decide I need to get my kicks somewhere else.

Yours sincerely,

Janice M

My fist balls the paper involuntarily as I lift my eyes to meet Pip's. She says nothing. I open my mouth to speak, and nothing comes out but a hitched breath as I try not to cry.

Finally, Pip speaks. 'I searched the title Janice mentions in the library catalogue. Fortunately, we have two copies, as one is out in your name. Several weeks overdue.'

'That, I will happily rectify—'

'Yes. Yes, you will,' Pip says firmly. 'But having now acquainted myself with the contents, you will understand that I will require an explanation, Meg. A strong one. For why I should allow Book Club to continue —'

'As Janice says, Pip, we are back on the straight and narrow. Margy has chosen the current book, and there is nothing titillating about it, let me assure you—'

'—And why I should allow your ongoing employment here, given what can only be described as gross misconduct.'

I swallow hard and try to stop my head from spinning. This can't be happening. First Johnno, then Elle, and now this, my job. Yes, it fell into my lap without me trying, and I whinge about it at every opportunity. But I was born to be a librarian. It suits me down to the ground, and I can't imagine doing anything else.

Pip's voice cuts back into my thoughts. 'I am giving you a week, Meg. There will be no book club this afternoon. Next Tuesday morning, we will meet. Bring your best excuses, and a support person. My decision on that day will be final.' She strides for the door, as tears well in my eyes, but she pauses with her hand on the knob. 'Good luck.'

***

A week to save my job. Seeing out the work week is tough. Being there is a constant reminder of the trouble I am in, and the hopelessness of the situation. There is no explanation. I chose a dirty, filthy book. I did it without telling Pip because I knew she would never allow it. And my proverbial chickens— who am I kidding? They are cocks— are coming home to roost. To make matters worse, the one person who would understand, and may even have an idea to get me out of this situation, isn't talking to me.

Come the weekend, my discomfort is not relieved. My efforts to avoid my family now need to be re-doubled. At home, I'm not a ghost, a zombie, or a corpse. I'm a stealthy beast, with sallow eyes and a milky pallor, stalking its prey— crisps and Twinkies from the pantry— capturing it, and fleeing with it at light-footed, break-neck speed back to my den. There I stay, with the blinds drawn, and a growing collection of crumbs in my bed, as I slowly waste away from a combination of malnutrition and melancholy. My room is starting to smell as odoriferous as the Alphabet rug. A rug I'm sure I will miss once it's no longer a regular feature in my life. I contemplate moving into the boys' cubby to avoid running into Mum when I do washing. But it's starting to get cold, and on top of everything else, I don't need to be cold.

No one even dares to disturb me for Sunday lunch. Dad knocks on Sunday afternoon for tea. I ignore it.

Chapter Twenty-Seven

I haven't told anyone what has happened at work, for obvious reasons. I can't explain the trouble I'm in without explaining what *Cloaked Lust* is and outing myself as a literary deviant. But by Tuesday, I have no choice. I need a support person, and Elle, who still hasn't been in contact, is out of the question.

That's why I decide upon the only other person I can think of who won't pass judgement. In fact, she might even congratulate me. I shoot off a text while I ready for work.

Meg

All right, Gabby? Hoping you might be free this morning. Can you meet me at the library at 9am? x

As expected, she doesn't reply straight away. When she does, it is discouraging.

Gabby

Huh?? x

Meg

Without going into details, I'm in trouble at work. Need a support person for a meeting with my boss. Are you in? x

I watch the three little dots as they pulse on the screen for what feels like forever, before finally, her answer arrives.

Gabby

Could be fun. But wouldn't Elle be better? x

A stabbing feeling hits me in the gut. Yes. Elle would be better. Elle would be amazing. Elle would charm the pants off Pip, and I would keep my job.

Meg

You will do. Meet me there at 9am. Don't be late x

***

To my relief, Gabby turns up at five to nine, and she looks the part. Or at least, she thinks she does.

'A suit? Really, Gabby?'

'Don't you think it has lawyer vibes?' she says proudly and straightens her jacket.

'It does. Yes,' I agree, without enthusiasm.

'Is that what you're wearing?' she asks, looking me up and down. In comparison to what I've been turning up to work in lately, I thought I'd done quite well. My blouse, with skinny jeans and flats. I've even straightened my hair. 'Do you want to borrow my jacket?'

'No. I'll pass. But...' I take a puff of a breath, 'Thanks for being here, Gabby.'

'Don't thank me,' she says, and she glances at her phone, before stuffing it into her pocket. 'Now, which one is your boss? I'll start the intimidation tactics now to soften her up.'

Right on cue, Pip comes from her office, an unforgiving look on her face. She strides in our direction and then beckons us with a jerk of her wrist to follow her into the conference room, where Book Club is usually held. I start to follow, but Gabby grabs my hand.

'Wait. Meg, you can't go in there like that.'

'Like what?' I ask, impatience slipping into my tone. Perhaps I would have been better off alone.

'Look at you! Your shoulders are slumped, your head is low. You have given up before you've even begun!' With her hands on both of my shoulders, she pushes them back, straightening my spine. 'Shoulders back, head up, balls of your feet, strong posture. Come on, girl! You know how to defend.'

'This is my job! Not netball, Gabby,' I say with exasperation.

'It doesn't matter. You have to move with confidence, Meg. Fake it until you make it and then fake it some more. This isn't over yet. Whatever you've done— very curious to know what it is, by the way— you have to fight. You like this job, don't you?'

'I do,' I admit, and I straighten a little further. I suppose it can't hurt.

Gabby pulls her phone from her pocket once more, glances at it, and puts it away. 'Come on.'

I step into the conference room and see Pip on one side of the long table. She motions for me to sit opposite from her, and I do, before turning around to look for Gabby. To my horror, a different sight meets my eyes.

'Not late, am I?' Bounding into the room, a cocky grin on her face, her blonde hair tied high in a ponytail, is none other than—

'Sophie,' I say darkly. 'What the hell are you doing here?' From the doorway, Gabby gives me a wave and then disappears.

'Gabby said you needed a support person,' Sophie says, and without pause, she makes her way to the table— the opposite side to me— and takes the seat beside Pip. 'Now, why on Earth would little Meg be needing one of those?'

***

I allow Pip the satisfaction of telling my sister all about Book Club, and *Cloaked Lust,* and Sophie soaks it all in with a look of glee on her face.

'Well, well, Meg. Here I thought you were the strait-laced one amongst us,' she says, drumming her fingers together where they rest in front of her on the table. 'I wonder what Mummy and Daddy will say when they find out.'

My blood starts to boil, and I bite down hard on my own tongue to stop myself from firing back at her in front of Pip. As it stands, I still have my job. It may be only for a few moments longer, but I have to hold on to that.

'Meg, I now invite you to say your piece,' Pip says, rather more gently than I was expecting. Perhaps knowing she is a lioness with her jaws poised wide open above my neck has triggered some sort of compassion within her. 'Why should I allow Book Club to continue?'

'Yes, Meg,' says Sophie, goading me with her eyes. 'Why should your smutty little club continue?'

That is it. That is truly it. I stand. My legs shake, and heat radiates from my face, down my chest. Everything that has happened in the last few weeks threatens to boil over into this moment, with my smug sister sitting in front of me, provoking me, shaming me, as she always has done. But this job is all I have left, and if she wants a fight, she is going to get one.

I straighten my shoulders, and lift my chin, ready to defend. 'Book Club is not a "smutty little club".' My voice, made strong by my anger towards Sophie, reverberates around the room. My hands clench at my sides. I lean into that feeling, letting it distract me from my legs, that feel weak, and my stomach that churns. 'Book Club was a chance for a group of women to get together and *unashamedly* share in the joy of a novel that— yes, was explicit— but was also engaging, and thought provoking. In that room we laughed; so hard that sometimes we cried. We talked about the book, and we talked about real life. Relationships. We shared wisdom, discussed morality and supported each other. I learned from the women in that room, and they even learned some things from me. We trusted each other. No opinion was too taboo. No question too silly. No shame. Only joy.' I pause for breath. Pip's expression is unreadable. 'Pip, I know I should have told you. But as much as I knew *Cloaked Lust* was what Book Club needed, I also knew you wouldn't see it that way, so I did what I did to save something I cared about.' A lump forms in my throat as I realise in doing so, I have probably lost something I care about even more. My job. 'I'm sorry.'

Slowly, I sit back down and lower my head into my hands.

'Well, she makes a strong case, doesn't she Pip?' I raise my eyes to see Sophie with a smile on her face, and her arms crossed over her chest. 'I think we should let her off.'

Confusion reigns. Pip stands. 'I—' she clears her throat. 'I suppose I hadn't considered things from that angle. I will be recommending the introduction of a consent form for all attendees, and identification checks to ensure no minors attend. But...I can see this means a lot more to you than I realised. By Janice's email, I assume it meant a lot to the attendees as well.' Pip walks over to me and places a hand on my shoulder. 'Keep your club, Meg. But don't let there be any more surprises, please. Take an early lunch with your friends. Compose yourself. Then back to work.'

As Pip leaves the room, relief crashes over me, and I let my tears fall freely. When finally, I compose myself enough to speak, it is Gabby I round on first.

'What the hell, Gabby? I asked you to be my support person and you send *Sophie*??'

'Brilliant, wasn't it?' says Gabby happily. Sophie still sits across from us, with a smile on her face, but at that, she stands and walks around the table to perch beside me.

'It *was* brilliant, Meg. Admit it.'

'I don't follow,' I say.

'I am the only person who can fire you up like that, Meg! If it wasn't for me, you would have given some weak excuse, like you forgot to tell her about it, or you didn't know the book was so dirty, and you would have lost your job. But once I got you going, you did what you never do, unless I'm involved.'

'Which is?'

'You fought!' She grins broadly. 'You fucking stood up for something you care about. You didn't let life just happen to you, for once. You took it with both hands, and you put it in a strangle hold. I'm proud of you, Meg.'

I am stunned into silence, not only be Sophie's words, but by the look on her face that can't be misinterpreted. She is, in fact, proud of me. But she isn't done. She leans in close to me and takes my chin between her fingers.

'Now, let me ask you this, little sister. What else do you really, really care about?'

***

What else do I really, really care about? Sophie, as much as it pains me to admit it, was right. That really was the first time I have ever fought for something, and not just let life 'happen' to me, and it has given me a new-found sense of peace to slightly off-set the emotional turmoil I have grown accustomed to of late. Everything else in my life might be a mess, but perhaps, in some small way, I have grown. Who would have thought it would be *Sophie* I'd have to thank?

Her question has reverberated in my mind, and a clear answer has arisen.

Coffees in hand, the three of us round the corner and head up the street until we are diagonally across the road from R.J. Ink. Johnno. That's what I really, really care about. And Elle, but of the two, Johnno is the most pressing because I don't know how much time I have. For all he has done, and for all the things he wasn't honest about, I still care about him, and maybe it's time to fight once more.

'There it is,' I say, and nod towards the shop front.

'Well, what are we waiting for?' says Gabby, and steps down the gutter towards the store. As she does, a man and a woman, smartly dressed, pause in front of the store. They look up at the signage and the bell tinkles as they make their way inside.

'Strange. They don't look like the type you'd see wanting a tattoo at—,' I quickly check my phone for the time, '—half ten on a Tuesday morning.'

'They're not.' Sophie points down the street about 50 yards to a marked vehicle. 'They got out of that car. They're cops.'

Chapter Twenty-Eight

Needless to say, my new-found sense of peace was short-lived. We couldn't stay for long outside R.J. Ink. I was needed back at work. By the time we left, the officers had not re-emerged, and we didn't get even a glimpse of Johnno. It takes all my effort to get through the rest of the day, and as soon as I finish, I make my way as quickly as I can back to the shop. I have to see him. I have to know he is all right. What if he isn't there? What if they took him?

When I arrive, that very fear is immediately stoked. Standing at the counter, on his own, is Miller. He looks up as I enter, and smiles, but not with the blood curdling glee of other occasions.

'All right, Miss?'

'All right, Miller,' I say stiffly.

'If you're looking for the guvnor, he's not here.' My heart plummets.

'Oh. Where is he?' Miller doesn't seem to know what to say to that. Surely, they should have a viable story ready to go. It seems a rookie error. 'I know. Everything.'

'Shhh,' Miller says urgently. He comes around the reception desk, quickly ducks back, pulling out a packet of cigarettes from behind the counter, then heads towards the door, beckoning me to follow. 'Smoko.'

He turns the door sign around to read, 'Closed', and I follow him a short way down the street, and then into a narrow space between two brick buildings.

'We can't talk in there,' he explains. 'Might be bugged. Can never be too careful.' I see. The rookie error was on my behalf. Miller places a cigarette between his lips, extends the packet to me in offer, and when I decline, lights his own. He takes a drag before continuing. He speaks no louder than a whisper.

'Johnno's shooting through.'

'What?!'

'That's right. We had a bit of a to-and-fro about it this morning, after...we had...visitors.'

'The police.'

'Aye. Sniffin' around. Johnno said he wanted to turn himself in. Said he might get less time if he does it that way. Said it didn't matter any more if he went back in, since you...you know.'

'Broke up.'

'Aye. I told him to hell with that. If anyone should go back inside, it's me. I don't mind the place.' Miller gives me a broad smile, with his cigarette still between his teeth. 'And Johnno's got Shae to think about. I told him, go. Start a new life. Take the pretty lass with you, guvnor.'

'Am I the…pretty lass?' I ask tentatively.

Miller grins again. 'Aye.'

'W-what did he say to that, Miller?'

'We argued for a good while, and finally he agreed to shoot through.' He gives me a thoughtful look. 'Thought he would've come straight to you. No point wasting time. Once the big boss finds out Johnno's gone…I said I'd keep the shop open for a few days, give him a head start. Tell the big boss on Monday. The least I can do to help him out, after all he's done for me.'

There has been not a flicker of resentment, or even inconvenience, in his tone or manner. Surely, he too is now in the shit. 'What will *you* do, Miller?'

Miller shrugs. 'Fucked if I know. When I tell the big boss, I reckon they'll either kick me out or make me take Johnno's place.'

'Hand the business over to you? As owner manager?'

Miller laughs. 'No love. I'd become Johnno.'

'You would…become Johnno?'

'That's right. Easier that way. And you wouldn't put Peter Wentworth in charge of a business.' He laughs again. 'No quicker way to get the pigs sniffin' around than doing that.'

'How can you just 'become' Johnno though?' I'm sure I'm being thick, but this is making no sense.

Miller holds out his right hand to me, as though offering a handshake. I do nothing. He nods towards his hand. I take it in my right hand. He shakes it firmly.

'All right? Nice to meet you. Johnno. Yeah, that's right. Short for Reed Johnson. How do?' Miller lets go of my hand and laughs again. 'If Johnno manages to get away, he's going to need a new name anyway.

And if he doesn't— well, I don't mean to scare you love, but he'll be dead if they get their hands on him. And there won't be a body to mess up their plans.' My stomach clenches, and I'm not sure if I'm going to vomit. My hand covers my mouth. Miller turns serious.

'Sorry love.'

I swallow hard so that I can speak.

'Aren't you...scared? Of what will happen when they find out?'

'Nah,' Miller says. He takes another long drag and blows the smoke out slowly. 'I'd have nothing if Johnno hadn't taken me in here. I'd have found a way to get back inside long ago. I've had a good run, working for Johnno. He's a good bloke. Not many like him on the inside.' He smiles, as though accessing pleasant memories. 'I owe him. I'll deal with what happens Monday when it happens. Worst case scenario I'll steal a car, and I'll have a roof back over my head by Tuesday.' He laughs again.

I have no further questions. At least, not ones I want answers to from Miller.

'Good luck. I...hope whatever happens on Monday is...what you need.'

'Ta, love,' he says, and I leave him alone to finish his cigarette.

I trudge back towards the library. What Miller has told me has rocked me to my core. Johnno is gone. By now, he might not even still *be* Johnno. He had told me he thought about leaving before he met me. What did I really think would happen to him if he ran? That they would just let him go? Accept his defection, with everything he knows? Not only would he be on the run for the rest of his life, but he would also be on the run with a target on his back. And if Miller is to be believed, Johnno is planning to ask me to go with him. What the hell do I say?

***

My mind is in a complete tailspin as I drive home. I take myself to my bedroom, where I collapse face down on my bed and put my pillow over my head, hoping to suffocate. It doesn't work. My stubborn lungs won't co-operate, and I have to breathe. So, I take the pillow back off, roll onto my back and stare at the ceiling.

What if he comes? What will I do? I have no idea. I stay like that for hours, with those questions revolving in my mind. Then, I do the only thing I think might help me to make the decision, before I'm faced with prospect of having to make it for real. I pick up my sketch book, and I move through the pages to the drawings of Johnno. They capture his likeness so well that I draw in a sharp breath as I look at them. God. He is still like a fantasy to me. How could it be that a short while ago, he was mine, and we were happy? The thought hurts but looking at the drawings has given me the clarity I need. I close the book, and stand. I look in the mirror.

For the conversation I need to have now, I need to look like I have my shit together. Like I am rational, and mature, and level-headed. Quietly dignified. I put some concealer on the dark circles beneath my eyes, and then I make my way upstairs, to Mum and Dad's room. I knock gently, and I hear Mum's voice.

'Come in.'

I open the door. They are in bed, with the lamps on their bedside tables throwing a soft light over them. Dad has his reading glasses on, and a finance magazine in hand. Mum is reading a book. She smiles and her eyes light up as I come in. Dad knows better. His eyebrows come together. He knows I don't come to see them at this time of night unless something is wrong. Mum is just happy to see me at all.

'Meg,' Dad says. 'Is everything all right?'

'Not really Dad,' I say, keeping my voice steady. *Quiet dignity*, I remind myself. 'I need to talk to you.'

Dad places down his newspaper, and swings his legs out of bed, and into his slippers. He is wearing long, flannelette pyjamas, and I curse myself for not thinking of that. He oozes quiet dignity.

'Let's make tea,' he says. He looks at Mum briefly, and they share a soft smile, and I swear it should be me, not Elle, who is the hopeless romantic, having grown up around these ninety-percenters.

Dad and I don't speak as we walk downstairs. We still don't speak as Dad boils the kettle, and I get the cups down. It isn't until we sit down in the front room, and I curl my legs beneath me on the sofa, holding me tea in both my hands to keep it steady, that Dad speaks.

'I've missed this.'

'Me too.' He waits. I take in a long breath, then let it out slowly. 'I know you won't like what I have to say.' Nothing. 'Johnno is leaving town. I found out today.'

'I'm sorry,' Dad says cautiously. He knows that can't be it, because so far, I've only said something he *would* like, very much, I'm sure.

'He's running. You were right about his business. It's not legit. It's some sort of...' I struggle to bring myself to say the words. I know what it is, but saying it sounds so...dirty. But Dad can't help unless I tell him. 'Money laundering. That's what it is. The tattoos are a front.' Dad nods slowly. 'Johnno set up the businesses when he came out of prison three years ago, with funds from people he met on the inside. He needed a way to make money, because he had nothing. He wanted to turn them into viable businesses over time, but it hasn't worked out. He is the face of it, but he doesn't have anything to do with the...background dealings.'

'This is very serious, my love,' Dad says. I grind my teeth a little.

'Before I say anything more, there's something you need to know. My chin goes up a little. *Quiet dignity, Meg.* 'Johnno may come to see me before he goes. He may ask me to go with him.' Dad's eyes widen. I forge ahead. 'If he does, I will have two options.'

'They are?' Dad asks stiffly.

'One. Go with him. Two. Help him with the business, so that he doesn't have to run.'

'Meg—' Dad starts to protest.

'—That's why I'm telling you, Dad,' I say, cutting him off before he can waste words on fruitless objections I am determined to ignore. 'Because I love him. And there are no other options. I can't let him leave, and never see him again. So, I need your help. Because I don't want to run. I want to stay and help.'

Dad is quiet, but I can see how tense he is. He has a vein on his forehead that pops out when he is mad, and it is visibly throbbing right now. I continue.

'Before we broke up, Johnno asked me to help. He asked if he could use my designs to boost the business, the tattoo side. To get more customers in, so eventually, he could start making money that way, pay out the current financers, and be free to run it as a legitimate business. I said no, because I was worried about getting involved.' Dad wants to speak. He opens his mouth. I continue. 'Of course, I'm still worried. But surely, Dad, there must be a way I can help, without attaching myself to it? This is why I'm asking you. You must know what I can do to keep myself safe.'

'Meggy, what you are proposing is a very valiant thing to do for someone you love. And I am sorry, sweetheart. I know he made you happy. But from what you have told me, I'm afraid there is no easy way out of this for Johnno.' He says it so gently, it's like he is breaking the news that a family pet has died. I feel the grief as though it had.

'What do you mean?'

'Based on my experience, arrangements like this are never simple to end. Money or not, what the...financers have with Johnno is...a dream scenario for them. He is the face of it all. If...when... authorities catch up with it, Johnno will be the one who takes the fall, along with anyone else associated with the business, and they stand to walk away. That is worth far more than any initial investment. I think Johnno will find it will be impossible to walk away.'

I can't drink tea anymore. I place the cup down on the ground beside the sofa, and stand. My quiet dignity is fading fast. In its place, panic.

'But Dad, that would mean— you mean to say— he's trapped, forever.'

'Trapped. Or back in prison. Yes.'

So long, quiet dignity. Tears fall thick and fast from my eyes. I pace several times back and forwards.

'Meg,' Dad says quietly. I can see the distress on his face, just as raw as mine, even though he doesn't cry.

'Dad,' I drop to my knees in front of him. 'Please. Tell me something. How can I help him? I don't want to get into trouble. I don't want to place anyone else— you, the family— at risk. But I *can't* do nothing.'

'Perhaps you should let him go, sweetheart,' Dad says, so gently. 'It may be his only chance to be free.'

I consider it for a moment, and then shake my head.

'No. It's not just me he would be leaving. He's a father. Think of Shaelea. If he runs, she will never see him again. And she has no choice in the matter, because she is in London, none the wiser. But if he comes to me— if— I can't let him go.'

Dad sighs, a long, resigned sigh.

'I won't have this taken as advice, Meg. Hear me now. My advice is to leave this well alone. But I hear you that you are going to choose a different path. So, listen carefully.'

And I do, while Dad tells me everything I need to know to aid and abet a criminal money laundering operation, without leaving prints.

Chapter Twenty-Nine

It is past half ten by the time I make it to my room after speaking with Dad. Quiet dignity is now restored. I know what I need to do. I know what I can offer, and what I can't. I open my window, and climb into bed, knowing I will lie there awake, waiting. Hoping he will come.

Eleven. Twelve. One. Two. Three. Four. He isn't coming. He's gone. My eyes drift close, and I fall into a light sleep. I wake at seven. I will be late for work.

I force myself into jeans and a t-shirt. I don't even bother with my hair, or with breakfast, and I don't have time for coffee. I make it to work ten minutes late. I plan to slip in unnoticed. I managed to avoid my entire family for over a week using stealth. Surely, I can get to the staff room, and out to the floor, without Pip realising I am late. I channel invisibility, letting my powers hum through my bod—

'Meg.'

Didn't work.

'Morning, Pip.'

She looks me up and down, and frowns. 'Is everything all right?'

Fucking awful. Thank you for asking. 'Fine.'

'You're late.'

Be grateful I'm here at all. I had plans for Russia. 'Yes. Sorry. Traffic was bad.'

'It's the school holidays. Traffic is considerably lighter than usual.'

'Or something. What can I do to make up for it?'

'First, fix your hair,' Pip says bluntly. 'Second, returns. And you can stay ten minutes late to make up the time.'

'Of course.' I head to the staff room and search for a hair tie in my bag, which is still slung over my shoulder. I find one, shove my hair up, and then head for the afterhours returns chute trolley. I heave it open. It's full to the brim, as no one got to it yesterday. I start to file books onto a set of wheeled shelves, but I freeze, and my heart sinks as I see the next three books lying on top. The *Eventide* Saga. Johnno was still here last night. He returned the books, after hours. It hits me. He didn't come to me because he didn't want to. Not because he was already gone. I stand there, staring for a long time before I can touch the books. But eventually, I pull them out, and file them with the others. Gone. What we had is gone.

***

Despite my impassioned speech to save my job, and my book club, I am just not in the mood this afternoon. But at three o'clock, just after

Pip has left for the afternoon, Gabby comes through the doors. She greets me and gives me a bright smile, but I am too distracted by what is on her face to respond in kind.

'What are you doing in glasses, Gabby? Did you go to the optometrist?'

She laughs. 'Course not! These are an old pair of Elle's. I popped the lenses out, see?' She takes them from her face and pokes her index finger through to demonstrate. 'These are just for the vibes.'

'The vibes?'

'Book Club vibes! Sophie filled me in on the details of your smutty little book club, and I'm on board. Can't believe you didn't tell me about it earlier.'

There is good reason for that. In fact, several. But the most obvious being— 'You don't read, Gabby.'

'No. But doesn't matter, does it? If you've all read it, I'll catch on. Or I could just read the good bits. That would work too.'

I groan internally. This is not what I need right now. Not when I'm still preoccupied with Johnno's disappearance. I'm in survival mode, and at this point, Gabby just feels like another existential threat.

'What is it, Meg?' she asks, and when I turn my attention back to her, I notice what might just be genuine concern on her face. 'Worried about Johnno?'

I might as well tell her. She will find out eventually. So I spill forth, in hushed tones, everything I swore to take to my grave, but have since now told three people. Gabby gawks at me open mouthed, but I continue. 'Yesterday, after work, I went back to the shop. Spoke to the guy who works for Johnno— '

'—The actor guy, from the prison show?'

'Sure. Him. Anyway, he told me Johnno is running. He thought Johnno was planning to come to me and ask me to go, so I went and spoke to Dad about it, so I would know what to do. I was all set to tell Johnno I'd help him with the business so he could stay, but then he never showed! And it's been all day, not a message, not a sign, other than the books he borrowed for Shae in the after-hours chute, proving he was still in town last night but didn't come. Maybe I didn't mean as much to him as I thought. But now I don't know what to do, Gabby. Do I wait? Do I give up? Do I call him— '

'Hold on a minute.' Gabby gives me a stern look over the top of her lens-less glasses. 'Did you just say, "do I call him"?'

'Yes,' I say meekly.

'So, you have been stressing for over 24 hours that he hasn't been in contact, but haven't thought to try his...you know... contact details?'

I hang my head. 'I'm sorry.'

'You should be!' Gabby snaps. 'Go and get your phone.'

I do as I'm told, and hand it over to Gabby, who promptly scrolls through my contacts to Johnno's number and calls it. I am so nervous as I wait for the number to connect and then...it doesn't. A cold, robotic voice, devoid of any mercy or compassion, informs us that this number has been disconnected.

I give a growl. 'She can rot in hell!' I cry.

Gabby looks startled. 'Now, now. There will be another way to contact him.' She takes the glasses from her face, and chews on the end as she thinks. 'Nope. No good. We need Elle.'

***

I protest strongly that Elle isn't talking to me, and with good reason, and that she won't want to be dragged into this fiasco, since it was this fiasco that made me blow up at her in the first place. All the while, Gabby, without pause, sends off a message to Elle, who arrives ten minutes later. When we lock eyes all I can see is hurt and betrayal there. Until she smiles. 'All right, Meg?'

Gabby responds for me. 'Meg's all right, but she's being insufferable about this Johnno character, and we need your help.' Gabby fills Elle in on the circumstances, since I don't seem to be able to speak to her. I know very well the only words that should be coming out of my mouth are, 'I'm sorry'.

Finally, after first addressing the obvious— Gabby's glasses— Elle then turns to my problem. 'So, we need a way of contacting Johnno. Letting him know that Meg wants to see him, to talk things through. But telecommunications are out...' She drums her finger against her lips, before exclaiming, 'I've got it!'

'You do?' I ask hopefully.

'Yes. It will only work if Johnno is still in town. But if he is, there is no way we will fail,' she says brightly. 'All I need is access to a laptop, and a printer, and...' she checks her phone, 'there's no time to lose.'

Chapter Thirty

'This is completely daft.' I shake my head for what must be the one hundredth time and glance up at the clock on the wall of the conference room. Five to four. Book Club starts in five minutes.

'It will work, Meg. I am confident. When have I ever let you down?'

A certain second cousin comes to mind, but I swallow my retort, because at least my best friend is talking to me again. Even if it is only to defend the most horrible idea she has ever had.

Our conversation is cut short as a group of Book Club regulars bustle into the room, and clearly, excitement is in the air.

'Meg!' *Janice.* 'You have outdone yourself, my dear!' she says. She takes a hold of each of my cheeks, and plants a kiss on each side before releasing me with a flourish. 'When I sent my consumer feedback to whom it may concern, I never expected this!'

'I don't think any of us were expecting it, Janice,' I reply, unable to mirror her enthusiasm.

'A live action version of *Cloaked Lust*!' The blonde lady with the red lipstick gushes. 'I am frothing at the mouth! And auditions start today!' She excitedly holds up an A5 flyer, one of the hundred or so Elle and Gabby frantically distributed around the centre of town, and all over social media, in the half hour before Book Club was due to commence, while I stayed in the library and rocked in the corner.

'Yes. My joy knows no bounds. But honestly, I think we should calm ourselves. In all likelihood, nobody will come, as it was very short notice, so perhaps we should take a seat and turn our attention to— '

The sound of a throat clearing stops me dead. It doesn't stop everybody else though. Excited squeals and giggles erupt, as I take in the tall, handsome figure leaning against the doorway. 'Is this the place for the auditions?' his deep voice rumbles.

'I thought Detective Martin had you, young man!' Margy cries, her eyes twinkling excitedly at this unexpected development.

I can't speak. It is too much. Elle quickly shepherds the rest of her over-excited flock to their seats around the long table, and then— the cur— looks at me expectantly. I give a shrug and turn to Gabby with the same look Elle has just given me.

'Not him?' she asks me.

I shake my head. Gabby, whose long legs were crossed in front of her where she sat perched on the table, stands, folds her arms across her chest, and approaches the man. 'Come in,' she commands. 'Name?'

The man pushes off the doorway, and saunters into the room. 'Dan.' Gabby begins a slow, appraising circle around him. 'Six foot something. Tattoos. Shoulder-length hair.' She moves back in front of him, and peers more closely at his face. 'Green eyes. You meet the description we requested.'

The man— Dan, *not* Johnno— looks pleased with himself. 'Have I got the part?'

'Not so fast,' says Gabby. 'We will need to see some acting first. You can act, can't you?'

This is getting out of hand, fast.

'Of course I can,' the man says, affronted. 'Tell me what you want, and I'll produce it.'

Gabby glances at Elle. This is where she may come unstuck, since she hasn't read *Cloaked Lust*. Elle rises to the challenge. She stands up, shoulder to shoulder with Gabby. 'The character you will be auditioning for is somewhat of a rogue, Dan,' Elle explains. 'Picture this. You, Patrick, have just climbed in the bedroom window of an unsuspecting, but highly co-operative woman, and tied her to her bed head.'

'I have?' Dan says, startled.

'He has?' Gabby says, her eyes lighting up. Elle nods in confirmation. 'Brilliant.' Gabby stands, removes the linen tie from around her waist that was clinching in her shirt, and pulls out a chair, positioning it so it faces the expectant audience. 'In that case, all we need you to do for us, Dan, is to demonstrate your competence with a single column tie, and then talk us through, in detail, everything you would do to—

'— "The Chosen One",' Elle supplies.

'— "The Chosen One" while she is tied to the bed head, should you be successful in earning the role of Patrick.'

I groan, a heavy groan, but there is no point in protesting. There are upwards of twelve eager faces in the room, itching for Dan to get started.

'Oh! And, if you don't mind Dan, it would be helpful if you would wear this.' Elle walks to the innocuous cardboard box in the corner of the room, where I stashed the LED candles, cloaks and masks after our final *Cloaked Lust* session. She takes out a cloak and a mask, and hands them to Dan.

'Any volunteers to sit in the chair?' Gabby asks with a grin.

There is no shortage of volunteers.

***

A string of men meeting Johnno's description, none of them Johnno, frequented Book Club this evening. With each one, my heart felt heavier than the last. The plan didn't work. Of course it didn't. It was a stupid plan, and Elle is daft. And to make matters worse, before she left to go home, all she said was, 'I'll see you round, Meg.' It was Gabby who told me she has abandoned her plans for Australia.

I am so tired by the time I get home I shower, change straight into my pyjamas, and fall into bed. The soft summer breeze through my open window plays with my hair as I lay on my stomach. I imagine it is soothing fingertips. Elle's, probably. Moments like these, she would stroke my hair, and I would feel comfort.

With less than three hours sleep the night before, and a full day at work, it takes no time for me to drift off to sleep. A heavy, dreamless sleep.

In the depth of the night, I jolt awake as a heavy, rough hand claps tightly over my mouth. My breath sucks in through my nose, but I can't scream. My eyes widen, and my pulse beats hard in the sides of my neck, as a figure on the bed beside me looms over me, and says, deep, and soft,

'Don't. Scream.'

Chapter Thirty-One

'D one?' Johnno asks gently, his hand still pressed firmly to my mouth. 'Can I take my hand away?'

I nod. Tentatively, he lifts it but keeps it hovering for a moment.

'It's OK,' I whisper. Johnno relaxes and drops his hand. He is lying on his side beside me, propped on his arm. So close, but he doesn't try to touch me. 'I thought you were gone.' My voice catches on the last word, and I bite my lip to hide the quiver.

'I came last night just after ten. The window was shut. I hung around another night. Hoping. I had to see you.'

I nod.

He reaches into the pocket of his jeans and takes out a folded piece of paper. 'I found one of these. Isn't this the book you were reading?' I take the flyer from his hand, in disbelief. The worst idea Elle has ever had worked.

'Yes, it is.'

'I would've been perfect for it,' Johnno grumbles.

I stifle a giggle. 'Johnno, there isn't going to be a live action *Cloaked Lust*. It was a way of trying to get in contact with you. Because I wanted to see you again, to talk to you...before you...'

'Really?' He swallows hard. 'C-can I kiss you?' he whispers.

'Yes,' I whisper back, and I pull him to me with a hand behind his neck. He braces his body over the top of me so I feel his heat, but I don't have his weight on me. His lips meet mine in a kiss so different than any he has ever given me before. Slow and gentle, as though he is savouring the sensation, trying to immortalise it. He can't kiss me without me wanting his body. I arch beneath him, searching for him. He threads his fingers through those of my left hand with his right and lifts my hand up beside my face. He deepens the kiss, slowly but surely melting every piece of me, but the gap between our bodies remains. God, I want him. But I don't just want his body. I want to hear his voice, and feel his heartbeat beneath my fingers, and stare into his eyes, and taste his...tears?

With my free hand, I run my fingers across his cheek. Tears. He is crying.

'Johnno.'

'I love you. So much. I know it isn't fair to ask, but Meg, I have to. Come with me. It will be hell, but if you are with me, it won't feel like it.'

'Johnno—'

'—I will look after you. I promise. I will never let anything happen to you. We'll make a new life. Somewhere. I don't know where yet. You and me. When the dust settles, we'll come back.'

'You know the dust won't settle,' I whisper gently, touching my thumb to his lips. 'And Shae.'

'She…she will barely notice. She hates me anyway. With good reason. She will be better off. If I stay, I'll only hurt her, like I've done time and time again.'

'That's not true. You're a good man. A good dad. You've made some…questionable decisions. But she needs you.'

Johnno lowers his head, and his forehead rests on my shoulder. 'I'm trapped, Meg. With no way out. *You* knew, within minutes of visiting the shop, that something wasn't right. The cops came by the shop the other day. They're coming back, with a warrant. One look at the books, and with my record, they will know. I'll go away for a long time. If I can't even make the place seem like a viable business to you, how the hell am I going to convince them?'

'I will help.'

Johnno lifts his eyes and looks into mine. 'I should never have asked that of you, sweetheart. I love you. I won't let this become your problem.'

'I've spoken to Dad.' Johnno's eyes widen in horror. 'It's OK,' I say quickly. 'You can trust him. *We* can trust him.'

'Meg, he's a fucking lawyer. I've never met a lawyer I could trust in my life, and I've met more than my fucking share.'

'Shh,' I say, pressing a finger to his lips. 'He's my dad. We can trust him. I promise. I had to talk to him. I had to know how I can help you, without becoming…'

'An accomplice.'

Ugly word. 'Yes.'

Johnno sighs. 'What did he say.'

I outline to Johnno everything Dad told me, being careful not to miss anything. My name cannot be associated with anything. That part goes without saying. My drawings can be used, if there is no link back to me. No payment will change hands, not even cash. And if things go badly, I am just a friend. Not a girlfriend. Not a partner.

'In the event things go badly, I don't know you, Meg. You don't have to worry about that,' Johnno says, without even baulking. He lowers his lips to mine. Again, so gentle. Apologetic, almost. 'Are you sure? I know I asked you, but I never want you to feel you did something that wasn't right for you, out of obligation, or duress.'

'I love you. I don't want to run. I don't want you to run. I want to try this way.' A slight smile touches his lips, the first since he has been here. 'I have just one question.'

'Go on.'

'What makes you think they will let you go, if you pay them back?'

Johnno sighs. 'I don't know for sure that they will. But I was inside with these guys, and a lot goes on in there. I owe them, for setting up the business, for keeping me off the streets, for paying me a wage. But they owe me for stuff that happened in there.'

'What kind of stuff?'

'I don't want to talk about inside with you, Meg. It was a dark time. I want to leave it in the past.'

'I want to know these things, though. You hid things from me before. Now, I want you to be honest.'

He gives a disgruntled grunt but tenderly brushes the hair back from my face. 'Fine. On the inside, I was a bit of an... enforcer, you might say. Because of my size, and because I had a good relationship with the wardens. I treated them like people just trying to do their jobs, and didn't assume the worst of them, like some of the guys do. Don't get me wrong, some are bastards, but plenty of them are all right.

'Anyway, the son of one of the guys I work for now ended up in the same prison as me. He was only eighteen years old. First time he'd been to adult prison, instead of juvie. It can be a rough place for young guys.

When you're green, you're an easy target, and his dad— my boss— had already been released. Boss asked me to look after his son, to keep him safe. And I did. For two years, until he was released.' Johnno chuckles. 'Funny how oblivious the wardens can be when they want to be. They never saw a thing, and there was plenty to see.'

Johnno's story, though it makes me a little sick to think about, and I squeeze his arm just to remind myself he is here, and not in there, is also the hope I needed. When Dad said there was no hope, he didn't know this. I should have known. Because Johnno is a good man.

'We're doing this then?' I ask. 'Together?' *But if the cops get involved then, you know, apart.*

'You sure you don't want to run? I hear there's a librarian shortage in the Scottish Highlands.'

'Are you thinking of becoming a librarian if you start a new life?' I ask.

Johnno smirks. 'Now that you mention it, I think I'd be good at it. I love books.'

'What would your librarian name be?'

He thinks for only a moment, and then says, 'Patrick'.

'Then I would be Bella.'

'And I would fuck you in the toy cupboard at least once a day.'

I bite my lip. 'You paint an attractive vision of the future. But there's something you need to know that I think will change your mind. It's about Shae.'

Johnno's smile fades, and his brow furrows. I'm about to betray a confidence. I don't feel good about it, but I'm sure if Shaelae knew the context, she would forgive me.

'Do you remember she asked to speak to me, alone, before she left?'

'Yes. Thought it was weird.'

'She wanted to see my drawings. Of you.'

Johnno is perfectly still. 'Was weird. Why?'

'She wanted one. She didn't want me to tell you. She thought it would be too…weird…to ask you for a photo.'

'She…she wanted a picture of me?'

'Yes. I drew her one of the two of you together. The same as the one I gave you.'

Johnno rubs his hand across his face. 'Fuck,' he says. 'That blows my mind.' I see his mind ticking over. 'She doesn't hate me?'

'No. But she is frightened of losing you. Of never seeing you again.'

I let those words sink in, and as they do, I know that Patrick and Bella will not be taking up employment in a Scottish Highlands library.

'Meg.'

'Yes?'

'You are incredible.'

'So are you,' I say, and God, I mean it. What a fool I was to doubt him. A selfish fool. Fuck. Elle. That train of thought is broken by Johnno kissing me, and I pull him to me, searching for the way he used to kiss me— rough and demanding, and he meets me there. My body comes alive, and I want to be on top of him. I attempt to roll him over, and at first, I think he is going to submit, but then he stops.

'Hold on. I almost forgot. I can't lay on my back.'

'Why?'

Johnno smiles. He sits up and lifts up his shirt. On the centre of his back is a perfect, beautiful tattoo of my naked torso, with bedroom eyes I'm sure I've never made in my life, but now adorn Johnno's skin. Right over the place where his heart beats.

I feel my cheeks warm. 'Johnno, you are a mad man.'

The way he laughs does nothing to dispel that theory. 'You like it?'

'I do. I'm honoured. Who did it? Not Miller I hope.'

'No way. I went to a woman in town.'

I breathe a sigh of relief. 'The cops aren't going to believe we are just friends if they see that, are they?'

'Better make sure they don't see it then,' he says. 'And you'd better let me go on top tonight, beautiful, and save your ride for another day.' His lips start their descent along my collarbone, and his hands, even lower.

'Fine,' I say.

Johnno freezes. 'I'll give *you* fine,' he says gruffly, and as his lips meet mine with a growl, something rare and fleeting occurs. I giggle.

***

I wake early, when the first daylight streams in through the open window. The weight of Johnno's arm around my waist and warm naked body against mine reassures me, as my eyes open, that last night wasn't a dream. I snuggle back into him, and he reciprocates. I roll to my back to meet his eyes that I couldn't see properly last night in the dark. There is the sweetest smile in them. I've never seen him look so soft. But as he looks into mine, his lips become tight. He pulls the covers down, right down to my knees, leaving us both exposed. I give a slight shiver from the cool air, and from his gaze, that is studying me closely.

He brings his thumb beneath my eyes and touches me gently.

'Your eyes don't look right.' His thumb travels down across my cheek bone, and then his fingers traverse my breasts, down to my ribs, that are more visible than they would have been the last time he saw me naked. 'You've lost weight.' His hand rests on my stomach. 'You haven't been looking after yourself.'

'I've been a little sad.' Even for me, this is an understatement.

His eyebrows come together, and I receive the same concerned look I've been getting from my family for the past two weeks. 'Meg, you can't let yourself fall apart over me. What we talked about last night, I want it to work. But until I can turn things around with the business, there will always be a risk I will be going away. For a long time. Last time was five years. If this is found out...it will be longer than that.' He brushes my hair back from my face. 'You will need to be strong, and you will need to be prepared to move on. I don't want you waiting for me, being miserable.'

'Johnno—'

'—No, Meg. Until everything is sorted out, I can't give you everything you will want. Everything you deserve. I can't marry you. I can't have a child with you. I won't leave another kid without a dad, and I won't leave you to handle it on your own. If things go badly, you need to forget about me. And whatever you've been doing to yourself for the past two weeks is not allowed.'

I nod, to ease his concern rather than in proper agreement.

'There is something I did want to ask of you though.'

'What?' I ask, touching my hand to the side of his face.

'I thought about what you said about Shae last night. She trusts you, and she likes you. And I wondered if you would be OK with me giving her your number, next year, when I see her again. I'd like her to have someone she can talk to if she ever needs to— if I go away. Someone who really knows me.' He takes my hand from his cheek and kisses my open palm. 'She might want that one day.'

'Of course,' I say. 'Are you frightened? Of going back there?'

'I never have been before. That's probably part of the reason I had trouble staying out. But now, yes, fucking terrified. I've got a lot more to lose now than I've ever had before.'

We lie together in silence for a while, and I think about Shae. Eventually I ask the question that has sat at the back of my mind for a while now.

'Do you not speak to Shae at all between visits?'

'I don't think I'm allowed. I get my two weeks, that's it.'

'That seems unusual, don't you think?'

'I don't know. I've only been able to take her on my own for a couple of years. I just assumed that was it.'

'I don't know a lot about it, of course. But I would have thought you could still speak to Shae, and maybe even visit, in between your two weeks.'

Johnno shrugs. 'I've got the paperwork. It's on the bike with all my stuff. I can't really understand it.' He adds, 'I hate looking at legal stuff. It stresses me out.'

'Do you have someone who helps you with this sort of thing?' I ask gently. 'Like...a lawyer?'

Johnno chuckles. 'Fuck no. Couldn't afford it, and even if I could, I don't trust them, like I told you last night. Scum of the earth. Mr Drury excepted. I represent myself.'

'Perhaps...you could show Dad. He isn't in family law, but he could understand the document.' Johnno looks like he'd rather chew his own arm off. 'What if you're wrong, Johnno? What if you think your two weeks is it, but it's not? Imagine if you could be there for other things in between.'

Johnno kisses me, and his hand, moves back to my stomach.

'I'll think about it. But I'm sure I'm the last person your dad wants to see right now.' I indicate my agreement with a tilt of my head, and a stifled smile.

'You will have to let him help you though, Johnno. With the shop. He will know what to do with the books.' Johnno opens his mouth to protest, and I stick my finger inside it to shut him up. 'You will have to let him help,' I repeat. 'The police are coming back, with a warrant. He is at work today and tomorrow, but on Saturday, we will come to the shop and get it sorted out.'

Chapter Thirty-Two

I spend the next two days, when I'm not at work or netball, draw-ing. I create as many new designs as I can, full size so they can be used for stencils, and I put them all into a black leather portfolio.

On Saturday morning, I am laying on my bed, putting the final touches on an intricate floral design when a quick rap on my bedroom door is followed by Gabby entering my bedroom. I am taken aback. Gabby, though she has been to my house before, has never been alone. Only ever with Elle, and never unannounced.

'Morning,' she says. 'You up?' Plonking down on the side of my bed, she studies her nails.

'Ah, yes. What about you? Are you up?'

'Don't be silly, Meg. I'm here, aren't I?' She stands, and starts to move around my room, picking up this and that, inspecting it, and putting it back down. 'Still planning to go to the shop this morning?'

I've felt it only fair to keep Gabby up to speed with all things Johnno since she played a part in helping me get in contact with him.

'That's the plan. Dad and I will leave in a half an hour or so. Once he's finished his brekky.'

She gives a seemingly disinterested 'hmph', then makes her way to my dressing table. The drawing I was almost finished is all but forgotten, my marker poised above the paper, as I observe the odd behaviour playing out before me. 'What are you doing here, Gabby?'

She doesn't say anything as she looks through my make-up bag, taking things out, and putting them back in. Then, she speaks. Not looking at me directly but catching my eye in the mirror in front of her. 'See, the thing is, Meg, I quite liked helping you out the other day. People don't often ask me for help. Don't know what it is. Could be that I have a short attention span—'

She cuts herself off as she applies my favourite red lipstick to her lips. She rubs them together, and seemingly satisfied, utters, 'Oooh.' Then the cow deposits my favourite lip stick in the pocket of her jeans, looking me straight in the eye as she gives her pocket a tap. 'Or maybe it's because I'm not the best listener. Whatever the reason, I'm not often called upon.' She returns to the side of the bed and sits back down. 'But it felt good, being a supportive friend. And it got me thinking—I should do more of it. And what better way than to spend more time with you, Meg. You have more problems than most, which makes you the perfect training ground.'

'I see,' I say blandly. Gabby's new-found interest in my life is concerning, but not as concerning as how I am going to get my lipstick back. 'The thought is certainly...noble, Gabby. But I don't need your help this morning. Dad and I can handle it.'

'Nonsense! I'm coming with you. You never know in what way I might be of use to you. And besides, I still haven't met Johnno, and

I'm dying to know what he's like, since I'm now so invested in this whole drama.'

'By drama, you mean my life?'

'Yes!'

I sigh. 'Fine. You can come on one condition.' I hold out my hand and wiggle my fingers. Gabby pouts, and my lipstick is restored to its rightful owner.

***

I can tell Dad is well out of his comfort zone as we step through the entrance of R.J. Ink. Johnno looks up from where he is standing at the counter, and smiles at me. I make my way to his side to kiss his cheek.

'Mr Drury,' he says, holding out a hand to Dad. 'Thanks for coming.'

'Dave,' Dad says stiffly, but accepts the handshake.

Johnno's attention catches on Gabby next. Gabby's attention has arrested on Johnno. She still stands near the doorway, mouth agog. I clear my throat. 'Gabby, this is Johnno. Johnno, Gabby.' I look apologetically at Johnno. 'She wants to "help".'

Finally, Gabby gives a quick shake of her head and turns to me. 'We will have words later, Meg. Not in front of your father. But there will be words.' Seemingly recovered, she starts moving around the shop with a similar routine to the one she performed in my bedroom earlier. She would have been a nightmare to take shopping as a kid. It's as though she can't help touching everything she sees. I decide to ignore her and focus on what is important— Dad looking over Johnno's books and getting out of here as quickly as possible. His discomfort has only grown in the few moments we have been here. His eyes dart around furtively. Checking for cameras, perhaps. As though he has read Dad's mind, Johnno says, 'We don't keep security cameras. Can't, with the plinth out here.'

Dad nods, and Johnno sends me a quick side eye. A plea for help. It prompts me to show him the designs. I hand him the portfolio. 'These should keep the shop going for a while, but I can always do up custom requests, if you can be the go-between with the customer.'

Johnno flicks through the pages and then places it down on the bench. He runs a hand over his hair, and I worry he doesn't like them.

'Meg, they're amazing. We'll have people interested, for sure.'

'No one can know they are Meg's.' We both turn to look at Dad, who stands stiffly behind us. 'It's very important, Johnno. Meg can't be associated with them in any way. If she is thought to be profiting from the...other side of the business...she will be in as much trouble as you will be.'

'I completely understand, Mr Drury. I promise, Meg's name won't cross my lips in relation to any of this.'

'No money will change hands,' Dad continues. 'Meg is doing this voluntarily, as well as anonymously.'

'Agreed,' says Johnno.

'And this will be her last visit to the shop. After today, she stays out of the business.'

'Really Dad—' I start to protest, but I quickly stop at the serious look on his face, and instead, I nod agreement. 'You're right. It's too risky.'

'Meg says you expect the police to return with a warrant.' It's as though every word is ground out from between his teeth, and his discomfort is now matched only by my own.

'That's right. I politely requested they obtain one,' Johnno confirms. 'They want a look at the books.'

'I think it will be best if I take a look before they do,' Dad says.

Johnno looks as though he might argue, but he glances at me and then turns to his laptop. A few clicks later, he has brought up a spreadsheet. He stands back, and Dad takes up position in front of it. Within seconds, Dad is frowning. 'This is it?' He scrolls down, and then back up, then drums his fingers on the bench. 'Where are the outgoings?'

'Ah...,' Johnno rubs the back of his head before answering. 'These aren't the only books,' he says. 'These are *my* books— the ones I keep in case of...visitors. All the overheads, and the wages for me and Miller are paid by my boss. I don't have access to any of that.'

'I see,' says Dad. 'That's a problem, Johnno. No legitimate business runs without outgoings. What about purchase of equipment? Consumables?'

'Business is...slow. We haven't needed to restock.' Dad looks up and glances around, and the tidy shelves tell the story.

'So, all these profits, services rendered, are...'

'Fabricated. To match the bank statements I get from the boss.'

'Let me see them,' Dad says shortly, then raises his voice. 'Gabrielle.' Gabby looks up from where she is sat perched on the side of the plinth, chaining safety pins together. 'I have a job for you.'

She jumps up and promptly discards the chain. 'I live to be helpful, Mr Drury.'

'I need you to make a mess. Put some gloves on, then put them in the bin. Open the wipes, use some, throw them out— that sort of thing. Do you understand?'

'Sounds fun,' she confirms, and sets to work.

Johnno places a pile of bank statements down, and Dad looks them over briefly. 'What are all these cash withdrawals? They aren't on your spreadsheet.'

'Yeah. There's a reason for that.' Dad quietly waits for explanation. Johnno shrugs. 'Because I haven't got a clue what they are.'

Dad sighs quietly and then cracks his knuckles. 'Right. Johnno, pay attention. I'm only going to do this once.'

***

Half an hour later, with Dad carefully explaining each and every change, Johnno's books are apparently in better shape than they were. Not that I would know, but Dad is much happier. He has added in costs for consumables, rent, wages and utilities and matched it all to the bank statements. And quietly, I think he has enjoyed his brief foray into criminal activity. Not that he will ever admit it.

Miller has joined us, and he and Gabby have embraced the task of making a mess with gusto. The shop now looks like tattooing takes place here, and though I would still take some convincing to let Miller come at me with a needle, other braver souls just might.

Johnno is in the process of thanking Dad, and we are about to make our escape, when a terrifying statement falls from the lips of Miller, who is near the front window.

'Fuck me. It's them. On a Saturday, the swines.'

Johnno looks at me with alarm and mutters a curse under his breath. He then springs into action, shoving Dad and I out the back, where there is a small room, with the staircase leading up to his living quarters. 'Stay out here. Don't make a sound,' he hisses. The stress on his face is obvious, and he cusses again, before going back to the shop floor. I can't even look at Dad, and alarmingly, Gabby hasn't followed us out back. I peak out, and my anxiety doubles, as I see her reclining on the plinth, with Miller by her side. I catch her attention and gesture frantically for her to join us, but she flicks her wrist at me in dismissal.

'Don't worry. I know what I'm doing,' she hisses back.

Nevertheless, I worry.

The bell tinkles— a sound I will now always associate with utter dread— and the same two officers who I saw enter the shop earlier in the week walk in.

The female officer speaks first, indicating seniority. 'Mr Johnson.'

'Sergeant Hathoway,' Johnno says politely— almost warmly. 'They haven't got you working on a Saturday morning, have they?'

'I'm afraid so,' the sergeant replies. She hands a piece of paper to Johnno, who takes it and scans it, before placing it down on the counter. 'I'm sorry about the timing,' she says with a glance at Gabby. 'I see you have a client.'

'Ah...' Johnno also glances at Gabby, who gives him a cheerful wave. 'Not at all. I'm sure we'll have this sorted quickly, once you see everything's in order,' he says smoothly, but his hand runs over his hair again— a subtle nervous tell. How does he do it? If I was under the amount of stress he must be feeling, I would be a puddle on the floor— or there would be a puddle on the floor. One or the other.

'Of course,' the sergeant says, and she smiles. Johnno smiles back and beckons her to move behind the counter, and together, they look at the laptop screen. I catch only bits and pieces of their conversation from my hiding spot. And bits and pieces of another.

'...my star sign. I'm an Aquarius. Can you show me some options?'

Oh, God. She can't be serious.

'A jug! I'm not getting a tattoo of a bloody jug! We'll have to choose a different one.'

'A *different* star sign, Miss?' Even Miller is surprised. But then, he has only just met Gabby.

'Ooh, I like this one. The scorpion.'

'Scorpio? I'm a Scorpio!' says Miller cheerfully.

'What a happy coincidence!'

From my vantage point, I see Gabby raise her shirt and then pull down her jeans just a fraction to reveal a spot on her lower abdomen.

'Here will do.'

Miller grins and reaches for the gloves, and then I can't watch. A heroic gesture, no doubt, to get a tattoo of her tattoo artist's star sign to convince the police the studio is legitimate. I will thank her later. But I can't watch.

I turn my attention back to Johnno. He has my portfolio in his hands, and I swear I can notice them shaking, even from here.

'The designs are all one-of-a-kind pieces. Once they're used, that's it, they won't be repeated. We can do custom as well. As I'm sure you'll agree, the higher than standard prices can be justified by the quality of the artwork we are delivering.'

The sergeant takes the folder. She flicks through the pages. It's impossible to tell what she is thinking. An art I'm sure she has perfected. She places the folder back down. 'Who is the artist?'

I can't breathe. I hazard a glance at Dad. His hand rubs across his face, and he doesn't meet my eyes.

'It's a freelance artist. No formal contract. Ad hoc arrangement. We didn't want to bind ourselves to one person. This way we have flexibility if we want to change things up.'

The sergeant nods and places the folder back down.

'Do you need me to follow up on that, Sarge?' The younger male officer, who has been taking notes of everything that has transpired, looks up from his notepad at his boss.

There is an agonising pause before the sergeant says, 'No. No, I'm satisfied.' And to my immense relief, she moves away from the computer, back to the customer side of the bench. 'I'm glad to see you doing well, Reed.' She holds out her hand. Johnno, who's hand is in a fist by his side, quickly wipes it on his shorts before accepting the handshake.

'Thank-you, Sergeant.'

'Stay out of trouble, won't you?'

'That's my intention.'

The officers leave the way they came, and Gabby's voice re-enters my consciousness, along with the buzzing of the needle.

'I thought you said this wouldn't hurt!'

Oh God, she is actually going through with this.

'I said there'd be a scratch, Miss. You weren't listening.'

Dad and I emerge from our hiding place. I move straight to Johnno and wrap my arms around him. His relief is palpable as his body relaxes into me. 'Fuck, I've never been so stressed in my life,' he says, and his lips press against the top of my head.

'You were amazing.'

He squeezes me tightly and then lets me go. 'Mr Drury, I can't ever thank you enough.' His voice is tight, clogged with emotion. 'You've...fuck, you've just kept me out of prison.'

Dad looks steadily at Johnno for a moment and then holds out his hand. Johnno takes it and shakes it. 'Sergeant Hathoway is one of the best operators in Leeds,' Dad says gently. 'Had she wanted to find something, she would have, mate. I think you kept yourself out of prison.'

I look up at Johnno with pride. For all the labels that might apply to him— criminal, arsonist, money launderer— the one I choose to focus on is decent human being.

'Are you nearly done?' Gabby's voice is laced heavily with impatience.

'Done? I've only finished one pincer!' says Miller. 'I'll need another half hour, at least.'

'Half an hour?' Gabby exclaims. 'I have to lay still for half a bloody hour?'

I bite my lip as a giggle threatens to escape. Heroes don't always wear capes.

Chapter Thirty-Three

Sunday morning dawns with a sense of peace I haven't experienced in some time. Johnno is across from me at the dining table, drinking tea. Safe. Not in prison. Not on the run. With me. Dad is...not overjoyed with how things have worked out, but more content than he was before the events of yesterday. I have my job, and my book club. Gabby, as far as I know, is afebrile—

'That Gabby's different, baby. Almost makes Elle seem lucid.' Elle's name, coming out of the blue as it has, jolts me back down to earth from the heights I had been sailing at. 'What's happened to her, anyway? I thought you two were joined at the hip.'

I groan in response, and Johnno raises his brows.

'I fucked up royally with Elle.'

'Surely it can't be that bad. What did you do?'

I tell Johnno the whole. From my efforts to convince her to stay with Joe, to the shameful insults I hurled at her in my weakest moment. And when I am done, he shakes his head. 'Yeah, you fucked up, baby.' He stands up and pulls me to my feet. 'Come on. We'll fix it together.'

***

Johnno, seated on his bike, pulls his hair into a bun at the nape of his neck. 'Where does she live?'

I show him on my phone, and get on the bike behind him, wrapping my arms tightly around him. He's about to start the bike, when he turns around, and lifts his visor up.

'Just so we're clear, you realise you have to let her go, right?'

I give a reluctant nod, he nods back, flicks his visor down, and we travel the ten minutes to Elle and Gabby's flat. I hope to catch Elle alone. But at the same time, I know I am not the only hurdle. Gabby, too, needs to be convinced that Elle should go.

It wouldn't be unusual for me to catch either, or both, walking around in their underwear. Since Johnno is with me, I knock and wait, rather than go straight in. Gabby comes to the door, sure enough, in a state of undress. When she sees Johnno, she quickly hides behind the door so that only her face is visible.

'Do you mind, Meg? A bit of notice would be nice,' she scolds.

'Sorry. Go and get dressed. We're coming in.' Gabby scowls, then shuts the door. I give her a minute, then open it. I move to the settee, and Johnno, noticing it is only a three-seater, brings a chair over with him from the kitchen table and sits down opposite. I smile at him gratefully. I don't want to be within swiping distance of Gabby for this conversation.

There is no sign of Elle, and I consider that maybe this is better anyway. Speak to Gabby, settle her down first, then talk to Elle. Gabby emerges a couple of minutes later in a singlet top and shorts and sits down on the other end of the settee to me.

'What are you doing here at this time in the morning, Meg Drury? I haven't even had coffee yet. Manners.' She shakes her head. 'I don't know, were you raised in some sort of asylum?' She raises her eyebrows at me as though I'm supposed to answer, all the while knowing I have been raised in a loving family with impeccable manners.

'We wanted to see Elle. Is she here?'

'No. She's gone to see Joe.'

'Fine. Perhaps that's good anyway, so we can talk. About Elle, and her plans for Australia.'

'Those are off. She's staying,' Gabby says stubbornly, almost as though she has pre-empted what I'm about to say.

'Because of what I said to her. Which wasn't fair. I was the one being selfish, not Elle.'

'Selfish *fool*, remember?'

I wince. 'Yes. Yes, I remember. And I've come to apologise, and to tell her that she needs to do what will make her happy.'

Gabby's eyes blaze. 'What, go to Australia? Leave us on our own? With miserable Joe?'

'It's her life, and she isn't happy.'

'Yes, she is,' Gabby says defiantly. 'I make Elle very happy.'

I take a deep breath. Gabby is frustrating. Oh, so frustrating. But I need to think of this from the kind, compassionate viewpoint. What would Elle say, if she was explaining Gabby's behaviour to another childlike person?

The strategy works. Of course, Gabby is frightened. Of being lonely. Of missing Elle, who has been by her side since they were kids. Of losing possibly the one person, aside from her Mum, who accepts her completely as she is, impeccable manners and abrasive personality included.

'I know this is scary. I'm scared too. We both rely on Elle, probably too much. She will do anything, for anyone. And in this case, she will stay here, even though she wants to go, because we've made it clear that we don't want her to go. And she will marry a man she doesn't want to, so that she doesn't hurt his feelings. We can't let this happen.'

I shuffle across on the settee and do something I have never done to Gabby before. I'm not sure how she will react. She might bite. But I put an arm around her shoulders. She is tense at first, and then I feel her relax.

'We will rely on each other. I will be just like a less bubbly, more morose version of Elle, with terrible manners, but a willingness to learn.' To convince her, I flash her my professional smile. She cowers and shrugs my arm off.

She looks at Johnno. 'Do you have any fit friends I can shag?' she asks.

Johnno seems a little stunned by the question. 'Ah...I could probably make some...if that would seal the deal.'

'Fine,' Gabby says, crossing her arms. 'Anyway Meg, that reminds me of what I wanted to speak to you about yesterday, at the shop. You told me Johnno was ugly! What were you on about? It left me totally unprepared for when I finally saw him.'

'Gabby, I never!'

'Yes, you did. Or at least that's what I heard.'

Johnno looks, understandably, appalled, and his expression demands an explanation.

'I said he is 'not half bad'! Which you, Johnno, know as well as anyone, is a very high compliment indeed, coming from me.'

Now, *he* crosses his arms, so I am confronted with two highly petulant adults who are pissed off at me. So, I cross my arms and lift my own chin.

We sit like that for a while, waiting for someone to break, before Johnno says, 'Guess you won't be getting *my* face tattooed to *your* body then.'

Gabby's face instantly lights up. 'You got a tattoo of *Meg*?' she cries, and I bury my face in my hands, because I just know she is not going to let up until she sees it.

The next five minutes pass with Gabby circling Johnno, simultaneously looking for the tattoo and trying to convince him to show her, and me telling him that he must, under no circumstances do so, until surprisingly, Gabby admits defeat.

She sits back down on the settee, and with a sigh, says, 'If we're going to let Elle go, then you'll have to be quick.'

'What do you mean?' I ask.

'She took off about an hour ago. She said it's about time she did something about the wedding, and then something about Scotland. I don't know, I wasn't really listening.'

I gasp. 'Gabby, you don't think—'

'— What? I think nothing.'

'You don't think she meant Gretna Green, do you?'

Gabby looks at me confused. So does Johnno. But I am suddenly flooded with panic, and I can't explain any further to either of them. I jump up from the couch and rush into Elle's bedroom. I look through her cupboard at a frantic pace. It's not there. Her white dress. The one she only wears for special occasions. It's her favourite— knee length, and feminine, with lace and floral accents. I've teased her before that she should get married in it. Fuck.

I look for her overnight bag. It's gone too. So are all her toiletries. Johnno has followed me into the room, and is sitting on the side of the bed, watching me. I put my hand to my mouth, and he stands up, wrapping his arm around my waist from behind.

'What is it, Meg?'

'I have a terrible feeling Elle is going to elope to Gretna Green with Joe. It happens a lot in the regency romance she loves to read. She mentioned the wedding, and Scotland, to Gabby. She's taken her white dress, and her overnight bag. It all adds up.'

Johnno seems doubtful. 'Are you sure? It sounds a little daft.'

'You've met Elle,' I snap. 'She *is* a little daft. This is exactly the sort of thing she would do.'

He sees the sense in that logic. 'Right. We go to Joe's then.'

***

We fly along the motorway. I'm sure Johnno probably has some traffic offences on that record somewhere he failed to mention, because he seems to have little concern for the speed limit. Elle, meanwhile, is a very conservative driver, especially since the accident, so it does give me hope we can catch her before she gets to Joe's. We slow down when we reach the market town of Skipton, at the edge of the Dales. The town closest to Joe's farm is Grassington, about another fifteen minutes on. Once we get through Skipton, Johnno picks up speed again.

We are minutes from Grassington when I spot Elle's silver hatchback pulled in at a petrol station. I urgently tap Johnno's shoulder and signal for him to turn in. Elle comes out of the shop as we pull up. I take off my helmet, and Elle's surprise is evident when she sees me. She comes straight to me with a sunny smile.

'Meg! What a surprise to see you here! All right, my love?' I swing my leg off the bike, and she gives me a kiss on the cheek.

'All right.'

Elle looks at Johnno, who has dismounted and taken off his helmet as well.

'All right, Johnno? You need to go south for Russia, you know,' says Elle, matter of factly. Johnno looks at her with confusion, and then to me for clarification. I smile apologetically as Elle continues. 'You've got two options: the Eurotunnel, or the ferry. I would suggest the tunnel, it will be quicker. You will board first, with your bike—'

'—Elle! We're not going to Russia. We've come to stop you,' I say, before she can get too much further.

'Stop me from what?'

'From making a big mistake.'

Elle laughs. 'I'm just going to Joe's. How is that a mistake? I thought you *wanted* me to stay with Joe. You said he could offer me everything I want, and I was a selfish fool to consider any other course of action. You said—'

'—Do you really just do exactly what people tell you to do?' Johnno asks, cutting Elle off.

Elle nods. 'I don't like to upset people. It's not in my nature.'

'That's not healthy,' Johnno states.

Elle shrugs, and says, 'Himph.'

'Stop. Elle, I was wrong, and Gretna Green isn't the answer.'

Elle stares at me, and then doubles over in hysterical laughter. When she composes herself, she says, 'Gretna Green? Oh, Meg, are you a few sandwiches short?'

Johnno and I exchange looks. He puts his fingers to the bridge of his nose, as though my stupidity has caused him a nosebleed.

'Gabby said you were going to see Joe, and you mentioned something about Scotland, and you took your overnight bag and the dress. The white one, that you only wear on special occasions.'

Elle starts giggling again. She stops briefly, wipes the tears from the corner of her eyes, and then starts giggling again.

'Meg, it's not the 19th Century, my love. You can't get married on the spot in Gretna Green anymore. You need to apply for a marriage schedule. It takes almost a month! Anyway, could you imagine Joe's face if I suggested that? He'd say, 'Can't be done, my love. We don't have a visa for Scotland.' More giggles.

'Well, why on earth did Gabby say you were going to Scotland then?'

'I did say that I'd *like* to get married in Gretna Green, and that I was going to see Joe to tell him we should set a date. Perhaps she got her wires crossed. She doesn't listen properly, you know. She hears what she wants to hear.'

'Why did you take the dress then?' I'm still not sure if I believe her. She might be trying to fob us off.

'It's for church. I thought, since I'm going to be a married woman, perhaps I should give God another chance.'

This is worse than I thought. Elle has been a terrible Catholic the entire time I've known her. If *she* is giving God another chance, then she must be truly desperate for salvation.

'You haven't been to church the entire time I've known you, Elle.'

'No. But God is good. He will forgive me, once I apologise pro-fusely and offer up my first-born child as a sacrifice.' She says it with a grin, which just reinforces that she is a terrible Catholic.

'I don't think you should do that,' I say, and then quickly realise it is largely beside the point. 'In fact, I'm sure you shouldn't do any of it, Elle. I was wrong the other day. I was upset, about me and Johnno, and I took it out on you. Of course, I know your heart is in the right place, and of course I want you to be happy.'

Elle looks from me to Johnno. 'I take it you sorted things out?' she asks.

'Yes.'

Elle shakes her head. 'It doesn't matter. I've made up my mind. You are right. I may never do better than Joe. The perfect love doesn't exist. Eighty percent is good enough. Eighty-five would be even better. That would be good enough to make the Yorkshire side—'

'—Stay focused, Elle! This has nothing to do with your shooting percentage.' I'm just going to have to come out with it. In front of Johnno, at a petrol station in Grassington. This is going to be a bold declaration, but it's what she needs to hear. 'And it does exist. Perhaps not perfect, but better than eighty percent.' I look at Johnno, and he smiles at me, and places his hand at the small of my back. 'You can have it, Elle. You can have someone who lights you on fire, who consumes your every waking moment *and* is your best friend. You deserve it. And so does Joe.'

Elle's eyes fill with tears, and with an unsteady voice, she says, 'I can't break up with him, Meg. Australia is the only way. If I stay, I marry him.'

I take a deep breath, and push the lump in my throat down, as far as it will go, so I can speak with confidence.

'Australia it is then.'

***

We follow Elle out to Joe's farm, a gorgeous 300-acre property amidst rolling green fields. The house is old. Probably a few hundred years, built of stone. There are several outbuildings, and a barn that has been converted to a studio for Joe's mother. They used to use it as a Bed and Breakfast, but Joe's mum has stayed there since his father passed away.

We pull up, and Elle lets us inside.

'Joe will be out in the fields. He comes up for morning tea around ten.' She leads us out the back to where there is a sitting area that looks out over the property. We sit down on the cushioned wicker chairs. Elle asks Johnno how he takes his tea, and then goes back inside. In the distance, Joe's tractor is visible, slowly making its way closer, surrounded by small white moving dots, and a couple of faster patchy ones. His Border Collies.

Elle returns a short time later with a tea tray and four cups. She sits down on a wicker loveseat opposite us and prepares tea for the three of us. She leaves Joe's cup empty, then tucks her legs up beneath her, and takes a sip of hers. She looks out towards the tractor, and a faint smile comes onto her face. She raises her hand to wave to Joe, and he lifts his hand back. It's adorable.

'This used to be just fine, you know,' she says. 'More than fine. This was what I wanted. A peaceful life with Joe. A family. Netball, of course. Joe has always said I wouldn't have to teach once we had children. There is plenty to do around the farm. I'd make tea for him and learn to bake. Write. Perhaps take up embroidery. At the end of the day, he would ride up on his tractor, give me a kiss on the cheek, and we'd sit and take tea out here, watching the sunset over the field. Then we'd go inside to a home cooked dinner. Hopefully Joe's mum would take care of that. Afterwards, we'd curl up by the fire and chat. And then...' She shakes her head. 'I think it was the accident that changed things. I thought I could go on without feeling that spark, to spare his feelings, but also because I loved the rest of it. How could I not? But since the accident, it just isn't enough anymore. Seeing how quickly life can change or be taken away completely. I couldn't ignore the feeling there was something more— something else that I want to experience before I could ever settle for almost perfect.' She sighs. 'I'm sure it is selfish. But Joe just needs to experience life without me for a while, to be able to see a different future. This is all he sees right now. To pull the rug out from beneath him... it would crush him. This way, he can adjust, and when he is ready, I know he will end it, on his terms.'

I feel a push in my back, and I know what it means. I stand and move over to sit next to Elle. I take her hands in mine.

'Elle, please let me take back those words. You are the least selfish person I know. I've never seen that more clearly than in these two weeks when we have been...estranged. I was the one being selfish. I hated the thought of losing you. But you need to do this, and I understand. I do.' I pull her into a hug, and she returns the embrace. 'I will look after Joe. I promise. And Gabby. We will look after each other, and everything will be OK.'

Chapter Thirty-Four

We stay for long enough at Joe's farm to have a cup of tea with Joe and Elle, before I quietly wish Elle good luck, and we leave. Joe will be hurting, but I'm sure Elle will wrap it all up in so much love that he will survive. I will check in on him early next week anyway, in case he needs a shoulder.

By the time we arrive back at my place, just past noon, my butt is proper hurting, and I am exhausted. I've never sat on a motorbike for so long, and I don't think it agrees with me. Johnno laughs at me as I rub my butt and reassures me that after a few months of dating him, I will develop callouses, and I won't feel sore anymore. I'm unsure if he is joking, but I sincerely hope so.

The house is quiet as we enter, but I can hear Mum and Dad's voices coming softly from the kitchen. We pop our heads in to say hi, and then head for my room. The events of this weekend are fast catching up with me, and I am shattered. Content. Happy, even. But shattered.

I notice Johnno hasn't put the chair against the doorknob, so I assume seduction isn't on his mind. I lie down on the bed and close my eyes. I hear Johnno rifling through the bag he brought with him, and then I hear him take his boots off, and his weight lands on the bed beside me.

'Meg.'

'Mhmm,' I say without opening my eyes.

'Is this a good time to show you this?' He sounds nervous. I open my eyes and prop myself up beside him. He has a white A4 envelope in his hands. 'It's the custody paperwork for Shae. I've been thinking about what you said. I don't want to show your dad, but I thought maybe you could have a read and see what you think.'

I lean my cheek against Johnno's shoulder and take the envelope from him as he passes it to me.

'I'm not sure I will be much help,' I say apologetically.

'You're smart.'

I open the top of the envelope and peak inside. It looks to be quite lengthy. 'Of course, I will read it, if you would like me to.'

'Yeah.'

I take the document out. At the top, it says, 'Child Arrangement Orders'. It is in the form of a contract, and I know straight away I am going to struggle to understand it. But I look through each page, trying to take in the jargon.

'This part here, supervised visits, does this still apply?' I ask when I am part of the way through.

'No. That was the old agreement, when I was first released. My ex told the court she didn't want Shae going with me on her own, so the visits had to be supervised for the first year. When I stayed out of trouble for a year, I challenged it and got the two weeks.'

After I read each sheet, I pass it to Johnno, and he scans it as well, so each of us are holding a small pile of paper in our hands when there is a light knock on my door, and it opens a fraction.

'Meg.'

I look at Johnno quickly, who looks as concerned as I do, and then call, 'Come in Dad.'

Dad pushes the door open and stops at the threshold. He takes in Johnno and I, knee deep in paperwork, and I'm sure jumps quickly to his own conclusion about what we are doing, because his eyes widen, and his posture stiffens.

'I-I just wanted to...never mind,' he says, and he steps back away from the door, pulling it shut behind him.

'Fuck.' I say to Johnno. 'I should tell him what it is.'

'Why? I'd rather not. It's my business.'

'Exactly. He thinks it's about your business. Did you see his face? I promised him after yesterday, I wouldn't be involved beyond my drawings, and now he thinks I'm in here, getting involved.'

A look of understanding comes over Johnno's face.

'Right. Yeah, you'd better tell him.'

I jump up, and rush for the door. Dad is at the end of the hallway when I open it.

'Dad,' I call. He turns. I walk down to meet him. 'That wasn't what it looked like. It's nothing to do with business. It's Johnno's custody paperwork for Shaelea. He asked me to read it.'

Dad looks surprised, and also relieved. 'I see. Why does he want you to do that?'

'He has never really had it looked at by someone who understands this stuff. He didn't have representation when it was drawn up. We're not sure if perhaps he might be missing something— in terms of how often he is allowed to see Shae.'

Ever-kind Dad immediately says, 'Why don't I take a look?'

I bite my lip. 'I'm not sure if Johnno...he didn't want to ask, since...recent events.'

'I should offer.' Dad starts back down towards my room. God, I hope I have done the right thing. Yes, I wanted to clarify to Dad what we were doing. But I was also hoping for exactly this, because I know I am out of my depth in trying to understand it. I just hope Johnno swallows his pride and co-operates. Dad knocks gently on the door again, and I open it. This time, he walks in, grabs my make-up chair, and sits down on it beside the bed. I sit down on the side of the bed next to where Johnno is reclining.

Johnno looks warily at Dad. 'Mr Drury.'

'Dave,' Dad says firmly. 'Meg has explained what you're looking at there. I'm happy to run my eyes over it if you like. Family law isn't my area, but I'm sure I can probably be of service.'

'I appreciate that, but you've given me enough free legal advice. Thanks anyway,' Johnno says. I'd like to throttle him.

'Show him,' I whisper.

'It wouldn't be advice,' Dad says. 'Think of it more as...an interpreting service.'

Johnno looks at me, and I plead with him with my eyes. I am pleased to find it works, and file that skill away for another day. Johnno gathers up my pile, and his pile, puts them together and hands them to Dad.

'Thanks.'

'Meggy, grab my glasses, they're by the sofa,' Dad says. Reluctant as I am to leave them alone together, I get up and walk quickly down the hallway, and back. As I had feared, I hear them speaking to each other as I return. I walk as softly as I can up to the doorway, then turn my back to the wall, and listen.

'...still have concerns.' Fuck. Dad is expressing his concerns. *Not part of the plan, Mr Drury. What happened to the free legal interpreting service?*

'I love your daughter. Meg and Shae are everything to me.' *My heart.*

'I appreciate that. But the situation you are in is precarious. I would hate to see Meg get caught up in it.' *Shut up, Dad.*

'She won't. I won't let anything happen to Meg. I promise you that.' There is a short pause. 'Anyway, she's listening outside the door.'

Damn it. 'How did you know?' I ask, stepping into the room, feeling the heat spreading across my cheeks.

'You're as light-footed as a moose, sweetheart,' Johnno says, shattering my own illusions of stealth, and even Dad smiles as I pout, sit back down and hand him his glasses.

Dad puts them on and sets to work scanning the document. He is a fast reader, spending all of ten seconds on one page before flicking to the next.

Finally, he says, 'There are some amendments here at the back. Much of this applies to when you were restricted to supervised visits.'

'Yeah, it was changed a couple of years ago.'

Dad nods and takes off his glasses. 'Back when the visits were supervised, your communication with Shaelea was limited to only those times. However, with the amendments, it is more like a joint custody agreement— albeit with a very unequal split. Certainly, the two weeks is the only time you are entitled to have Shaelea live with you each year. But in between times, there is nothing to restrict your communication with her, or to stop you from visiting.'

Johnno looks disbelieving. 'Really? You mean I can call her?'

'I believe so. Just as anyone else is legally allowed to contact her, you are as well. This agreement doesn't preclude that in any way.'

'Right. And you said visit.'

'Of course, a lot depends on how cordial your relationship is with her mother. I would suggest keeping her informed if you are planning to visit, to save any conflicts arising. Perhaps keeping to things like school events, or sporting events, where it's expected that both parents might attend.'

Johnno nods, and I can tell he is shaken. He rubs his hand across his face and looks at me like he isn't sure what to say. I take over.

'Thanks Dad,' I say, and hold out my hands for the agreement. 'That helps a lot.'

'Yeah, thanks very much, Dave,' Johnno says.

Dad stands. 'Happy to help.' He leaves without saying anything else, shutting the door behind him.

I lay down the paperwork and climb onto the bed beside Johnno. I wrap my arms around him and snuggle into his side, and he puts an arm around my shoulders.

'Are you OK?' I ask.

'Yeah. I just feel a bit stupid that I didn't investigate this sooner. All this time...no wonder she's pissed off at me. She probably knows I could've been there more than I have.'

'Do you think so?'

Johnno shrugs. 'I don't know.'

'There is no time like the present, Johnno. Send her a text.'

'What the fuck do I say?'

Good question. 'Ask how her holidays have been.'

Johnno doesn't look convinced, but he picks up his phone anyway, types it out, and presses send. Then he puts his phone on my bedside table and rolls onto his side to face me. He looks at me with those magical green eyes. I soak him in.

'You really are not half bad, you know,' I say.

'Really? Well, you, Meg Drury, are a work of art,' he replies. He kisses my bottom lip, and I feel the touch of his teeth, suggesting that seduction may now be climbing up his list of priorities.

'You exaggerate.'

'You've changed my life, sweetheart. And no, I don't exaggerate.'

My heart is swelling. 'You have changed mine too. I barely recognise the girl I was when I lied to you about my name while wearing a name badge. And you know *I* don't exaggerate.'

Johnno smiles, at the memory perhaps, or perhaps back at me, because I can't keep the smile off my face.

'You were perfect then. You are perfect now,' he says. 'My fantasy girl.' Then there is a slight shift in those magical green eyes, and I feel the heat rise in my cheeks. His tongue touches his bottom lip, the way it does when I know he wants me. 'Do you think your second cousin can stay out of trouble long enough for me to tie you up and have my way with you?'

'I don't think we will be hearing from her anymore. But just in case, I will turn my phone off.'

'Fine,' Johnno says, with the hint of a teasing smile on his lips.

'Just fine?' I ask, with a raise of my eyebrows.

'Good.'

'Great.'

Also by

Rubi Somerton

Contemporary Romance

All Things Imperfect Series
The Eighty-Twenty Rule
Perfect the Next
Coming Soon...Before We Were Finished

Regency Romance

Ladylike Pursuits Series
The Art of Ruin and Other Ladylike Pursuits

www.ingramcontent.com/pod-product-compliance
Lightning Source LLC
Chambersburg PA
CBHW030530190726
48283CB00006B/1852